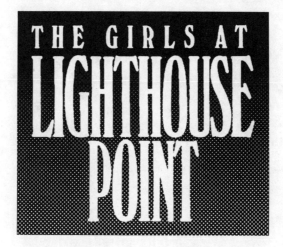

THE GIRLS AT
LIGHTHOUSE
POINT

THE GIRLS AT
LIGHTHOUSE POINT

BEVERLEY GASNER

E. P. DUTTON   NEW YORK

Published in the United States by E. P. Dutton,
a division of Penguin Books USA Inc.,
2 Park Avenue, New York, N.Y. 10016.

Published simultaneously in Canada by Fitzhenry and Whiteside, Limited, Toronto.

Library of Congress Cataloging-in-Publication Data

Gasner, Beverley.
The girls at Lightouse Point / Beverley Gasner.
p.   cm.
ISBN 0-525-24849-8
I. Title.
PS3557.A84475G57   1990
813'.54—dc20   *89-23420*
                                                          CIP

Designed by Margo D. Barooshian

1 3 5 7 9 10 8 6 4 2

First Edition

For Steve, with
love and gratitude

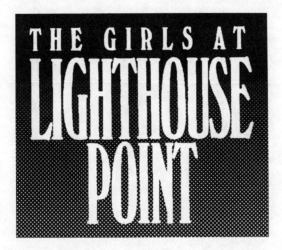

THE GIRLS AT
LIGHTHOUSE
POINT

The accident itself was a simple tragedy, as slim and quick in its dimensions as the lovely girl in its spinning center. But the scandal that followed spread like a fire storm that time could only enlarge. It blazed on and on in the public eye; it was the story that had everything: sex and death and fame were there, the power of great wealth, and the doom of high ambition. Mystery fueled it with a hundred questions asked and never answered, and even today people still sift those ashes in search of a clue, a hint, a charred, suggestive ember.

"The truth?" people ask. And then, "No way, forget it; the truth never came out."

It didn't.

We hid it. We thought we had to. We were young, ignorant, frightened.

But at least the fire storm was so bright it blinded everyone.

1

In that lurid glare, who could see a single candle burning low? Who would even think to look for it? Only we knew it existed. Love was that candle, and any truth worth knowing about Lighthouse Point must begin with its old flame.

We loved Justin Lambert. Lighthouse Point ended all of that, and we thought, as the years passed, that our lives had diverged forever. We were wrong, and so the truth begins its telling ten years later, that night in April when I saw him on TV.

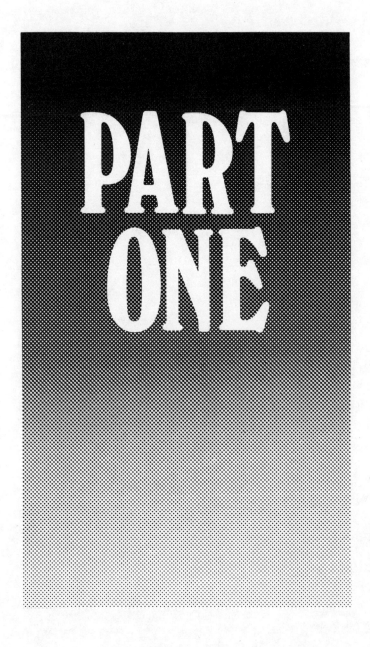

PART ONE

I was dressing for a faculty party, a dinner for which I was not really qualified. Vanderbush, the head of our department, always invited full professors to his house to celebrate Shakespeare's birthday, and my new full professorship was still a month shy of being official.

"You must be with us anyway, Rachel!" he had said. "I insist. A note of youth, at long last. You shall glow in our midst 'like a rich jewel in an Ethiop's ear.' "

I was thirty-six, and it was never unpleasant to sound the note of youth. I said I'd be there, and at seven o'clock I was dressing, with the TV on and the news coming over it. My head was deep within the challis folds of my dress when I heard, "The Secretary of State was on hand to introduce Justin Lambert."

I yanked my head free. There he was. I was looking right at him, breathless with intent.

Don't go. Stay there, shining on the glass screen.

Age and extra weight and the sly pull of gravity hadn't damaged the camera's favor. The fullness of his mouth was just diminished, not pinched, and the Viking planes of his nose and jaw were as bold as ever. It was a good, generous face, and the voice was a silver bell with a call in it.

"I am honored by this task," he was saying. "I expect to do everything in my power to bring some clarity of purpose to America's concern for the victims of this disaster. Goodwill is not enough."

It was the famine in Africa. Weeks ago I had read in the newspapers about the possibility of this presidential commission and Justin as a candidate to chair it. I had even felt a little preternatural thrill of coincidence, when Vanderbush quoted that line from *Romeo and Juliet*. I still had a few of those habits, seeing signs and portents everywhere.

Justin will get it done, I thought now. It's the kind of job that's right up his alley. He'll work twelve hours a day and plead and bully, and he'll write personal checks for the payoffs if he has to. Other men might have to use cash, but even in Africa a Lambert check will look good as gold.

The whole clip—a rerun of the morning swearing-in—was on for just thirty seconds. I can still gauge a clip, and I do exercises in class to teach my media students how to do it too. TV sells time, not space, and I want the kids to get used to the idea of writing for dollars-per-pulse-beat.

My own pulse was racing. I saw him so seldom on TV; it wasn't like the old days when he was Governor Lambert and got all the time he wanted. But there had been occasions. Even after the accident, the public life still claimed him.

There's more to public life than politics when you're a Lambert, and a man like Justin. He knew how to serve, and he couldn't serve without leading, and every year he'd add another cause or charity or select committee to his schedule. He was a Lambert, born to wealth and power; he was Justin, destined for deference and the top of every letterhead.

And if, in the fastness of his heart, he yearned for privacy, how could he demand it? He didn't believe he had any right to

6

privacy, or to respite from the limelight. He didn't think he deserved the very air in his lungs. I knew that. I used to weep over knowing that.

"Don't worry, Rachel," he'd said to me, almost at the end, when we were standing near the black-green pool. "I'll never take that way out. I'll go on. I'll serve my time."

And so he'd gone on, and I could still see him sometimes, a face made of dots on the glass screen, a body on a podium, trying not to yawn.

Oh, Justin.

But it was seven-ten, and I still had hair to do, and makeup, and Vanderbush himself was punctual as royalty. I began to rush, grateful for the pace and the worry about being late. I didn't want to think about Justin Lambert.

I used to want to, even long after Lighthouse Point. I used to live my inner life like some priestess of love and sacrifice who tended a sacred flame. I'd blow on it till the old joy and the new pain blended and warmed me. I would imagine what he was doing that very minute; I would think of him lying sleepless, as I was, saying the same things to himself that I did.

All over. We're out of danger. But it has to be this way now.

Silence and separation. That was our way, and it was narrow. I had the past for company; I had the *Clarion-Dispatch* as well, sent to me by mail. I didn't have to read it with a fine-tooth comb, as I read *The New York Times*, looking for Justin's name. The *Dispatch* was home-state, Lambert territory, and if there was a Lambert wedding, party, or demise of a second cousin, it made the news and rated a picture. There would be Justin and Tandy welcoming their guests at Burning Brook Club; Justin at his daughter's college graduation; old Henry Lambert cutting the ribbon on the new hospital wing. If there was no hard news, I could always settle for a smaller fix: what Lambert Industries was selling for, or what was playing at the Lambert Arts Complex.

When did I begin to let those papers in their brown wrappers start to pile up, unread? When did I stop inventing pretexts to put Justin's name into my letters to Bitsie and Caro and Amy, those letters that flow among the four of us like streaming sound?

We write as people must have written before the phone was in-vented; ever since the time our phones were tapped we've been super careful. We do call one another, but we keep important things for letters. The letter rules are easy: each of us must get a photocopy of every letter, all mailed on the same day; we put in pictures when possible; we can keep the pictures but the letters must be trashed after two readings. I can't remember just when it was that I began writing things like this to my three friends:

"I don't dwell on Justin much anymore. It's all getting blurred, really, and sometimes I feel ashamed, forgetting to re-member. But I guess that's what happens. It solves a lot, this getting older!"

Perhaps that sounds more cocky than I actually felt, but all the same it became true. The silence and separation did their work—and after all, it was only what Justin and I had both hoped for.

"It's for your sake," I'd said. "Think how you'll be watched."

"Mine *and* yours," he'd answered. "You're young. You can have a beautiful life."

Those words stayed with me and were the charm I could invoke, a loyal priestess, against self-pity. But little by little I stopped using them. The charm failed. The priestess, now and then, was known to snarl and show her pointy teeth. A hag.

There was gall in that silence.

After ten years, Justin and I seemed as safely separated as two stones flung from an airplane, but across that final distance I wanted a journeying word from him. Just a word. Something spe-cial: if not caring, then curious at least? David Freed could have brought it to me. I still saw David whenever I went up to New York, and lately I'd feel my mouth puckering and drying before-hand, anticipating disappointment.

"You're looking great, Rachel," David would say, almost at once, getting it over with. "I'll tell Justin. I like what you've done to your hair."

(Or your skirts, or your perfume.)

"Thanks," I'd say. "Feeling great, too. This tan is from the ski trip to Vail."

(Or skin-diving in Aruba, or Christmas in Marbella.)

8

"Justin's looking fit, too. Gone on another diet, if you can believe it."

(Or off a diet, or out of squash into racquetball.)

"All's well, then."

"All's well."

I would never embarrass David or myself by probing or asking for more. I'd roll my martini on my dry tongue and fish out the onion and crunch it, wincing.

Gall.

But it wouldn't last, not when I was with David. We had a past of our own, David and I, and it was sweet with trust and friendship. With the hard part out of the way, we'd get to drinking and laughing and reminiscing and growing visibly younger under each other's eyes.

Mine are black-brown, nearly as dark as my hair. But David's are a sunny hazel-amber; with lids lowered, his thin, bony face looks sardonic, but the eyes make all the difference. His curly hair has gone frosty with crimped silver wires.

"Distinguished," I always say.

"Extinguished," and he always sighs.

I never minded thinking about David. But seeing Justin on TV had left me a little shaken, and I wanted both of them out of my head. It wasn't difficult. When you're rushing off to dinner over four blocks of bumpy brick in three-inch Maud Frizons, you can't think about much else except not breaking your neck.

I enjoyed the faculty dinner, but I was too keyed up when I got home to go to sleep. That was partly the aftermath of seeing Justin on the tube but mostly because I'd met someone new. He was a visiting lecturer from Harvard, a wrinkled pixie with a wise grin named Julius Cohen, and we'd monopolized each other all evening. So as usual whenever I meet someone new that I like, I had to sit around afterward, drinking weak tea and going over the number of lies I'd told him.

"Rachel Warshowsky," he'd said. "Rachel-from-Warsaw, right? So where can I get some good Jewish rye bread in the middle of Pennsylvania? You're divorced? That's one heck of a ring, anyway. So young, and an orphan too. How does that happen?"

The questions, of course, didn't come all at once. They never do. I just file them together automatically.

My name? A lie. But it was legal. The name's implications were theater, and theater so old I could hardly remember opening night.

A divorce? There hadn't been any marriage, much less a divorce, but I wore the diamond because I loved it. It was a big, badly cut, flawless stone that had once belonged to Justin's grandmother, and besides, its glitter was useful. I like my lies on the thrifty side, and a brief marriage in my dim past explained my expensive clothes, my good vacations, my always-almost-new car. The big ring said it all: Took him for a bundle.

Orphan? True, but I kept changing the cause of my father's early death. I favored "heart attack," which was nearly correct, if you come down hard on the word "attack."

So just three lies tonight, and with the tally made I clicked off my mental abacus. Bitsie and Caro and Amy know I do this, and they laugh at me for it. But it's only natural. Of the four of us, I was the one most at risk for disappearing totally into our fog of deceit. I often envy Caro because she has the church and her deep faith in some celestial bookkeeper who counts the lies and forgives them anyway.

The phone rang. I jumped, startled, because it was late, and then I felt a flash of guilt; was it Professor Cohen? A single woman gets that feeling. You think you've flirted just a little, but maybe you overdid it.

It was Amy. Because we use the phone so seldom I sounded worried.

"Don't panic, Rachel," Amy said. "Nothing serious. But my girls went to Grandma's, to sleep over."

That meant there'd be no eavesdropping. But our conversation was guarded anyway.

"I saw Justin on TV," Amy said. "He's off to Ethiopia."

"I saw him too," I said. "It's terrific. A big job."

"Did you catch it on NBC?"

"Nope. I'm loyal to our local station, in all its blow-dried beauty."

Amy giggled. She lived in a small place too, and she was

familiar with anchormen in cardboard suits who combed their hair funny.

"So you missed some action. NBC had a remote afterward, from Washington. Tom Braddock and Harry Llewelyn, gabbing away. Guess what they gabbed."

"Too late for guessing."

"They started punditing about the President's health. And how he may not be well enough to run again. And who might the party put up if the incumbent withdraws."

"I get it," I said slowly. "Harry Llewelyn mentioned Justin. They usually do. Then someone brings up the accident. Cheap thrills."

"Not this time. Leave it to Harry. It was straight puffery. Youngest congressman ever from the state. Two-term governor. The Lambert magic, and how the party can use some."

"Really beating the drum?"

"Loud. And for some parade: President!"

"Shit. Well, the Lamberts. They don't quit, do they? But this will end on the cutting-room floor, like always."

"Probably. But you know, Rachel, I need a vacation."

This was one of our code phrases. It meant that Amy thought we all ought to meet, and if I agreed I would say, "Me too. I'll put some ideas in the mail."

I said it. The first thing I did when I hung up on Amy was to run get my diary and check when I'd last seen David Freed. There it was: three months ago, January, and we'd had a big time going from mellow to maudlin over steaks and wine. But David was in constant touch with Justin and the Lambert group, and he hadn't said a word to me about floating Justin's name for any office, from dogcatcher on up. I went scrabbling through the piles of old magazines I keep for student critiquing until I found what I was looking for: the issue of *Newsweek* that broke the story about the President's visits to NIH, the tests, the X rays.

The issue was from February. So David hadn't been holding out on me. Nobody knew, back then. Nowadays, the President was carrying on bravely, but he looked puffy-eyed and pallid and the doctors were still puzzled and plainly concerned.

The primary was just a year away. The Veep was a nonentity.

11

The nomination was starting to look like a bride's bouquet, ready for the toss.

I began to dust my apartment, if "dusting" is the word for snapping a white rag at the windowsills. I cursed myself for missing Harry Llewelyn, that old pimp, fiddling with his glasses and slipping Justin's name—oh, quite casually—into the standard list of contenders. It was the kind of move, low and slow, the Lamberts knew how to make, and they always had people like Harry Llewelyn to do it for them. Tom Braddock wasn't going to snicker at Justin's name on prime-time TV, not in the face of dear old twinkly elder-pundit Harry Llewelyn.

President! Dusting was no help. I threw away the rag and sat down at the typewriter.

"Dear Ones," I wrote. "It's after midnight and I've just done talking to Amy. She caught Justin on TV and heard Harry Llewelyn put out his name, on NBC yet, for the big primary. Just a mention, but still! Let's do our worrying together. With Jean-Claude away, my weekends are free. Could we aim for Saturday the 2nd, or the 9th if necessary?"

I wrote out the envelopes in longhand; a typed envelope can too easily be opened by the wrong person. Amy's went to Port Jervis, Bitsie's to Frederick, Caro's to Philadelphia. If you looked at a map of the mid-Atlantic region, you'd see what a neat parallelogram our addresses made, four dots in three states, all about a hundred miles from one another. It wasn't planning; it was fate, coincidence, happy chance.

I washed my teacup, face, and hands and got into bed, prepared to lie awake. I wasn't used to an evening so full of incident, particularly these days, with Jean-Claude gone to teach for a term at Stanford. Thanks to him, I'd had a lively winter. It wasn't love and it didn't have to be, either. Oh, no. By no means. . . . One yawn and I was fast asleep.

But the dream waited, a courteous demon, until morning light. It was an old dream and I knew how it would end. We were all out there on the lawn again, all five girls, all three men, throwing the Frisbee and laughing because it was so hard to see in the fog and the gathering dusk. I laughed the loudest but I was worried. I thought we were one person too many, and I kept trying to count us up and no one would stand still long enough to let me do it. Then I stopped trying because I knew. The Judge was there. He had put on Vinnie's fishing hat; he was pretending—in the fog and the gathering dusk—to be one of us.

As soon as I realized this I woke up. I always did. I woke up on my feet, out of bed, trembling all over and drenched in the simple sweat of animal fear.

So much time had passed since the accident, and still the Judge's words could clothe themselves in nightmare images.

"You won't make it, you know," he'd said. "You're so damnably young, and you think this is the hardest life gets. Believe me, it gets harder. A conspiracy is only as strong as its weakest link. One day one of you will find life too hard. And break."

He paused, testing us. We sat in silence, resisting him. Then he'd gone on.

"You can tell me the truth now. I couldn't betray you even if I wanted to, and I don't want to. I want to help you. There are ways of safeguarding your secret, ways I know and have used to help others. Tell me. Tell me and protect yourselves against a dangerous future."

I was still the spokesman for the four of us. There was a fire crackling in the library's fireplace, and I listened for a moment

14

to its popping sparks. Then I said, "We've told you all we can. There isn't anything left to say except how much we appreciate what you're doing for us. All of us. Justin could not have had a better friend."

Then for the first time since we'd met him we became our natural selves, babbling, laughing, raising our voices; he was great, terrific, we couldn't thank him enough, now or ever! Bitsie got up from the sofa and kissed him, crying "Blondes first!" and then we all did. The Judge colored and made deprecating noises but he looked beaten all the same, and later, at lunch, he ate without saying a word.

And years afterward, when we remembered that morning, Amy said, "That old fox. He sat there and ate his veal and looked so sad, and all the while he was planning to tap our phones."

The Judge died five years ago. Amy had already begun her clipping-service business, and she sent us copies of all his obituaries. She thought it would do us good to read them; I wasn't the only one still haunted by his words and by his sleek, commanding presence. There he was, embodied in long columns of black type setting forth his age and honors and associations with power. Presidents had confided in him. People like the Lamberts were his friends. He must have taken a hundred important secrets to his grave, but he didn't take ours. We told him only what we wanted him to know—what we wanted anyone to know!—about that bright afternoon at Lighthouse Point and the blind black night that followed.

It was some damned miracle, how the four of us managed to set up a date so quickly. After I spoke to Amy, our letters crossed and recrossed and there were the usual misunderstandings, but in ten days' time we got it fixed: May ninth, at the Matron's Place, at noon. I canceled out of my Saturday bike-club trip; I said I couldn't miss this important auction of Amish quilts. So I dressed on the morning of the ninth with a high heart, thinking how ridiculous I'd look if I were really going to spend the day in some moldy Lancaster County barn. I shook the new dove-gray suede skirt out of its tissue paper and added a blouse of heavy white silk and snakeskin shoes so glossy they looked wet. I was the one who

15

always cared most about clothes, and I knew my friends would be dressing and wondering, What's Rachel going to have on this time? I scrubbed the diamond ring with ammonia and water until it sparkled enough to send casual rainbows all over the dashboard of my car, and I drove through fields of alfalfa and wheat stubble singing loudly and badly, along with the radio. I was happy. We were going to meet.

Close as our letters keep us, they're not enough. After a few months we begin to hunger for the sight of one another: a pigeon-toed walk, a grin, a Chicago accent. We didn't meet a tenth as often as we wanted. We had varying work schedules and vacations; there were Amy's children and Bitsie's son-plus-husband; Caro's convent was abysmally strict about giving her free time. And we all had to meet together or not at all; that was one of our rules, and perhaps the most important one. No one must ever feel left out. No one must have to hear things secondhand. The sacrifice had a single purpose: a seamless unity of trust. In days so distant we could hardly recall them, we had not been like this. Bitsie and I were openly, exclusively, best friends; Amy and Bitsie kept a grudge going over the time they were dating the same man; Caro used to tell the others that she found me hard to deal with. All that was over. "Dear Ones," we wrote, to our dear and absolute equals, every difference subsumed in the kind of love that patriots feel, and impartial mothers.

And successful conspirators, gladly gathering.

The Matron's Place was once a plain farmer's hotel. Tourism and prosperity had plastered its grimy walls with copper weathervanes and stenciled proverbs in Pennsylvania Dutch. There was a round table in an alcove and Bitsie had requested it. She was already there when I walked in. I could see her from the entrance, a tall, preppy blonde who could still get away with stick-straight hair and a silver barrette.

It was five to twelve. We kissed. We were still standing when Amy walked in, and then Caro. We were together.

When you see people you love—after some absence—you feel unready. We're always awkward at first. Bitsie will immediately start to study the menu as if it's written in Sanskrit. Amy may start a hopelessly boring story about her office staff. Caro will try to

16

beam that abstract goodwill you expect from a nun—even if the nun, nowadays, wears pants and a turtleneck and Arpège. I am always the quietest. You'd think the hostess had seated me with these women by mistake.

A drink helps. We ordered two daiquiris and two vodka tonics and sipped them gratefully, in a rush of feeling: the warmth of one another, eyes, smiles.

As always, we started trading the minor indignities. Bitsie is the oldest of us, nearly forty, and she was dyeing her hair now. She hated it. She wanted her own dirty-blond back and they wouldn't give it to her.

"You've still got the legs," Amy said. "Walk on your hands and no one will notice your hair."

"Rachel doesn't even need touch-ups," Bitsie said. "See those two guys at the bar? They put down their beer when she walked in."

"Amy's an ad for that new diet."

"Caro's still a size eight and she eats like a horse."

The immediate pleasure we took in one another's appearances was like visible light, playing over us, and it brought another rush of well-being—and hunger. Out of the quaint misspellings on the menu ("Mama's Chiggen, Choost Like") we devised a three-course meal and ordered a good bottle of wine. Then, to the beat of dishes thunking off the relish tray, we went right into the news about Justin. Bitsie had seen NBC too.

"Rachel, you didn't say much in your letter," Caro said. "I mean something personal. About how you felt. Hearing it."

They gave me time.

I said, after a moment, "I was confused, I guess. All those old emotions. And then . . . angry? Yes, a little. Ten years, and I haven't seen Justin, or heard a word from him, and goddammit, why do I have to worry what he does do, doesn't do, will do, won't? Okay, I got through that. It's a given. Next step: my own judgment. And my own judgment says it's nothing, or soon will be. Justin doesn't want to make a comeback. Not on that level! He has to know he'll get pasted. So maybe a few party pros—his diehards, anyway—will push at him to take a chance. And maybe he'll act like he doesn't mind being pushed. It won't last long. He's

17

too intelligent. He'll know he can't dodge Lighthouse Point, and that will be the end of it. It's not wishful thinking on my part—well, maybe a little. But mostly it's common sense."

Caro shuddered. "How could he stand it? Having the accident thrown up in his face again."

"Forget him," Amy muttered. "Think of us. Of Rachel. They'd start digging, looking. . . ."

Everyone nodded; the agreement was general, but it was plain that further speculation could only ruin our lunch. We knew we needed more hard information, and the good news was that I'd get it soon. I had another textbook in outline, and I was going up to New York next week to see my publisher. New York meant David Freed, and David Freed meant access to Justin Lambert's plans.

"I'll get the story," I said grimly. "I'll get it if I have to wring David's neck."

"Oh, Rachel, you can do better than that," Amy teased, and made a kissy-mouth, and then they all joined in until I flushed scarlet. I usually did, when they got going on David. He hadn't married even once since the old days, unlike Amy and Bitsie, who were two for two; he hadn't taken holy orders, like Caro; clearly the man was waiting for unmarried me to fall into his arms. I countered with news of David's latest live-in, a gorgeous model with a bogus Brit accent. She said things like "I should have went" in it, which David told me, snorting. We told each other everything, I said; we were like family, for the love of God.

"So why the red face?" Caro asked sweetly.

"Thoughts of incest, Sister," I answered.

We all laughed, and Bitsie said, "Oh, this is so good, we should do it more often. Ten years, it's been ten fucking years! Who gives a damn about us anymore? Justin: all right, I agree; my rotten kid should be President ahead of Justin Lambert. But us? Who still cares?"

We took up the theme, grumbling and cursing, letting the liquor do the talking. Yeah! That's right! Who gives a good goddam—sorry, Caro—about us anymore? And this too, like the teasing about David and me, had become something of a ritual, without depth or substance. We knew who still gave a damn. We kept to the code and the habits that had kept us safe, and that was that.

It must have been some vague thought of this kind that reminded me of my dream. I told it, quickly.

Caro shook her head and several pins fell out. She could never manage all that thick red hair. She sighed. "Oh, the Judge. You know, I wish *I* could dream about him. But not some scary dream like yours. Because I miss him. Yes, really. He made me feel . . . not so vulnerable."

"Well, he's up in heaven, isn't he?" Amy asked, but wryly. She was still a militant atheist. "He must be happy, now he knows the whole story about Lighthouse Point. What's a heaven for, if not to find out all the old stuff you wanted to know?"

"People have the weirdest ideas about heaven," Caro said. "The old stuff doesn't go on mattering. The old stuff is exactly what you leave behind."

I think all of us—even Caro—tried to imagine a heaven so different from this world that the Judge, on entering, would leave his supple, inquiring intelligence at the door, like a useless umbrella. It did seem ridiculous.

"I was thinking of Lucia and all her nicknames," Bitsie said. "How she'd make up new ones all the time and then get to hate them. Like Lulu. First she loved it; then it drove her bananas."

"Right," I said. "She asked me a hundred times to quit calling her Lulu, but I kept forgetting."

And then we were all back in time, remembering Lucia and marveling. Was it possible we were ever that young? Lucia was still putting her monogram on everything and trying out different styles of handwriting. Lucia was still taking the tests in *Glamour* magazine and begging us to confirm—was she more the Timid Tease or the Sexy Pal?—because her scores came out even.

We laughed; we laughed too loudly, as we usually did. The details of Lucia's youth were like little keys that still unlocked what was noisy, giddy, dopey in us.

But then we were too quiet, remembering, and Bitsie broke in, saying, "Quick, Amy, do the dumb reporter with the stutter! That's my all-time favorite."

Amy put down her cranberry muffin and obliged. The reporter had said he was "in advertising"; Amy had met him at a party soon after the inquest into Lucia's death. He stuttered, but he was a real hunk, and Amy went out with him a few times before she discovered the tape recorder in his pocket.

They were up in her apartment. He was saying, "You're such a sweet kid and you've been through so much and I know there's things you want to get off your chest."

"Sure," Amy had answered. "Your hand, for starters."

Then she'd grabbed the clumsy box from his pants pocket and run to the window and tossed it three stories down.

Now she imitated his look of horrified hunkness so broadly that we all whooped, and people turned to stare. But what could they see? Four women unwinding over a Saturday lunch. Maybe someone's birthday, baby, promotion? Nobody could guess what it meant to us, still, to meet in public and make noise.

"Point of order," Bitsie said. "Amy broke the alphabet code. She called Rachel first, after she saw Justin on TV."

The alphabet code—ABCR—was another rule of some importance; that strict, impartial order of telephoning summed up the very essence of our bond. But Amy only sniffed.

"Of course I called you first, dumbbell. Nate answered. He said you'd gone to bed with a migraine but he'd tell you in the morning."

"Oh. He didn't tell me. Let me make a note: Brain that rotten kid."

"Then I called Caro," Amy said, "but Our Lady of Curfews wasn't taking personal calls. So I went on to Rachel. Say, before I forget. My service is sending you all a clipping about Boozadora. The creep got herself named Woman of the Year by the Epilepsy Foundation. She must have given them a pot of money."

Boozadora was our code name for Edith, one of Justin's three sisters. Caro made a face.

"Money?" she asked. "I bet they got ten bucks and a picture of her ugly mug to put on their stationery. Listen, I know those people."

Caro did fund-raising for her convent's outreach program in the slums of Philadelphia. Caro said, with what he knew about the rich, Jesus was Dick Tracy.

20

"Oh, Sister!" we said, because nuns are not supposed to say mean things about anyone. But Caro looked so feisty and freckled in her indignation that we drank to her wisdom: the rich are cheap and have ugly mugs.

So we went on laughing and talking and getting into one another's desserts, and the westering sun gilded our table, a benediction, a reminder. The afternoon was ending.

"I think it's time to drink to Lucia," Caro said. She always knew when it was time for that. I called to the waitress to clear our table of everything but the wine bottle and the glasses. For a minute or two we sat quietly. This time I was the one who felt her first.

"She's here," I said, when I was sure. "She's glad we're together. As we are and always will be."

We lifted our glasses, held them up to the light, drank. There was never any more to it than this. Lucia just arrived, slipping among us like a silken scarf. Death had kept her supple; death had kept her young and fair and exempt from shame and scandal. She didn't know why Lighthouse Point was famous and why she was famous too.

The last of the wine went down; it tasted of her gaiety and greediness, her careless, reckless youth.

Our youth.

After that came the sorrow. It rose around us, lapping and lifting like water, and it was so pure it felt like a kind of holy joy.

In the parking lot of the restaurant we wandered around for a while, checking out one another's cars and talking and touching.

Only Amy went off by herself, then came over to say, "I hate this part; it's so crappy. Look at me. I never cry."

"Does you good," Bitsie said. "Blow your nose, it's dribbling."

We always saw one another, at first, as the girls we once were, but when we had to leave we became avid for reality, and we marked and memorized the changes, what had thickened, faded, hollowed down. We saw one another then for what we had become: strong women, fit to go on leaning against the chilled gates of an old hell. I had once been our spokesman at those gates. They always let me end it.

"Kiss good-bye," I said. "We've got long drives, and this is enough for now. Remember, I'm seeing David next week. I'll hear about Justin. Big letter follows."

Bitsie held up both hands, with fingers crossed.

We kissed and parted.

I met David for lunch at Windows on the World, that restaurant that seems to float 110 stories high in the sky at the tip of Manhattan Island. Like the Matron's Place, it attracts hordes of tourists, but if I worked on Wall Street I'd go there often. Space is what New Yorkers starve for, and there you have it: sky all around, the dizzying view of the Narrows, the earth beyond the Jersey shore seeming to curve all the way to California.

"Sorry I'm late," David said, pretending to huff and puff as he sat down at our table. He always reserved the same one, next to a window, with the Statue of Liberty looking small as a chess piece below.

"No problem," I said. "I've been busy trying to read my new book contract. It won't make me rich, but it sure makes me feel important."

"Don't sign it without sending me a copy first," David said.

"I'll get someone in the office to look it over. Someone with publishing smarts."

"Oh, good idea," I said. "Not too much trouble?"

"Not for you," David said, but his smile seemed to flicker on and off like a flashlight with battery problems.

I patted his hand. "Yes, dear, I did see Justin on TV. He's left for Africa, hasn't he? Excellent timing. I didn't catch Harry Llewelyn diving for pennies on NBC, but Amy and Bitsie did."

"It wasn't my idea, Rachel."

"Didn't think it was. But I met with the troops last Saturday, and I've been delegated to grill you for the inside skinny."

"You'll get it," David said. He ran one thin olive-hued hand through his hair. "For what it's worth, anyway. Waiter? Vodka martini with an onion. Tio Pepe for me. With soda."

I whistled. "Oh, boy. Your stomach's on the fritz again. Harry must have given you some nasty surprise."

"Yes, but I should have been prepared. Because two months ago—after the story about the President's health broke—the Lamberts started sounding some of us out. They got me and Vinnie to fly down to the Lambert estate for a meeting: Old Henry, Uncle Benson, Smith, and Trager. We spoke our piece at the top of our lungs, but it was four against two and they outshouted us."

"Justin wasn't there?"

"He was in Canada, scouting up extra wheat. He was already working unofficially on the famine. But I talked to him twice on the phone, and each time he said not to worry, he'd nixed the thing for good."

"He told *you* he nixed it. Maybe he wasn't sounding so positive around his father."

"Maybe. But you should have seen Old Henry. He was being Mr. Genial for a change. Smiling at me and Vinnie and saying, 'Easy, boys, it can't hurt, can it?' Can't hurt! What assholes they are."

"So they tried it out. Maybe they're right. It'll come to a big fat zero anyway, won't it? David? Look at me."

"Who the hell knows," he mumbled, not looking. When the waiter brought our drinks he knocked back the sherry and ordered himself a vodka martini. Then he grinned at me. "Nice to see you, Rachel."

24

"Nice, yes, but I hate being a bad influence. I thought the ulcer was gone."

"Gone but not forgotten. 'Can't hurt.' Listen. . . ."

I listened until we were both almost through with our red snapper. It was an obvious relief to David to groan and curse in my company. Shit, he said, did the party need this? Everyone knew who the two real contenders were, and they were both good men, with solid organizations. It would be all the excitement the voters could take, a primary race between a couple of stars, no dumb dark horses, no outside spoilers. If there was any place for the "Lambert magic" it was to wave the wand over one of them, maybe broker a little, come out medium early. Instead there was this! When everyone knew Justin didn't stand a chance! But the Lamberts had gone crazy. Talking like ditsy women. No, snorting and rearing in their stalls like old cavalry nags, sniffing gunpowder. Charge! Go for it! David and Vinnie had felt like they were plugged into some bad movie.

"David," I said sternly, "quit it. You're exaggerating. You've seen them go through these fits before."

"This is different." He looked drained and disgusted. "This is for President. They're out of control."

"I'll buy that," I said. "At a better price than 'ditsy women,' too."

"Pardon the sexual put-down." David sighed. "But one more remark like that and you can read your own contract."

"Poor David. You really are upset. What else? Tell. Give your ulcer a break."

He sighed again. The table was cleared now, and he kept drawing lines on the tablecloth with his fork. He took my hand, dropped it, squirmed in his chair.

"Rachel? I can't sleep. I'm feeling it too, a little. I keep thinking about the old days. Campaigning. And after. Running things. It's getting to me; my stomach knew it before I did."

"Your own job doesn't help. I know that."

"It's no help at all. I can't make it mean enough. Inside, where it counts. A job that anyone in this city would kill for."

I pressed his hand; I didn't have to comment. David was the acting head of the Lambert Foundation on Fifth Avenue, a place that was part think tank, part philanthropic gusher. He hired Nobel laureates; he dispersed millions of dollars every year. He had power, real power, and he used it with the absentminded competence of a bored, honest clerk.

"I understand," I said. "How you're feeling. Just remembering the old days makes you feel so . . . is it young? Vital? Something. Hard to keep throwing cold water on it."

"You can't feel it that way, Rachel."

"I feel it my way. Differently, but I feel it."

For a while we sat stirring our coffee in easy quiet. We could sit for long stretches like that. Sometimes the past was a pillow; we'd put back our heads and rest on it.

Suddenly David stopped slouching and sat up straight. "Listen, Rachel. And don't get mad, either! That next summer, after the inquest was finished, when you moved to New York and started living with Sidney Miller? Seems like he puts out a book a year these days. Well, I've always wanted to ask you. You didn't give anything to Sidney to go on, did you? A writer and all. I see him, now and then, because he sits on one of our foundation councils, and I always wonder. How *did* you handle it, with Sidney? He must have asked a million questions. Don't get mad."

I gulped some coffee and put the cup down hard. "I'm not getting mad," I said coldly. "I *am* mad. What a creep you can be. Implying I'd talk to Sidney about the accident."

"You lived with him for two years. Christ, you even thought about marrying him! Why shouldn't I worry what you talked about?"

"Some piss-poor worrier you are. If you were so concerned, why didn't you ask me years ago?"

I kept up the sarcasm for another minute or two, but I couldn't keep it going. David didn't deserve it. The past might be a pillow at odd moments, but mostly it was more like a cheap old mattress, poking at us with its busted springs. This business about Justin and the presidential primary was digging at David, making him squirm, reviving old worries by way of fresh anxieties. David was one of us; his fears were ours too. And who was I to fault him, me with my drenched dreams about the lawn, the fog, the Judge?

"All right," I said. "I know what you mean. The accident.

And we never were explicit, were we, about how we would handle the important people in our lives, people who were close enough to ask for the 'real story.' Ha ha. In quotes. Well, Caro and Bitsie and Amy and I used to compare notes. I had Sidney—we all had someone like that—and we wanted our stories to have some consistency. Give us some credit! But after I walked out on Sidney there was no more need for mine. There wasn't anybody, later, who had the right to ask."

"You didn't fall in love again, after Sidney."

"If it *was* love. It was more like . . . shelter."

"He wasn't good enough for you."

"He got me through a bad time. No regrets."

"His last book got terrible reviews. No regrets."

We started laughing. David ordered more coffee and folded his arms, so I knew he wasn't letting me off the hook.

"Oh, shit," I said. "This is embarrassing. How I handled Sid. Well. David, I'm not proud of knowing this, but I do know it: the best way to keep a secret is to bury it in irrelevant detail. I swear to you, I gave Sid so much background stuff he used to beg me to quit. And I wouldn't. I'd tell him he had to get the whole picture. How young we were and enthusiastic, five girls all working our butts off to make Justin a winner. Even if it was for his second term as governor, the race was tight, what with Polsky having so much upstate support. People like Sid think it's all so easy! That always annoys me. So there we were, Bitsie and I as paid staff, and Lucia and Caro and Amy volunteers. How close we got. And how we felt when Justin won and Bitsie and I got great jobs. Politics? I'd say to Sid. Oh, sure, everyone has a hand out; that's the game, and I knew how to play it.

"And oh, yes, how we all idolized Justin. That was important. How he didn't forget us, after he won. My troops, he called us, my mascots, my luck. Tandy too; I'd always bring her in: Mrs. Justin Lambert. I gave her the credit for getting us invited to all the picnics and parties at the governor's mansion and how whoever didn't have a date or something better to do would dress up and go and maybe lend a hand if one was needed. We never thought of ourselves as guests. We'd fill in for the coat-check girl who didn't show, or help the caterer, or warm up the floor if there was

27

dancing. We'd get there early and give the high sign to the guards to let us park up front. And then, going home, we'd brag to one another about how we'd met this big wheel in the party, made some time, worked the room. . . .

"My God, this is embarrassing! Because we really were like that. I was showing off to Sidney, what an insider I was, what a real pol!

"Well. Let me get this over with. I told Sid a little about Vinnie. More about you, but that was natural. And then I'd tell about the next three years, zipping past, and then that summer. The accident. The inquest.

"I knew I had to be careful with Sidney about the inquest, and not just because he was a writer. He'd had a year of law school. He had plenty of hotshot questions, you can believe it. But I moved first. Fast. I took the bull by the horns. No, I took the bullshit by the horns. 'Listen, Sidney,' I said, straight out, 'I know that everyone and his brother thinks we were bribed. Call it suborning a witness if you like, but who doesn't think the Lamberts wouldn't have tried it? And gotten away with it too. They run that state like it's some feudal fief, and what they don't own they can buy and what they can't buy they can ruin.

"'But the Lamberts are just rich,' I said to Sid, 'and they're not dumb. They don't buy what they can get for free. We told them what we knew. They got the whole truth from us, and I'll say this for them: they believed us. Granted, they're not nice people. Granted that Justin is the best of them, a sport, a freak of plain decency. At least the Lamberts and their crowd stood by us. They didn't leave us alone to stew in the mess and the misery. They didn't hound us and vilify us, like the press and the public. The press!' I said to Sidney. 'If we answered a question in the same way, they said it was obvious we were coached. If we differed on some point or some opinion, they yelled for blood. Who was lying?'

"I did a damn good job, David! And as for writers . . . I'm one myself, remember? I had it *down*, all four of us had it down, the innocence and the injury and—goddammit, David, this is really unpleasant. Look what you've gone and made me do."

My eyes were stinging. I rubbed at them.

"I am so dumb." David groaned.

28

"No, you're not," I said. "You're just as nervous as a wet cat, and I am too, and I don't have as many reasons as you do. David? Was Justin lying, two months ago, when he told you he'd throttle those primary plans?"

"That never occurred to me. He sounded one hundred percent sincere."

"He can always do that. He's a crowd-pleaser."

"That's a bitchy thing to say," David said. "I'm in the crowd? You think that's the kind of relationship I have with him?"

"No. You're friends. That was bitchy. But he's weak."

"He has been. He was."

"I'll throw up, here and now, if you say he's changed all that much."

"You're in some mood. I wasn't going to say that."

"You were thinking it. Wishful thinking."

"Screw off. You don't have a license to read minds. Why don't you just spit it out? You think Justin can sucker me."

"He can sucker anyone. That's what the 'Lambert magic' really means."

We were glaring at each other. David switched his glare off first.

"Nervous isn't the word for it. Be a sport, Rachel. Don't catch the afternoon train. Stay in town and go to a museum. Do some damage in the stores. After work, we'll have dinner."

"Can't. I have a meeting at nine. My Senior Honors List, all one of him."

"Well, anyway, this was good. You've got what to tell the troops. And in spite of my gut, and remembering the old days, I want them to know Vinnie and I are on the record. You should have heard us with the Lamberts. Screaming and shouting. '*No go! He can't run!*' "

"Oh, shut up already," I said. "I believe you."

I did, of course, and he knew it. He called for the check and paid it, and we walked to the elevators. We looked down at the tiny tugboats and the bridges and the water winking in the thin May sunshine.

"I hate to tell you," David said, "but you've smeared your mascara and you look exactly like Rocky Raccoon."

29

"You go down," I said. "I'll go to the ladies'. Thanks for the lunch, and don't be stingy with the phone calls. You're in touch with things and I'm out in the boonies. Any news, good, bad, or indifferent, I want to hear."

"Will do. You just remember what side I'm on. And if the news should be bad . . . well, you know what comes next. Brace yourself."

"Lighthouse Point," I muttered, just as the elevator came.

"Lighthouse Point," David repeated, and he hit me twice on the upper arm and grinned at me from inside the elevator. "Two for flinching," he said, and then the doors closed.

I needed a subway, a train ride, and an hour and a half's drive to get back to Columbus College, but I didn't feel in the least sorry for myself. It's what's at the end of the trip that matters, and I liked where I lived. The college was home to me. It's just a few quadrangles of gray stone set down in the badlands of Pennsylvania, a small oasis between a pair of coal-dark mountains. It says THIS WAY OUT to the sons and daughters of the miners, and the children of their former bosses too, because the region is seriously depressed. You wouldn't know that from the atmosphere on campus. The kids are so hardworking and hopeful, and the local people—meaning residents who live within a hundred miles—flock in for adult ed and film festivals and poetry readings and little theater. They come with an air of expectancy, and a willingness to be puzzled as well as pleased. They're plain people and it's a plain place, and I feel about it as I do about love: it's not Harvard and it doesn't have to be.

When I came here, nearly four years after Lighthouse Point, I knew that some of my notoriety would precede me. That story might be ancient history to my freshmen lit students, but the faculty would have longer memories. There'd be the look that lasts a second too long or the absentminded reference, covered with a cough. But I also knew I wouldn't have to handle any hard questions. I'd found out for myself how much curiosity gets muffled by shyness and good manners. That ordinary American kindness is so valuable I don't think it should ever be called "common."

So I sat easily in the train, marking up some student essays, and then I read and then I dozed. But I woke up feeling headachey and irritable, and when I got off the train I had to hang around the Kiss 'n' Park for a while, drinking vile coffee from a vending machine and washing down the aspirins. When my head cleared, I started the drive, knowing full well that my headache wasn't the half of it.

There were no pills to take away the sharp exasperation I felt with myself. I knew I'd nursed a hope that should never have been born: that David would tell me what I wanted to hear. Hey! I'd wanted him to say, don't tell me you're worried about what that gas bag Llewelyn leaked! Nothing to it! The Lamberts are furious with the old geek. A joke, a mistake.

David hadn't said anything of the kind.

David was so worried his ulcer was back.

He was so worried he'd even let slip that unguarded "maybe," when I'd suggested that Justin had caved in to his family's pressure.

The Lamberts. They didn't just sit securely on their money and power. It wasn't old money, or refined old-boy power, either. It was a brass tank, made to move and crush, and they rode it up and down the eastern seaboard into banking, real estate, insurance, politics. And if you didn't go along for the ride, you had better get out of their way.

Oh, Justin. He *was* the best of them. It wasn't love and it didn't have to be, because memory is all it takes to do the trick. I wanted to hit him, kiss him, pull his hair, stroke his cheek. *Don't!* Don't let them run you. You know you don't need it or want it and you can't have it anyway, not after Lighthouse Point, not even ten years

32

after. The story of Lighthouse Point will always be there—two stories: the one the world knows, and the one *we* know, Caro and Bitsie and Amy and Vinnie and David and I—and you, Justin, you. It lives for all of us in that monstrous twinship, and that summer I went to Rome—oh, it was awful—I took an excursion to Pompeii and the guide kept us in a museum room with calcified mummies and he went on talking and I thought I'd faint, then and there, because I couldn't tear my eyes away from the glass cases, those pitiful bodies all curled up with their arms over their heads, trying to ward off that deadly rain of fire and ash and caught for all time in their last moments of suffocating agony.

I was doing seventy-five. I might have gone to ninety if I hadn't heard the wail of the trooper's siren, and I pulled over onto the shoulder of the interstate and took my ticket without a word of excuse. I was only ten miles from the campus and I crawled the rest of the way, trembling and ashamed because I had abandoned myself so dangerously, so mindlessly, to kiss and claw at the shade of a man I hadn't seen or heard from in ten mortal years.

But that was my doing too. There was all that "your sake" and "my sake" and our vow to separate forever, and what else did I have to be faithful to if it wasn't that final promise to stay apart? That I might have to be drawn publicly into his orbit again for a fool's game, a brazen gamble. . . .

I went right to Barber Hall and my nine o'clock appointment with my honors student. Then I went home. Ten-thirty found me in the bathtub; at eleven I went to bed; at eleven-thirty I was up and vacuuming the living room. I knew I was being ridiculous but I didn't care. There was no one to laugh but me. And I did feel like laughing, even though I knew I was out of control, mumbling and cursing, wishing and wanting, defrosting my refrigerator at I-can't-believe-it's one in the morning.

Well, it happens like that sometimes. The past just comes on to you like some flamboyant jerk in a nightclub and whirls you around, and even while you're crying Let go! you only hold on tighter. Because of the music. Because you know all the steps. Because you haven't danced for such a long time and it makes you feel exactly twenty-three years old.

33

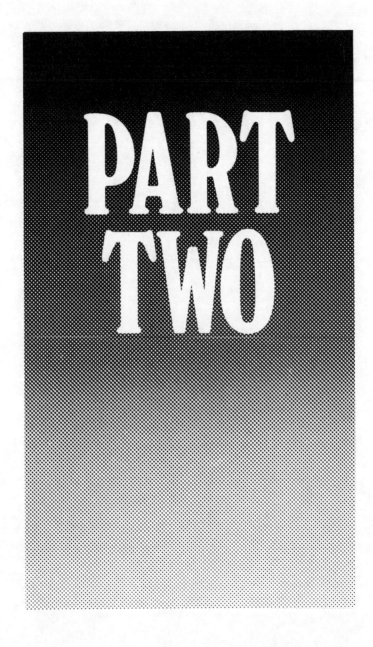

PART
TWO

5

Justin and I fell in love at first sight. He is a large man and I am a small woman, so it wasn't easy. He stood up behind his desk when I came into his office and he looked right over my head. I looked right into his tie. We both laughed.

"This is Rachel Warshowsky," David said. "Myers recruited her from Tillman's group in New York. You remember. Rachel is going to do women's issues, PR, and the suburban advance stuff."

"I hope that's not all," Justin said. He came around the desk to shake my hand. "Myers told me about all the other good work you did for Hizzoner. I hear you can polish a mean speech." It was his second campaign for governor.

"I can do that too," I said. "David said he'd let me help out wherever."

"If that's a wish I'll see that you get it. You'll be sharing an office with Bitsie Ames. She's in charge of scheduling. I'm sure you'll like her."

"Oh, I think I'm going to like everything."

He laughed. "I think I won't disillusion you. But to tell the truth I was expecting someone older."

"So was I," I said, and that's all it took. Funny, David told me later, I could feel it too. I thought it was only because the Orioles were two runs ahead.

He was married. He had three children. The first time I saw Tandy—it was a nickname for Alexandra—she'd come to our shabby campaign headquarters to pose for some poster stills. I watched her being photographed with Justin and thought how much they looked alike, brother-and-sister alike, two large, fair people with heavy limbs and narrow, wide-spaced eyes that scrunched nearly closed when they smiled.

"She's very nice," Bitsie said. "And very dumb. Everyone knows that."

Bitsie and I had become roommates; she'd invited me to share her apartment. She needed a roommate to help with the rent, and she said that if we could get along in the cramped slum of a campaign office, we were a cinch to share a bathroom. I loved living with Bitsie. Aside from herself and her nice apartment, she was fifth-generation in that city and knew everything about everyone, or seemed to.

So when she said Tandy was dumb, I didn't argue, although Tandy hadn't struck *me* that way. I merely asked, with real curiosity, why a man like Justin Lambert would marry a stupid woman.

"He got married when he was twenty-two," Bitsie answered. "He got a homecoming queen with *Mayflower* connections, and don't think *that* didn't knock the socks off his old man. The Lamberts have been marrying up since they got off the boat. Which was not named the *Mayflower*. Don't blame me, Rachel, I'm quoting people."

"I'm not blaming you."

"I hate sounding like a country-club twit. Even if I am one. Anyway, they were in love then. Everyone said so and the wedding was lovely; my mother went. But he was twenty-two! I mean. Please."

We agreed that that was awfully young to get married. And when I knew Tandy better—she played her dutiful part in our strategy for the women's vote—I had to admit that she wasn't all that bright. No one took her seriously. She simply contributed, much as if she were writing a check, her large, fair presence where it was needed and everyone accorded her the unambiguous affection you give to a lovely child or a beautiful pedigreed animal. Tandy didn't care about politics; that was the main thing. She didn't have a particle of interest in the process, or the prerogatives either, and in the atmosphere of a campaign headquarters—my atmosphere—this attitude was a sign of such profound otherness it made her seem to belong to a different race.

Yet she awed me. I had come up in the world, much more than I ever let anyone know; she had been born at the very top, and the whole world knew it. Next to such quiet self-possession, such bland benevolence, I often felt like a yapping little terrier trying to get Lassie's attention.

I tried to copy her quiet voice and her manners. I tried to walk more slowly, like she did. David asked me once if someone was slipping Valium into my coffee, but I didn't stop trying to imitate Tandy's serenity until the night Justin told me he loved me.

That was three months before election day, when the countdown frenzy was starting, the longer hours, the late nights, and the polls showing up all the weak spots. In the middle of all that frantic patch-and-dab, the flu started going around and our people started dropping in their tracks, tossing—with awful groans—their card files at the still standing.

One day Bitsie announced that she couldn't help it, I would have to pitch in and do the advance when Justin swung through Forrester County, in the westernmost corner of the state. I couldn't find it on a map; I couldn't pronounce it properly, either. (You said "Foster" or they'd laugh you into West Virginia.) But I borrowed a car and I went and booked four rooms for the entourage in the only hotel in the county seat. Then I lined up the Elks and Rotary and the Future Farmers and the Sons of Erin; I made sure of the chairs and the coffee and the banners for the windup banquet, and when Justin got to his first stop, three days later, I had a high school band playing "Hail, Columbia" on the steps of Our Lady of Blessed Counsel.

The weather was wonderful. The sun shone in golden spangles on the trumpets and the tuba. The district leader took Justin's arm when he stepped out of the car, but the other arm was free, and when Justin saw me he touched his head and pantomimed a wild cowboy wave. Hats off.

After that the weekend went off without more than a couple of bad glitches, and by Sunday night we were back in the county seat. Vinnie had come along this trip; all the overnight trips had Vinnie or David on hand. The two of them had Justin's fullest confidence, and the locals knew they could make their needs and suggestions audible to a pair of ears that were as good as the Governor's, almost.

By the time the last bannered banquet was over I was exhausted, not so much with the work—I was used to work—as with the strain. I'd driven hundreds of miles around that huge, unpopulated county; it was a far cry from organizing in the capital suburbs. I was not a good driver or map reader, either, and I was in knots trying to keep to schedule.

People were clearing out of the hotel banquet room, and I was thinking of sneaking off by myself to go upstairs when Vinnie came over to me.

"The Guv wants to talk to you. Hang around a few minutes. He thinks you did a terrific job. We all do."

"Thanks, Vinnie. But he already told me."

"Well, it must be something else then," Vinnie said. "He was very definite. Just hang around a few minutes."

I hung around. The hotel help dismantled the head table with its dinky sateen skirt and stiff little flower arrangements and bulbous old-fashioned mike. Justin was at the door, saying goodbye and shaking hands with the last of the regulars.

Then he came over to the table I was sitting at, a forlorn couple of planks now that its tablecloth was gone. I loved him so much I had no thoughts other than how tired he looked and how well his speech had gone over. He sat down opposite me.

"I love you," he said. "I have to tell you. It's making me sick, how much I love you."

He sounded perfectly matter-of-fact, and I answered in the same way, the way you find yourself speaking in a dream, no matter how absurd the circumstances.

40

"You can't love me," I said. "You're married. I can love you but you can't love me."

"I don't seem to have much choice," he said. "I actually enjoyed it, at first. When you first came down from New York. I enjoyed it. Now it's just making me sick."

"I'm sorry for that," I said. "It doesn't do that to me."

We sat for a minute or two without saying anything. Then I just said I was too sleepy to talk anymore and I got up to go to the elevator. He followed me into a creaking old box that smelled of ancient cigar smoke and machine oil, and then he followed me to my room. The corridor of our floor was very dark, and the old boards beneath the shabby carpet creaked at every step. At the door to my room he put his arms around me and kissed me very gently on the mouth. I must be dreaming, I thought, but the kiss was so shy and tentative—a boy's kiss, uncertain of its welcome—that I didn't stiffen. I had a quick premonition: an immediate future just as shy and uncertain as that kiss, full of lingering looks and delicate confusions and what-if's and yes-but's, a high school girl's fantasy of romance to embroider and embellish as she sits dreaming away another study hall.

"Good night," I said, and turned and opened my door and went into my room. But I didn't close the door on him. He was right behind me, and his hands were on my shoulders and he was whispering into my hair.

"It's love, Rachel," he said. "I know it, trust me. I'll guard you with my life and keep you safe forever."

He hugged me so tightly I felt my breath go short. But even so, I knew I wasn't being overpowered. I was dazed with surprise and exhaustion; I didn't feel a flicker of desire; I was perfectly capable of telling him to go. But I knew, as even girls in high school know, that it was just a question of sooner or later. And that there would not ever again be a time for the two of us to be so alone in a place so far away, at least until the election was over. After all, I knew his schedule by heart. And so did he.

Had Justin and I become lovers sooner—at this point we were barely ten weeks from election day—perhaps it would all have been different. I had a talent for secrecy and also for making friends—the second point follows from the first—on a carefully

41

superficial level. I could have kept the affair very neatly to myself. But months before that night I had moved into Bitsie's apartment and we had become real friends. We worked well together, too, and had such a good time we seemed to affect the whole office. It was a happy place; before long we were the nucleus of what we called the Corps, five young women all caught up in the excitement of a winning campaign. And we weren't so young that we didn't know how lucky we were. How often does it happen? To work hard for a cause you believe in, surrounded by the people you like best in the world?

There was Bitsie Ames, first, with her boarding-school baby voice, wicked legs, and streaky-blond hair. You had to know her to understand how soft she was, inside. Like Justin, she'd led a privileged life; like him, she seemed to wear a perpetual top hat of self-assurance.

Amy Shillitoe came to campaign headquarters as a one-day substitute reporter for the *Dispatch* and got hooked and became a volunteer. No matter how much cynicism and foul language she threw around, Amy was doomed—by her elfin frame and horn-rims—to be the Cute Kid in every office.

As for Caro Fitzhugh, she was just the opposite of Bitsie. All her softness was exterior; she had a large, languid body and a redhead's fragile skin and such a mild manner you'd think she was shy. She wasn't; she used her volunteer status to lobby relentlessly for preschool education, and with her passionate pestering she got Justin to mention it in half his speeches.

Next there was me. I think of those little bios the newspapers ran under our pictures, after the accident.

Rachel Warshowsky, 26, former consultant on Governor Lambert's second campaign, presently Associate Director of State Board of Trade. . . .

"The dark one," *Time* magazine called me, subtly slandering all brunettes. "Miss Warshowsky wore a flowered print dress that enhanced her gypsy looks."

The four of us were so tight you'd think there wasn't room

enough for a toothpick in our midst, let alone another girl. But Lucia Bennett wasn't just another girl.

Lucia waltzed in one day and sat on Bitsie's desk and asked if she could help out. The volunteer coordinator was out to lunch that day, and Bitsie and Caro and Amy and I were sharing yogurt and carrot sticks in the office. It was a Sunday, a quiet day with time to breathe and shuffle paper.

"Glad to have you," Bitsie said. "What would you like to do?"

"Carry the Governor's briefcase," Lucia said. "He is *so* dreamy."

"He carries his own briefcase," Bitsie said tartly. "Anything else?"

"Clean the bathrooms," Lucia said. "Get coffee. Honestly, I'll do anything. Point. I'll do it."

And before we could all do any more eye-rolling and snickering up our sleeves—Lucia was wearing torn jeans that day, a dirty T-shirt, and a gold Rolex worth more than our combined bank balances—she told us that she wanted to work on the campaign because it would "sound serious" to her brother and sister-in-law who had been her guardians since her parents were killed in a plane crash years ago, when Lucia was eleven. They still thought they ran her life; she had dropped out of college; they wanted her to go back and no way, José, she had gotten print poisoning from a year of reading horrible books.

You had to laugh. You had to like her. Bitsie gave her the worst work in the place: cold-calling registered past contributors who hadn't coughed up dime one this time around, and Lucia sat down then and there with a card file and started calling and kept at it—with some success—till dinnertime. She invited the four of us for pizza and beer, paid the check with an astounding tip to the "cute waiter," and then had to borrow five dollars from Amy to put gas in her brother's MG.

When she roared off into the night, Bitsie watched her go. "Ten dollars says she doesn't show up on Monday."

"She lives in Fort Leeds," Caro said. "She has to return that car to her brother tomorrow, and I'll bet she doesn't come back too."

But Lucia not only came back, she came back on a Trailways

43

bus, a means of transportation as exotic—to her—as an elephant. And she took the grungy hall bedroom in the house Caro and Amy shared with two other girls and paid them three months' rent in advance.

"It's my insurance," she said proudly. "If I don't have that money, I won't spend it. Works like a charm."

Armed with her "sounds serious" position in our office, she had wheedled a small living allowance out of her brother. To everyone's amazement, she treated her volunteer status as if it were a paying slot from which she could be fired at any minute. She worked with all the energy and enthusiasm you'd expect from an ex-cheerleader with a real brain, and before long we were each of us taking credit for her and including her in everything and planning how to get her something substantial to do when the campaign was over. She wouldn't go back to college. And we didn't want to lose her.

Justin told me that Vinnie and David knew how he felt about me. But even without that, I would have told my friends. And then my love for Justin, and his for me, bloomed for us like some private garden, embowering everyone, hiding us all. It was a scented, secret kingdom for a royal pair and our friends were our courtiers, canny and protective. No one had to say a word about what would happen if even a whisper of an "office affair" got out! We were now two months from an election, and Justin was both our center and our future. To protect him might seem like a matter of duty or self-interest, but it was more than that. We *believed* in him; we had a faith in his worth that was nearly religious. So in the next two months I saw Justin alone just twice, and each time represented a consensus of caution to which I willingly agreed. Once he came to my apartment when Bitsie was out. Once I was "assigned" to drive him to a county fair, and in a traffic tie-up that lasted for over an hour we sat speechless with delight, holding hands.

That was Caro you saw on TV, the night he won, holding up a little girl from her Head Start program for the Governor's big kiss.

That was Amy who did the article in the *Dispatch* about how the New Politics attracted young people.

44

That was Lucia, smiling in the photograph above the article, described as a girl who took "time out from books for a real-world experience."

Kings have divine rights. Justin was governor for a second term and he loved me, not Tandy. But queens live in the great governor's mansion with its stone pillars and its ten servants, and the princes of the blood rest their fair young heads against the folds of her velvet skirt on ten thousand Christmas cards with a facsimile signature on the bottom.

Governor and Mrs. Lambert wish you peace and prosperity in this joyous holiday season.

The king's favorite lives in a row house within walking distance of her new job in the State Capitol Annex. She has a cat named Forrester and a housemate named Bitsie who is often elsewhere and has an equally good, equally new position over in Parks and Recreation. In spite of her long hours working on the Board of Trade, the king's favorite has an active social life. She is often seen at parties, discos, and restaurants with David Freed. She and David hold hands a lot. They're an item. They have been heard talking about marriage, but not soon, not till they both feel it's the "right time."

Oh, Justin. The care we took, the false trails we left. We did the necessary: we hid our love in plain sight, always in a crowd. We pulled together like a fine pair of matched dray horses, and our shoulders were grooved to the harness of a long, clandestine affair. That harness chafed him more than it did me. I was only twenty-three when we met, and I couldn't count the cost of love. No price seemed too high for it, not if it would keep him safe. He was the Governor; he was a Lambert; he would be a senator next, and there were people—smart, powerful people who had seen them come and seen them go—who said he was on his way to the White House. Divorce was no longer considered an impossible handicap in politics, but it had to be an *old* divorce, all passion spent, long past the headlines and settlements and faces of hurt. When Justin spoke about divorcing Tandy and marrying me, I thought I had no other option but to soothe him.

45

I didn't believe him when he said things like, "Oh, let's shove it, Rachel. Tell them all to go to hell! I don't really like the game anymore. I don't think I ever did. I was just so young when I got started. Listen, if my father had had three sons and one daughter instead of the other way around, you think I'd have chosen to live in a goldfish bowl?"

"You'd have been the best of them. If he had seven sons. You're a natural. Everyone says so, and you know it too."

"You can be good at something and not like it. You can be good and still know it's not good for *you*."

I used to laugh when he said things like that. I'd say, "See what I mean? It's part of being so good. You always seem as if you can do without it. Reluctant. Not all eaten up with ambition. And it's true and I love it and so does everyone else."

"You don't understand what I'm saying. That's okay. Half the time I don't understand it myself. But I never forget it. Never."

"We'll get married. We just have to wait. I don't think I want children. You've got three. Waiting's not so hard. I'm yours forever, and that's what matters."

And I'd tell him about old Mrs. DeVito, a fortuneteller who read my cards when I was little. You'll be loved well and truly, she told me, but it ain't gonna be like in the commercials.

He'd laugh and kiss me and the mood would be over.

He got the big old dirty diamond ring out of the family vault and hung it on a platinum chain, a long one, so that I could wear it all the time. It fell between and below my breasts, where no one could ever see. He put it around my neck and said that I was Rachel Lambert now, and instead of "I do" I said, "I am." I cried for happiness that night and he rocked me to sleep in his arms before he went back to the great house with the stone pillars.

That was fair, that was right. I didn't question the privileges of his queen. She deserved the warmth and bulk of him in their legal bed. And although I never asked about it, I knew that she deserved the slow kiss and the gentle hand when she wanted that, as well. She was his dim, distant, undemanding queen, and without ever putting it into words, I somehow thought of her as my other self.

I accepted her rights with such serenity I suppose you could

46

say I was still trying to imitate her. If so, it must have been best for us both. I never complained or asked for more of him. Tandy never guessed about me. It seemed fair. It was, at least, the way you see "fairness" when you're that young, that happy, that much in love for the first time in your life.

Soon after Justin gave me the ring—it was during our first year together—he told me about the gun. No, it was me who went first: I told him my real name. But whatever we had shared till then felt small and unimportant, compared to what we felt for the wounded children we could see in each other's eyes.

6

The house Justin bought for me was a brand-new row house, the last in its line, on the corner. I didn't know then—and I don't really know now—what complexities of dummy corporations, private trusts, or Swiss bankers arranged the purchase, but I signed some papers and put the deed in a drawer and paid the property taxes in my own name thereafter. There was no mortgage. It was mine to delight in and to furnish—much to Justin's amusement—with things I found in thrift shops and garage sales and country auctions. "To keep myself honest," was the way I put it to Justin, when he offered to help, and Bitsie, when she took the second bedroom, insisted on paying me rent. These sops to conscience satisfied us both, and we could revel in the pleasures of a beautiful kitchen, central air-conditioning, and walking to work.

You could walk back from work too, if it wasn't getting dark. In spite of its proximity to the gold-domed state capitol and its sleek modern annex, the neighborhood was seedy. It was just starting to attract the developers and the rehabbers and the kind of smart young people who would rather risk an occasional mugging than move to the suburbs or to the bland high-rises on the "good" side of the city. The process of gentrification was just beginning, and Bitsie and I could scurry past the winos and flowing trash cans and feel like pioneers. And I could grumble, on cue, about being an "urban guerrilla" and making a "risky investment," for all the world, as if it were really my money I'd used in the interests of equity real estate. But all that was just window dressing, not calculation. I never thought of the house as anything other than Justin's house, no matter whose name was on the deed. He'd chosen it. He'd chosen me. We were both part of his domain.

The best thing of all was the private garage, under the house. The only drawback was neighborhood curiosity, because neither Bitsie nor I owned a car. But once or twice a week that empty space would contain, for a bare minute, a car, driven by Vinnie or David, and in perfect privacy Justin would leave that car and put his key into the door that led to the kitchen. The car would pull away. Later, it would come back for him. I would watch, from the living room window, its two red taillights winking at the corner stop sign.

Sometimes we'd have only an hour or two. Sometimes he'd leave past midnight. We never minded much if it was one hour or five; happiness and gratitude were what we offered to the gods of chance and their blessing on our safety.

He'd always call me in plenty of time to plan. Bitsie would arrange her time elsewhere. I'd have a day or two to think, like any prudent housewife, of the casserole I'd leave that morning to defrost in the kitchen sink. Chicken cacciatore. Beef à la mode. He liked rich, spicy meats that fell apart at a touch. The smoking-hot wisps of steam would catch in my hair as I served him. All day, at my desk at the Board of Trade, I would find myself thinking of the food I had ready for him, ready now, thawing, melting, falling apart at a touch.

After Justin gave me the diamond ring, I felt I couldn't wait any longer. It was one of what we called our "lucky nights," when we had hours and hours. I wasn't even afraid. I took his hands and opened them and kissed the palms. "I love you," I said, "and my real name is Robin White."

I told him everything. He was the first person I'd ever told. I saw his narrow, blue-gray eyes grow big behind the tears.

I'm not Jewish and I'm not from New York, I told him. I'm from Dover, Delaware, and I grew up in a trailer park so rag-ass it didn't have a name. "Tin Town" is what people called it. "They live over in Tin Town, and pity the poor postman."

I wish I could say that was the worst thing I heard about my home. But it's the worst thing I'm going to tell you.

See this scar on my leg? That's from the time my father threw a hot frying pan at me because I made him two eggs, not three, and one with the yolk broken.

My father drank, I said. He had a truck and he ran bootleg whiskey and untaxed cigarettes up from North Carolina. Sometimes he'd do honest work, like hauling up Christmas trees, but Mama said that was on account of the other woman, in Greensboro.

Poor Mama. She took it and took it. She worked six days a week in the beauty parlor, downtown, and she was proud her customers couldn't guess she lived in Tin Town. She was proud of me, too, and my good marks in school. She was proud I was an only child. There were packs of seven and eight brats in those tin cans.

We were in a good school district, though. Mama impressed that on me, and I couldn't tell her how I wished we had a school of our own, just for trailer kids. That way I wouldn't have had to see those others, from nice homes. If they had a big black-and-blue mark on them, you knew it came from falling off a bike. You knew they had parents like on TV. "Dear, would you answer the door?" "Dear, did you get the station wagon fixed?"

Bad enough, seeing that on TV.

He put my mother in the hospital once.

I'm coming to the bad part. But first the Warshowskys. That's the good part.

The Warshowskys were an old couple who'd once owned a big on-time furniture store in Dover, but they sold it when the neighborhood changed. They needed help in their house and yard, and I answered their ad on the Safeway bulletin board. I was twelve but I looked sixteen. I had my full growth: hips, bosom, all as much as they ever would be. Anyway, they hired me, and I kept the job for five years. I loved them. I loved their house. I went there every day after school, to clean and iron and rake and polish everything till it shone. I'd eat my supper with them. They had a canary. They'd tell me stories about Russia, where they came from, and they'd make me tell about school and what I was reading. They loved books. Tolstoy. Conrad. Isaac Singer.

They'd never pry about Tin Town, either. Only they'd ask, How's Mama? She's good? That cough, it's better?

They taught me about the special Jewish holidays and what they signified. I picked up some Yiddish too, funny words like *gonif* and *chutspah* and *meshuggeneh*, and when I asked them to take me to their synagogue for services, they did that too, whenever I wanted. I'd get dressed up on a Friday night and tell my folks the Warshowskys needed me to wait on table because they had company.

Go ahead, my father would say. I like their money more than I like them. It was Ikies started World War Two.

I don't think he was born that dumb. It was the life he led, and the drinking. He even believed they paid me fifty cents an hour. It was $2.50, and Mama banked it in a special account he couldn't touch. She hoped I'd go to college.

All right. The bad part.

He had done ninety days once for running whiskey, no time at all, and it made him reckless. There was money in it. He talked too much.

Two days after he put Mama in the hospital, the troopers came to the trailer. I said he was away, but I knew he was making a run. So they left, and they went around Tin Town asking questions. Sandy White? Ever buy any booze from him? I knew what they were asking.

I was crazy with worry about Mama. He'd broken her jaw.

I heard his truck coming up the road. I knew the sound of it.

I could have warned him. Instead, I ran and hid in the woods and when the troopers came back there he was, opening a crate.

51

I could have warned him.

He got three years this time, but he served only six months. He got in a fight and another prisoner broke his rib and the rib punctured his heart.

I would have done just what you did, Mama said. Cry for yourself, if you want to, but not for him. The road patrol spotted the truck anyway, doing eighty. You couldn't have saved him.

The Warshowskys' daughter was a guidance counselor at the high school. She got me to prepare for the SATs; she got me to apply for the scholarship to Barnard. I changed my name when I won it: White to Warshowsky, how's that for a switch? Mama thought it was a nutty thing to do, but she understood. I loved them.

All my friends at Barnard were Jewish. I was a new person. If anyone asked me what my father did, I said he was dead but he used to own a little furniture store in Dover.

Mama moved to Cape Canaveral. The Warshowskys died, one right after the other. I never went back to Dover.

I was a new person, *Spiegel-neu*, mirror-new. I had school, friends, a part-time job in the student aid office, and oh, New York, and being young and dating nice boys with good manners, clean hands. Gabe Lewis got me my first real job after college, in his father's firm. Political PR, that's how I started, first crack out of the box.

I sent Mama fifty dollars a week until she died. Of the usual.

He loosened my teeth once, but she got the wired jaw.

When he wasn't drunk, only mellow, he used to play twelve-string guitar. He would sing, too.

I could have warned him. I have to live with that. But I think, I was only fourteen! And if they hadn't put him away, he'd have done something worse. Mama always said that. Something worse. Maybe to her? Maybe to me.

Justin called me Robin then; he kissed the whitened scar on my leg. I was a whole person to him, with nothing left out, and for the second time in my life I felt *Spiegel-neu*, mirror-new.

"The two of us," he murmured, "the two of us. I know what that guilt feels like. I'll tell you about it sometime."

"Tell me now," I whispered, and he did, and for years—two years—I truly believed I could do for his pain what he had done for mine.

I was too late.

I killed a girl, Justin said. I was thirteen. It was an accident.

She was one of the maids. Mother used to send servants ahead of us to the lodge. We only used it in shooting season. Duck.

I didn't mind going down ahead of the others with Mother and the servants. I'd go to the blinds by myself and hunker down and pretend I was bagging one after another.

I'd been shooting since I was ten.

That morning the cook and the chauffeur went into town to buy food. Ginger stayed back. She was cleaning the gun room when I came in. She was wiping the handle of the old Matlock.

You're not supposed to touch the guns, I said. Put that back.

My dad was strict about that. I felt important, telling her what to do.

They're not loaded, she said. She was wiping the handle.

Hand it over, I said. I wanted to open it and make sure it was empty. I wanted to show her I knew about guns.

She must have cocked it. Or it was cocked already. When I took it—I must have grabbed it too hard—it went off. There was a shell still in it.

Mother came running into the gun room.

Ginger was on the carpet with blood on her neck.

I was holding the gun.

Mother put it on the table. I don't remember handing it to her.

She called an ambulance. She said I must be brave and listen to her.

I heard her on the phone saying Ginger had shot herself.

She didn't, I said. I told her to give *me* the gun, and it went off.

She did, my mother said. It's nobody's fault. An accident.

I was too frightened to say more. I thought that Ginger

would tell the truth, when they fixed her up at the hospital. Mother would have to know Ginger was telling the truth.

I didn't realize that Ginger was dead. Mother did.

He was silent, sitting next to me on the sofa in the living room of our little house. In the lamplight I could see how pale he was. I had to ask him several times, "Then what happened? Justin? What happened next?"

Nothing, he said. We rode with Ginger in the ambulance. At the hospital, the sheriff came. He was a pal of my dad's. He told Mother to lean on me until my father got there.

Oh, Charlie, my mother said. That sound. I thought the boiler had exploded.

Nobody asked me anything. My father just told me that night that Mother had done the right thing and it was over and done with. If it's anyone's fault, my father said, it's mine; that's *my* gun, on *my* property, and I'm responsible.

I didn't know Ginger that well. She'd only been with us two years.

I suppose he gave her family something.

I suppose I wanted to think it was his fault.

I told Mother I didn't want to go shooting the next day.

You have to go, she said. You don't want any questions.

So I went.

Such a sparse, dry accounting it was. Only his pallor and the wetness of his hands in mine made me feel the presence of the boy who had to go out the next day to handle a gun. I hugged him to me; his back stayed straight and braced, a wall within my arms.

I saw a shrink, he said. Later, when I started screwing up at school. He was a cousin, and I didn't have to be told that I could be honest with him. He was family. I was safe.

The dream was making me crazy, always the same. I grabbed the gun and shot myself in the dream, and then I'd wake up soaking with sweat, thinking it was blood and screaming. But you know how it is in a dream. You think you're making this horrible noise but nothing comes out except little squeaks.

We'll work it through, the shrink used to say. It's painful, I know, but it's for your benefit.

Working it through means going over it, again and again. And talking about my parents. I guess it helped. I got my concentration back. I stopped hassling my teachers. I'd say it helped. But after a year I told my parents I didn't want to go to him anymore.

You can bet they were relieved. I knew how they felt about shrinks. My father used to say that psychiatrists were crazier than their patients.

The dream never stopped, though. It just got more and more infrequent. I still have it sometimes.

"You won't have it anymore," I said. "You've told *me*, and it will make all the difference."

He smiled then. He said a curious thing. He said, "No, it won't. I think I like having it."

So then we knew each other, Justin and I, in total nakedness, and our private garden became a spacious place, a better Eden, with room in it for every truth. I could tell him about the old hurts and envies and the guilt that still wrapped my father's memory. I could make him laugh with Tin Town stories, the fights, the rackets, old Mrs. DeVito scamming her clients with those phony fortunes. But the advantage of honesty was all to my benefit; he would never talk anymore about the shooting and what it had done to him. I'd try, but I didn't seem to have the art, or the tact, to make it different, and once he said to me, "I don't enjoy all this morbid curiosity. I should never have told you."

His tone was so cold, so flat and final, it nearly stopped my heart. It stopped my clumsy probing forever. I felt crude.

But there was one way the matter stayed alive between us. He'd often tell me how much stronger I was than he was; he'd praise me for it. I was a "little rock," I had guts, I'd come so far, all on my own. The superficial truth hid a deeper one that we never talked about, but that we both knew. Because when I had told Mama how I ran and hid in the woods when the troopers came, she didn't tell me I hadn't done anything. She didn't say I'd had no choice. All she ever said was that she'd have done what I did, and that was that. Yes, I hurt. Yes, I'd heal.

Whereas Justin had his mother lying on his behalf and his father denying him his own responsibility. That tough old buffalo, stooped beneath the hump of his wealth and power, had to be the boss always. And when Justin needed help they turned him over to a psychiatrist, one of *them*, a Lambert. He was probably better than no help at all, but he hadn't healed the boy that was Justin. The wound stayed open and the infection went on working to raise strange fevers, foul dreams.

In any event, I knew I'd once held Justin's soul in my hands and seen it close, and full of shadows. I thought that love would lift them and that in time I would find the right words, or the right moment, to help. I told myself that he was older, prouder, more reserved than I was and I must give him time.

So I waited, thinking I was learning something about patience. I wasn't doing that, of course. I was only being timid and loving. I was only being twenty-four, twenty-five, twenty-six. And then came Lighthouse Point.

7

The high winds of political triumph had shaken a real plum loose for me. The head of the Board of Trade was Murph Steuben, a dear old hack who told me that the harder I worked the better it would be for his golf game. I had my own secretary and one assistant and a free field to show what I could do.

By dint of pestering every contact we had, Bitsie and I even got Lucia on the state payroll, another triumph, considering her aborted education, two-finger typing, and devout aversion to reading. She was a capitol statehouse tour guide. It paid beans; it was supposed to be a stopgap. But Lucia loved it. She could sleep late. The tours—mostly grade-school kids and an occasional busload of senior citizens—didn't start till ten, and she had the rest of the day to hang around the PR office, doing her nails and using the phone to set up the evening's schedule of partying.

When we nagged her to start looking for something better,

she'd say, astonished, "What could be better? You know another line of work a woman can do on three hours' sleep and a snootful?"

We moaned and groaned. Caro would say, in total exasperation, "Can't anyone reach that jerk? She's just vegetating in that dumb job. She could at least learn to type."

"She says typing is terminal to her nail wrap," Amy would say. "And now that she's come into her own money—her parents should have tied it up for another twenty years—it's worse."

"She's good at it, anyway," Bitsie would add. "They love her over there. She gets fan mail from the Golden Oldies."

"Not a heavy hitter," I would say, in my turn. "Well, so what. It's kind of nice, having a playgirl for a friend."

And it was. Money or no, Lucia still lived with Amy and Caro in that tumbledown house for the fun and the company of it. She lent her car, her clothes, her superfluous boyfriends, and her irrepressible good nature wherever they were needed, and she'd even sit quietly through the lectures about Growing Up and Using Your Brain.

"I know." She'd sigh. "You're right, I'll start looking Monday. Maybe I'll go back to school. I'm a dyslexic orphan with terrible asthma, but I should try harder."

But if the asthma was bad, and there was a tour to give or a party to go to, she wouldn't give in to it. Her voice might get smaller, and her motions slower and more precise, but she wouldn't give in. Her purse clanked with inhalers and sprays and pills and capsules. "You have to show it who's boss," she'd say. "Give this mother an inch, it'll take a mile."

So Justin was in the third year of his second term and our Corps was tighter than ever. That spring got Amy a big raise on the newspaper and a broken heart from a law student. Caro was supervising the Head Start programs for the whole county and still writing letters to the hometown honey she didn't want to marry on alternate Tuesdays, and Bitsie was totally involved with a totally unacceptable person who wore turbans. As for Lucia, she was still making speeches about the famous WPA murals in the statehouse and how a bill becomes a law; she was still saying that with all the gorgeous men around, commitment could wait.

58

As for me, I had Justin, and I lived my life—compared to my friends—with elderly decorum. I saw Justin when I could; I worked long hours; I did a lot of traveling around the state so I could write up its untapped attractions—and handsome tax incentives—in glowing language. I had a gold membership in a Holiday Spa and I was learning to cook things like Peking duck. I was happy. We all were, even Amy with her broken heart. Time flew and stood still for us, defying all the laws of physics and adult wisdom. The only time we cared about was the present moment, and the only plans we had for the future consisted of reminding one another to shop early for bathing suits; all the good ones were gone by June. Summer was coming. What a beautiful word. Summer.

But that was the summer that began in May with a heat wave that set a record for the century. The heat wouldn't quit, and every weekend brought reports about monumental gridlocks on the highways to the shore. That was the summer we all cut our hair and started wearing linen, a real craze, as in "crazy." You had to iron the stuff every night or you'd look like an unmade bed. Bitsie and I—liberated women, fashion victims—used to iron in our underwear after dinner, watching television and cursing the pleats.

Heat. Pink and blue and beige and white linen. The smell of steamy cloth and occasional scorches. "Are you taking in laundry or what?" Justin used to ask, knocking over the ironing board. "Don't you ever put this damn thing away?"

I'd tell him he had some nerve complaining, him with a closetful of fresh suits in the office and a valet at the mansion, as well.

I'd never known him so tense and irritable. The housing scandal that had begun in April wouldn't go away. It was all we talked about. He'd had his share of crises before, but this was the first one that featured his family, the Lamberts, at their high-handed worst.

The State Housing Authority had bought some land from one of the Lambert corporations. The Lamberts had taken themselves a tax abatement they apparently weren't remotely entitled to. It amounted to some six million dollars.

I say "apparently" because the Lambert lawyers were making a strenuous case for their right to the abatement. But it was, politically, too strenuous by half; it put Justin on the griddle; in spite of his honest distance from the sale, he had to speak as if his family's fortune were his own bank account. And even if the state-house people knew that Justin had no part in the deal, the taxpayers needed reassurance and the opposition needed ammunition. So the story played and played and kept on being news.

Justin's father—Old Henry to the rank and file—made a couple of outrageous statements Justin had to publicly disown. Old Henry accepted a muzzle after that, but he'd still call his only son five times a day, snorting and stomping, a wounded buffalo with blood in his eye and a battery of expensive lawyers, making noise.

Well, you ride such things out. You try to swivel heads and push your own agenda. But it adds to the workload and it compounds the pressure, and there's only so many times you can have your secretary say, "The Governor's in a meeting, Mr. Lambert. I have you on the top of his list."

"Rub my neck," Justin said, flopping down next to me on the couch. It was July; the light outside was brassy, still, with sunlight. "And my shoulders too. Dig in. I'm in knots."

Hot as it was, I'd turned off the air-conditioning and opened the windows to let in some fresh air. On the front sidewalk we could hear kids jumping rope, and there was a pleasant smell of asphalt from a newly paved part of the street. The tarry smell had the beach in it.

Justin was tieless and shoeless, and because he was dieting we'd had our spartan supper off trays in the living room. The ironing board had a pitcher of iced tea on it. It jiggled when he flopped on the couch. I thought how tired he looked. He was too busy to play tennis, and the heat had cut down his jogging. That one afternoon sailing on the Bay with Tandy and the kids—pictures of them were in Monday's paper, pointing up Clean Bay Month— had given him a peeling sunburn and a false glow of health.

"Tandy's saying she might not go to Brittany after all," he murmured. "Hot as it is here? That's how cold it is in France."

My heart sank. These plans of Tandy's were precious to me; for a year she'd had the rental in France set. She had friends there; she was taking the children. Justin would be alone.

"Oh," was all I could say.

Justin put his head in my lap. He hugged my knees tightly.

"That coast? I warned her. The weather's tricky."

"Oh," I said again. I was too choked up to say more. I had been waiting for those four weeks like they were thirty days of sheer Christmas. I had silly dreams and sober plans. He might sleep over. We might get up to New York. We could get together at the shore for a weekend. We'd done that twice before, at Sea Pines, where the summer festival always got the Governor to judge the parade, with the floats and the bands. It was a tradition in the state, and because Tandy didn't have to go, she didn't.

We'd gone, all of us, and stayed in the same hotel, hidden in plain sight, invisible in the light of the fireworks, for two whole days.

I felt like crying until Justin said, sleepily, "Not so much to ask. Just a change in the weather. Hell, I need to have the decks cleared. I need to be alone."

I knew he meant alone-with-me. He closed his eyes and I stroked the thick hair that hardly showed the gray except at the temples. I felt peaceful. I was twenty-six, and all I needed to be perfectly happy was for the weather to get better in France. Meanwhile, I knew that Vinnie or David would pick him up soon, and that we wouldn't make love, and that I'd see him again when I got back from the Mid-Atlantic Trade Conference. Virginia was hosting this year. My boss, Murph Steuben, would make the talk I'd written about the work I'd started with the Japanese. He'd get the applause and then he'd look down from the podium and give me his Big Finish wink.

"Politics, darling," he said, and often. "You do your best, pay your dues, and wait your turn."

"Can't say I'm in any hurry, either," I'd answer, and that was politics too.

Once or twice, in strange tandem, Murph Steuben and Justin would tell me the same thing, on the same day: "How did I ever live without you?" Love and politics. I lived in them, between them, with their peaks and lulls, their claims on loyalty and patience. The dues had never yet seemed too high.

So I sat quietly with Justin's head in my lap, and I was glad he was sleeping, because the TV was on, and the seven o'clock news had a local segment with the State Minority Leader, Matty Ferguson, in the studio and Louis Kahn, the Attorney General, on remote. Matty was mean and Louis was bland and it was nothing earthshaking, but who needed it?

"Just how long," asked Matty meanly, "will it take before your office steps into this investigation?"

"No longer than it takes to come up with evidence of intentional wrongdoing," answered Louis blandly. He reminded Matty of several laws that distinguish our great state from states in other countries, like Russia. So Matty reminded *him* of how hard it is to do a good job on such a sensitive issue, particularly when Louis must be concerned about his good friend the Governor.

Justin sat up, yawning. "I wasn't really asleep," he said. "Louis sounded good."

"So did Matty." I sighed. "He's such a horsefly, though. You can't twitch him off."

"He hates Louis's guts," Justin said. "It's personal."

"He's getting miles of name recognition out of this," I said. "He'd keep it hot even without hating Louis."

"The tax ruling is months away," Justin said. "I have to live with his noise. It's getting to me."

I went over to kiss him. He was putting on his jacket. He tasted sleepy.

"You do need a rest," I said. "You're letting Matty and his boys get in too close."

"Them and my old man," Justin said. "He's got this racking cough he uses on the phone now. He's working the sympathy vein for a change."

"Let him. At least he's not roaring."

"I'm just sick of it," Justin said. "Are you sick of hearing me say that?"

"I love you."

"I love you. Hug."

"Listen, I've got a premonition," I said. "The sun is shining in France right this minute. Tandy won't change her plans. We're going to have some lovely times."

"Name one," he said. "I'm flogging Vinnie and David to death. Matty is flogging me. I don't have time to breathe. So go ahead, name one."

"The beach," I said. "I bet we get a whole weekend at the beach," and before he could argue the buzzer sounded, two short, three long—Vinnie's signal.

"Dream on," he said, but he sounded happy. He had his hand on the door when he looked around the living room. "Rachel? You're feeling trapped?"

"A little. Same as you. We need some . . . sky."

"Talk to David," he said. "You're right. She'll go."

I could usually avoid a certain thought. This time I didn't. I thought, Poor Tandy.

David and I had a standing date for brunch on Sundays. It only worked out to once or twice a month, but we both always enjoyed it. We'd try to remember to hold hands occasionally and give each other meaningful looks. We laughed a lot, but that was real. We were friends. David loved Justin too. He'd look deep into my eyes and squeeze my hand and whisper, "This is the fun side of politics."

For the last year we'd been meeting at Chatterton's; it was nearly the first of the new downtown "fern bars." The old pols wouldn't set foot in it, naturally, not with all that glass and glare and sissy waiters. The old pols stuck to Bevin's, which was dark as a dungeon and had thick carpets to muffle voices and served real food, like liver with smothered onions.

But the younger people from the statehouse had made Chatterton's their own. We didn't need dark corners and cigar smoke to tell us what business we were in. David was a star of the first magnitude at Chatterton's; at Bevin's, men clapped him on the shoulder and called him "Sonny." They didn't care that he was Justin's right hand, either. He'd be Sonny until he got elected to something, or at least ran for it.

Naturally David had his own table at Chatterton's. That Sunday was burning hot as usual, but we still killed a jug of wicked sangria, and we smiled and waved at people, and we did a few fast breaks, hopping up from the table to say something to someone at the bar, someone-I've-been-trying-to-reach-all-week, goddammit.

We'd smile at each other, too, meaning, Can you believe this bullshit? David was just thirty; we weren't either of us above showing off.

"Here's his schedule for August," David said to me. We were pleasantly buzzed and full of omelette.

I studied the photocopied calendar pages.

"Too bad about the summer festival," I said. "Damn. I was counting on that, at least."

"Good for Louis, though. It's his fiftieth birthday, and he was born when Sea Pines incorporated. A natural. He gets to be Numero Uno this year."

"I can't help feeling cheated. It was so easy."

"For you, maybe. It's still work for the Guv. Listen, maybe it's for the best? What Justin needs is a rest. Real rest."

"Oh, does he. David, I'm worried. The land sale. His goddam family."

"Go fight city hall," David said. "It's his Achilles heel, sure. You think he's bad now? You should have known him when he was running the first time for the House. Rich man's son. Silver spoon. Never worked a day in his life. He'd *fold*."

"I don't mean that. Or only partly. No, it's this thing. The pure pressure. He can't seem to get his mind off it. He talks and talks about it. He follows every blip."

"But that's how he's always been. No balance there. He either pretends the other Lamberts don't exist or acts like they're all joined at the hip."

"That's right. A love-slash-hate thing. It's like . . ."

And we were off and running, talking about Justin, rolling his name on our tongues like coarse salt off a German pretzel. It was our specialty, analyzing him, studying him, exchanging our portraits of him so we could take him back with a new detail added, a color more finely shaded. David wasn't married; he didn't have a wife or special girlfriend to talk to. He needed me for this, and I needed him. To see Justin through his eyes—the eyes of an intelligent, faithful man—seemed to open my tight, secret world. I could share that world with my women friends, but that didn't make it larger. I knew, for myself, everything a woman could know about Justin Lambert, or at least I thought so. David knew him differently; in my heart of hearts, I had to acknowledge he knew him better. I never mentioned the shooting accident, though, and neither did he. I knew intuitively that Justin had never told David about it.

David had been with Justin when David was still a kid in college and Justin was running for the House seat. There were just two other party regulars who could claim the honor of being with Justin on the equivalent of Mao Tse-tung's Long March, and none whom Justin trusted so completely. Sometimes I was jealous of that trust, but I never thought it wasn't deserved, and David knew that. It made us feel so close that we really did appear to be lovers when we weren't even trying.

"This weekend," David said. He pointed to the calendar. "Look here. That's the one. He's got that luncheon to dedicate the library at Dyer Community College. Ever been to Dyer? It's a wide place in the road down on the Bay. Okay—I move him off these two numbers, on Saturday, no sweat. All clear."

"For what?"

"A rest-and-recreation period. All alone. Just him, me, and Vinnie at Lighthouse Point, down the road, one hour, no traffic that early Friday afternoon. I put it out: quiet time. Family place. The Guv gets some space."

"With a bunch of Lamberts all around? David, don't be ridiculous."

David pretended to twirl an imaginary mustache. "You un-derestimate me, my lady. Lighthouse Point is empty and will stay empty till Labor Day! They opened the house and had it cleaned for July Fourth and they all went down, and now they're not going to use it all summer!"

David had it all taped; I myself had the information, but I'd never bothered to put it together. Justin's mother didn't want to go to Lighthouse Point anymore. Her heart trouble had gotten worse over the winter, and she wouldn't stay there, with no doctor nearby, and only a ferry to deal with in case of emergency.

Mr. Lambert was "Old Henry"; Mrs. Lambert was "Missy." Sometimes that was "Poormissy": one word, as in "Damnyankees." Sympathetic people—or just plain people trying to be knowing about the Lamberts—murmured that it was a shame; she used to be a real person, but now you wouldn't give her spot to a leopard, being married to Old Henry! He'd knocked the stuffings out of her.

Sometimes, when I heard these things, or when Justin said a few words about his mother's health, I'd remember a woman who could take the gun from the hands of a frozen boy, and lie through her teeth, and know that the power of her family was all the law she needed. She must have been a real person then. She must have thought she was the most important woman in Old Henry's life, in spite of the others. He had a weakness for singers; "chanteuses," as they were called then, orchidlike beauties who did two shows a night in fancy supper clubs in Manhattan. He'd be photographed there, with Missy smiling bravely at his side. One of them was supposed to have a daughter with the Lambert teeth, the Lambert jaw. Justin said it was a dirty story and not a word of truth in it—the daughter part anyway, he added.

Missy had gone the invalid route. She wore out Christian Science; she went from Mayo to Mayo and back again. "Mother's heart" was a family phrase. She'd been interviewed once, during the campaign I worked on, propped up in bed, with a nurse knitting bed socks at one side of the room. "Still beautiful, and determined to be brave," wrote the reverent reporter, duly noting the number of pill bottles on the night table.

"Mostly tranquilizers," Justin told me. "She might be addicted. I don't think her heart is really bad. None of us do."

But none of them tried to change her. If she wanted to be an invalid, let her be one. The family motto was *Suit yourself and don't come crying*.

In this case, everyone was suited. Lighthouse Point was unpopular, David said, with all of them now. It was too isolated. They got on one another's nerves. The kids wanted to be closer to the action on the boardwalk. And they had two other summer places anyway.

"David," I breathed. "You, okay. But us? How?"

66

"A snap. You and the troops go to the shore Friday. Check into a motel near where the main beach ends. Come over on the ferry, bold as brass, for my birthday party on Saturday."

"Your birthday party?"

David tapped a square on the calendar.

"This number is my birthday! And you and my old campaign buddies are coming over with a steak and a big cake for a celebration! You can stay till ten, when the ferry shuts down. With my birthday in place, you can come back Sunday morning. A favor to *me*, from Justin, see? My pretty almost-fiancée and her friends. *My* friends too."

"We might have to announce our engagement," I said, laughing, but I felt queasy, with the wine and the mounting excitement.

"I have *that* in reserve." David was smug. "In case anyone important gets wise."

"See how Justin feels about it," I said. "Tandy will have been gone . . . how long by then? Two weeks. That's all right."

"Right," David said happily. "I thought of that. One week would look bad. Like we were waiting for Tandy to leave. Two weeks is fine."

"Neighbors," I said. "There aren't any!"

"A couple of houses a mile off. The ferry guy's family and some clammers with squatter's rights. Not that Old Henry couldn't throw them off if he wanted to."

"The beach is public," I said.

"You'll get all the beach you need in front of your motel. On the island, you'll swim off the dock. The main house dock, on the Bay side."

"The main house," I said dreamily. "Are there others?"

"Lots," said David. "Cottages, built for the second generation. Neat. All woody, but with these great kitchens. Like they have on the estate. Missy got Old Henry to build them. She says the grandchildren make so much noise she gets palpitations."

"Poor Missy," I said, and I shivered. It was a great shudder, and David noticed and asked me what was wrong.

"Nothing," I said. "It's the excitement. Or maybe somebody just walked over my grave."

8

I didn't tell my friends about David's plan for many days. In the first place, I was afraid something would come up to sink it. In the second, Justin's "might be okay" was not the reaction I'd hoped for. But after a while I understood his lack of enthusiasm. He was irritable and overworked, and he didn't enjoy our many references to his irritability and overworkedness.

"I don't need a rest, goddammit," he kept saying. "I need some cooperation around here, that's all, not bullshit sympathy!"

But he came around. One boiling-hot evening in early August—when Amy, Caro, and Lucia had come to my house for a dinner of take-out Chinese—I announced the plan. Everybody cheered. Lucia did a cartwheel on the living room rug.

"A motel near the end of the beach?" Bitsie groaned. "Oh, Jesus, Rachel, why didn't you tell us sooner? We'll never get in. The whole shore is booked solid."

I pulled an envelope out of my pants pocket. More cheers. When I left David that Sunday in Chatterton's, I'd gone straight to the phone and lucked into two rooms at the Dune Deck, last motel on the beach, water view, cot in the second room at no extra charge. The envelope held the confirmation.

We gave high fives all around. The Dune Deck was the best. We all had stayed there before. It had no charm but it was cheap, and on a clear day the lighthouse looked close enough to touch.

"Justin didn't have any objections?" Caro asked, biting into an egg roll.

"Not a one," I said. "The only thing he didn't like was our saying how tired he was and how much he deserved a little time-out."

"How's he doing?"

"Time-out is what he needs. The land sale, damn it."

"It'll blow over. Bet they split that six million down the middle."

"If Matty Ferguson doesn't hold out. That creep."

"What are they saying over in your department?"

"You must be kidding. Those bozos don't talk about anything but their lawns and the pennant race."

"Who here knows how Lighthouse Point got to be an island? No takers? Well, it was the big hurricane of 1938. The ocean just broke through the dunes at the end of the main beach and ripped the whole point loose. Only the Lamberts owned that end anyway, so what did they care? They just started their own ferry service. There was this big lawsuit—maybe in the fifties?—that made them make the ferry available to the public because the beach perimeter belongs to the state. They charge ten bucks to bring a car over! Typical."

"You've never been there, Bitsie?"

"Nope. They say it's lovely. I'm so excited."

We all were. We cleaned up the soy sauce and cartons from the dining table and started a bridge game while Amy did her home permanent. Amy, Caro, and Lucia always used the bathrooms in our house for their size and privacy and reliable hot water. This time Bitsie begged Amy to stay in the bathroom with her smelly head; the last time she did a home perm she'd made the whole house into a rotten egg factory.

We played my old Doors tapes while we played cards and we talked through the game, over the music. David's birthday? Okay, we'd all bring presents, little ones, but in big boxes, for the effect. Balloons. A cake from Schumachers; they were the best in the city. Angel food with chocolate frosting? No, chocolate, all the way through, with praline between the layers. Bitsie suddenly put down her hand, held her nose, and walked into the bathroom where Amy was putting goo on her hair. She came back grinning broadly.

"Angel food," she said. "Three against two, so there."

"Oh, I know what you were asking Amy, really," I said. "About the pot. And that guy in her newsroom who sells it."

"You didn't complain last time," Bitsie said. "Not Rachel but everyone else. Even Justin liked it."

"He was just being nice," I said. "He really didn't feel a thing. I don't get what there is to like, anyway. First you laugh like a hyena and then you fall asleep. Big deal, dope."

"That's not it anyway," Bitsie said. "Remember, angel food."

Caro was writing a list on the back of the score pad.

"Cake, big presents, balloons. Steaks for the cookout Saturday night. Cooler to carry them. Roadside stands on the way down for tomatoes and corn."

"Oh, corn, I could eat a dozen ears."

"Write down 'big pot,' Caro. We'll need a huge pot for the corn water."

"Don't be dim. You think the Lamberts don't own a big clam steamer or something?"

"All right, don't write it down. We'll be boiling water in ten dinky saucepans and you'll wish you'd listened to me."

"Who wants to hold the kitty? We'll give Amy a break, though, it's her car."

"We'll pay for the gas but split the food. Booze?"

"Maybe some beer. David said the house is stocked and we can use what's there."

"Do the schedule again."

"Wheels up Friday noon. Check in at Dune Deck. Call David

to say we've arrived. Saturday morning, do some beach and call David again to say we're leaving for the ferry. He'll meet us on the other side of the channel and show us the way to the house. We'll have the whole afternoon and the evening till ten."

"Do you think Vinnie will come for sure?" Caro asked me.

"David said so. You can wear that plaid bikini."

"I certainly will not. I'm sorry I bought it anyway."

But she didn't sound certain at all, and we laughed. Caro had this dopey crush on Vinnie. He reminded her of a cousin, one of those cousins you fell in love with when you were ten and he was eighteen.

Then Lucia said she'd seen this movie that was supposed to take place in England, only they filmed it in Brittany. So now she knew what Brittany looked like. It was gray. They had funny square umbrellas on the beach. It was such a lousy movie you noticed things like square umbrellas.

"I want to go to Monaco someday," Bitsie said quickly. "Antibes; Nice. That's where you get the good weather."

"I want to do Spain. My Spanish is better than my French, but that's not saying much."

"I think you can get by anywhere if you speak English loud and slow. Who dealt this mess?"

So we got off Brittany, and not by accident. Brittany meant Tandy. Tandy was there, and she was a nice woman, and we were nice women too. Men don't own the word "chivalry." We felt it. It's the debt you owe to the weaker person, the unregretted, absent, ignorant.

There but for the grace of God go I.

We seldom referred to her. It was a point of honor, not even to appear to gloat.

Caro left early that night, leaving her hand to Amy. Before she sat down, Amy whispered something in Lucia's ear, and Lucia whispered back, and they both giggled.

"What the hell is that about?" I demanded.

"Oh, Rachel, do you have to know everything?" Lucia asked. "It's a surprise. You just be sure to get some kind of white cake."

She mugged and made slurping noises. Everyone laughed but me. I took my bridge game seriously, and from then on we played for real and kept it going till midnight, although the next day was a working one for all of us. But we didn't care. We could always catch up on sleep. That was when we still had all the time in the world.

Without Vinnie and David, without my four friends, Justin and I would never have made it through those three years. I was too young; Justin was too important; the passion we had for each other would surely have made us bold, impatient, and stupid. Secret lovers, alone with their secret, lose touch with reality; they lapse into illusion and the carelessness illusion breeds. But Justin and I were the center of a loyal court that had made our welfare their own, and it was thanks to them that we never made a slip. They restrained us; they made a game of going out into the world like Indian scouts and coming back to us with news of the territory. David and I must be seen at more parties, more double dates. Justin should use a different car from time to time, when he came to the house. "You danced twice with him at the mansion, Rachel; don't have even one dance this time."

Now and then I used to wonder: did David and Vinnie ever wish that Justin and I had never met? I never wondered that about my women friends; like all young women we shared a fatalism about love. We often sounded cynical, but all the same we were romantics. Love to us was like the wishing ring in the fairy tale, and even if you wished for the wrong or painful thing, the ring itself could never be refused. But Vinnie and David were men.

I asked David about it once. We were dancing; it was one of those nights when we'd been invited to the governor's mansion for a buffet honoring Veterans Day, the VFW, and local brass. A Marine Corps general was guest of honor, and the ballroom glittered with uniform braid. It was the kind of event "the troops" got invited to: no sit-down dinner, no receiving line, Justin and Tandy appearing just for an hour or two, for a waltz and a wave and an early exit.

"I know it makes your life more complicated," I said to David. "It makes me feel guilty."

"It does do that," David said. "The worry. If it got out. But that's only one part. The other is that he's never been happier. Or

72

more productive. Or more appreciative of *me*. And if that sounds hard-nosed, I'm not apologizing."

"How about Vinnie? I sometimes think he's judgmental."

"Wrong. He feels like I do. His nose is even harder."

I knew I'd gotten an honest answer. I closed my eyes—Justin had left already—and pressed my cheek to David's. It was a slow dance, the only kind he could do. Bitsie came by in some uniform's embrace and gave David a tap on the shoulder.

"Hey, you two," she said. "Save something for later."

David gave her a wink and we went on shuffling cheek-to-cheek. Foot-on-foot, too. He was a terrible dancer.

We managed it like that for three years, and they went by so quickly I can hardly separate them anymore. Justin and I were restrained and circumspect and that, of course, is why the years blended. Passion feeds on continence. Every time we made love was like the first time, a fever dream, always new, never cooling. There were never even any seasons in those years, for us or the others. Our secret garden was always green, and all eight of us had taken root in it.

It rained the whole week before we were to go to the beach. But that Friday dawned a more promising pearly gray. I put out extra food and water for the cat, and by noon—we'd all taken time off—we were jammed like anchovies into Amy's Ford with our legs curled over bags, the Polar-Pak, beach mats, and towels. Five huge boxes, all wrapped and bowed, were in the trunk; we made a stop to pick up the cake; Amy used the stop to blow up one of the balloons she had bought. She had twenty, and they all said Happy Birthday David.

Early as it was, there was beach traffic. But when the Bay Bridge went up to let a big tanker through, we boasted of the time we'd saved, leaving this early. A tanker going through could tie up the traffic for two hours on a weekend evening.

The sky and the bit of the Bay we could see were the same color, a pink-shot gray. You could feel the sun trying to come out, and we went ahead singing all the songs we knew that had the word "sun" in them: "Here Comes the Sun," "You Are My Sunshine," "Sunny," "The House of the Rising Sun."

"Lulu?" Amy demanded, from the driver's seat. "Let's hear it, you know the words to everything."

"Can't," Lucia said. "I'm saving air right now."

"Oh, shit," Amy said. She was a doctor's daughter, and she took an exasperated interest in Lucia's asthma. It was her opinion that Lucia went from denial to overdosing, with nothing in between.

"Did you take some medicine?" Bitsie asked.

"Not yet. It's mostly Caro's knee in my stomach. Plus the car. I'll be fine when we get there."

After the bridge, we started arguing about where to stop for the vegetables. Lucia liked the stands with the misspelled cardboard signs: Last Chanse Corn, Good Watermellons. She believed they did it on purpose, to make you think some little kid wrote it.

"Wait for the Greek place after the Exxon. They're the best."

"No way, there's chickens walking around; I hate them."

But Amy had the wheel and she passed up the cute signs and the Greek and we bought eight bags of corn and tomatoes from Smiling Pa Parker, the worst phony on the strip. After that came the farm with the Historic Windmill, the new Waterslide and the old Kiddie Zoo, and then the highway narrowed down, straight as a ruler, to the ocean. The Shore Road always came as a surprise; you always thought it was farther east.

And then we were on it, with the telephone poles whipping by and sailboats dipping in the inlet, the whole of the mighty Atlantic heaving and sighing across the dunes.

We sang. We sang, "We're here because we're here. . . ." We staggered into the Dune Deck Motel to sign the register and cart the bags up to our second-story rooms. Bitsie dropped a sack of tomatoes; they fell through the wooden stairs and splattered on the sand.

We thought this was very funny. Amy got a picture of Bitsie hunkered down on the sand, gathering tomatoes. We washed them in the sink and ate two each and snaked suits out of our bags and went running down the stairs onto the beach.

It was five o'clock. It was actually raining. The sand was the color of pockmarked lead. But we walked over it seeing it the way it had to be tomorrow, bright white, fine as powder, with the sun putting diamonds in it, the sun that would toast us brown in a day and make us gorgeous for the whole next week at work.

Lucia passed us all, running. She got to the water first, diving into a wave with perfect timing, clean as a knife.

Then she stood up, calling, "It's warm as spit! What are you waiting for?"

9

The sun woke us up at seven Saturday morning, and we didn't waste a minute. The sky was clear, but there was a line of gray in the northeast where the bad weather came from. We grabbed some "complimentary breakfast" from the motel lobby—it was a closet with a desk in it—and carried Styrofoam cups of coffee and stale doughnuts out to the beach, screaming as the hot coffee slopped our legs. Then we threw down our mats and towels, oiled one another up, and begged the rays to do their worst.

The sea was flat as a saucer; the waves hardly bothered to break. We went swimming and oiled up again and sweated and swam, and by ten-thirty Caro's freckles were having freckles. Lucia flagged down the cruising chair-and-umbrella truck and we got an umbrella, and when the boys had finished putting it up for us, Lucia followed them down to the water's edge where their truck was. I can still see her sitting on the fender, swinging her legs and braiding her hair so it would have a wave in it when it dried.

"There's a party at their house tonight," she said, when she came back. "Brian's the tall one; is that a fox or not? All of us invited. Let's see, if we're back from Lighthouse Point by ten-thirty, eleven, we can make it."

"*You* might." Amy snorted. "Not us. They're kids, Lulu. High school, even."

"Not kids," Lucia said. "I asked. All seniors at State," and we hooted, because it was an axiom at the beach, how all the boys lied about their ages. Besides, even seniors were too young! "Not for me, Grandma," Lucia said. "I like 'em young. They can dance. Show me one of your three-piece suits that can dance and I'll reconsider."

We talked about what happens to all the good dancers from high school. They disappear, we grumbled. They get laid, they get lazy. "So how come the gay guys are such good dancers?" Lucia asked, and we all laughed and she said she was going to make that party and Brian had better watch out.

By eleven-thirty the sky was striped with more gray than blue and we bought some hot dogs from another truck and I went in to call David and say that we had beached and lunched and could make the twelve-thirty ferry. It was only three minutes' drive down the road.

The sign to the ferry was so small and faded we missed it and lost a little time. You had to make an abrupt dogleg down a thin dirt road that ought to have been paved just as the sign ought to have been bigger. There'd been complaints for years, Bitsie said, but who was going to force the Lamberts to make changes? What county supervisor wanted to tangle with Old Henry over a lousy sign? They got along just figuring that most people with ten bucks for the ride had brains enough to find the turn.

The inlet between the barrier beach and the island that had once been part of it was only a hundred yards or so in width, but the current could be fast and tricky. The ferry was really a large raft with a diesel engine, and the landing reeked of oil. The ferryman took our money through a window in a shack that might have been a toolshed if not an outhouse.

"Very low rent," Amy muttered. "Considering the price."

"He's a nasty old boy," I muttered back, because Lucia had

asked him for a glass of water to wash down a pill and he'd grunted and said, "No water," and sold her a Coke for a dollar.

The ferryman jerked a thumb at our car, the only one in the parking space.

"You all have to get in the car," he said.

"All get in!"

"No standing on board. Regulations."

We packed ourselves back into the hot car and rumbled over the steel plates. The diesel roared; we settled down, disgruntled. We agreed it was a plot on the part of the Lamberts, taking the fun out of it to discourage people. But we hung out the windows anyway. In spite of the overcast, we needed sunglasses against the glare, and when the ferryman passed from stern to bow, Amy asked him, politely, what did he think the weather was going to do?

"Fog coming," he said, with relish. "Might be real bad."

We forgot to groan because we were near enough to see David standing on the opposite dock, a mirror image of the one we had just left, with another dirty shack and rutted parking lot. Three cars were in it, and a bunch of people waiting for the ferry.

"Leaving early," the ferryman said, pointing. "Sand flies got 'em."

He gave us a big toothless grin. Amy announced, in rather a loud voice, that it would only take a small tornado to make his day.

I got into David's car and the others followed behind. David told Amy to drive carefully over the channel bridges. They were only wide enough for one car at a time, and you had to stop first and honk three times before you crossed.

Bridges? Bridges over channels? I had never dreamed the island was so big. The postcards of Lighthouse Point made it look like just a clump of rock with a meadow attached; I had guessed the Lambert place would be right behind the meadow, with the lighthouse itself out front like a gigantic garden ornament. But David told me it was a mile long and nearly half a mile wide and the Lamberts owned everything but the acre around the lighthouse and the beach on the ocean side. Justin's grandfather had been a yachting buddy of J. P. Morgan, and he'd bought the property with some idea of creating a private yacht and fishing club. He'd gone and dredged and bulkheaded a couple of deep channels from the Bay side, but long before the hurricane of '38 the plan had fizzled.

"Not that he cared," David said. "Those were the days. They didn't know what the hell to do with all their money. I think they paid their taxes out of petty cash."

We went rattling over the first bridge. There was nothing under it except mud and cattails.

"All silted up," David said. "The channel under Camel Bridge is the only one still open."

Camel Bridge had a high hump in the middle. Heights are not my favorite thing, and I only took one look at the water underneath. I could see that it was deep, though, black water moving fast.

"Oh, look, it's hilly!" I cried as we came off Camel Bridge. The road went straight through the island's center, and now there was a little hill and a miniature moorland stretched on either side, with coarse golden grass all over and tangles of wild rose and scrubby pine trees gone humpbacked from the wind. And all around it, olive green in the glare, the wide Atlantic like a skirt of wrinkled silk.

It was so beautiful I wanted to stop and stare. But Justin was waiting.

"How is he?" I asked.

"Fine. Just fine."

"Not fine. I know that tone of voice."

"Oh, well, he got up at five this morning; I heard him. He's supposed to be taking it easy, for God's sake. Instead he goes out and clears some brush and goes jogging and says he didn't sleep a wink anyway, so why stay in bed?"

"He always says that." I sighed and then the road veered north and dipped steeply toward the Bay, and the lighthouse—it had always been in view—vanished from sight.

Amy was dawdling behind. David stopped to let her catch up. Then we turned into an unmarked lane paved in slick gray stone.

"Oh, my God," I breathed. "Is that the house?"

"You sound disappointed," David said. "Do you have some objection to castles?"

We got out of our cars and just stood there, gawking. It was a huge stone building with six chimneys and innumerable windows of leaded glass. The front door—doors—were dark wood studded with rounds of iron; they were big enough to drive a car through. No, not a car. Horses in velvet blankets with knights in full armor on them.

"Ten steaks," Amy said. "We should have brought a whole ox."

"Disney World," Lucia said. "I can't believe it."

I got the nervous giggles. I wanted Justin.

"He's out back," David said. "Fishing off the dock with Vinnie. Well, at least he's sitting still. Come on, where's my famous cake?"

I was taking it out of the trunk when I felt Justin's arms around me, bare, wet, fishy arms. I shrieked. I said, "My God, Justin, this place!"

We beamed at each other. His eyes were full of mischief.

"How do you like Grandpa's idea of a summer bungalow?"

Then he made his big podium voice boom across the cobbled courtyard.

"Leave your stuff in the car! Line up! The grand tour starts here!"

They weren't using the main house at all; they'd made themselves comfortable in a cottage. But Justin knew we'd want to see the inside and he took us through the great hallway, living rooms, dining room, and the cavernous kitchen with its flagstone floor. He put on a British accent and pretended to be a guide.

"Please observe, ladies, that the living room had four walls and not a single comfortable chair. The books were bought by the yard and have never been opened in living memory. That picture—"

He told us about the drunken butler and got us laughing and loosened up and asking questions. How many servants? Who had the pony? What's a Japanese lantern? We burst into applause for the best thing of all: a genuine throne of a toilet in the master bathroom, encased in mahogany and set on a carpeted platform.

The bathroom window was all stained glass. It streaked the white tile with trembling color.

"Sun!" Bitsie cried. "Quick, let's catch it before it goes in again!"

"Go out the front door and snake left around the house," Justin said. "David's got the beer ready."

His eyes signaled me: Stay. I signaled Amy: Go.

The four of them went clattering down the stairs. Justin took my hand.

"My old room. This way."

"You look wonderful," I said, as he opened the door. "You did so get some sleep."

And it was still only one-thirty on a summer Saturday and we were alone on an island, and we could make lazy love and doze a little and make love again and even then it wasn't three o'clock. Twilight was ahead; we'd have that. Hours of night were ours, too; the last ferry left at ten. After twenty minutes in that immense stone folly of a house, I felt as if I had learned everything there was to know about being rich.

10

I never wanted that afternoon to end. I still don't. Let me stay there for a while.

A rough lawn ran behind the main house down to the Bay, and three neat cottages were scattered on the sides of the slope. The lawn was already dotted with blankets and books and cans of beer, and when I went into the cottage the men were using—we had a room to ourselves for changing—I could see that the dining table had been transformed with piles of presents and balloons and crepe paper streamers linking chairs.

"Party party!" Bitsie yelled from the bathroom, and I put on my bathing suit and we went running to the water. We went swimming and wading for clams and had a contest for the longest cannonball off the dock. We threw a Frisbee. We drank beer and wore a path to the cottage bathrooms and came out and did it all again. And Justin was in the middle of everything, with a boy's energy. I loved seeing him this way; big as he was, he was faster and lighter on his feet than any of us except Lucia.

But after he won the cannonball contest, Justin elected book-and-blanket, and I stayed with him. I read; I watched the gulls wheeling over the Bay and my friends playing in the summer afternoon. Vinnie and Caro were fishing off the dock; Bitsie and David were throwing the Frisbee; Lucia was flopped, at a discreet distance from us, on another blanket, offering her back to the sun and turning the pages of *Time*. Sometimes she'd catch my eye and smile shyly. She changed when she was near Justin and me, even in the anonymous spaces of the mansion ballroom or the state-house lawn when we had that picnic. She wouldn't squeal, mug, or jump around. I knew why because she once told me.

"I've never been in love, Rachel," she said. "I just pretended when I was younger. But I look at you and Justin and I say to myself, That's what it's like. I'll know it when it happens because I've seen you and Justin."

I don't remember what I answered, but I know I was touched. And amused, sometimes, like now, because I knew she was only pretending to read. She was imitating me and getting more bored by the minute, and after a while she jumped up and joined the Frisbee game.

Justin soon fell asleep. When I looked behind me at the immense stone house it seemed ordinary, just another element of our protection. It enclosed everything Justin and I had starved for: to be together in the open air, to act silly and carefree in the company of our friends.

I'd seen a meadow full of wildflowers from the window of the cottage bedroom, and I had a sudden urge to pick some. Not that the table needed more decoration, but because Caro had a flower press back home and I could borrow it and preserve some for a souvenir. Already I could feel the afternoon ending. I got up quietly from our blanket and walked around the back of the house. There was Queen Anne's lace, goldenrod, blue chicory, purple clover. . . . I was making a bouquet when Lucia joined me.

She was red as a beet. I could hear the wheezing.

"Bitsie's got the worst chicken arm," she said. "She throws so crazy she's worn me out."

"You don't sound so great," I said. "You ought to stretch out and rest."

"I'm okay," she said. "I've switched medicines. I'm doing Beconase now; that always does the trick."

To look at her you wouldn't suspect anything. She had such a lithe gymnast's body, sturdy with muscle and not an ounce of fat.

"Well, quit running around for a couple of minutes. If you're not careful you'll need a shot, and you know how you hate that stuff."

She shrugged and looked embarrassed.

"I left the kit back at the motel. Took the bottle, forgot the needle. Just as well. You know I'm not supposed to give myself shots anyway."

"Oh, shit," I said, getting angry, just like Amy always did.

"I'll lay off the beer, promise. And Bitsie's going to make Bloody Marys in a tin bucket and I won't have any."

"How about the pot? That could really do you in."

"Not a hit, swear. I won't ruin your day. Oh, Rachel, it's all just . . ."

She waved around the meadow, the Bay, and the clouded sky as if there weren't any words for it. She said to watch her later, she was sure to cry; she always did when everyone sang "Happy Birthday."

It was four o'clock when I came back to our blanket, and now the sky was a full sheet of tarnished silver. Our blanket was damp when I sat down on it.

"There'll be a fog later," Justin said, yawning. "It's funny out here. It starts from the ground up."

"That's what the ferryman said," I answered. "Is he ever a troll. Does he hate that job, or what?"

"Simon?" Justin laughed. "Simon's my pal. He's just an old clammer with job security. Been with us forever. When we were kids—me and my sisters and the cousins—he'd always cover for us. He'd take us over to the mainland after we'd promised the grownups we'd be back at midnight. Only we'd call him on the phone at two or three in the morning and he'd come and get us and never snitch. Cuss us out, but not snitch."

"God, Justin, you were rich. Chauffeurs, even on the water."

"If Simon heard you call him a chauffeur, he'd throw you overboard."

"Guess I'll get dressed. I'm chilly. Look, all the sailboats are heading home. Who's doing the charcoal for the steaks?"

"Vinnie offered. I'd better get over there. I like to start it with twigs."

We were soon all jammed in the bedroom, taking showers and turns with the hair dryer and fixing assignments. Bitsie was for the drinks, Amy for the corn, Caro and me for the salad and tears while slicing onions. Lucia came out of the shower and fell naked on a bed.

"Oooh, I'm sleepy. It's the Beconase; I can't keep my eyes open."

"So go to sleep," said Amy, but not kindly, adding that Lucia would get a nice moon face from popping so many steroids. Plus leaving the emergency syringe back at the motel! "Denial," Amy said, "pure and simple denial; get a book, ask a shrink."

"Oh, dry up, Sigmund." Lucia giggled. "And get off the Wheeze Patrol, I have three real doctors."

"None of whom happen to be here." Amy snorted, having the last useless word, and Lucia threw a pillow at her and got up to boogie to the radio while she dressed.

We'd all brought sweaters and we were glad of it. The chill and its foggy threat had gotten into the house. Justin built a fire in the living room and showed me how and he kept marching out to the grill on the lawn to correct what Vinnie was doing. I had never seen him behaving like Harry Homeowner before; I got a kick out of it.

The cottage was just as David had described it to me, all woody and rustic except for a big modern kitchen and dinette. Around the fireplace a bench of fieldstone had been built, and there were thick cushions on it so you could sit close to the fire. I suddenly wished it were my house. I drowned the wish in one of the Bloody Marys Bitsie dipped out of a tin bucket and passed around.

Amy lit a joint and that got passed around too. I waved it away; among other things I hated the smell. We all sprawled lux-

85

uriously on the cushions and sofa and started teasing Vinnie about his sneakers. He grinned and reddened. He had forgotten to take them off when he did his cannonball. They still squished.

I know I've said very little about Vinnie. I didn't know him very well; none of us did—not even Caro, with her burgeoning crush. But he was as close to Justin as David was, with this difference: next to David's intense volubility, Vinnie seemed nearly mute. He was Justin's chief legislative aide, and if you saw him in the statehouse corridors—a swarthy little guy in a shiny suit with papers falling out of every pocket—you might take him lightly. People with experience took him seriously. He was smart. He had an incredible memory. He liked to deal and he liked to fight, and Justin said he had a perfect record so far, choosing which for when.

But socially he was a cipher to us, because if he wasn't talking politics he wasn't talking at all, and the teasing was our way of bringing him into things. One year it was his sideburns. One year it was his car. I would never have dreamed of asking Vinnie if he wished that Justin and I had never met. I could barely get up the nerve to ask him how his wife, Brenda, was, and the two kids. Caro thought he was shy and Amy thought he was tough as nails and Lucia thought it worth bragging about when he waved to her, once, in the statehouse cafeteria.

"I don't mind that he looks like a Sicilian hit man." Bitsie sniffed. "I mind that he obviously thinks we're a bunch of ditsy broads."

But we didn't speculate much anymore about Vinnie. He was just always there, a quiet, sensible married boy of twenty-nine whom Justin trusted as he trusted David. They were young, certainly, to be part of the inner circle; even party people said so. But Justin was young, too, for the office he held, and I was young to be his lover. If Vinnie or David or I had been older, would we ever have been all together that summer evening, smoking dope at Lighthouse Point?

I doubt it. And if we'd all come of age ten years earlier, we wouldn't have been so casual about pot. Or hash. Or how that copy boy in Amy's newsroom could afford such sharp jackets, such good shoes.

As it was, we knew just enough to be careless. To take drugs for granted—not coke, though, that came later—and act unafraid. Like it or leave it. No big deal.

No way out.

Let me stay there awhile longer. It's all voices. Vinnie is calling for the steaks because the fire is ready. Caro is calling to Bitsie to tell me not to touch the corn till the last two minutes. Amy is calling from the porch that there's this terrific light; she wants us all for a picture. We love taking pictures. We go running out to the porch, wetting our lips and poking at our hair.

"Not such a good idea, boss," Vinnie says to Justin.

"Relax, Vinnie," Justin says. "This picture isn't even going to come out."

The light is terrific and also weird. The sun has poked a narrow hole in the cloud layer, and just a piece of it glows like a chip of red-hot charcoal from the grill. The lowering sky looks purple around it. We gather around the grill with Justin on one side of Vinnie and David on the other and the rest of us leaning in. It's automatic: I place myself at the end of the semicircle, away from Justin.

Amy yells, "Say prunes!" There's a loud pop. She used a flash. "It'll come out fine," she says proudly.

It does come out fine. There we all are, grinning, with Vinnie in the middle brandishing the stick he used to poke the coals. Bitsie is holding the balloon she grabbed on the way out. The picture is so crisp and clear that when they blew it up to show at the inquest, the writing on the balloon is perfectly legible: Happy Birthday David.

I can't delay any longer. There's just the dinner left.

There wasn't time for David to open his presents because the steaks got done so quickly and the corn hardly needed cooking, it was so sweet and fresh. We made toasts. We laughed a lot. Justin and I held hands tightly when the cake and candles came out, and after we sang "Happy Birthday" I called to Lucia, "Hey, Lulu! You're not crying. You promised to cry."

"Too whoozy," she said, in a small strangled voice, and although we were whoozy too, with the sun, the beer, the pig-

87

out, we caught it and shot one another worried looks. Lucia raised a hand, signaling, Not now.

But when we were all dumping paper plates in the kitchen, she said she might have to go back early and give herself a shot. If the last pill didn't kick in, anyway. She'd give it another half hour to work.

When she went back to the table for more dirty plates, Amy said, "No sense getting mad at her anymore. Maybe the next pill will do it. I've seen it happen. She gets bad and badder and then, click! she's breathing normally."

"She could take our car if she has to leave early. David will drive us to the last ferry and to the motel."

"No problem, then," Bitsie said. "My, my, what have we here?"

She took a small aluminum cake pan from the fridge.

"Brownies," I moaned. "Who'll want them? We have half a divine cake left."

Amy and Bitsie smiled broadly. "Hash brownies," Amy said. "For later. Or now. We got the recipe from Bitsie's cousin. Bitsie tried them at her cousin's place."

"Oh, I remember," I said. "Back in May? Yeah."

"That's the surprise," Amy said. "You get this lovely mellow floaty feeling."

"I heard all about it," I said. "Oh, for God's sake. Justin will probably have a fit. Vinnie will have two."

All the same I was intrigued. I told myself, I won't try one if Justin doesn't.

Just then Lucia stuck her head in the door. "Six o'clock and all's well. I did some of that iced coffee and I'm perfectly fine!"

"Iced coffee my ass," Amy muttered, but she rolled her eyes in relief.

Justin was intrigued too. Amy gave instructions, importantly, when the presents were all opened, the table cleared, and we had all gone back to sit in the living room. It was nice, having dinner over so early. We felt at home. The fire was crackling and Justin's face was all smoothed out, relaxed and rosy-brown in the firelight. We sat close.

"There's enough for two pieces each," Amy said. "Now what you do is just nibble. Then sort of let the crumbs melt on your tongue. Little bites, see?"

She did some dainty mouse nibbles. She said that Lucia couldn't have any.

"Oh, rats," Lucia wailed, and we all laughed. Amy relented. "Half a piece for you."

The pan went around. We were all as sober as children learning a new game. The half-filled pan went on the coffee table, and then we waited for something to happen. After a while the waiting seemed ridiculous. No one felt a thing.

"I think I measured wrong," Bitsie said, dejected. "We must have got grams and ounces mixed up."

Time went by. I felt sorry for Amy and Bitsie and their flop of a surprise. I thought I'd comfort them but I was distracted by how the sofa felt under me. It was so very very soft.

"Well, let's finish them up and see."

The pan got picked up. I waved it away.

"Lucia's gobbling," Vinnie said. "Amy said to nibble. Nibble is not gobble, isn't that something we agree on?"

"You made a speech, Vinnie," Justin said, laughing. "You made a goddam speech."

"Thank you," Vinnie said. "I really mean that."

Lucia stood up. I said, dreamily, "Where are you going, Lulu?"

"I'm getting my pills. Boy, is it ever hot in here!"

"I thought you were out of pills."

"Did I say pills? I meant my inhaler, the Cremolin."

"I thought you said you were feeling fine."

"I was until I started sitting in the fire."

David was in a chair near me. He started laughing. I narrowed my eyes to watch his laughter. He looked like a braying donkey. They're ugly animals with big teeth. I thought, David must have donkey blood.

I felt afraid. I stopped looking at David and the feeling went away.

"There's a piece left," somebody said. I was surprised to know that I couldn't tell whose voice it was.

"It must be mine," I said. "I don't want it. I feel really strange this minute."

A gentle chorus of "Me too"s went around the living room.

"All gone now," someone said, and giggled.

That was the end of the good part for me. There was this sensation of being cradled in air and a rubbery languor in my arms and legs and the fire looking like a single scarlet flower. But when I tried to speak the air cradle rocked and made me queasy, and I whispered, "The house is moving. I want it to stop."

No one seemed to hear. Bitsie passed in front of me and said, "Go to sleep. You're dreaming."

I wanted to go over to Justin, who had moved to a chair near the fire. At the same time I was overwhelmed by a terrible premonition of emptying my bladder, then and there, and I fumbled my way to the bathroom and forgot what I'd come for. I washed my hands, went back to the sofa, and felt the cradle rock. I thought, *This is no fun* and *Don't tell Justin* and I kept repeating these two sentences over and over to myself, like a mantra, but glumly, as if someone had assigned them to me to write after school. It was boring.

"Rachel? Hold my hand."

Justin was sitting next to me again. I asked him how he felt.

"I feel funny," he said. "My heart is too noisy."

"Me too," I said. "Let's not wake the others."

Everyone looked like they were asleep, even Vinnie, who was standing at a window, even Amy, who was talking about baseball to David. I heard the screen door to the porch bang.

"Who went out?"

"Bitsie," Justin murmured. "People keep going in and out. In and out. So stupid. We stay put."

I laughed politely and dropped his hand. It seemed to have a glove on it.

Vinnie was making coffee in the kitchen when I came out of it. The process was gradual. First I smelled the aroma of the coffee, and then I noticed the scratchy feel of the sofa's upholstery. After that, I walked quickly to the bathroom and didn't forget what for.

90

When I came back everyone was stretching, yawning, and knocking at the bathroom doors.

Bitsie and I went into the kitchen to help Vinnie. He said, "Jesus, that was some stuff. It knocked me for a loop."

"Me too," I said. "I just fell off the world."

"It wasn't anything like the first time," Bitsie said. "I wasn't just floating, I was *paralyzed*. What time is it?"

Vinnie looked at his watch and compared it with the clock on the stove. It was seven-fifteen. We looked at one another in absolute bafflement. We'd passed the brownies when? Say twenty of seven? We could all have sworn we'd been out of it for hours.

"It worked so fast," Bitsie said. "Must have been all the beer we drank before. *And* the Bloody Marys."

"Live and learn," Vinnie said. "I'd better check the boss."

He came back to the kitchen followed by David and Justin, both a little bleary, both looking sheepish.

"Coffee, quick," Justin said. "If I ever write my memoirs, I'm leaving this out. For a while there I thought I'd turned to stone. I thought I was a statue with someone inside it."

"Blame me, if you're mad," Bitsie said, handing him a cup of coffee. "Watch out, hot stuff."

"I'm not mad. I only might be if Rachel had a better time than I did."

"Never fear," I said. "I've had better times on No-Doz."

Amy put her head around the kitchen door. "What's keeping the coffee? And Lucia . . . anyone seen her?"

"I did," I said confidently. "Wait . . . she was getting a pill from her purse."

"That was way back," Amy said, and we made a tray of cups and coffee and brought it out. Everyone grabbed, blew, took two sips, and said, "Ahh." Everyone felt awkward; we were all thinking of things we hoped we hadn't said out loud.

Caro took her cup and went around the bedrooms, calling, "Lulu?" and Justin raised an eyebrow at all of us.

"She was with us when we went out to look for the sunset," Amy said. "She came back in with us, too."

"I went out again," David said. "Beats me what for. I was alone, though."

"Hell you were alone," Bitsie said. "I was with you."

"Maybe she slipped out again by herself," I said. "She could have fallen asleep in that wicker chair."

Amy went over to open the door to the porch. As soon as she switched the porch light on we could see the fog, the empty chair, and David's Olivetti on a wicker table. It was beaded with fat droplets of condensation. Justin went out on the porch, to peer into the gray twilight. It wasn't dark yet, but the fog was disorienting. It lay over the wide lawn in thick clumps and thin ones with patches of clear in between so that you could see big pieces of the Bay.

David muttered something about drying off his typewriter, and Justin said gruffly, "Forget it. We're looking for Lucia."

Then we realized that that was what we were doing. There was no basement; we'd gone through the house twice.

"There's a couple of flashlights in that broom closet," Justin said. "Get 'em, Vinnie."

There were three flashlights. The three men took them. The four of us fanned out around them, calling.

"Lucia!" we called, softly at first and then louder. "Lucia!"

We went across the lawn; we went down to the dock. Behind us the outline of the big house hulked, a swath of darkness in the fog. We were looking up the slope, from the dock.

"Could she have gone up there?" Justin said. "The doors are locked. She couldn't have gotten in."

"I don't think she'd do that," I said. "That junk scared the hell out of me. She wouldn't want to go that far away, all alone."

"It affects different people differently," Amy said. Her voice had a quaver in it.

"She was sitting near me for a while," Caro said. "I was scared by the sound of her. Wheezing and coughing, too."

"I think it was her took that last piece," Bitsie said, and for a minute we all just stood there, thinking of Lucia wandering around in the fog, mindless, frightened, wheezing.

Justin said, "Vinnie, you and everyone else check around the three cottages. Rachel and I will go up to the house. It's possible she might have had some dumb idea of taking a car."

"Yes," I said eagerly. "She was talking about going back if she didn't feel better. Let's go."

We were halfway up the slope, skidding a little on the wet grass, when we heard Vinnie yell.

"Over here! Out behind our place!"

I felt a great *whoosh* of relief. That was where the meadow started; I could imagine Lucia wanting to get some flowers, like mine.

"Vinnie shouldn't shout like that," I said to Justin as we started back. "Someone could hear."

But no one was within a mile of us to hear. And Lucia couldn't hear anything, not even after Vinnie had turned her over on her back. The three flashlights made jumping white circles over her body and what surrounded it: a small grassy patch behind the house, next to the meadow, with the ground all churned up so that it looked more mud than grass. She had rolled on it. Even without the flashlights, there was light enough to see that she had rolled on it. She had torn out chunks of turf, flailed, kicked, clawed, trying to get up.

We stood in a semicircle, looking down at her. It didn't take a split second for all of us to understand what had happened. There was a thin strewing of clover and chicory in the mud. There was a vile, overpowering odor. There was the sight of her face, a featureless mask of mud and vomit, all over, in her hair, her open eyes, her open mouth. She was buried in it. She was completely buried in chocolate-brown death, and before she'd given in, she'd struggled through a final agony of suffocation.

11

Horror is heavy. David and Vinnie staggered, carrying Lucia inside the cottage. Caro had raced ahead; she had done some nursing in the Peace Corps; she knew what to do. She made the men hold Lucia upright while she swabbed her face with a sponge and a bucket of water, asking for more water, wet towels. She worked fast; in a minute she had them double Lucia over the back of a chair and she pounded Lucia's back and squeezed her, hugging her from behind. Then she had her laid face up on the rug in front of the fireplace, and she started the CPR, saying, "Down, up, one-two-three. Down, up, one-two-three."

Bitsie knelt at Lucia's head, sponging.

"See that her mouth is open," Caro hissed. "Turn her head to one side."

I put my hand between Lucia's parted teeth and pulled hard. A little gush of clotted brown slime came out.

94

"Her nose is still blocked. Get a Q-tip from my purse."

Amy ran and got it and worked the stub inside Lucia's nose, moaning. "Oh, shit, I think I'm pushing it farther in."

"Let me."

All the while Justin was on his knees at Lucia's side, moving his fingers over her wrist.

"I can't get anything. Try her neck, her heart."

Bitsie put her hand inside Lucia's blouse. She drew it out, crying, "I can't feel her heart!"

Justin sank down heavily on the rug. He took Lucia's wrist again.

Caro signaled to Vinnie to take over without losing the rhythm. "Faster, faster," she said. She was sweating and trembling in the fire's heat. She pinched Lucia's nose shut and put her mouth over Lucia's. She blew into Lucia's mouth, great breaths that made her own face contort. Then Bitsie took over. Then I went and then Amy, while the men did the CPR. We were too intent to sicken from the smell. Her eyes were open and imploring. It went on for fifteen minutes.

"Oh, Lulu," Caro whispered, sinking down at her side and stroking back her wetted hair. "Please breathe, darling, please breathe."

She looked up at us defiantly.

"That was a prayer, goddammit. That was a prayer."

Vinnie pulled her to her feet and put his arm around her. David bent to close Lucia's eyes. We all looked toward Justin.

"She's gone," he said. "Passed out, vomited, choked on it."

"It nauseated me too," Bitsie said dully. "I remember wanting to throw up."

"Her medicine," Amy said. "I kept warning her. She was doubling up on everything."

I looked over at the big tin bucket with the cup still in it.

"She swiped a drink," I said. "I saw her."

Amy hissed something and walked stiffly to the front door. She opened it; cold air swept through the room. The porch light was diffused through swirling fog.

"I knew she was dead when we found her," Caro said. "I'd try all night if I thought it would make a difference."

"You did your best," Vinnie said. "None of us would have even known how to try."

David had a sheet in his hands. We looked at him, dumbly. What would he want with a sheet?

He laid it gently over Lucia's body.

We all looked at Justin.

"Let's sit in the kitchen," Justin said. "Get some coffee going. It's eight o'clock. We have to think."

"We have two hours till the ferry," I said.

"Simon shuts down at nine-thirty if there's no car in the parking lot. Did any of you girls tell him when you'd be leaving?"

"We didn't say anything to him," I said. "I just checked the schedule on the wall, where he sells tickets."

"That's good," Justin said.

He was grim and calm. I know what I looked like because I could see the others. Our faces were flaccid, stupefied. But Justin didn't have that dazed expression. He put his arm around David and David nodded. It was some kind of signal and we took it.

Lucia was gone. We were left. We had to think about us. Starting now.

We sat in the kitchen drinking coffee until we hummed with it. "Wired and tired," we used to say during the campaign, veteran crisis junkies and proud of it. We used to laugh after some setback or piece of bad news from the other side. We used to say that running scared was the name of the game.

We couldn't be less than that, could we? Everything we had learned, everything we had shared, was there for us, including Justin, calm and grim at the head of the table.

David and Vinnie had their yellow pads out. It was team routine. Write it down. Get it in focus. Don't argue until we list all the options.

It was too new for grief. We were too numb to cry.

"Nobody's to blame," Justin said. "That's first. You kept nagging her all day. We heard you. 'Don't drink. Lie down.' I saw Amy split that piece of brownie much less than half. I noticed that."

"I baked it," Amy said.

96

"I did too," Bitsie said. "And I made the Bloody Marys that she couldn't ever resist."

"She wouldn't even have been here except for me," I said.

Justin rapped the table impatiently. "Over," he said. "No more of that. David? The most obvious things, please."

Like Caro, David had raced ahead. His pad was covered with writing.

"Call a hospital. The nearest is at Talcott on the mainland. We lost time giving her CPR, and that's why we didn't call immediately. I figure it would take an ambulance forty minutes at least to get here."

Justin pointed to the phone on the wall. "So we call now," he said. "Then what?"

"We'd have almost an hour, maybe. To clean up. Get rid of the beer cans and the booze. Dress."

He looked at Bitsie, whose sweat shirt covered her shorts. She looked naked under it.

"Oh, Jesus," she said. "What a scene!"

"Two calls," Vinnie said. "I remember that much of my law. The police. Accidental death, sudden death, violent death. The police."

Justin nodded. "Which station?" Amy got the phone book. The police station was in Seaview, fifteen miles closer than the hospital.

"They'll be here first," David said. "Not much time, then. Another call to the ferryman to meet them."

We were silent for a moment. Vinnie spoke to Caro.

"What do they do with the body when they get it to the hospital?"

"It wouldn't be a Code Blue anymore," Caro said. "Not an emergency. They'd take her to autopsy. Do blood, stomach, the works. Vinnie? You knew that."

He knew that.

"This is trouble," David said. He seemed to be talking to himself. We looked at one another. The horror was lively now. Five young women. Three men, two married. A dead girl with alcohol in her, and illegal drugs in her, at the Governor's home, with the Governor there.

97

I wanted to bolt for the front door. I wanted to go to the ends of the earth and die in a ditch. I had ruined him.

"Don't, Rachel," Justin said, putting his arm around me.

"We'd have to tell them about the asthma," Caro said. "All that medicine. Beconase, Cremolin, the other steroids . . . they have to look."

"No matter how much she vomited, there must be hash in her lungs."

"They'd be thorough," Justin said thoughtfully. "In this case they'd have to be very thorough."

He asked David to read his notes back.

David read. We imagined. There would be the police in the cottage. And the words, in black caps, speeding to the wire services. A search. Fingerprints, mine and Justin's, in his old room. The sheets on his bed. I wanted to wail with anguish but instead I cried out in anger.

"Oh, why didn't she leave when she *knew* she should!"

"Don't, Rachel." This time it was Caro. "It's my fault. I talked her out of leaving the first time, after the cannonballs. She was so full of beer I thought she'd pile up the car. Or drive it off a bridge. I said *I'd* drive her back to the motel, and she got mad at me. She said I was making her feel like she was ruining my day. So then she said she felt fine."

"She said that twenty times."

"But I should have insisted. I gave up too fast."

And then we didn't need Justin to rap the table. We fell silent. We had the rest of our lives to fault ourselves.

"The autopsy, Vinnie," Justin said. "Can we put pressure to avoid?"

"I'm thinking about it. We could make sure the hospital releases the body to the county coroner's office, for the autopsy. Then reach someone there."

"Possible?"

"With the right name. I'd need a day for that, a working day, and tomorrow's Sunday."

"Let's talk about that," Justin said. "Making some time. We don't have to rush it."

"Like we haven't found her yet," David said eagerly. "Yes,

that was in my mind too. We could always say we found her later. That we looked longer. Time to think."

"We have to consider the worst. Let's hear, Vinnie."

Vinnie wiped his forehead with his sleeve. He said, "Felony drugs, on your property. Contributory negligence. I don't have the tort law pat. But I think we'd have to worry about manslaughter too, just in case."

"They'd throw the book at us," David said.

Suddenly Caro spoke up loudly. "But it wasn't the drugs, it was the medicine, I'm sure of it! She was *chewing* that Theo-phylline, and it gave her palpitations every time. With her lungs blocked and a bad arrhythmia, listen to me, she could have choked on a glass of milk!"

Bitsie reached across the dinette table to hold down Caro's hands, waving wildly. "Hush, Caro. It's still what people will think."

"They'll think the worst," Vinnie said. "About everything here. About all of us."

"Naturally," Justin said, and he leaned back in his chair. He rolled a pencil on the table. His voice was low and measured, but somewhere, in the back of my mind, was the thought that he sounded different.

"We have two outboards down at the dock. One's a big Boston Whaler. So we don't have to worry about the ferry. We can get the girls back to their motel. No hurry. Let's agree, first, that we'll say we found her later than we did."

He looked around the table. We all nodded. Agreed.

"The hospital autopsy," Justin said. "The chocolate stuff. If it weren't for that part I think we could survive."

Agreed.

"So I'm for thinking about it," Justin said. "Any idea, for consideration. Suppose this. Suppose that. Let's see if we can come up with some damage controls."

We all murmured that we'd try. It was a relief to have something to set our minds on. There's always something to sal-vage. The flames of hell were licking at our feet, and if we just stood there we'd burn.

We'd already agreed not to tell that we'd found her at

99

twenty to eight. That was the first step. They say the first step is the big one.

So we took it. And then we ran scared. We ran and ran until we reached Camel Bridge and the deep black water under it.

At first it was like a game, a game with stakes so high it couldn't seem real. It was like a lull in a nightmare. Suppose this. Suppose that. Who knew Justin was at Lighthouse Point? Who knew we were? Was there a way to get Justin off the island? If he could drive back to the city without being seen, go to my house, wrong, reach his father, wrong, a sister maybe . . .

Suppose this. Suppose that. If we really hadn't found Lucia yet, where would she be? She could be anywhere out there in that emptiness around the lighthouse. There were the marshes and the meadows and the thick shrubs around the big house, the beaches, the Bay.

Such an empty island. Such a thick fog. A sickened stranger on those dirt roads, stumbling, lurching, weaving. . . .

Caro's vision became Lucia's ghost, beckoning.

What Lucia could have done became what Lucia should have done.

Did do.

She left in Amy's car and drove off Camel Bridge and the strong salt waters held her and washed her clean and they would call it death by drowning.

Say she left around eight, promising to call us when she got to the motel and took her shot. We'd wait and we'd worry, and— waiting, worrying—we'd miss the ferry. We'd insist on going back before midnight, in the Whaler; we'd all walk back to the motel. But we wouldn't find Lucia or the car, and we'd call the hospital in Talcott. She might have driven herself there. And then we'd be annoyed; we'd guess she'd forgotten to call us and felt perfectly fine and had gone off to the party the umbrella-rental boys had invited her to that morning.

Oh, we'd be annoyed with her. So thoughtless! We'd go to sleep. We'd call the cottage in the morning and hear the awful truth. Someone would have seen the car by morning.

Awful. Awful, tragic, magnetizing vision drawing us closer and closer until we couldn't see anything else.

How? Easy. The fog, too. Use a broom.

The tide. There was a tide table on the kitchen bulletin board. Full moon behind the fog, and full high tide in an hour.

We argued, went forward, drew back. We wove it, unraveled it, wove it again, tighter yet. David wrote. Vinnie wrote. Then Justin said, "It's ten-fifteen. Let's take another fifteen minutes. I'm for it, but I will not do any persuading."

Time stopped. Nobody said anything. It's true, believe it or not: your whole life flashes in front of you.

I spoke up first.

"I'm with Justin. I know he has the most to lose if we play it straight. But we're just as much in it as he is."

"One working day," Vinnie said. "That's all I need. If the coroner says death by drowning, I won't even need that."

"She choked. It'll work," David said. "And it won't make any difference, to her."

So we were four. The others followed. Seven. And the flames froze because suddenly we were all encased in the same cold shield of resolution. Nothing mattered now but being quick, because the fog could lift, the tide run out, the ice melt.

The radiant heat of the dying fire was enough to have kept her warm. We put pennies on her eyes, and then we lavished her again with soap and water, everywhere, even her nails where the mud had crusted. We washed her pants and put them back on her. Her stained blouse was exchanged for Caro's blue sweater. We combed her hair and kissed her. The skin of her forehead was like satin. Caro rolled up the sleeves of her sweater, too long for Lucia.

"Sleep, dear," she whispered. "We love you. Sleep."

Justin and Vinnie carried her out. David had her pocketbook with the room key we'd put in her wallet. The faint sound of Amy's car starting up didn't stop us as we went on scrubbing away the stains in the rug, straightening the bedrooms and baths, leaving the balloons and the crumples of wrapping paper conspicuous on the dining room table. It was another nightmare lull, and in it I cried, "Oh, if someone sees them!"

"They'll say they just found her and they're rushing to rout up Simon for the ferry."

I bit my tongue until it hurt, so as not to cry out the next thing: *If someone sees them stopped on the bridge!*

There was no answer for that.

"Ten more minutes," Amy said. "They have to walk back through the swamp on the Bay side."

Five minutes passed. Caro used the hair dryer on the dampened carpet. Amy put the sheet back in the linen closet.

"Four more minutes," Bitsie whispered. "Please, God."

The minutes passed. We heard steps on the porch.

"No one saw us. It took a minute. Less, even. The car turned over."

Their legs were streaked with mud from the marsh. I could feel Justin's heart pounding when I put my arms around him. David marched to the broom closet and put away the broom. They'd used the broom to hit the gas pedal. One of them had reached into the open window on the driver's side.

I had the action by heart. Position the car facing the water. Keep it in gear. Hit the pedal. Jump back. Watch the throbbing hulk, like a blinded animal, lurch forward.

Like a person diving? Like Lucia, diving into the ocean yesterday, a slim knife. Just yesterday evening.

Vinnie got some brandy out of the wet-bar closet. He poured three shots and they all drank. David said again, to no one, "It didn't make any difference, to her."

"Everyone?" It was Justin, speaking over his shoulder. He was building up the fire, with kindling that caught at once; in the glow his hair was reddish-gold and curly with damp night air. "Everyone come and sit around here," he said. "We'll take another fifteen minutes. I want to go over the next part again."

We went over it again.

I had a minute alone with Justin before we left. I let the others go ahead to pick their way through the fog down to the dock, and I clung to him and kissed him.

"It's going to be awful anyway," I said.

"Yes," he said. "But not the worst. Nothing criminal."

"We'll make it," I said. "She'd want us to make it."

"I think so too," he murmured, and then he turned me around and gave me a little push in the direction of the dock. But his hands held me and he whispered in my hair, "The hospital. Not the police. Let the desk clerk at the motel see you come in. Ask him about her."

I swung around, shaking his hands off.

"We've been over that," I said. "Over and over. One call to the hospital. One here, tomorrow morning. Justin? You sound funny. What is it?"

"What's what?"

But I didn't answer because I didn't know, and I ran down the lawn to the others. The motor of the Whaler was still warming up; Justin had told David to give it a few minutes to clear the lines. Justin knew about boats; David and Vinnie didn't, but it was too risky exposing Justin in an open boat, even at midnight, even in a fog. I ran, worrying that David and Vinnie couldn't handle the Whaler. And I worried about the bad feeling I'd just had on the porch. It had something to do with Justin's voice. It had something to do with his face when he kissed me. It had felt as if he were smiling. . . .

The six of us huddled in the big boat. Vinnie pushed off and the current pulled us west toward the inlet. It changed in the channel and went against us, and David muttered, "Here goes nothing," and gunned the motor. The Whaler leaped and pitched, and in a minute we were sopped and shivering. But the trip was over in another minute and it wasn't hard for David to steer by the big red light at the ferry landing. "Ladder to the left," Vinnie said, and David cut the motor and we scrambled up the mossy rungs. David tossed our beach bags over the bulkhead.

"All set. Call tomorrow."

"Watch yourselves walking."

"Take care of him."

I said that. I said it instead of doing what I wanted to do: jump back into the boat and go back to Justin.

It was a fifteen-minute walk back to the motel, but we made it faster, trotting. No cars passed us, coming or going. The lights of the Dune Deck Motel were the only ones we could see, but barely. The fog had become a hard drizzle.

There was an old man sleeping with his head in his arms in the motel lobby. We asked softly, then loudly, till he stirred.

"Did our friend come in a few hours ago? A little blond girl?"

"She checked in with you?"

"Sure. Last night."

"What would she come in this way for? Nobody comes in this way. This is a motel."

He yawned and stared at us. A mistake, asking that. I tried to think through the chill. A mistake. So soon?

It was Caro who spoke up, smartly. "She was supposed to call us. She'd have to use the phone."

She pointed to the pay phone in the corner. There were no phones in the rooms.

"Nobody used that phone. Not since I came on. There's another one up top."

"She just went to sleep, I guess," Caro said. "Give us the passkey so we don't have to wake her up. Room two-twelve."

"Bring it right back."

We saw the phone at the top of the stairs. Bitsie pointed to the big trash can near it.

"Before I call the hospital let's get rid of the garbage."

We took the beer cans from our beach bags and dumped them. Caro had Lucia's blouse in a plastic bag.

"I can't," she murmured, but Amy took it from her and threw it in.

Bitsie phoned the hospital. "B-E-N-N-E-T-T," she spelled. Lucia Bennett. Around nine o'clock, maybe. Maybe later.

"That's that," Bitsie said, when she hung up. We went into our room. In a few minutes Amy and Caro knocked and joined us after having returned the passkey. They had Lucia's suitcase and the bathing suit she'd left in the bathroom to dry.

They were crying. Bitsie and I said we didn't dare; if we started we might not stop.

It was past one in the morning. It was the sight of Caro's quivering shoulders that undid me. She was always such a placid person. She was big and strong, too. She'd helped deliver babies in the *favelas* outside Rio, in the Peace Corps; she chased a purse-snatcher on the beach once, and caught him and sat on him till the police came. The clipping was in her Peace Corps scrapbook, in Portuguese that she translated for us, giggling. The headline said: AMERICA IN THE SADDLE.

I wept. So did Bitsie. We put the TV on to muffle the sound; I don't know how to cry quietly. We didn't talk about what we'd done after Lucia died. We talked about calling her brother in Fort Leeds. We talked about her funeral. We talked about Tandy in Brittany and when she'd hear and what would they ask Justin and what would he answer and Brenda, Vinnie's wife, and Mrs. Freed, David's mother.

105

And we wept again for the harm we'd done to so many people and for dread of the morning.

Finally we became so exhausted that we were ready for sleep. We bunched together in two beds, grateful for the crowding. Amy and Caro could not go back to their room. They couldn't look at the empty cot.

I slept till eight the next day. I was the one who had to call the cottage and tell them Lucia hadn't returned.

"Quick, Rachel, they'll be waiting," Bitsie said. She had been awake for hours, and she handed me a couple of quarters for the pay phone.

"So ten more minutes," I said. "I want some coffee. I feel sick."

We all felt sick. Amy went down for coffee and doughnuts and the sugar hit me like a blow to the stomach. I dressed slowly, drank some water, and went to the phone. It had a booth of wooden slats around it but there was no real privacy.

Vinnie answered on the first ring. I spoke loudly.

"Vinnie? Listen, we're petrified. Lucia's not here and we don't think she came back all night."

"They found the car," Vinnie said. He seemed hoarse. "The ferry guy, Simon, saw it on his way to open the ferry at seven o'clock. He turned around and drove here to tell us."

"Oh, my God," I said. "What do we do now?"

"Stay where you are," Vinnie said. "Go out on the beach. Act normal. Rachel, something terrible happened."

The new blue sky tilted over me. The smell of wet tar from the parking lot made me dizzy.

"What happened?"

"Justin didn't sleep all night. He started acting crazy. We didn't dare go to sleep, either."

"Crazy," I repeated. "Didn't sleep."

"You heard me. Walking and walking. Babbling things. Saying it was all his fault."

"I'll come right over."

"Stay where you are, hear me? He's gone."

"Gone? Where?"

"To the police station. Rachel, hang in. Listen. When Simon walked in and told us there was a car in the channel under Camel Bridge? He said he remembered that car. It had five girls in it. So Justin just stood there and said that one of the girls was still in the car! The car that *he'd* been driving! That *he'd* run off the bridge in the fog! And he got out and tried to save her but he couldn't."

"How could you let him say that?" I whispered.

"We tried to get him aside to stop him. We couldn't. He kept talking to that old guy like the old guy was the police!"

A family with little children kept padding back and forth to their room. They kept forgetting things. I hissed, "So who's with him? David?"

"David and Simon. They took the ferry and Simon's car. They left at eight. Christ, if only David would *call* me. Maybe he got Justin calmed down. Or hit him with a brick."

"Don't hang up, Vinnie. Talk to me."

"Hit him with a brick. I wanted to do that all night. He went out of his fucking mind, Rachel. He kept calling that old ferry guy 'sir.' 'It's all my fault, sir. I killed the girl. I killed her.' "

"You have to do me a favor, Vinnie," I said. "I'm calling Bitsie to the phone. You have to repeat it all to her. Tell her what happened, all right?"

I left the receiver dangling. I ran to our room and said to the others, "One of you pick up the phone. It's Vinnie. Something bad."

They all went running. I must have been white as a sheet. As soon as I was alone I looked around the room, chose a place, and fainted.

By ten-thirty we were all on the beach, lying with our heads toward the pole of the umbrella like spokes in a wheel. We knew it was too early, but we listened to the radio anyway, for news. We were right in front of the motel, where Vinnie could find us easily; he'd only been waiting in the cottage for our call before taking their car and going to the police station. He'd find us. It was our turn to wait.

We went swimming. The water had gotten colder and it stung us into ravenous hunger. But we had no car to go for food in, and when the hot-dog man arrived we mobbed him and lay down again with the radio. We hardly spoke. I think we were all in the same state of uncanny calm; it was a form of exhausted indifference to reality. Lucia was dead. Justin was crazy and talking to the police. They might come for us next. The numbness was merciful.

I told the others about the girl Justin shot. Then I told them about his voice the night before, and how I'd thought it sounded strange. They took it in, and for a long while we just lay there, saying the same things.

"We can't let him take the blame."

"We can't ever tell the truth."

"He's been working too hard, we all saw that."

"Cracked."

"Snapped."

"Breakdown."

"Vinnie's there now. Maybe David did something."

"Cracked. Snapped. Breakdown."

Fainting had done me some good. I said I wanted to kill Justin, and Caro pressed my hand.

"I keep trying to pray," she said. "Only I don't know what for."

None of us could tell her. None of us knew what to do with the feeling we had. Vinnie had told Bitsie more than he'd told me. Vinnie said that Justin was not only convinced that he'd caused the accident, he told Simon that he'd come back to the cottage and found us gone, and Vinnie and David fast asleep.

Us gone. Them asleep. We couldn't have known anything except that he'd left with Lucia, to drive her back to the motel.

If he stuck to that story we were in the clear.

We didn't know what to do with the feeling. We couldn't talk about it to one another. I had it too. Oh, yes. I loved him but I had it too.

Amy saw Vinnie first, walking with his shoes in his hand across the beach. There were people all around us, and we made a tight circle under the umbrella.

"I've got his statement in my pocket," Vinnie said. "David swiped the third carbon. He did some job, our David."

"Statement," I repeated. "He made a statement!"

"Couldn't stop it. Not after he'd called the police and said he was coming. Not after he walked into the station house. Too late. But David did what he could. He told the sheriff the Governor was in a state of shock and might have a concussion. So David got the sheriff to let him, David, do the writing."

"You mean he got Justin to shut up?"

"Not exactly." Vinnie bit his lip. For a minute I thought he'd cry. So I wasn't surprised when he said, "Justin stopped talking on the ferry over, David told me. Only blinking and muttering under his breath. I saw for myself when I got there. Rachel? I don't think he knew who I was."

He looked around to see if we understood and took a deep breath and went on.

"He signed what David wrote. What David wrote had to stay in line with what Justin already blabbed to the ferry guy. I've got it in my pocket, but I won't take it out. Who knows who might remember seeing us. But it said that Lucia was so sick Justin had to drive her back. It was so foggy he went off Camel Bridge. Somehow saved himself and kept trying to save her. Doesn't remember anything after that. Can't say what he did for four hours before coming back to the cottage. Sat around, maybe, then. Maybe slept. Then woke us up and told David and me."

Bitsie tried to laugh; it came out barking. "Oh, for the love of God. Amnesia! Who the hell's going to believe it?"

"Who the hell can believe any of it?"

"You saw him at the police station," I said. "How is he?"

It was a stupid question, considering the circumstances. But Vinnie knew what I meant.

"He really looks the part. Dazed. Zonked. Like he's been through some awful . . . thing and it's confused him. Rachel? I thought of Billy."

Billy was Vinnie's little boy. Billy was six years old.

We sat dumbly, listening to Vinnie. They'd already been in touch with Old Henry. The Lambert family's private turbojet was on its way. The sheriff couldn't hold Justin, not with his voluntary statement and the way he looked.

Suddenly Amy said fiercely, "He can't be crazy! It's all too goddam pat."

"I want to think that," Vinnie said. "I do. But listen to me, how hoarse I am. David and I were up all night, talking to him, arguing with him. He was wild. Raving. A couple of times we had to hold him down. You hear? Hold him!"

"I have to see him," I whispered, and Vinnie took some car keys from his pocket and started to hand them to me. Then he obviously changed his mind. He looked at his watch.

"Justin and David are in the air by now. You girls have to follow by car. I rented a green two-door Mercury. It's out back. Pack, pay up here, and drive like hell to the Lambert estate. We'll meet there. You can make it in six hours."

"You can't come with us?"

"No. My job is to stay here, with Lucia, through the postmortem. One of the Lamberts already got hold of her brother. He got permission to have the body released to me. So after the coroner does his examination, they'll send another plane. For both of us."

He looked over at Caro shyly.

"I'm a Catholic too," Vinnie said. "I know it's not right to leave them alone. I'll be with her. All the way."

Them, I thought. *Them* must be dead people. All morning long I seemed to hear things that needed laborious translation before they could register in my brain. When Bitsie cleared her throat, I even thought she was touched by Vinnie's statement, but of course it wasn't that. She was angry.

"All this shit is coming from the Lamberts. Do this! Do that! Supposing I don't *want* to drive six fucking hours to their place? Suppose I want to call my parents, or go to my house or their house or any goddam place I want?"

She glowered, pulled at her yellow bangs, and blew a mean stream of cigarette smoke in Vinnie's face. She'd never liked him, but she'd never showed it either.

"Oh, Bitsie, shush," Amy said quickly. "Be realistic. How can we separate now, with everything up in the air? With decisions to make? And this place will be crawling with press any minute."

"Amy's right," Caro said. "Anyway, at least we know what to do next. Pack, pay up, and drive. We need a map."

"I made one on the back of Justin's statement," Vinnie said. "Here, take it, with the keys. You've got the whole trip to get it by heart. The statement, I mean."

"We can't let Justin take all the blame!" I cried, and so, in their own words, did Amy and Caro and Bitsie. But my voice was loudest.

Vinnie's hand was a sudden vise on my arm. "If you think we have any choice at this minute you're crazier than he is."

He glared at us. Purplish shadows looked like bruises beneath his eyes. Girls! his eyes said, and I knew he'd been dreading some kind of hysteria, the kind women were prone to and men could cure with a quick slap.

I glared back. I wanted to tell him that hysteria would be a relief, compared to what I was feeling! But I just said, "Stuff it, Vinnie. I know exactly where we stand now. But it could change. Any minute, if Justin's that unstable."

Vinnie dropped his head and mumbled an apology that I cut off. Caro hugged him.

"We have to stick," he said softly. "Until and unless Justin changes his story. Retracts. Leaving all of us—"

"Where Caro is," I said dully. "Not even knowing what to pray for. Vinnie, listen. Did Justin ever tell you about what happened to him when he was thirteen? An awful thing."

He'd never heard about it. He listened in silence, impassive as a Buddha, and when I finished all he said was, "I'll tell David."

Then he said he had to get over to the coroner's office, and it was odd, how suddenly it heartened us all to know that Lucia was really out of that car. She was somewhere dry and in daylight and she wasn't going to be alone, either. Vinnie would be with her, dear, exhausted Vinnie, who was getting up, brushing the sand from his pants, and pulling Caro to her feet. Even without shoes, she was half a head taller. They held each other's hands; for a moment it was as if they were alone on the beach. We all felt it.

"Don't worry about the coroner," Caro murmured. "It will go all right. I'm sure of it."

He turned up his palms in that universal gesture of uncertainty—Who knows?—and walked off.

But it did go all right at the coroner's office, as we soon heard. The coroner was a young man, and inexperienced, and when he pressed down on Lucia's rib cage, and the white towel under her head turned gray with wet, he said there was certainly a lot of water in this one! That was his inexperience. He got huffy with the undertaker's assistant, who was standing by and saying that in *his* opinion there wasn't a lot of water at all, and what there was was coming mostly from the stomach, not the lungs. But the coroner knew that the Governor was involved in the accident; he preened in the approaching spotlight; he was not disposed to back

112

down in favor of some funeral-parlor employee. That was his youth. He couldn't admit a doubt about his first impression. Death by drowning, he said. Sign and seal it: death by drowning.

Vinnie was right there. As soon as he saw the postmortem report typed and signed, he found the undertaker's assistant and asked to buy a coffin. But he was told a coffin wouldn't fit into the little plane that was due to take him away from the shore, and so together they wrapped Lucia in a length of thick green plastic and the ambulance drove them to the airfield, where the plane was waiting. Lucia was laid in the aisle next to Vinnie's seat. She left Lighthouse Point, flying. She might even have flown over the four of us, as we drove north along I-95. There was so much traffic it took us close to seven hours.

She flew. We were merely fleeing.

"Oh, God," Caro said, slowing the car. "What the hell is all that?"

Vinnie's map showed a three-mile piece of back road before we hit the Lambert estate. We'd clocked it; we were almost there. But up ahead of us, plain to see in the thickening dusk, were a whole bunch of cars in the road and people milling around.

"Press," Amy said grimly. "Pull over, Caro. What do we do?"

"They know about us," I said. It had been on the radio; we'd heard the bulletins, over and over, switching stations.

"A tragic accident ended a birthday party for Governor Lambert's aide, David Freed, and his fiancée, Rachel Warshowsky. Four other young women attended the party that ended in death last night—"

It was always the same. David had managed it. But there

114

was no managing a follow-up, ever. You could only guess the approach and react.

"They can't know we're coming here," Bitsie said. "They'll be busy checking motels all day. Justin's statement didn't name where we were staying."

"It's not just us," I said. "It's only they know that Justin's up there, inside. They want to keep track of people coming and going."

"If I know about Old Henry," Bitsie said, "they've clocked ten lawyers in already."

"We could be lawyers," I said. "We've got our city stuff on."

"We're the four girls, is what we are," Bitsie said. "We could be cleaning help, maybe. But *four*. They've got our number."

"So make it one," Amy said. "Rachel and me scrunched on the floor, Bitsie lying down. Throw the mats and bags on us."

It didn't take a minute. Vinnie's map had the fence, the gates, the word GUARD in front of the gates. Caro could whisper her name.

We started up. We could hear voices, loud.

"Who's this? Green Mercury."

"Get the driver."

There were people around the car, on the sides, running after. We could hear the sizzle of the flashes and the guard, shouting, "You stupid assholes will get yourselves killed."

"Assholes is right," Amy muttered.

"Hold it!" I heard a man shout, right in my ear. He was leaning in through Caro's open window.

"Oh, really!" We heard Caro snort and a grunt from the man as she swatted him. Then the guard was at the window, and Caro was whispering, and then the gates opened and we drove through. We didn't even sit up until we were under the white portico in the driveway.

Vinnie and David were there, waiting for us. We hugged them.

"Just leave the car," David said. "Grab your stuff and follow me. There's a back way in."

The six of us went around the farthest wing of the house. It wasn't a stone house. It was white wood, a mile of white wood.

115

We followed them through a screen door and up a winding, narrow staircase, uncarpeted and steep. We kept going up. Finally, Vinnie opened a door to a big, bare room. It had four small bunk beds in it, covered with Indian blankets, and beat-up bureaus and shelves full of books and toys.

"My old room," I heard Justin say, but only in my imagination. Justin wasn't there.

"He's asleep," David said. "A psychiatrist met the plane. Gave him a horse needle full of something to make him sleep."

"They held dinner for you," Vinnie said. "I told them you'd have eaten, on the road."

"We didn't," I said. "But my God, Vinnie. Dinner with them? What do we say?"

"Good question," David said. "I've been thinking. I think you should stay up here. Ask for sandwiches in the room. Just say you're too upset to talk now."

"You mean you guys go down and tell them that?"

"Yes."

"Sounds fishy."

"What doesn't?"

Vinnie and David left. We unpacked. We pulled a low table and four nursery-school chairs to the center of the room. We sat in them, waiting.

"Like jail," Bitsie said. "Kiddie prison."

David and Vinnie came back with trays, and we fell on the food and the coffee. Bitsie asked David to go down for some wine. There must be wonderful wine and she wanted some.

"Vinnie and I made a pact," David said. "Not to drink. Same for you guys, if you know the score."

"Good idea," said Caro. "What did you tell them?"

"You're all crying. You can't face people. If they cared, they didn't show it."

"Who's they?"

"Old Henry. The psychiatrist and a regular doctor. One of the sisters, Edith. The brother-in-law, her husband, whom they call Jimbo. There was a lawyer too, but he left."

"Missy's not here," I said.

"They left her in Deal with the two other sisters. That's the beach house they were all using: Deal. It was easy to get hold of them."

"There'll probably be more people tomorrow."

"Old Henry's got his hooks out. He'll call in the Marines if he thinks they'll do Justin some good."

"At least we can be together for a while," I said. "Tell us exactly what happened. Please."

Vinnie threw himself on one of the bunk beds. "Let David talk. I'll close my eyes for a minute."

"You could lie down too, Rachel," David said. "You don't look so hot."

"I'm all right. Please, David."

"I'll give you the details. But nothing makes any sense."

They knew that something was wrong with Justin when they brought the Whaler back to Lighthouse Point. He was washing the rug again, making a mess of soap and water. He was hyper. He went around checking ridiculous things and pacing and talking a mile a minute. They gave him some more brandy and they all got undressed for bed. But they couldn't shut their eyes. As soon as he was alone in his own room, Justin began shouting that he'd killed her. Or that she was still alive and he had to go back there and save her.

They wanted to lock him in the bathroom but they were afraid he'd break a window and jump out. So they just stayed up with him, talking and arguing, and in desperation they told him they'd do what he wanted: call the police in the morning. That quieted him. They got him to sit down on the sofa between them, each on a side, holding him. He didn't seem to notice the restraint. He went limp; his eyes were wide open but he seemed to be asleep. And the night wore away and they thought the worst was over. At first light they got him dressed and they made breakfast and ate. He said normal things like, "This is good coffee," and he noticed the sun. Then Simon came in, talking about a blue car turned turtle under Camel Bridge, and before they could stop him Justin was on the phone, dialing 911. "There's been a fatal accident," he said. "This is Governor Lambert speaking. A car accident. I was driving."

117

The black stubble on David's cheek was wet. He mumbled something about "no sleep," and we all looked elsewhere until he could go on talking.

"We felt so helpless," David said. "Simon was right there! What could we do? Anyway, that was the last of Justin's babbling. He went limp again and stopped talking altogether, and I had to practically lift him out of the car at the police station. That's when I got the idea about the concussion. The sheriff let me write the statement and read it to Justin. I think the sheriff was in shock too. Letting me write the statement for Justin to sign. Letting him leave the beach without more questioning. You know that statement's not worth a nickel? Not with Justin acting deaf and dumb and signing it like a robot. But that's no help. No help at all. They tape all nine-one-one calls at the police station. They've got his voice on tape saying he was the driver."

Vinnie's snores were loud in the silence. We were all cramped from sitting in the tiny chairs, and we got up to open the windows and leaned out. The night was starry and clear, and the low Appalachian foothills that we couldn't see sent their warm winds stirring in the trees. Our shoulders touched and we looked ahead, like passengers at the rail of a ship.

"You didn't put what time they were supposed to have left, Justin and Lucia," said Amy. "You left that out on purpose, right?"

"I wasn't thinking that straight. Just being vague as possible. The part about his wandering around the marshes . . . that's from him, Justin. That's what he was raving about, during the night. Wandering in the marshes. He kept asking us to look at the mud on his legs."

"You did a good job, David," Amy said. "But he's not crazy. You wrote what *he* wanted you to write. A crazy person couldn't make it that goddam *neat*."

"You're a nice kid, Amy," David said. "Shut up for a while and think why a sane person would pretend to be crazy."

"He wants to save us."

"We *were* saved."

Amy shut up. For a minute we all looked into that hall of

118

mirrors and then gave up. It was more important, even to me, to listen to David talking about tomorrow and the Lamberts. They'd want to see us. They'd ask us questions.

"How did you and Vinnie manage so far?"

"Total stonewall. Old Henry is ready to lynch us. But we won't say anything until Justin comes to and speaks for himself."

"How long will that be?"

"God knows. A day, maybe longer."

"What do we do? The same?"

"Vinnie had a better idea. You have to insist on not talking until you can contact some lawyers. You're so upset, so frightened, et cetera, et cetera. You have to pretend you haven't seen Justin's statement but you know he made one and you want to read it for yourselves. I'll drag my heels providing it. That should get us through tomorrow."

"We'll have to call our offices. Families. Say what?"

"Say you're here. Tell everyone not to speak to the press. About anything. Don't make any promises about when you'll be back and don't give any information about the accident."

"Okay. David? *Do* we need our own lawyers?"

David yawned. It was midnight. He went over to wake Vinnie, and Caro got a washcloth and patted Vinnie's face.

"Lawyers, Vinnie. Do the girls really need their own?"

"Mother of God!" Vinnie groaned. "We may all need three lawyers each! You think the Lamberts give a damn about us? They only want to save what they can of Justin."

"But they'll need *us* for that."

"Don't count on it. They'd use us to get him off, if they thought of a way to do it."

"Don't get paranoid, either, Vinnie," David said. "That's all we need. You know we're holding cards."

Vinnie nodded. "Guess so." He looked out of it; he hadn't slept for thirty-six hours. But he said, sharply, "I've got another idea. The four of you: pick one person to do all the talking. Even if it's saying you won't talk at all. Insist on that. Don't let them take you aside separately. One talks for all. That'll show them right off the bat. They can't make any deals here."

"We'll do that," Caro said. "It'll be easier, too."

119

"There won't be an autopsy," Vinnie said. "We have to keep remembering that. It's important. You understand?"

"Hush, Vinnie," Caro said. "David, get him to sleep. You sleep. Don't worry. We'll do everything you say. We'll get through tomorrow."

They left and we undressed and took long showers in the adjoining old-fashioned bathroom. There was plenty of hot water but the towels were threadbare, and Bitsie said we must be stuck in the wing where the help lived.

Amy walked around in her nightgown brushing her hair and repeating, "I have to wait until I've spoken to my lawyer."

"Say 'we' have to wait," Bitsie said. "We, we, we."

"We also need a spokesman," I said. "Let's elect."

We got into our beds, two on each side of the room. We turned out the light and whispered in the dark. We decided it made sense to have "David's fiancée" do the talking. It would look good. It would distance me from Justin.

I said fine, and Caro said, "Lucia would like that. Remember how she came to hear Rachel talk to the Clairmont Club? She said Rachel should run for something herself."

"I remember." I sighed.

"Where is she?"

"David said another undertaker met the plane. Somebody local."

"They won't do anything else to her."

"Embalming. That's all."

"They've called her brother. It doesn't bear thinking."

"That flowered cotton she wore from work. She should wear that."

"It's in her suitcase. Don't forget."

"And sandals. The white ones."

We went on murmuring in the dark from our narrow beds. The words connected us to Lucia and one another. We all lay in the dark, all together, resting peacefully for the moment, weaving the first threads of a spell that would bind us forever. We praised her, an elegy of praise, for everything she had been, a fond, foolish, brave girl. She was still so near to us that we imagined she

120

could hear us, and so it didn't even seem odd for Caro to hear her.

"She doesn't think it's her fault anymore," Caro said. "She did, but she doesn't now. She knows it wasn't anybody's fault. It just happened."

I woke up the next morning with a feeling of such anguish that it hurt to breathe. "I hurt," I whispered, just as Bitsie ran past my bed, to the door, to pick up a note that had been pushed under it. She and Caro were already dressed; Amy and I listened from our beds. It was from David.

"'Breakfast, dining room, eat fast, get out quick. Will try to see you upstairs soonest. Stick together! Let Rachel say about lawyers, waiting for statement. Don't answer questions! Watch out for Hofstedter. The Judge. A heavy. Extra care around him. Lunch at one on terrace. Rachel: kiss me. Remember: stick together!'"

It seemed a long note, considering, and we guessed that David didn't have much hope of seeing us before lunch. Amy remarked that David had apparently guessed that I was to be spokesman; she sounded annoyed; I snapped at her for it.

"Cut it out," Caro said. "So who's this Hofstedter?"

"Used to be a senator. Big buddy of Old Henry's."

"Senator? I thought he was once an ambassador."

"That too. Then why 'Judge'?"

"Dunno. Didn't know he was still alive, actually."

"Well, we know we have to watch out for him."

"Him and the rest of the immediate world."

"It's Old Henry I'm scared of. He's got some rep."

It was nine already. Amy and I dressed quickly.

"Maybe breakfast is over," Amy said hopefully. "We won't see anyone. Just grab some coffee and dash back up."

"Oh, why does it have to be such a beautiful day?"

The nursery was drenched in sunlight and fragrant with grassy air. From our windows we could see the distant, hazy hills and hear birds singing, a horse whinnying.

"Stables must be over there." Bitsie pointed. "I think this used to be a stud farm. Mellon money. Old Henry bought it just ten years ago."

So those weren't Justin's books on the shelves, Justin's blanket on my bed. I brushed my teeth thinking, David didn't mention Justin. I did my hair, thinking, How is he? Where is he? How is he? But I didn't say these things, or others like them. The words in David's note stopped me.

Stick together!

It had to be total. I had to make it my job, and when I said "us" I had to mean only me and Bitsie and Caro and Amy. For the time being, I had to pretend that our safety was my only concern.

"There must be another staircase."

"Left. There it is."

"Oh, shit, this shirt is filthy. How did I miss it?"

We went slowly down the broad, carpeted main staircase. Before we reached the dining room I knew I wasn't pretending. The vaulted stairwell, the chandeliers, the Persian rugs on the glowing, mellow floorboards: this was the famous Lambert estate, a county's worth of it. This was no musty grotesque of a summer place, either; it glowed with care and luxury and incalculable wealth. Old Henry was known to be mean as a sick skunk toward

123

people if he didn't like them but lavish with money and influence if he did.

Justin was his only son. Justin didn't need me. I had nothing to offer him here. Whatever strengths I could call on I could use in my own behalf. Our behalf. Because if there was any conflict between what was good for us or good for Justin—

"No one here, good," Amy whispered, peeping into the dining room at the foot of the stairs. "Come on, it smells wonderful."

There was an acre of mahogany table in front of us, and French doors open to the terrace framing big tubs of flowers. There was a sideboard full of gleaming, steaming silver dishes and a pile of newspapers all over the table. We didn't know what to grab first, news or food. But suddenly there was Edith, Justin's sister, coming in from the swinging doors that must lead to the kitchen.

"Oh, goody, you're up. You must be famished. Heavens! We need more plates! John! Plates!"

She was tall and skinny, a windmill of waving arms and exclamation points, and she insisted on serving us, dabbing and exclaiming.

"Eggs! Bacon! Gluey porridge, awful, don't touch. Sit there! Sit here! Papers, papers, you'd think it was Sunday. Try a muffin."

She had Justin's imperious nose, but she was much older and the wavy blond hair was more gray than gold. Ropy veins stood out on her bare legs. She had a toughened, weatherbeaten face, but her voice was sweet and girlish, and when she sat down she just flopped and sprawled, fishing for a slipped shoe under the table.

"Now you just have a good breakfast. I'm Edith Frayn, Justin's sister."

"How do you do," we chorused, and introduced ourselves.

"Caro Fitzhugh."

"Rachel Warshowsky."

"Amy Shillitoe."

"Bitsie Ames."

"I think we've met," she said. "During the last campaign."

None of us remembered meeting her. We murmured polite assents, and she beamed. We began to eat quickly; we wanted those papers almost more than the food.

"Such a terrible thing," she said. "You have all my sympathy."

"We still can't believe all this."

"It's a tragedy."

"It doesn't seem real."

All of us wanted to ask about Justin; none of us knew how. What should we call him? Justin? The Governor? Your brother? The Guv?

"My brother is still sleeping," Edith said. "I saw him for a minute. He was . . . distraught."

"So awful," Amy said. "What are they saying? In the papers?"

Edith gestured to the pile. "Nothing that makes any sense," she said. "See for yourselves."

We each took a paper. It was too early, we knew, for more hard news. But there was plenty of speculation, on the same variant headline words: GOVERNOR GIRL CAR BRIDGE DEAD DROWNED. The birthday party was described as an "engagement celebration as well." There was a description of Lucia that could have come off her driver's license. And one paper had our names, too, the "four surviving friends of the victim," which had to have come from Dune Deck Motel. No mystery there: the key with the motel's name on it had been in Lucia's purse. One of the more enterprising reporters had gotten hold of the fact and gone over.

We read in silence, exchanging papers and not daring to look at one another. All the papers said that Governor Lambert had made a statement to the police implicating himself in the accident, or words to that effect. But what the statement said wasn't given, and we could only assume the sheriff had made himself, or had been made, unreachable all Sunday.

We were so absorbed in reading we almost forgot that Edith was with us. She wasn't reading herself. She smoked and drank coffee and stared out the windows, but we knew it wasn't tact or good manners that kept her quiet. She kept up an irritable drumming of her fingers on the table. She kept clearing her throat. Finally, she banged down her coffee cup like a gavel.

"Well, surely, you've read enough by now! I don't believe a single word of it! Drove off Camel Bridge? He's been driving over that bridge since he was twelve years old!" Then she added, "I don't care *what* David says, Miss Shapiro!"

Edith was staring at Amy, whose name was nearly Shapiro.

"I'm Amy Shillitoe, Mrs. Frayn," said Amy. "Rachel War-showsky is David's fiancée."

Mrs. Frayn's grimace was not embarrassed. It was annoyed; it said that she could not be expected to keep these peculiar names straight. She turned to Caro. Caro pointed to me.

"We haven't read your brother's statement," I said. "We want to. David is going to get a copy for us."

"Do you need to know it word for word to say it's not true?"

"We'd like to see it. We can't discuss anything before we get in touch with our own lawyers."

"Your own lawyers!"

"Yes. Have you seen David this morning?"

"I have, for what it was worth. He's not being any more helpful than you are."

"We want to be helpful," I said. I tried to sound placating. "We want to help in any way we can. Oh, please understand. It's so awful. We need advice. Advice on how to help. Help us. Help you."

"Your own *lawyers?*"

She was stuck on the word. She was frightened and unhappy, and from the looks of her eyes she hadn't stopped crying until recently. There were many excuses for her behavior, but none for her character; she was a spoiled brat.

"You won't get away with this. Letting my brother take the blame!"

"We're not doing that."

"Yes, you are," Edith said. "She was your friend. You knew all about it."

"About it?"

"About your friend. What she was up to."

She looked around the table, trying to catch our eyes, each in turn. She gave the table a smart slap.

"Birthday party my *eye.*"

She thought she had it all figured out. She was stupid too. I said, "Please, Mrs. Frayn. It's bad enough."

"You're making it worse!"

"When we see Justin's statement, we'll know how to help."

"We will."

"You'll see."

"We're so terribly sorry for *everything*."

It didn't work. She glared.

"Bitches," she said.

Somewhere in the house, on this same floor, a door opened with a bang. Someone said, "Get that thing fixed." Someone else said, "Let's sit outside. I want a long, smelly cigar." The voices were men's voices; the rumbling carried.

"Daddy!" Edith cried, jumping up. "In here! They're in here!"

I leapt to my feet. I said, "Out!" I grabbed the nearest papers and we ran through the open French doors, left on the lawn, and left again to the narrow door at the end of a mile of white wood. Then up the three flights of stairs and into our room.

"What a scene!"

"She must be so upset."

"We did all right. Rachel did fine."

"Get out the radio. Look for news."

I had two papers. We had three hours to read them. We took turns reading out loud and listening to the radio. We went over the stories line by line, looking for the gaps that would be filled in. The very gaps made a big story bigger; a thousand reporters knew what they wanted to be first with. They had the Who and the What and the Where in place; they would know the Why when the details about Lucia's asthma showed up in Justin's statement; the When was the only fact that could still be invented.

"We should make it around eight or nine," Amy said. "If we say any time later, it will look like we intended to spend the night there."

"Get the statement, Bitsie. Of course it has to be before ten; that's the last ferry."

Bitsie got the statement out of her locked suitcase and we read it again. We knew how much David had done to make it coherent, but even so . . .

It was the neatness, the very clarity that confused us! We had to make those concise paragraphs fit, somehow, with a man David and Vinnie had called not much less than a babbling, raving lunatic. We couldn't do it; the lies and the truth were too freshly mixed; we went back to the papers with Amy, the good reporter, taking notes.

The newspapers were scattered all over the nursery floor. Bitsie found some blunt kindergarten scissors in a cup on a bookshelf and let Amy go through the pages, cutting.

Whenever I get an item from Amy's profitable clipping service, I think of her as she was that morning, sitting cross-legged on the bare floor, cursing those tiny scissors.

"Here's something we missed," she muttered. "Some smart stringer interviewed the scuba diver who found her."

It was a bordered box, on an inside page. The headline said, SEAVIEW MAN USES SCUBA SKILLS DIVING FOR VICTIM'S BODY.

The story stated that Lawrence LeMay, a member of the volunteer rescue squad, had been called to accompany the tow trucks from the police station to the site of the submerged car under Camel Bridge. Mr. LeMay dived to report the position of the car and to retrieve the victim's body. Mr. LeMay said the victim was wedged on the floor of the front seat and all the car's windows had been blown out on impact. . . .

I heard the roar. An avalanche of black water, tons of it, rushing, pinning, holding. Tons and tons of cold black water.

I buried my head in my hands. When I looked up, I saw everyone through water.

"Read the last part again, Amy," Caro said. "Rachel wasn't listening."

Amy read, " 'In a private interview last night, Mr. LeMay dismissed rumors about Governor Lambert escaping from the submerged car, saying that it would have taken a miracle for anyone to have got out alive.' "

We stared at one another. Bitsie's barking laugh broke the quiet.

"You see?" she asked us. "Not neat. Not neat at all. Only crazy."

"Let's put it aside," I said. "One guy. Back page. We have enough to worry about; it's almost twelve-thirty."

We spent the rest of the time trying to make ourselves look decent, in spite of stains, wrinkles, a lost belt, a single shoe.

Don't separate. Rachel answers direct questions. Trust David and Vinnie and no one else.

We still hadn't called our homes and offices, but it didn't matter. Everyone would know, from the newspapers, that we must be with the Lamberts. They would certainly think it was the best place for us.

But my cat, poor Forrester! Bitsie reminded me that her mother had an emergency key to our house. Her mother would take Forrester. Bitsie would call her, right after lunch.

"All ready? Rachel, kiss David."

"My hands are shaking. I wish this skirt had pockets."

"No drinks. Not one."

"That Edith. Watch out for her."

"She's just a jerk. Hofstedter. That's who."

"Old Henry. Oh, dear."

We went down to the dining room. We heard David's voice on the terrace. We walked out on the terrace, squinting in the sun.

I did kiss David. We didn't smile. The terrace was crowded with people; the terrace was empty of Justin.

"Mr. Lambert? May I introduce my fiancée, Rachel Warshowsky."

I went first, with the others in back of me. Each of us stood for a minute in front of Old Henry's chair, saying "How do you do" and feeling the tug of his hand. We had seen him before. He was shorter than he looked in his photographs, more humped of shoulder, more domed bald head than the camera could catch.

"Judge Hofstedter."

The Judge was tall but half as wide—a long drink of water, as my mother used to say. From a distance he might have been a youngish man with an old face; up close, it was his skeletal frame that seemed old, with a young face on top of it. There was youth in his blue eyes and white, crowded, prominent teeth. He showed them when he talked. He was still handsome and he knew it. When he looked at you it was an invitation, to look back and keep looking.

There was a psychiatrist, Dr. Mellors. There was another doctor, Dr. Smith. There was Jimbo Frayn, husband of Edith, and

129

Mr. Delano, who turned out to be a lawyer, from the attorney general's old law firm. And there was Edith herself, restored to her girlish, breathy voice and exclamation points.

"Oh, we've met! We had a nice breakfast together! What will you have? Here's sherry! Here's Dubonnet! Here's the G and T!"

Edith had a gin and tonic. We looked at her with envy; she was flushed and chatty, and it was probably not her first.

I was the last of us to be introduced to the Judge, and when David tried to draw me away, the Judge said, "Now, now, David, let me have the pleasure of Rachel's company."

He patted the place next to him on the cushioned iron bench. It was like a ballet; everyone of us was swept to the side of a different man. The lawyer had Bitsie; the two doctors took Amy and Caro; a man in a white coat brought us Cokes and tiny tomatoes filled with flakes of salmon.

"I would congratulate you on your engagement if I didn't know how painful all this must be," the Judge said.

"It seems so unimportant," I said. "But thank you anyway."

"You've known David for a long time? He's a fine young man."

"I met him when I came down from New York to work on the campaign."

"Your family must be happy."

"I wish they could be. I lost my mother almost four years ago. My father eleven."

"Don't say it doesn't matter. Love is very important."

I looked down; I sipped my drink. He had that quality. I almost blushed: a girl, getting married soon, enveloped in the world's approval. He seemed to have the world behind him.

The Judge remembered his own engagement. It was a century past! Things were better now. He'd hardly known his future wife.

"I think I know David pretty well," I said.

"Much the best way," he said. "Your poor friend . . . was she engaged too?"

"Oh, no," I said. "She was very young. Only twenty-one. The youngest of all of us."

130

"So unfair." The Judge sighed. "And these old bones, trying to get warm in the sun."

He stretched his long, long fingers. I shook my head; I said he shouldn't talk like that! Because that was the quality: he drew you in, close, caught on the hook of his sublime self-possession.

"I suppose you've been speaking to David," he said. "This awful business. That David won't explain. Not to my satisfaction, anyway."

"He wants to wait till Justin can speak for himself," I said. "That's natural, isn't it? There's so much confusion! And we—Caro and Bitsie and Amy and I—want to read Justin's statement too."

"Didn't David tell you what the statement said? I believe he wrote it."

"He just says wait. He'll get us a copy this afternoon. I think that's what he said. Judge Hofstedter? I think David doesn't *want* us to know the details yet. He thinks we'll be . . . safer."

The Judge nodded. I felt cunning. I had scored my point, but softly.

"I'd expect as much. As I said, he's a fine young man. Protective. Taking the brunt of it. What time did Justin and Lucia leave the cottage?"

"Around eight o'clock."

The words were out of my mouth before I knew it. I had taken the question like the flick of a whip, and I had jumped to reply, and I didn't know if I'd made a mistake, answering right, answering wrong. I wasn't supposed to answer at all! I had been in his company for five minutes and I was already screwing up.

I blushed crimson. He turned his head deliberately to look at me.

"Not 'Judge Hofstedter,' please. Just 'Judge.' "

"Just 'Judge'?"

"Oh, if you like, 'Judge, dear.' "

I felt frightened. I looked around at the others, talking to doctors and lawyers. Vinnie had come out; he was with Old Henry. Who was screwing up at this very minute? Who else?

I leapt to my feet when Edith called, "Luncheon, everyone! Sit anywhere! Liberty Hall!"

"Sit by me," the Judge murmured, but I pretended not to

131

hear. I collected Amy and Bitsie and Caro and we went inside together. I caught David's hand and pressed it on my way into the dining room, and I stopped myself from turning to see if the Judge was looking.

"What's he like?" Caro muttered to me.

"Don't ask," I muttered back. "Sit together. Kick me under the table if you think I'm screwing up."

16

Nervous as I was, that first lunch—luncheon?—absorbed me. The servants were so deft and quiet you could hear the starch creaking in the white apron, the white jacket. There were place mats, shaped like flat shells, of palest yellow organdy so sheer you could see the table through them. The silver fork seemed twice as big and twice as heavy as any I had ever held, and when the plates were gone glass bowls of water were put in front of every mat. Just water, except for a floating leaf. A real leaf. Green.

"Finger bowls!" Edith cried. "Oh, yes, the drumsticks. John, you think of everything."

She dabbled the fingers of her right hand. We all followed her. I crushed the leaf and smelled lemon and saw one white apron clear the sideboard, another enter with a silver tray of fruit salad for John to serve. He was the butler. There was plenty of opportunity to take in the details because the talk was only about the food. A cascade of comment greeted every dish. Everyone admitted hunger.

"Try just a bit more of this salad."

"So delicious, summer tomatoes."

"Let me tell you what my mother used to do with drumsticks. She'd take a big bowl of Chinese rice vinegar. . . ."

The weather came up, and summers much hotter than this one, for all the talk. Seemed hotter, anyway, before air-conditioning. You wouldn't be drinking hot coffee in the summer of '53, no indeed, you wouldn't touch a cup; it was all iced tea and lemonade, and not much ice either, come to think of it.

And while the light, banal remarks floated around, I thought of the servants and what they were thinking. They read the papers, they had the radio. Justin was upstairs and there were doctors in the house and four young women had sneaked into the nursery at nightfall. GOVERNOR BRIDGE GIRL DEAD DROWNED.

And everybody in the dining room talking about the weather and dabbing their lips with pale yellow organdy napkins.

"John, shut the doors. All of them, tight. Send everybody out of the kitchen too. Leave the dishes for later."

John didn't say, "As you wish, madam." That must be only in the movies. He just went around shutting the doors, and in a minute the big dining room was dusky-dim. The French doors were curtained inside and there was no other window.

The central chandelier clicked on and Edith said, "There. We can't be more private than this."

I counted thirteen people around the table. It was bare now. The two doctors and the lawyer had serious expressions. The Judge and Old Henry compared cigars. Edith rolled the ice impatiently in her glass. The rest of us looked however it is you look in a falling elevator.

We weren't ready. An hour of fine food and obsequious service and idle, easy chatter had made us the willing dupes of their willful illusion: we were their guests. But now we knew we weren't. Nobody had to tell us. Without the shifting of a single chair by a single inch, we could sense the Lamberts and their experts moving as far away from us as they possibly could, short of throwing us out of the house.

134

We were "the girls" now. There were no servants to put on a show for.

"We're going to get to the bottom of this," Old Henry said, "if we have to sit here all day."

He pointed to Vinnie and David and looked hard at us.

"It's a conspiracy," he said. "A goddamned conspiracy!"

"It's no such thing, sir," David said. "Vinnie and I have one loyalty. To Justin. And until we know what he wants, we won't speak for him or for ourselves."

"And them?"

"The girls are frightened. Can you blame them?"

"Not so frightened they didn't ask for their own lawyers before they'll say a word to help us!"

Edith smirked. The Judge sighed.

"Speaking of conspiracies, Henry," he said, "didn't we have one ourselves? Didn't we decide that I was to take charge?"

Old Henry subsided, a volcano fuming blue cigar smoke. "So take charge, dammit."

"*I* spoke to them at breakfast. *I* saw right through—"

"Shut up, Edie," the volcano growled.

Amy giggled and Caro kicked her. The Judge unfolded his length and angles and stood leaning on his knuckles behind the table.

"Let me begin by saying, and firmly, that I take everyone's goodwill as a given. Everyone's. We all want the same thing: a clear passage through this situation. For everyone. No exceptions. Does that seem reasonable, as our mutual goal?"

After Old Henry's explosion, it seemed more than reasonable.

We all nodded vigorously. That's what we wanted.

"Justin's statement will appear in full, in the papers, tomorrow. David has given me his best shot at remembering what he wrote. He will make a copy for these young ladies when we adjourn. So we will all have the same information as the public will have tomorrow. We will also release the reports of Dr. Smith and Dr. Mellors. Dr. Smith?"

Dr. Smith was ready. He read from his notebook.

" 'I examined Governor Lambert at two-thirty P.M., Sunday,

August fourteenth. He appeared to be suffering the effects of either a mild concussion or severe mental stress. A small hematoma over his right ear was reduced with applications of ice. Due to his mental state, X rays of the affected area were deemed inadvisable. Other fresh bruises were noted on his right femur. Dr. Mellors completed the examination.' "

Dr. Smith sat down.

Dr. Mellors stood up. He had a notebook too.

" 'I examined Governor Lambert at two-fifty P.M., Sunday, August fourteenth. He appeared to be in a state of shock, resulting from either physical or mental trauma. Tics manifest: abnormal blinking, pacing, tremors of left leg and both hands. He complained of wandering pain in neck and head. Time and space disorientation. I judged the patient to be incompetent both for further intake and consent to treatment. Consent was obtained from patient's father, Henry Lambert, to administer two cc's of diazepam in solution. Patient remained in deep sleep for following twenty-four hours.' "

"I want to thank Drs. Smith and Mellors for their care and concern," said the Judge softly.

Dr. Mellors stayed. Dr. Smith left. For the first time I noticed the sound of an engine humming in the driveway behind the closed door. I thought, So smooth. Imagine, how smooth.

Now it was Mr. Delano's turn, as lawyer.

"There are varying penalties in this state for leaving the scene of an accident. Circumstances are to be taken into the judge's discretion in sentencing. None can exceed three months' imprisonment and a five-hundred-dollar fine. A first offender, absent legal levels of intoxication, can expect a short suspended sentence, plus full fine.

"The test given to Governor Lambert in the sheriff's office showed no level of alcohol at all. The report also stated that the subject did not appear to have been drinking heavily the day before.

"In my opinion, an inquest can be expected. But an inquest is not mandatory because of the coroner's p.m. Nevertheless, the unusual circumstances surrounding the manner of the decease will almost certainly raise questions, and these should have a full hearing, in my opinion. Some delay may be expected, if not actively sought for. But *avoidance* of an inquest should be avoided, in my opinion."

The Judge smiled. "That's three in-my-opinions, Barney. Isn't that excessive?"

Old Henry snorted appreciatively.

Barney Delano said he was on retainer, so three, six, twelve, he wasn't counting. Then he left too.

As soon as he was out the door, the Judge said, "So. There you have it. We have doctors to make the case for the extenuating circumstances *after* the accident. I doubt the Governor would receive more than thirty days, suspended."

"Call him Justin," Old Henry said. "For Christ's sake, Leland."

"Justin, yes. I wish he were here with us. Dr. Mellors is very reassuring on that score. He should be fine. Soon. And so this is what we will have to live with: a birthday and engagement party and an isolated place and a young woman suddenly taken ill. Very ill. And a generous, responsible man—Justin—rushing to get her to her medicine, or a hospital, on a foggy road that only he knew from past experience. But the accident happened anyway. One victim. One survivor, so dazed and shocked he wandered around the marshes of Lighthouse Point until he found his way back to the cottage and collapsed. And revived in the morning. And reported the accident to the proper authorities."

The Judge nodded then, as if approving his own summation. You couldn't blame him. I think we all felt that same surge of admiration. It was so clear, so plausible!

He gave us a full minute to enjoy it, and then he said, "They'll cut it to shreds. They'll slice it six ways from Sunday: the press, the other party, the public. Wolves. Howling."

I couldn't breathe.

"You don't deserve any better, do you? Every one of you is guilty. *You* involved Justin. *You* arranged the party. *You* put a man who lives in the public eye in a damning position. Five young women! Two wives, both elsewhere. A place so private, so secluded. You cannot expect a drop of mercy from the public. You didn't show a shred of respect for appearances.

"I am sorry for you. You have an ordeal to face, different

from what you've been through already, but very bad. You will say you were innocent bystanders, but you will not be believed—except by people like myself, people who know Justin: a family man, a prudent man, a loving husband. And just because he had nothing to hide, he went along with your plans—"

"No, Leland!" It was Edith, rapping her glass on the table. It was full; she'd had it replenished. Limpid pools of spill shimmered on the dark wood of the table.

"Edie," Old Henry growled.

"There was someone! I know it! It had to be *her*, that one—Lucille, or Lucy, or whatever the hell her name was."

"Perhaps you should go out," said the Judge. "Edith, my dear, you're letting your imagination get the better of you."

"I'll say what's on my mind!" she cried. "On your mind too!"

Jimbo Frayn had played football at Duke. I never heard about any of his other good qualities; there may have been none. But he walked past Edith's chair and hooked an arm around her torso and simply lifted her up. Before the chair had time to fall on the floor, they were out the door.

Old Henry put his head in his hands. The Judge bit his lip. Then he made a mistake. He said, "Your poor friend is gone and can't defend herself. Believe me, none of us thinks that. None of us."

So then we knew they all thought that. They had only planned not to say it until Justin came to and could answer questions.

Until then, they'd pretend to take us at face value. Nice girls. Old campaign buddies. One of them is actually engaged.

"De mortuis nil nisi bonum."

The Latin tag rolled smoothly off the Judge's lips. Of the dead, speak naught but good. Vinnie's hoarse voice broke in, rough as granite.

"Nobody asked Dr. Mellors exactly how long that shot lasts. So I want permission to stay in Justin's room. Sit there. Sleep there if I have to! It's important. I don't want him to wake up so—"

Old Henry did a curious thing. He got up and walked over to Vinnie's chair and leaned down and hugged him.

"Tough guy," Old Henry said. "Sure, do it your way."

Then he went back to his armchair at the head of the table and lit another cigar. I watched him. I thought of a bull in the ring, with ribboned darts sticking into his back. He shakes his body; one or two darts fall out. Something had given Old Henry relief. Vinnie?

"Go ahead, Judge. We've got the picture. Now, the funeral: where does that stand?"

"Delano has made the arrangements. Miss Bennett's body will be driven in a hearse tomorrow to Fort Leeds, where her brother lives. Delano's been in touch with her brother. Funeral will be on Wednesday, day after tomorrow."

"We have a dress for her!" Caro cried. "We have to make sure she wears the dress."

When you don't use your voice for a while, and you're very nervous, it comes out funny. Caro sounded shrill.

"John will take it over," the Judge said.

"I want to be sure. I want to take it myself."

The Judge gave Caro a sad look. "I think I understand your concern," he said. "But you don't want to leave here. You'd have to drive through the front gate. I get reports from the gatehouse. At last count there were seventy-two reporters in fifty-some cars."

Caro subsided. The Judge asked if any of the other young ladies had a request or a contribution.

Amy asked for a place to phone from, to families, offices. She asked about her car. It was her car that Justin "used." The mention of it made small beads of sweat break out on my palms.

Did it make sense for Justin to have used Amy's car? That made sense if Lucia had been driving. But Justin?

I could hardly hear the Judge's answer for the clamor in my head. Phones? Of course. Take the small study for an hour. The car? Towed somewhere. Vinnie?

"I'm not sure where it is," Vinnie said. But he looked at the Judge and not the owner, who was Amy. What did that mean? There was no time to think about it.

"Rachel," the Judge was saying, "what time did you tell me it was? I mean the exact time that Justin and Lucia left the cottage."

I was glad to get it over with. I even stood up.

"I'm speaking for Amy and Caro and Bitsie as well as myself. We're not sure of the time. We're not sure of anything, and we don't want to answer any questions until we've seen Justin's statement and talked to our own lawyers."

Old Henry thumped the table. Clearly, Edith had his bratty manners.

"So get your own lawyers, goddammit!"

"We don't know any lawyers. We have to find some."

"Find some!" he sneered. "Where? In the Yellow Pages?"

"Maybe Mr. Delano could recommend someone. Or maybe we could ask him to give us advice. Legal advice. We can't go ahead without it."

Old Henry pointed an accusing finger at David. David shrugged, as if helpless in the face of my stubbornness, and sank lower in his chair.

"Mr. Delano will be representing Justin," the Judge said. "Let me recommend something. It's in the nature of a favor. I don't want you to call any lawyers—or call *about* any lawyers—for the next twenty-four hours. In return, I promise that no one here, including myself, will bother you with questions. Since I understand that you have all agreed to remain with us until after the funeral, I think that's a reasonable request."

A loud cough from David informed us of just who had told the Judge that we'd be willing to stay until after the funeral. So we'd stay, then. As to the lawyers, I gave David a publicly beseeching glance, fit for a fiancée; I got back a masterful men-know-best nod of affirmation. I thought that Old Henry was watching the byplay with approval, but he wasn't.

"Waste of time!" Old Henry roared. "Dammit, we need a few facts. We need the truth!"

When the Judge chuckled, he sounded like a purring cat.

"What we need is patience, Henry. These young ladies have to trust us first. Isn't that right? David? Vinnie?"

His tone was friendly. It sent its warmth around the table, enveloping the six of us. Such friendly warmth.

I was still standing. I said, "All right. No lawyers or anything. No questions either."

"I appreciate that," the Judge said. "We all do. A terrible

thing. Tragedy, yes; the press got that much right. I hope you're not being too hard on yourselves. Such harsh consequences. Grief. Shock. Fear. I understand."

He was a master of that tactic. He was adept at telling you what you shouldn't feel, thereby reminding you to feel it. Fear, particularly. Oh, but not *too* much fear. He didn't want us to be afraid as Edith was afraid, and stupid with it.

It was past three o'clock. The Judge advised us to use the phones now and then take advantage of the rest of the afternoon. There was the swimming pool, the rose garden, the famous maze, and perhaps we could all relax a little. All except David, the Judge purred, who had to stay inside and spend the next few hours trying to do an exact reconstruction of the statement he gave to the sheriff.

The statement *you* want to read, the Judge said gravely, and we gave him a chorus of guilty nods, each of us thinking of the carbon upstairs in Bitsie's suitcase.

Everybody was standing now, and I shifted awkwardly, not knowing if I should go over to David. But doing nothing was best. David came to my side of the table and tipped up my chin to look searchingly at me. It was a loverlike gesture, but I could only hope I looked better than he did. His face was drawn and greenish-pale.

When he took my hand I felt a scrap of paper. When the four of us were alone in the small paneled library with the phone, and the doors shut, I read it out loud.

" 'Swim. Avoid house! Meet at Maze, six.' "

"Could be worse. A swim is just what I want."

"Can they get us to Fort Leeds for the funeral? Two hours. Oh, sure, what am I asking, they must have ten cars."

"Seventy-five reporters, the Judge said."

"Seven hundred at the funeral, I'll bet. Awful, awful."

"Make your calls, Amy! You're staring into space."

"Rachel did fine. We all did fine."

" 'Meet at maze.' Give me a break. Meet at *maze*? It's all absolutely unreal."

"It's real. We can't all be having the same bad dream."

Released from the restraints of other people, we let go. We didn't even try to tame the thin, high hum of suppressed hysteria,

141

and it lasted until we were in our bathing suits and out of the house. A long flagstone path led to the pool; a tiny iron marker— it said POOL—showed us the way. I had never seen a pool like that. The sides and bottom were painted gray, so it didn't sparkle like those aquamarine pools whose white sides reflect the light. This pool was a deep, mysterious green, and it was shaped like an irregular oval with rocks at one end heaped into a high mound, for diving. It was meant to look as if they had dammed up a pond or a natural spring. It was beautiful.

We swam laps until we were exhausted. We stayed in the water till our fingers turned pruney, and then we sat in the sun on the grass. No one had remembered to bring the radio or something to read. It wasn't deliberate, but we sat in a circle, close enough to touch, hands, feet, shoulders.

"We're in a prayer circle," Caro said, after a while. "That's what this feels like."

We gave one another furtive looks. We all said we understood Caro's "spiritual side," but of course we didn't. We could barely accept it at a safe distance. It smacked too much of Sunday school and organized religion and other anathema, including embarrassment.

To show that she wasn't embarrassed, Amy said she didn't pray ever, purely on principle.

"You can make a wish," Caro said mildly. "Same thing."

Amy wished it was Friday again. Bitsie and I wished for a couple of miracles, one for us, one for Justin.

"You atheists always ask for such impossible things," Caro said. "I pray only for what I know I can have."

"Like what? Like what, now?"

"Like we stick together. Like we don't forget Lucia."

She bowed her head; her sincerity was so matter-of-fact that all of us, even Amy, followed suit. It seemed so little to ask for, compared to what we needed.

We were all too young to know that it wasn't little at all. Even now, when we have what we wished for, it's only Caro who gives God any credit, and it's to Caro's credit that she'd never embarrass us by saying so.

17

At five we left the pool to look for the maze. We had jeans and shirts to put on over our bathing suits, so we didn't have to go back to the house. But we didn't want to be seen wandering around outside, so we struck out for the woods that began where the pool and its patio ended and we worked our way back parallel to the house.

The woods were lovely. "Like France," Amy said; she had lived there for a year. The lower branches of the trees had been lopped off to let light filter through their leaves, and the ground between the trees was a rich carpet of pine needles and moss. You could have walked on it barefoot, there were so few twigs. This great semicircle of manicured woodland surrounded the back of the estate, and behind it the real forest began, like a wall of gray-green bark, circle around circle, one swimming in dappled light, one dark and tangled with choking vines.

143

We went to this outer circle to squat, one at a time, the others keeping guard. David's plan had neglected human nature. We felt invisible, even in the sunlit woods. The trees were huge; the careful thinning had let each develop a thick round bole. They were like cathedral columns, and we strolled from one to the next, spying out the rose garden and a vegetable garden and a great square of flowers growing in careful rows.

"The cutting garden," Bitsie said. "Flowers for the house. Can you imagine what it takes to keep this up?"

Bitsie knew about things like cutting gardens, but she had no more idea than the rest of us as to what it took to keep twenty acres tamed to perfection. She'd heard about the maze, too, yet she didn't recognize it first. We passed it several times, looking; it must have been very old, from the Mellons' time, or before; it had no real relation to the rest of the landscaping. It seemed, from the woods, nothing but a wall of something green and solid, higher than Caro's hand when she raised her arm. And though we were nowhere near the stables, the air was thick with animal warmth, a horsey pungency.

"Boxwood," Bitsie said. "Boy, is this ever old! Come on, there's the opening; let's try it before David gets here."

Big as the thing was, it hadn't been neglected; the paths between the walls of green were clear. But they had narrowed over the years, and you had to walk nearly sideways to avoid being nicked by the boxwood branches. At first we followed Bitsie till she hit a dead end; then we took turns going our own ways. It was interesting; by peeking under the thinned-out bottoms of the shrubs you could see the little paved clearing in the center; nevertheless, we tried for ten minutes with none of us getting to it.

"Let's crawl through," Caro said. We were all perspiring in the heat and liberally nicked.

"No fair," Amy said. "I think there's a formula, though. I think you have to make every turn to the left or every turn to the right. Let me try."

She went in, and not a minute went by before she called, "Right turns only!" The central clearing was paved with weathered brick and had two tiny stone benches and a statue. The statue knelt between the benches, a stone nymph holding a stone plate.

The plate had shards of silvery glass stuck to it, and bits of silvered glass lay at her feet.

"She was holding a mirror," Caro said. "Somebody smashed it."

The sapphire-blue sky of summer evening rose above us. The walls of black-green box enclosed us. We sat on the two stone benches, hushed by mystery. Who smashed the mirror? What were you supposed to see when you found your way to it?

"You twist and turn," Amy said, after a while. "But you always come up against yourself at the end. That must be what it means."

"I hear David coming," I said. "Come on, let's get out of here. It's hot and creepy."

"You look like you're going to faint again."

"No, it's the heat. And this place—"

"You're right, it's morbid."

"I feel claustrophobic."

We straggled out. David was walking up the lawn, whistling. None of us mentioned the round face and the antic grin that made the little stone nymph resemble Lucia.

"What went on after lunch, David?"

"I sat down with the Judge to try to reprise the statement, but after ten minutes the phone rang and I didn't have to bother. The sheriff had just released the statement to the press. A copy for every vulture that's been down at the shore, waiting. But one of Delano's lawyers was waiting too. He grabbed one and phoned it in to the Judge. Old Henry's secretary is making the copies now."

"Let's make sure we get to read ours in private," I said. "I don't want the Judge watching our reactions."

"Listen," Amy said. "I don't get it! Jesus, these people are *powerful*. One word from Henry Lambert, and that hick sheriff would have been happy to call him yesterday with Justin's statement."

"The Judge is too smart for that," David said. "He didn't want it on the record, calling the sheriff for a favor. I had given him the gist of it. And he was pleased as punch already with the kid-glove treatment Justin got. I told you. Some hard-ass cop could have kept Justin down there for more questioning. But this guy thought Justin was going to keel over any minute. He was sorry for him. Not to mention that he's the Governor, for God's sake. So the sheriff did the decent thing. Poor bastard, he'll probably regret it."

"Can he ask Justin to come back now?"

"He signed Justin off. Unless there's new evidence, Justin doesn't have to go back until he's arraigned for leaving the scene of an accident."

I could feel the panic flutters easing. Amy asked about her car, and then she pulled the clipping about the diver out.

"Did you see this?"

"Read it ten times. The *Washington Post* had it too. Look, what are we standing for? I took a nap after lunch but I'm still groggy."

We all sat down on the lawn. David said the story about the diver was just the beginning.

"Beginning of what?"

"The whole version of the accident. Checking it out. The police are looking for skid marks on the bridge. They're looking for Justin's tracks on the banks of the channel and in the marshes. It drizzled the whole night, that's their problem."

"They won't find any skid marks, either."

"No kidding."

"Oh, sarcasm. Great."

"Let David talk."

"Amy's car. The same lawyer that got the copy of the statement? He saw the car in back of the station house. Being photographed. Fingerprinted. So he asks the sheriff, What are you going to do with the car? And the sheriff says he has to hold it until the owner settles up with the township for hauling and towing."

"How much?" Amy asked.

"Three hundred dollars. Delano's man paid it and sent for a private company to take it away."

"I don't want to see it," Amy said and stood up and walked away and then walked back.

The body was wedged in the well of the front seat. . . .

"I'm not crying for my fucking car," Amy said.

146

"Oh, we know that," David said. He squeezed her shoulder. "But Amy? Delano's man did a cool thing. The Judge was glad. The Judge wants the car junked."

"It looked that bad?"

"Well, no. But we don't want a bunch of smart-ass newsmen crawling all over it. Trying to fit through a window. I mean, it had to be through a window, right? He couldn't have opened the frigging door in ten feet of water."

Justin was a big man. We thought about it.

"It can't be impossible, can it?" I said.

"The statement doesn't even use the word. Window."

"So maybe the door flew open."

"So how did it get shut tight again? Please."

A maze is a labyrinth. It winds and doubles back and does tricks, and there must be mazes so complicated they hold you fast in the center.

"We're talking about something that never happened," Caro said, softly. "I keep losing track."

"We've got one another to hold on to," David said grimly. "But don't think Old Henry and the Judge haven't been smelling a rat. They're working alone now; they've given up beating me and Vinnie. But that diver's statement gave them a clue. I ran into that psychiatrist, Mellors, when I woke up from my nap, after lunch. I asked him what everyone was doing. Calling insurance companies, says he."

David looked around at us to see if we understood. We didn't. Amy said her company was Apex Mutual.

"They're going through Mammoth State," David said. "That's the insurance company the Lamberts *own*. They're trying to find out if Justin could have done what he said he did."

"Oh," said Caro. "I get it. They'll go into the computers. Go through accidents. See if anything like it has been reported before."

"Very good, Caro," David said. "Vinnie said you didn't know what to pray for? Well, you can pray that they come up with some big guy who got out of a car that turned upside down in ten feet of water. A car that fell in, not slipped in. Fell through the air off a bridge."

147

Bitsie had been very quiet. All of a sudden she jumped up, crying, "Oh, for God's sake! There's a first time for everything! And if he didn't do it, why say he did?"

"It's Catch-22," I murmured. "Catch-22. The logic."

"I'm speaking for Vinnie and myself now," David said. "We follow Justin. If he sticks, we stick. If he tells the truth, we tell the truth: the drugs, the cover-up, his crazy behavior, all of it."

"He'll come to soon. Okay, same for us. But Rachel's part . . ."

Everyone looked at me.

"We can still hide that," I said. "What we've got is bad enough."

We all nodded. Agreed.

"I've got the extra whammy," Amy said. "I bought the joints, all rolled up. And the hash. If it was hash. It looked like ordinary marijuana."

"What's the difference?"

"Who the hell knows. But the guy from the copy desk I bought from? Very bright. Goes to State on a full scholarship. If he reads the papers, he knows where I was and what I might have had with me."

David said he and Vinnie had already been up that tree. If the kid wanted to come forward and admit he was dealing—

"It might be wishful thinking," Amy said, "but I don't think he'll talk. He lives in a project and he's got a connection, but he's ambitious. A hard worker, days, nights. Would he blow his scholarship just to make trouble for us?"

Bitsie put her arm around Amy. "Poor Amy. She's been sweating this."

"Didn't want to talk about it," Amy muttered. "Makes it more real, talking."

"Leave it alone for now. I wish we could ask the Judge for advice! Isn't he a piece of work?"

"Is he really a judge?"

"Was for years," David said. "Trial lawyer before that in upstate New York. Somehow he got Old Henry's attention when he was still a young man. Married a local girl, moved down here, and got the party's backing for the Senate."

148

"A carpetbagger. That wasn't common back then."

"What's the ambassador part?"

"Not a country. The UN for less than a year."

"What hasn't he done? He's a name, all right."

"There's ten just as big the Lamberts could have down here right this minute. You should see the phone messages. I keep sneaking looks. Everyone but the Pope, and he's in Australia. But Old Henry's too smart to let anyone else in on this. He trusts Leland Hofstedter. You got him, you don't need any chorus of second-guessers."

"You're getting a crush, David."

"Don't remind me. I'm starting to do the drawl, too."

"Justin's still asleep?"

"He woke up for a few minutes and then conked out again. Vinnie is keeping close. Justin recognized him. That's good."

"Now what happens?"

"Now dinner. We've got the Judge's word: no questions. But let Rachel handle anything tricky."

"What time is dinner?"

"Eight. Seven-thirty for drinks on the terrace. Cokes all around, right? Come down late, if you want."

"No way. I like the hors d'oeuvres. But could I ask that Mellors for a sleeping pill? I'll need it. I'm wired."

But David answered that the only thing he'd ask Mellors was what to wear to dinner, and he'd already done that. The drill was "informal" and "tell the girls not to fuss." So we went back to our quarters to paw sullenly through our clothes: city things all wrinkled, and beach stuff heavy on the Mickey Mouse T-shirts and cutoffs. We fussed. We borrowed and improvised, and by seven-thirty we could see one another—with freshened sunburns and neat hair—all decently covered and looking as if we didn't have a care in the world.

"You're not drinking, Miss Warshowsky?" Dr. Mellors asked me, on the terrace where candles burned in ruby globes and a big table was set for dinner with rustic pottery and thick green-glass goblets that looked Mexican.

"Sure I am," I said. "This is Tab."

149

"I notice that you and your friends are teetotalers," the doctor said, smiling. "Couldn't help noticing, with this delicious wine going around. A particularly good French Chardonnay—one of my favorites."

"We do drink sometimes," I said. There didn't seem to be any point fencing with Justin's doctor. "But in these circumstances . . . it wouldn't feel right. I think if I had a glass of wine I'd start crying."

"Alcohol does that," he said. "It's a solvent of the emotions."

"We're dreading Lucia's funeral," I said.

"It won't be easy," he said. He sounded kind, but he didn't look it. His face was too intent, and too close to mine. "But funerals help with grief. They're a punctuation mark. A true full stop."

"Not for us. We won't stop grieving. Ever."

"Your friend wouldn't want that. She would want you to go on living and remembering her when you're happy."

It was true and I even believed it. I just didn't like this chubby man with the intent eyes. I'd never met a psychiatrist before. I had the feeling that he was judging me.

"We're grieving for Justin too," I said. "It's terrible, what's happened to him. How is he?"

"Resting comfortably," said the doctor. The bland formula stung me.

"He can't be," I said. "After what he's been through."

"You'd be surprised."

"Surprised?"

"Human being are resilient," said the doctor. "Particularly if they're what we call *intact* people. People with well-organized personalities. Justin's a man of that type. I got to know him really well, when he was a teenager."

"Did you go to school together?"

"No, I'm years older. We're cousins. Missy is my aunt."

I understood. *This* was Justin's psychiatrist, back then *and* right now. He was the one Justin saw after the accident with the gun, the one Old Henry could trust because he was family. There was no sense or fairness in it, but I wanted to hit him. I wanted to slap his face and watch his glasses fly off and smash on the slate terrace. He hadn't helped Justin. And he could sit there and talk about that terrified boy, that dazed man, as a "well-organized personality"! I knew nothing about psychiatry, but I knew this: no one in the Lambert family had ever really wanted to deal with that old tragedy, and even now they wouldn't acknowledge its new and twisted face.

It must be what you feel for a child in pain. You have to watch, in helplessness. I thought of Justin waking to the heavy nightmare feeling, and this man again, this voice, and the nightmare feeling was mine too, and it must have showed because Mellors was staring at me, leaning so close that I could feel his breath.

"You're not feeling well," he said. "Here, sit down."

It was too dim in that corner of the terrace for anyone to see him take my arm and ease me into a wrought-iron chair. It was a help, just sitting down. He sat next to me and kept quiet for the minute or two that passed until Edith's girlish voice announced dinner and no Liberty Hall tonight; she would show us where to sit.

Dr. Mellors helped me to my feet. "Eat very lightly," he said. "And no coffee, hear? Then go up and lie down right after dinner. Even if you're not sleepy. Just lie down.

"Terrible strain," he added. "I wish I could do more for you."

He smiled at me as Edith led him to the other side of the table. He seemed to mean that he wished he could help more. All the rage and horror suddenly vanished, and for a minute, when I looked around the table from my seat near the Judge, everyone, even Edith, looked ordinary. Here was his sister, father, brother-in-law, cousin, old friend of the family—just family, just people like us, full of confusion and worried to death and trying to hold themselves together for the sake of a man they all loved.

It would happen like that. The solvent was love, not alcohol, and every once in a while it would dissolve the boundaries. I loved him and so did they and we were all on the same side.

Then the oldest instinct of all, blinder even than love, would assert itself, and I would feel their power. Vinnie had defined it: they'd throw us away if it meant rescuing Justin. We were expendable. And we were to blame.

Fear is the real iron curtain, the one around the heart. There are no people on the other side, only enemies.

The most dangerous enemy of all was saying to me, "Rachel?

Could you have a word with me after dinner? Just us. No questions, as I promised. I'll just talk and you only have to listen."

"If my friends say it's all right with them. Why just me?"

"I feel more comfortable talking to someone who can talk back. It's evident that you're the one. You've arranged that, haven't you?"

Apparently it was too evident to deny. I said yes, we had decided that I would speak for all of us about anything that concerned Lighthouse Point. But that didn't mean I was in charge! We made all our decisions together.

The Judge gave me one of his approving you-get-an-A-and-a-gold-star looks.

"Very wise. And a neat division of labor too! I mean separating the girls from the boys."

"We don't think of it that way. David and Vinnie have an obligation to Justin that's different from ours."

"Do you always call the Governor 'Justin'?"

"I guess it does sound funny. But when we were all working on his campaign he made everyone call him Justin. We wouldn't do that in public! Like bragging."

"What was your role in the campaign?"

"PR and speeches and organizing the suburban coffees. I did women's issues too."

"Oh, a feminist. I should have guessed."

"You'd have guessed wrong. I wasn't hired to be an advocate. I was the women's-issues analyst. The polls, the surveys. What would work, what wouldn't. The numbers do the deciding."

"An unprincipled feminist! The very worst kind."

He was teasing me. He was enjoying me, looking at me, trying to hold my attention. When John appeared with a wicker tray full of coffee cups, Dr. Mellors called to me, from the other end of the table.

"No coffee, Rachel. You promised. You girls drink too much of that diet stuff, too. It's loaded with caffeine."

And Edith chimed in, asking us if those beds weren't too dreadful, and did we need more pillows?

Not a word was said during dinner, not to any of us, to make us uncomfortable. It was all a tissue of gentle flattery, and care, and the concerns of hospitality.

Old Henry ate and talked in low tones to Vinnie and Jimbo.

Even the candles in their ruby globes had a caressing glow.

Vinnie ate a few bites and then said he was going up to Justin.

"Good person, that Vinnie," the Judge said to me. "He'll be missing the TV. A friend of ours at CBS called to say some pictures will be on at ten o'clock. The bridge. The car coming out of the water. The tow people took some providential movies. They do that, for insurance purposes, and CBS snagged the use of the film. Must have cost them a pretty penny."

"Oh," I said.

"And the usual aerial views of the Lambert place and the lighthouse. Plus a short interview with the sheriff which I believe is innocuous."

"Innocuous," I repeated.

"The best we could hope for," the Judge said. "You've done public relations. *Innocuous* is fine. Considering."

This time the terrace doors were shut from the inside. The Judge didn't stand up but everyone turned to him, automatically.

"I was just telling Rachel about the TV story. The statement will not be on tonight. They'll use it tomorrow. At least Dr. Mellors has good news."

"Justin's coming around," said Dr. Mellors. "Not clear-headed yet, by any means. But the signs are encouraging."

Old Henry snorted. It was not an encouraged noise.

"I ought to go up too," Edith cried. "And Jimbo, yes, Justin adores him, they're more like brothers, really."

"Leave him alone, Edie," Old Henry growled. "You stay out."

She was just where she had been at lunchtime, mixing it up and spilling liquor. This time she subsided gracefully in all action except speech.

"Old Simon! Did they ever get to him?"

"No, Edith," the Judge answered. "The media—for want of a better word—haven't been able to contact the ferryman. As yet, of course. So far we've been fortunate."

"You told me that," she simpered. "I forgot."

She shot a wandering glance at us, the "girls." We hadn't been told. She knew more than we did. One more G and T and she would stick her tongue out.

153

"Getting on for ten o'clock," the Judge said. "Let's head for the television. Rachel? Please ask your friends for the little favor I want. After the broadcast." Each in her turn, Caro, Amy, and Bitsie got a sweet, supplicating smile. The Judge added, "I'll be much obliged to you."

"Favors!" Edith announced to the night sky. "All these *favors*. I must say, it's getting on my nerves."

We were solemn with misery after standing with the others around the TV set in one of the living rooms. Nobody could sit down, not even Old Henry. Out of fear, respect, dumb dismay, we stood, watching the car with the chains around it come out of the water. The pictures were poor but you could see the car and its open windows like the holes in a skull. Mud and water poured from it when it lurched up. It didn't matter that we knew for a fact that Lucia was no longer inside. She had gone in an ambulance to the coroner's office. It didn't matter. We felt her in the car with the flattened top that had burrowed into the mud down there. No matter where they put her, that, for us, would always be her real coffin, of twisted tin, sunk in the mud.

We could hardly hear the voice-over. All of us got different bits and pieces. Governor exhausted with possible concussion resting in family home. The sheriff saying that the Governor had been forthcoming and cooperative. State of shock, very obvious. The sheriff was young; if he wasn't sick, he had no reason for looking so haggard. David's prediction was coming true. People were talking about the Governor's quick disappearance from the shore, and this was the man who had let him go.

I went over to David when it ended. I leaned on him, visibly. He whispered to me, "Poor Rachel."

I turned to face him so the others couldn't hear.

"The Judge wants to see me alone now. Without the others," I said.

"No way," said David. "They go with you."

I went around to the others, saying that David said I mustn't be alone with the Judge.

The Judge, seeing us clumped together, came over and took my arm.

154

"I'm sorry, Judge," I said. "You have to take all of us."

It came out sounding like a line from a corny Western. The Judge didn't show any disappointment. He even smiled.

"I understand. But it's been a long day for me, and I think I'd rather postpone our meeting until tomorrow. Ten o'clock, how's that?"

"That's all right," I said. "Wait. The funeral."

"Tomorrow is Tuesday. The funeral is on Wednesday."

"I guess I do need some sleep."

"Perfectly natural. Till tomorrow. Ten."

He went over to talk to David. I rounded up the others and told them about the date, and then Amy and I said we were dying, we had to go upstairs and lie down. Bitsie and Caro were wide awake and wanted to stay downstairs and see if there would be anything new, on other channels, at eleven.

"So stay," I said wearily. "Come up later and tell us how the Judge worked you over."

But we all wound up going upstairs. We got undressed.

"I won't sleep," I said. "I can't stand it. I want to see Justin."

I didn't cry, I just kept trembling. They pushed me in and out of a hot shower and wrapped me in blankets.

"You'll sleep," said Caro. "I'll sit here next to your bed. I won't sleep until you do."

We turned out the lights at eleven. Caro sat at my side in one of the little chairs. She had her rosary in her hands; the tiny clicking sound was a comfort in the dark. It was a comfort, just knowing that Caro could pray. I fell asleep thinking that she was praying for all of us, because it wouldn't be like Caro to pray only for herself.

18

We met the Judge in the smaller library; the bigger one was Old Henry's domain and we never went into it. I caught just a glimpse, once, of the ranks of file cabinets, the computer, the desk only a little shorter than the table in the dining room. It was his head-quarters, and with the door open we could hear him growling or roaring at his secretaries. He hated the heat; the big wooden house wasn't cool enough for him, even though it nearly vibrated with the constant hum of the air-conditioning. When we sat down on the couch in the little library, the slick leather felt like ice.

The Judge half sat, half stood against an old desk with a green felt top. He kept swinging one long slim foot, in an elegant moccasin. His blue-veined ankle was as slender as any of ours. And no matter what he said, in however stern a voice, he kept that air of quietly savoring something: this burnished, paneled room, these young women, his own finesse.

"Please don't be uneasy," he began. "I've promised not to ask questions and I won't. Just hear me out. You may know this: I used to do a fair amount of trial work. Mostly criminal. Funny line of work! Your clients are mostly criminals, about nine out of ten, average. The pleasure of having a client who's been wrongfully accused—I mean the professional pleasure—is pretty rare in those courtrooms.

"Your client's done something legally wrong. But what's the degree of culpability? Did the client know he—or she—was doing something wrong? That counts. Is the law on the matter ambiguous? Can I make this case look different from others like it? That's the attorney's job. That, and knowing how to present him—or her—as a candidate for the lesser sentence. Or even the better prison. Big difference, between this prison and that one.

"Oh, I knew my work. But I never got over one kind of nervousness. No good lawyer ever does. You worry and you stay worried that something will come out during the trial that your client knew and didn't tell you. Like a jack-in-the-box. Ugly. Sudden. Even something good can do it to you. Because you weren't pre-pared. I've stood absolutely speechless, hearing something like that. What do you young people say? A bummer.

"So you see what I'm driving at. I'm not asking any ques-tions. I'm telling you that there will be an inquest, and no matter how many roadblocks we can legally make use of, we can only hope to win extra time to prepare. Preparation. That's the key.

"An inquest is not an adversary procedure. It's a system of fact-finding designed to clear up the circumstances around a death. Not any death. Only one that might have been caused by a wrongful act. So the county coroner—the boss of the coroner in Seaview, in this case—will appoint a judge to hear testimony. If the facts seem plainly to point to natural or accidental causes, the matter ends right there. But if the facts are confusing or suspicious, or the people involved contradict one another on important aspects, then the judge has to say to the state's attorney, Clear this up! Make a case. Prove it beyond a reasonable doubt.

"The facts in this case are certainly confusing. They must look suspicious. We have a sober man driving on a familiar road. He drives off the bridge into ten feet of water. His passenger

157

drowns. He escapes from the submerged car and wanders around for hours in a state of amnesia. Then he goes to his residence and falls asleep and wakes up to report the accident. It's outlandish. It's incredible. It's unreal.

"And that's like life, isn't it! Things happen all the time that beggar the imagination. All the time. And we must stretch our narrow minds to accommodate the facts, and not vice versa.

"You see I'm starting to walk around the room! Pacing. Like in a courtroom. I'm acting like Justin's lawyer, at Justin's trial.

"But we don't expect a trial. I firmly believe that the inquest will not lead to a trial. That is, *if* the facts, *however* outlandish, are corroborated by the people involved.

"You are the people involved. You will be told the penalties of perjury at the inquest and sworn in and made to testify.

"It's a serious matter, taking the oath.

"The coroner will take the oath too, and do we have any reason to suppose he'll change his findings? Of course not. And thank heaven, too. Because in this whole horrible affair, with a poor dead girl, and a man who can't even remember what he did for hours after the accident, that coroner's finding is the one clear fact the inquest judge can grasp without difficulty.

"It's a rock, that finding. A solid rock in a sea of quicksand.

"I am speaking to you of these things because I know you are innocent bystanders and intelligent people. Unfortunately, neither of those qualities means much next to this one: you are inexperienced. Young. Unaware. I'm giving you food for thought. About surprises. About confusion and contradictions. About decent young people making mistakes that can cost them immense regret."

It was weird, we said later to one another. How none of us wanted him to stop talking, even though we heard the sinister music under the kind and caring words. There were deep, threatening bass chords in the middle of "prison" and "oath" and "trial" and "perjury."

But it was his music, that was the point. He had command of it, and it was a siren song, holding us to him.

It said, Listen. Follow me. Dance.

158

Don't contradict each other.

Don't contradict the coroner.

Don't say anything to anyone you haven't said, or will say, to me. You have nothing to say now? So be it.

I saw it suddenly: his "promise" not to ask us any questions was not just a promise, it was a strategy. It was a tactic for dealing with "the girls" until Justin came forward. He had decided that unless one of *us* had been driving that car, and wanted to admit it, we couldn't add any details that would make a bad case better.

We might only make it worse.

Amy's eyes were red. Someone had brought a portable TV into the dining room, and at breakfast the pictures of her car were shown again. They got her name from the registration, and it was the first time one of our names had sounded on television. It was a bad sound.

"Miss Shillitoe? Amy?" the Judge said. "I'm sorry about your car. Not the *thing*, of course. Just that it was yours, and you had to see it. It was just fortuitous. *Un*fortuitous. Justin could have grabbed any car keys, but yours were what he took. I suppose that's how it happened, anyway? I suppose one car is as good as another, in such an emergency? Yes. But did David ask you about having the car—uh, junked?"

Amy nodded.

"So much damage. I haven't got the figures, but it must come to nearly totaled. Even if not . . . you can get a new one."

"I don't want to see it," Amy said.

"Let me take care of that. Here. Just sign this. All done."

All done. Including, we knew, the matter of what business Justin had using Amy's car. He'd just grabbed the first keys that came to hand. All done.

So we knew then and there how final it was. Justin's story was being nailed into place, beam by beam, board by board, hour by hour, while he slept upstairs, unable to add or amend or contradict or retract. . . .

We would be safe inside that structure. We'd have what was left of Justin for company.

We could be safe, if we just went along.

We'd go along. It was finished. When Justin was himself

159

again, the Judge would tell him just what he'd told us. And Justin would understand, just as we had understood. *Sufficient unto the day*. . . .

I didn't trust the Judge. Even if I'd wanted to, I wouldn't have let myself trust him! But at least I understood what kind of relationship we had. He *liked* us for making his job easier. It gave me confidence to know it wasn't all acting, and out of that confidence I asked, "What's the worst that can happen? To any of us, including Justin. If there should be a trial."

The Judge winced.

"A circus. A long, drawn-out horror. The State would ask for the body to be exhumed. Then an autopsy. Every one of your lives would be picked over with a comb and a magnifying glass. The district attorney would turn Justin's life inside out, looking for some relationship with your poor friend. A reason for wanting her death? Even that. Oh, I know they wouldn't prove anything. They'd lose. But I hate to think what it would be like, for all of you."

"I see," I said. "The worst. Yes."

"Dismiss it from your minds. What I have today is a dazed and mentally disturbed eyewitness to a terrible accident. The *only* eyewitness. That's quite enough, for what's under these gray hairs."

"But if he's out of his mind—"

"I'm sure that he'll be well restored to it before he's questioned," the Judge said, and I was going to ask him about finding our own lawyers when there was a knock at the door.

The Judge opened it. Vinnie stepped in.

"He's been up for an hour," he said. "He wants to talk to you."

"Thank God," said the Judge. "Vinnie? You too. Please."

"Two secs. Let me talk to them."

The Judge was a blur of seersucker leaving the room in two long lopes. We could hear him running up the stairs. Vinnie closed the door.

"He's sitting up. Ate a lot. Talking normal."

"I'll get you some coffee," Caro said.

"Vinnie. What does he know? What's he said?"

"He knows the whole thing," Vinnie said. "I was alone with

him. Mellors was in the room, not twenty minutes before, and Justin just kept mumbling to him, 'Go away, go away, I want to sleep.' "

"For real?"

"For fake, is what I think. But I don't know. You think I asked him if he was faking?"

"Don't get angry."

"I don't know what I'm getting. A stroke maybe, ha ha. As soon as Mellors left, he called me. 'Vinnie!' His real voice. He asked the day, the time. He even asked when Lucia's funeral was. Right off the bat."

I sucked in my breath. Caro came in with the coffee, and I grabbed the cup before Vinnie could take it.

"Go on."

"I asked him if he remembered what he'd said in his statement to the police. He remembered some. I had the newspapers upstairs, thank God. I read the statement out loud, fast. I don't know if he got it all. I was worried someone would walk in on us."

"Did he remember then?"

"Absolutely. All of it. Even the sheriff's name. The plane coming here. Just the plane part: he thought *here* was some kind of hospital. Thought the butler in the white jacket was a doctor."

"He thought that then."

"Right. Oh, shit, I didn't know what to do next. David was outside, on the terrace with Old Henry. I had to play it by ear. I didn't know what to do. All that time, *sitting* up there, and when it happened, I lost it. Just lost it."

"You didn't," Caro said. "You didn't have many choices."

"I just wanted not to make it worse. For him."

"You couldn't do that if you tried. Then what?"

"Vinnie!"

It was a call from the Judge, at the top of the stairs.

"I'll make it fast. He said he was sorry. He asked about Rachel and you all. I said you were all here, tight together, and the family was being nice. He said that was good. He said—"

David was in the library doorway. Vinnie pointed: *Up.* Then he grabbed me by the shoulders.

"Don't ask to see him, Rachel! Keep cool. I swear, he's himself. When I told him the Judge was here, he actually smiled. Said to keep Mellors away and get the Judge. See? Isn't that good? He knows where the help is."

"Yes, that's good," I said, and Vinnie said he would see us at lunch, maybe, and shot away. We were alone, looking at one another, wrapped in the same feeling. A kind of numbness? A hard, stony feeling. Final.

Bitsie rallied first. She said we should get our minds on important things, like what a mess we'd look at the funeral. An ironing board, a washing machine. . . .

"Let's find one of the maids," Amy said.

"Then let's hide out at the pool," I said. "If I stay here, I'll go bananas."

"But he might ask for you," Amy whispered.

"You heard Vinnie. He's himself. He won't ask."

When we went upstairs to the nursery—by the back staircase, so as not to pass Justin's room or anywhere near it—we found a tall elderly woman supervising a young Spanish-looking girl in remaking the beds with fresh sheets. There was another little TV set on the table.

"I'm Mrs. Shearing," said the elderly woman, who wasn't in uniform. "I'm the housekeeper and this is Rosa. Mrs. Frayn told me to bring you the TV set. And some better pillows."

"Thank you," I said. "Thank Mrs. Frayn, too."

"Mrs. Frayn asked me to tell you that the bathroom at the end of this hall is yours too. It has a nice big tub in it, not just a shower. Four girls in one bathroom . . . I have three girls of my own, so I know."

"Well, we've been managing. But that will be nice. Thank you."

"We are all worried about the funeral. Our clothes are not what they should be. But we could be presentable if we had an ironing board. And could use the washing machine too."

"Rosa? Give me a pillowcase."

Mrs. Shearing asked us to put the washable things in the pillowcase. She'd have them back to us by evening. What we couldn't wash we must give to her too. She would have them sponged and pressed. Shoes?

We looked at one another dumbly. What could she do with shoes? But we meekly handed over our city pumps.

The bedmaking went on. There was no news at eleven in the morning, but Bitsie put on a game show. We stood watching it in silence until they left, and then we put on our suits and went out to the pool.

Edith, Jimbo, and Dr. Mellors were at the pool. By the time we saw them, it was too late to turn around. We marched forward.

"Oh, here you are!" Edith cried, as if she had been waiting for us. "Let's all take advantage. Did you hear the weather? Storms tonight and then a cold front tomorrow. And good riddance, is all I can say. This heat has gone on forever."

"We don't want to disturb you," I said.

"Oh, heavens, room and to spare. I've been out since nine. Early breakfast. I just had this feeling. Stay out of the house. Come back, and there will be Justin, good as new! Down for lunch, right as rain! Didn't you promise, Harve?"

Harve was Dr. Mellors. He said he hadn't promised. He only hoped.

"I popped in and he told me to go away," he said. "Good sign. Annoyed. Speaking quite clearly, too."

"I looked in," said Jimbo. "He was asleep."

"A great medicine, sleep," said Dr. Mellors. "Nature's own."

I took the chaise longue next to Edith. I told her how nice Mrs. Shearing had been to us, how nice they all were. I laid on the appreciation with a trowel.

"Oh, it's the least we can do!" she said. "For Justin's friends. I did everything with Tandy in mind. As *she'd* want it done. You'll be meeting her. She's flying in. She'll be here tomorrow morning in plenty of time to be with Justin at the funeral."

I was going to say that we all knew Mrs. Lambert when Jimbo said, from his wife's other side, "For God's sake, Edith, stop saying things like they're facts. Tandy may not have gotten on that plane. Justin may not be able to go to the funeral. You just set yourself up. For being disappointed."

"Harve said he would be able to go!"

"If the trend continues," said Dr. Mellors. He was in the pool, letting himself down the steps very gingerly. "*If* it continues."

"I hope Mrs. Frayn is right," I said, and Edith gave me a pat on the arm. We all went in swimming. Then John appeared carrying a tray and glasses. He must have known we were there. There were four Tabs and a recognizable gin and tonic.

We all took our drinks. Edith sipped hers daintily; her quotient, I guessed, until lunchtime.

"I'd like to see the rose garden," I said. "So soothing! Flowers!"

I was starting to talk like her. We pulled our towels around our shoulders and walked in the direction she pointed.

"Tandy's coming," I told the others. "They want her here. They want her with Justin at the funeral."

"Oh, sweet mother of God," Caro said. "Does he have to do that? Does he have to go?"

"That must be the drill. Unless they put it out that he's too sick. Then they'd still need her. To represent."

"As if Lucia gave a damn. It's all for the looks of it."

"It's going on. I can feel it. Like swirls. How they're . . . orchestrating."

"Is it all the Judge?"

I had been thinking of this. It kept me from thinking about Justin.

"I don't think so," I said. "He's only . . . well, like he was an ambassador? And they're his country. The Lamberts. Old Henry, his brothers, their children. He represents them. He carries the flag. But the bottom line has to be that he does what *they* want. He's just in charge of thinking how to get it."

"David said the Lamberts backed him for the Senate. He must owe them a lot."

"Not just Old Henry, the whole family. There's Benson, the one who runs the real estate."

"The big bank guy. I forget *his* name."

"And E.J., the congressman."

"Like the Rockefellers. Only fewer. Well, so what, this state is tiny, compared to New York."

"Justin's himself, Vinnie said so. That changes everything."

"Or nothing. We'll see."

"Funny, I'm starting to feel at home here. Crazy."

"Me too. Not crazy. It feels safe. Think of that crowd at the gatehouse."

"Oh, please. *Not* think."

We walked right past the rose garden without noticing it. We went back to it. It was a long rectangle divided by paths made of wood chips. You could walk between the beds and see the bushes from either side. Bees hummed around the flowers, undisturbed by our presence, intent on their work.

You can only look so long at roses. We didn't want to go back to the pool and Edith. We sat on the grass and looked at the sky.

"I don't think she hears well, that Edith," Bitsie said. "Look around. There's not a cloud in the sky."

"But it's hotter than hell. And so still. I wish we could swim."

"Let's go over what the Judge said."

"What's to go over? We got the message. I certainly did: *Shut up.*"

"He knows there's more."

"He couldn't guess the truth."

"He came down sort of hard on the word 'autopsy.' "

"I didn't hear that."

"I did. But it could be my own . . . imagination."

"Autopsy. Vinnie would have fainted if he'd been there."

"Oh, come on. Vinnie and David got that speech before we did. And not in baby talk, either. Vinnie passed the bar, even if he never practiced."

"Same message, bet on it."

"Bullshit. I bet the Judge really gave them a grilling."

"Bullshit back. Why would he want to hear from them what he doesn't want to hear from us?"

"Oh. Yes. I have to keep reminding myself. It's not the truth he wants. What did he say, yesterday? 'Clear passage through.' "

"I saw a movie once. This crooked lawyer tells Paul Newman not to tell him the truth. Because then he'd have to go to the DA with it."

"Is that the law?"

"You're asking *me*? It was just in a movie. But it must be a real issue. About legal ethics. Let's say the Judge finds out."

"Oh, God. Just saying. Okay. Then if he doesn't tell the DA what he knows, he's a what? An accessory?"

"That's right. He'd be an accessory. To a . . . a . . . crime."

"But it wasn't a crime! She was dead."

"Not a crime. Something, though. Could we drop this?"

"In the movie, he got disbarred."

"Some bluff, getting our own lawyers. We don't know chicken salad from chicken shit. What would we say? To some . . . stranger."

"Vinnie and David. We'll see what they do."

It's hard to remember how ignorant we were, how soon we learned. Inquest, perjury, accessory, self-incrimination; hearsay, demurrer, deposition, and the fine lines between can't remember/forgot/didn't notice/never knew. You have to know which. Your life can depend on it. But we didn't know then, and we had no one to ask but the Judge, and we couldn't trust him either. Not yet. Not till we knew what Justin would say.

In those first days it was always Caro who brought Lucia back. It was Caro who wouldn't let her disappear.

"We have to ask the Lamberts for money," she said. "A loan. So we can buy our flowers for the funeral. I've got only ten bucks left, and I know Bitsie is flat."

"We could write checks. Use American Express."

"I didn't bring any checks."

"It's a bitch, but we have to ask Edith. Not the Judge, he's up to here. Edith's the one. She'd know where to get them."

"All these gorgeous roses."

"Rose petals! Look, all over the ground. Beautiful. We could gather them up. Scatter them? Where they bury her."

It was something to do. Up and down the paths we went, using Amy's tote bag. We gathered up handfuls of petals from the ground, and when those were all gathered, we shook the spiny stems of the bushes to make more shower down, opulent confetti: burgundy, red, scarlet, coral, and then gold to yellow to cream to white. The sun blazed on our backs and arms; we breathed an air so thick with heat and fragrance we could almost taste it.

And so little by little everything fell away: the fear and the worry, the Judge, Justin. Only one thing mattered and we knew it; even I, dazed with fear and worry for Justin, knew it. We were alive in a world still filled with sun and roses, and Lucia was dead at twenty-one. We could have put back our heads and howled. Instead we went around picking up petals and wiping away the sweat and tears with our towels. Nobody made any noise. We wept silently and so much there was nothing left for the funeral. The press called it "composure."

19

Tuesday's lunch was easy. We had taken so long to dress and make our faces presentable that we found the dining room empty, with just a tray of sandwiches and plates left out on the sideboard. We took our plates to the terrace, but through the open French doors we could hear the great white house throbbing and humming; it felt like an ocean liner must feel when the engines open up. People kept running down the stairs. Phones rang many times before they were answered, and out front cars crunched on the graveled drive-way, doors slammed, voices raised. We all knew Old Henry's roar.

"Not that car, you idiot! I said the big wagon! You want her to leave half her luggage in New York?"

Tandy.

"She grabbed the first plane. They have to send a car all the way to Kennedy."

"Hours and hours on the pike. Rush hour in the tunnel."

168

"So Edith was right. She will make the funeral."

"Rachel? You holding?"

"Sure. Look, Tandy belongs here. I've had practice, understanding that."

Bitsie got up and closed the French doors.

"Paranoid," she said. "But be careful. Talk low."

"I am talking low," I said. "I'm talking sense too. I'm glad she's coming. He needs her, not me."

"You don't really mean that."

"Every word. She's his real life."

"He loves you."

"He doesn't need me. Not in a thing like this. A thing that wouldn't have even happened if it weren't for me. Me. *I* wanted to be with him. *I* was feeling cooped up—"

Amy gave a couple of disgusted snorts.

"You're chickening out, Rachel. Doing a number on yourself. I suppose you're also wishing you encouraged him, last year, when he was going on about divorce and leaving politics. Giving up the throne like what's-his-name, *you* know; talk about wimps!"

"The Duke of Windsor."

"That's the one."

"I couldn't let Justin do that," I said. "Maybe I should have. Oh, I was stalling, superstitious maybe. I thought when he won next year for the Senate—"

I shook my head, wryly. We all knew the primary was less than a year away. We didn't have to say what this situation had done to his plans for the Senate.

"He's young," Bitsie said. "He can afford to wait a while until this is history."

"He'll wait with Tandy," I said. "We're over, Justin and I. You can see that. We won't even want to go on in the old way, and can you imagine what it would look like if Justin went and married one of the girls at Lighthouse Point?"

"Lousy. Yich. Hate to say it."

"I can see how you feel right now," Caro said hesitantly. "But it could change. In the future? Love is—"

"Not worth it," I said.

I was calm; it felt good to say these things out loud to

169

friends who wouldn't blame me. And yet I didn't quite believe what I was saying; it was like a rehearsal for a bitter part I might someday play. I was only sure that even without Justin I would never be alone.

I felt grateful. I took a deep breath.

"You guys have done so much for me already," I said. "I don't want to go on keeping a secret from you. I want to tell you my real name. It's Robin White. I changed it when I went to Barnard."

It didn't take long to tell about Tin Town and how my father died. It wasn't hard, either. I felt it again, that shipboard sensation, as if the Lambert estate were one of those mighty liners you see in old black-and-white movies, a fantasy of power and luxury, out of time and space. On these green lawns, like those green waters, the rules were special. You could lie through your teeth or tell the truth and the only rule was their motto: *Suit yourself and don't come crying*.

"That's why Justin told me about the shooting accident," I said finally. "I went first. I wanted to be honest. I wanted him to know me. I guess he felt the same."

"Funny how things work," Amy said. "If you hadn't told him, we wouldn't know about his killing that girl. But we do know. And it makes sense."

"His going crazy makes sense?"

"Yes," said Amy stoutly. "And now that I think of it, when you put it together with—oh, forget it. I shouldn't say it anyway."

"Say it, Amy," Bitsie said. "You took off your glasses; it must be important."

Amy looked at me uneasily. "Rachel reminded me. Of how often Justin used to say he wanted to get out of politics. Quit the grind. Try something else. Well. See? That's just what *this* is going to let him do."

"So maybe he's not crazy," Caro whispered. "Only pretending."

Bitsie held up her hand. "We'll all go crazy, thinking about him and what he's done! Listen, I'm going to tell why I got kicked out of boarding school."

* * *

170

I knew about the incident, but Amy and Caro didn't. They got furious, hearing how the boy got off with just a term's probation. After they calmed down, Amy said she'd tell us why she really went to France in her junior year.

It was a sad thing. A few days ago, all four of us would have thought it was the saddest thing in the world.

"I guess it's my turn," Caro said softly. "I do really love Vinnie. I want not to, but I can't. I think he knows it, too."

We were quiet for a few minutes, feeling the strange new weight of one another's regrets.

"Let's make a deal," Bitsie said abruptly. "A deal for the rest of our lives. No secrets from one another. Not just this. Everything."

Amy dug her ubiquitous pad of paper and a pencil stub out of her pants pocket. "Write, Bitsie," she said. "We'll sign it. Like when we were kids. A club. First rule: No secrets."

That's how it started. We added two other rules then and many more later, but the essentials were there, short enough to sign, memorize, and then tear up. Because that was one of the original rules: Tear up anything written.

"I won't see Justin alone," I said. "You'll have to help me. Even if he asks for me, alone. It must be all of us. So we'll all hear the same thing. So we won't have any doubts."

"Oh, Rachel."

"I mean it."

"Okay. The ayes have it."

"May I have a vote?" It was Dr. Mellors, smiling up at us from behind a great urn of pink geraniums, only a little pinker than his face. "Good news," he said. "Our patient is doing very well. But I suppose you knew that already?"

"We heard. It certainly sounds good."

"Tandy will be here around midnight. So Justin will have her support at the funeral."

"He'll really be well enough to go?"

"Absolutely."

"But what an awful strain."

"At least there'll be no TV coverage of the funeral. We have assurances."

"Assurances?"

"The Lamberts have very good friends in Fort Leeds."

I suddenly saw, upon the convex surfaces of Dr. Mellor's face, the narrow, snappish smirk of Edith Lambert. The doctor was relishing this: his famous patient, the family's clout, his own importance.

"Oh, Dr. Mellors," I cooed, "what are the papers saying? We haven't seen any this morning."

Dr. Mellors went at once to tug a cast-iron bell on the terrace wall. A maid opened the French door.

"Celia? Bring us some of the morning papers."

The maid came back with an armload. Dr. Mellors took a chaise longue and a chorus of thank you's. He didn't read himself. He watched us reading. He watched us looking at the front pages and the pictures.

The car coming out of the water. The bridge. Neat diagrams full of dotted lines connecting locations marked with stars, with bullets, with arrows. The cottage, the ferry, the bay, the inlet, Justin's face, Lucia's face, a groaning board of visuals for the hungry public.

"There's a nice editorial in our *Dispatch*," Dr. Mellors called. "Who's got the *Dispatch*? Oh, Rachel. Read it out loud."

I read it out loud. It said that every citizen of our state wished Governor Lambert well in his hour of tragedy. It asked its readers not to rush judgment until all the facts were clear. It announced that Woodrow Lester, the Lieutenant Governor, was at the helm until Governor Lambert was fully restored to health.

Oh, it was a nice editorial. The Lamberts owned the paper. It said "health" and not "sanity." The news story on the front page mentioned a "mild concussion" in the very first paragraph.

We traded papers. We didn't expect the tea-and-sympathy approach from any other paper, and we didn't get it. Bourbon, neat, was the order of the day. There'd be the word "party" without the word "birthday" in front of it. There'd be the descriptions of the Governor: young, handsome, rich, a scion, an heir, a political star. We were variously campaign workers, volunteers, staff, friends. We weren't, as yet, individuals with real jobs. We were females, young ones, the five girls at Lighthouse Point.

But only Lucia was pictured. The wire services all had the

same cut from the same Fort Leeds paper. It showed her in her cheerleader's uniform, with outstretched arms, pom-poms, and bright blond hair flying.

She would have hated it! She always said the cheerleading was "first phase." It was the asthma, she said. It was the doctors, always telling her what not to do. She had to show them. She had to show more pep, jump higher, yell louder, to prove herself, to be a person without a handicap.

A person who always felt fine.

"Rachel? A penny for your thoughts."

"Lucia," I said to Dr. Mellors. "I'm thinking about her."

Everyone said they were thinking about Lucia. Bitsie said that didn't do any of us any good, and let's flip for who gets first crack at that big old bathtub. A good long soak.

We flipped for it. I won. I got up and said, "What's happened to the weather?"

It had been clear when we started going through the papers and we'd gone slowly, practically moving our lips in the hope that Mellors would get bored and go away. Now the sky was plum-gray and the green lawn had an oily sheen.

"Storm coming," Dr. Mellors said. "Those are real old thunderheads. Well, we can use the rain."

The first rumble of distant thunder sounded. When Dr. Mellors turned in its direction, I saw Amy take a page of newspaper and fold it fast and stick it in her pocket.

"See you," I said, and went in.

20

We had been together in the house, the four of us, since Sunday, always close enough to call, to touch. It felt odd, being alone; I felt it as I crossed the dark dining room. Someone had put on all the lights in the hall, and I entered it, blinking. Then I stepped back into the shadow of the dining room door. I could hear the Judge's voice and Old Henry's, coming from the big library.

"E.J.'s got them all in line. For the time being."

E.J. was the congressman, Old Henry's brother.

"They'll hold for him. He's got the Whip's ear, thank God."

"Matty's willing to shut up for a while. A week or two, he says."

"That son of a bitch."

"He's not dumb. Jump on Justin when he's down? Not that dumb."

174

"Eight weeks till the inquest. You couldn't do better."

"Henry, I've made myself clear. I *could* do better. I don't *want* to."

"All right, all right. Give me that telegram."

The front doorbell rang, melodious chimes that brought John running. I could see the back of his white jacket and Delano, the lawyer.

"I'm late," he said. "Where are they?"

"The library, sir."

"You took your goddam time."

That was Old Henry. The door slammed. John disappeared. I came into the hall on tiptoe and went as quickly as I dared to the back stairs. I knew the way now: past the main staircase, through the long glassed-in porch full of wicker and hanging plants, into the butler's pantry, and up the back staircase to join the one we had used that first night.

Thunder rumbled outside. I paused, listening. That sound goes into you like a message drummed on the skin around your heart. I wondered if Justin heard it. I wondered because he seemed so far away.

I started running my bath first, and then I went into the nursery to collect my terry robe and a bra and underpants left drying on the shower door. Then I went back down the hall into the big bathroom and turned on the light. Even as I did this I thought, That's funny. I thought I left the light on. I closed the door.

I smelled her before I heard her. The sweet stink of gin was swirling in the steam.

"I guess you can turn off the water. The tub's full."

It was Edith. She was sitting on a little stool, and the closed lid of the toilet was a table for her glass.

"Mrs. Frayn?"

"Edith. Please. Isn't this cozy? A nice place to chat. I saw you go in to run your bath and I said to myself, Now there's a nice place for a chat!"

"It's not such a nice place."

"Come to my room. Jimbo's downstairs, watching television."

"Oh, no, this is fine, just fine." I was totally flustered. She looked really drunk, slack in the mouth, giggling over how hard it was to get a cigarette out of a new pack.

When she lit up, she said, "Guess what I've got in my pocket."

I couldn't guess. I said so.

"A check for ten thousand bucks," she said. "All yours. Just fill in your name. Our little secret. Your friends don't have to know."

"What for?"

"Just for telling me. It won't go any further than *here*."

"There's nothing to tell."

"He got her pregnant, right? Knocked her up. So she killed herself. Drove the car right off Camel Bridge."

"No! Never. Anyway, he was driving. He said so."

Edith stood up, taking her drink with her. She waved it at me. "Bullshit. I knew. Tandy knew. He had someone on the side. He got her pregnant and she committed suicide."

"He was driving," I repeated, backing away. "You know that."

"Bullshit. He wants to take the blame because he got her pregnant. I know him. Goddam overgrown Boy Scout. He's telling crazy lies to cover up the truth."

"You don't know what you're saying."

"Oh, don't I? They do that. Get a belly and kill themselves. All you sluts. Slutty secretaries. Out for what you can get. Ruining people."

It was a big bathroom. She came closer. We were circling one another like a pair of mismatched dogs, one tall, one short.

"Edith," I whispered, "stop this. You're not right. Lucia was absolutely innocent. Really. Truly. She never even had a real boyfriend."

"I'm going nuts with your lies! I knew. Tandy didn't want to know but I told her. I know the signs; oh, boy, I know the signs; this is Edith Frayn you're talking to."

"I won't listen to this. I'm going to my room."

"This is my father's house. You'll go when I tell you to."

It wasn't smart, but I tried to push past her and make a grab

176

at the doorknob. She saw me coming and threw her drink in my face.

It must have been mostly gin; it stung my eyes like acid. I knew I had to wash them out, fast, and I let her watch me do it. The burning subsided. I turned from the sink, plucked the glass from her hand, put the glass in the sink, turned again, and slapped her face. She swung at me, missed, and fell to her knees, clawing at the hem of my robe and pulling me down on top of her. I rolled off. She rolled on. We both banged our heads on the side of the tub, and I scrambled to my feet and picked up the first thing that came to hand.

It was the bath brush. We would laugh about it, later. Because Caro and Amy came upstairs then and heard the thunks and opened the bathroom door. They saw me standing over Edith.

"I'll use this if I have to," they heard me say. "I swear I'll brain you with it if you don't leave me alone."

It might just as well have been a gun. She got to her feet, and we saw the blood on her chin. She must have bitten her lip when she fell.

Amy ran to get Bitsie, Edith staggered out, and then the four of us were in the bathroom. Bitsie leaned on the sink, Amy took the toilet, Caro sat on the floor, and I got into the tub and told them the dialogue.

"Let's call her back," Bitsie said when I finished. "We can take turns, beating her up."

"Alcoholic. Brain-damaged. That's what happens to them."

"Vinnie and David have to know. She's a lunatic! Dangerous. Some creep reporter could get hold of her when she's drunk."

Amy reached into the tub and pulled my arm up. "The winner and noo champeen . . . Warshowsky!"

The encounter had given us all a lift: the fight, the bribe, the "slutty secretaries." We got dressed quickly; we talked loudly; we were crackling with malice and adrenaline, and it felt good. It blocked the sight of the clothing the housekeeper had brought back, and our shiny shoes, polished and ready for tomorrow and the funeral.

Caro joined in, but in such an absentminded way I had to ask her what she was thinking.

"It's Jimbo," she announced, sighing. "I didn't want to bring it up before. He was patting my knee under the table at breakfast. When we were watching TV and the car? Pretending sympathy. He wouldn't stop so I changed my seat."

"A chaser," said Bitsie. "You bet. He chases, so she drinks. Or maybe the other way around. She drinks so he chases."

"Screw them both," Amy said. "That bitch. Running to tell Tandy the *signs*. What signs, for God's sake?"

"She might really have noticed something," I said. "He had to say he was working late, those nights."

"Oh, very revealing," Amy said, dripping sarcasm. "Earth-shaking clue. All the other governors quit at six, every night of the year."

"She's jealous of Tandy," Caro said. "I caught that before. Say, do you think Edith's in love with her brother?"

"If she is it's a one-way street. I don't think he ever mentioned her name to me. Not in three years."

"Rachel has all the luck. She got to hit her."

"But what a sleazeball. Trying to mix Lulu up with Jimbo's kind of stuff."

We couldn't let go of it. We felt we were protecting Lucia, just as if she were still alive. When Vinnie came into our room he said he could hear us laughing clear down the hall and what the hell did we think we were doing, late for dinner, making noise?

"You're late too," Caro said. "Vinnie, wait till you hear—"

"No time," Vinnie snapped. "David's eating in Justin's room. I get to go downstairs tonight. Before we go, there's one part of our story I want to get straight."

"Shoot."

"He left with Lucia around quarter to eight. He insisted on driving because of the fog. He said he'd be back by ten, but if he missed the regular ferry he'd just call Simon and get him to make a special trip. *That's* why you girls kept on waiting for him. You thought he'd get Simon to make a special trip for you too. But toward midnight you were too tired and worried and insisted we take you across in the Whaler. You all know the drill after that."

We flattened out. Vinnie looked awful, with those purple puffs under his eyes. His sport shirt was visibly soiled and looked even worse for being teamed with the pants to his office suit. But he wasn't hoarse anymore; his sharp staccato was all business, and when Caro put her hand out he didn't take it.

"Don't be a bear, Vinnie," she said. "We had a good reason to laugh. You're telling us what to say, so I guess we can answer them now, right? It's all set, isn't it?"

"All set," Vinnie said. "But for the time being, Rachel will answer questions for all of you. In front of other people, that is."

He hesitated. Then he put an arm around Caro's waist.

"I already told the Judge that he can be our lawyer. The six of us. He offered. I can tell him you've changed your minds, if you want. But don't. He's our best chance out."

"He gets us and Justin's story?"

"Yes."

"But if Justin——"

"Changes the story? He won't, Rachel. I was with him all day. I won't say he's himself; that was wishful thinking. But he's lucid. He says that what we did Saturday night was all for his benefit anyway, because he had the most to lose from the truth. And he says any change that takes him away from the scene of the accident will look like—get this—a cover-up."

"How is he?"

"He looks good. Still on the tranquilizers—pills, no shots—so he's talking kind of . . . heavy. He keeps apologizing because he knows he's out of the Senate race. He keeps apologizing to *me*. Like it's *my* loss. Oh, hell, I don't know what to think anymore; it's a Chinese puzzle. I used to say I knew him inside and out——"

He threw up his hands. For a moment he looked like an old man, old with despair, old with confusion. I kissed him.

"You love him, Vinnie," I said. "That's enough."

"Vote," Bitsie said. "Do we take the Judge?"

The vote was unanimous. We filed out, down the dark hallway to the top of the great staircase. Amy and Caro and Vinnie went ahead; Bitsie and I hung back, looking down. The storm had turned the summer dusk inky black and the chandelier was fully lit; it glittered on the silver tray the butler was carrying; it made the tall vase of fresh lilies on the center table shine like snow.

179

"Those flowers are new," I said. "From the cutting garden, I guess."

"Lambertland," Bitsie said. "They do it right, don't they? They take care of themselves. They'll take care of us."

"Lambertland," I echoed. I felt numb. I said, "There was never any choice, was there?"

"Never any," Bitsie said. She squeezed my hand. She said, "I knew that before we even got here."

If there had been a cocktail hour that night it was over when we got downstairs. John was at the dining room door, to show us where to sit and pull back our chairs. Old Henry was already at the head of the table in his big wing chair, flanked by Delano and the Judge. No Edith, no David, no Dr. Mellors. The first two must be upstairs, the one to sleep it off, the other to buffer Justin from the hovering psychiatrist. The four of us understood it all without saying a word, and a kind of rag-doll relaxation took us over. Justin safe with David. Edith elsewhere. Soup with bits of something savory floating in it (Bitsie knew it was marrow) and fluffy brown rolls and the strong light from the central fixture making the candle flames pale.

It was not the kind of night you want only candles to see by. There was a new, high wind behind the rain that was falling in sheets. The wind drove the water against the French doors in pailfuls and made the trees groan. Once there was a loud snapping sound that made us jump.

"Goddam maple," Old Henry said. "Lousy tree, maple. Can't take wind. I'm going to get rid of that one near the driveway before it keels over."

"The Crimson King?" the Judge asked. "You'll regret it. Sight for sore eyes in October. I paid eight hundred to have mine shored up."

"Who do you use?" Delano asked.

"Chris Jensen. He's no bigger a thief than the rest."

All through dinner the Judge had made a special effort to include us in the conversation. He brought up newspapers for Amy and child care for Caro; he too seemed relaxed, but his avuncular attention signaled a new way of relating to us. He was treating us as clients.

180

Now he said, "I'd like to show you young ladies my own place someday. Just a summer shack, compared to this! I built it down the road a piece, and it's on a real ridge. Practically alpine, for these latitudes."

"And a driveway so steep you need a Jeep when it shows," Old Henry said. "Some ridge. You would have done better with the Lee property."

"Jealous, jealous," the Judge said. "You're in a sump down here, Henry; you want us all dug in with you."

They traded insults. It must have been an old argument, and for a moment I warmed to them, Old Henry particularly. For all the men around him in his trouble, there was no woman at his side. He had to join in the conversation, look strong, sound positive, while his wife took Valium and the daughter who drank made a fool of herself.

I thought of Tandy. I thought of Justin saying once, casually, "Dad thinks the world of Tandy."

Tandy would be with him tonight. She had not one but two men to be there for. It was no wonder that Edith's nose was permanently out of joint.

And mine? Mine only ached from the pressure of an invisible pane of glass. I was outside with my nose pressed to the window, looking in at Justin's real life. A family man. A member of a family that held together, the weak with the strong, the fools with the foxes, and Tandy was one of them. Had our luck held and our love deepened, Justin's wife would still have had all that power on her side, to keep him where he belonged. A family man, a Lambert.

I didn't know the word for what I felt then, but I know it now. It was resignation. You submit. You relinquish. And in return you get to keep the kind of dignity you won't even value until you're much, much older.

I must have been staring into space over my coffee. Bitsie kicked me and I saw that John was gone, the doors were shut, and Old Henry was pouring from a decanter that looked like molten ruby.

"Port," he said. "Very fine, if I must say so myself. Or are you people still conducting an AA reunion?"

"We're not AA," I said. "It looks delicious. We just don't think liquor would do us any good right now."

181

"Neither will lawyers. Have you decided what to do?"

The Judge raised his glass to the light. "I have a happy surprise for you, Hank. These young ladies have accepted my offer to represent them, if such representation is ever needed. And to accept my advice, in any case at all."

It was the first time we'd seen Justin's father smile. My heart turned over. He looked like Justin around the eyes.

"That's good," he mumbled. "By God, that's good."

He drained his glass.

"I won't forget this, Vinnie."

"It was their own decision," Vinnie said, and then it was my turn, to say what else I'd been thinking of all through dinner.

"There's just one thing. David and Vinnie have been with Justin constantly. We want to see him too. Alone. As soon as possible. Until we see him, it's all . . . provisional."

"Conditional, Rachel," the Judge purred. "That's a condition, not a provision."

"Just so it's understood."

"Of course. Let's see. I suspect it's too late now, because I believe Dr. Mellors wants Justin asleep by ten. The funeral is tomorrow. The timetable means we all leave here at nine-thirty to be at the chapel in Fort Leeds by eleven-thirty. Then the cemetery and then back here. Let's say six o'clock tomorrow night. Will that suit you?"

Bitsie and Caro and Amy nodded vigorously. Caro winked across the table at me: *Good move.*

"Okay," said Old Henry. "Let's go into the den. Let's get some real work done. Is Rachel going to do all the talking?"

"Yes," said Bitsie smartly. "Any objections?"

"No, no," he said. "Just asking. I'll leave all the objecting about *that* to David."

He smiled again. We trooped into the den and sat down. Funny, we said later, this time the men did all the writing too. Even Vinnie, and he was so tired he kept dropping his pen.

"The time that Justin and Lucia left," the Judge said. "Do you agree with Vinnie and David that it was between seven-thirty and eight?"

"Yes. We can't be more precise. We all have different ideas but it's within that half-hour."

"There was some discussion? Argument? Why didn't all of you just leave together? The girls, that is. All the girls together."

"Justin wouldn't hear of it. There was the fog. We didn't know the roads, the bridges. And he was so concerned about her, he didn't even want to wait a few minutes so we could pack up, collect our things."

"If she was so sick, why weren't you all more concerned?"

"We were worried. But we were used to Lucia. The asthma, the wheezing and coughing: we'd seen it all before. Like last New Year's when their house gave a party. We had to drive her to All Saints for a shot."

"Did she often forget her medicines?"

"She was always forgetting. If not the shot, this pill, that pill. She'd go out with three inhalers, all empty. She was careless. I shouldn't say that."

"You may have to say that."

Delano was writing it all down. The Judge concentrated on the questions. Did we have all her medicines in her suitcase? Her doctor's name? How long would it have taken to show Justin she was out of danger? Had she been drinking? Was she a heavy drinker?

Vinnie interrupted. "This is Mickey Mouse. I don't like it." His voice was loud. It sounded artificial, warning me.

"An honest mistake, Vinnie. I thought you'd told the girls. About the blood test. Well. The medical examiner had one done. Routine, but we didn't have the result until this morning. Miss Bennett—Lucia—had point one percent. Stiff drinking, and over the legal limit if she'd been driving."

"My fault," Bitsie said. "Those damn Bloody Marys I made."

For some reason the Judge seemed satisfied. "A birthday party," he said. "Special occasion. And it wouldn't take much, a little girl like that."

"Was Justin drinking?" Old Henry was staring at me from under his beetling iron-gray brows, and I tried to look puzzled.

"Drinking? Like a lot? We would have noticed. He had some beer that afternoon. A Bloody Mary for the toasts. We didn't have any wine, we forgot to buy it."

The Judge took a different tack. Where, exactly, did we think Lucia had gone, when we got back to the motel and didn't find her? Gone to the hospital with Justin? What time did you make that call? So then where did you think she was? A party! Another party? With some boys she'd met on the beach? What were their names? What was the name of the company on their truck?

The questions came at me like baseballs, too fast to catch the windup. The Judge wasn't fooling. This is what it will be like, he seemed to say. It's what you're up against. Old Henry's bald dome swung back and forth: me-him, me-him. I was rapt, absorbed, cold with concentration, a rock climber looking for a handhold in every question.

"Let's go back a bit," the Judge said. "You four are at the motel. There's no Lucia, no Justin, no Amy's car. Lucia could be in a hospital or at a party. She's *not* in the hospital. So where did you think *Justin* was?"

"We couldn't imagine. We knew he could get back to Lighthouse Point any time he wanted, just by calling Simon on the phone to come and get him. But we really weren't thinking about him at all."

Amy broke in. "I did, Rachel, don't you remember? I thought maybe she got *really* sick and he rushed her to some doctor, closer than the hospital. The hospital was all the way over in Talcott."

"Yes, you said that. And then, yes, there was always the chance that we just missed him. He could have been driving toward Lighthouse Point just as we got into the Whaler."

"But of course you were focused on your friend and how she was," the Judge said. "And then you decided she'd gone to the party. With the—um, beach boys. Well. There's still no car. Justin, presumably, is using it to go back to the island. So how in the world did you think your friend *got* to this other party?"

I knew from the tone of his voice that he thought this was a tough question. I nearly laughed out loud, telling the truth.

"You didn't know Lucia. If she wanted to party she'd call a cab. And if she was out of money, she'd hitchhike."

It was wonderful to let the truth of Lucia snap in his face like a bright banner: her enthusiasm, her bravado—reckless, careless, greedy for the music and the noise and the phone ringing off the hook with all the new boys she'd meet. Hitchhike to a party when she felt better? Goddam right she would. Ask anybody about Lucia. Look at her picture. Ask the world.

184

Even—when I finished—ask Old Henry and the Judge, their eyes lowered, their faces stilled. I made her real to them.

"I take your point, Rachel." The Judge's voice was soft and saddened. "I'm sure you all tried to warn her, many times. But for her sake it would be better, if you're asked, to mention only a possible taxi to that party. Not hitchhiking. It's prejudicial."

"I see. About her character. Nice girls don't hitchhike. Or take a drink too many."

"Something like that."

"Lucia was a virgin. What does that say about her character?"

A great groan escaped Vinnie. Old Henry put his head in his hands, and the Judge's cheek was stained with mottled red. I had embarrassed them all. For a minute even Leland Hofstedter was at a loss for words.

"You have me between a rock and a hard place on that one," he said finally. "Whatever I say, I'm convicted. I'm taking the Fifth."

David stuck his head in the door. "Justin's sound asleep. Do you need me here?"

"We're breaking up," the Judge said. "I suggest we all make use of John to bring us a drink. Let's turn on the TV and watch something mindless. We have the funeral to get through tomorrow."

David put his arm around me. "Let's walk somewhere," he said. "We're engaged. We've got a right to be alone."

"It's still raining."

"Your room. Let's go."

We slipped away. Before we got to the nursery I had told David all about the incident with Edith.

"A loose cannon," he said glumly. "I'll have to tell Old Henry. He'll handle her. Christ, what we have to handle! Don't think the reporters haven't been pestering my mother. Thank God I got to her early."

"What did you tell her?"

"That you and I are not really engaged and the papers got it wrong, but it's not the time to make denials of anything. I told her to say she liked you."

"She does like me."

"She likes Hilda Samson better. She's rich and ugly."

David flung himself on Amy's bed. I sat on a chair and described the session with the Judge. I said, "Is Vinnie right? Justin's sticking?"

"Absolutely. It's not Justin, only. It's the Judge. He warned Justin. Oh, very gently. But he warned him. This is it."

"Now what?"

"The arraignment's on Thursday. He has to show up before a magistrate and be sentenced for leaving the scene of an accident. The fix is in, from what I hear. Fine and a suspended sentence."

"And then?"

"He goes back to work Monday morning. Mellors says it's okay, for what *that's* worth. It's the family. *They* want him back on the job as soon as possible. They don't want him to look as if he's hiding out."

"They don't want to admit he's sick! He is sick, isn't he?"

"Mental? Who knows. It's all so weird, Rachel. Sometimes Vinnie and I think he's—"

"Faking," I finished. "I know. That's wishful thinking, David. I believe he went crazy. Just broke down under it."

"I don't trust Mellors. I don't even think he's got another patient, or even a regular job. He's a parasite. But believe me, he's still the best Justin's going to get. Old Henry will see to it."

David closed his eyes.

"Next step is the inquest. They're going to let the heat build. The Judge and Delano will make statements, huff and puff, just a show to make the DA look good. Then they'll be gracious and back down. 'Interest of full and frank disclosure' and other bullshit. The inquest will be early October, I think."

"That's something else to dread."

"Don't, Rachel. Unless some Martian in a spaceship saw us, we're all right."

"I asked to see Justin. All of us. It's set for six, tomorrow night."

"You pushed that? I'm glad. It's *you* I want to see him. It's your opinion I want. Rachel? He keeps asking about you."

"Not *for* me, though."

186

"No. But about how you're doing. Can you sleep. Things like that."

"You have to be reassuring."

"It's not hard. All of you have been great."

"Not as good as you and Vinnie. You were up front."

"I guess you could call it self-defense. But it's more than that. It's what we've all been to one another."

"I know. But now I'm resigned to losing it. I'll never be with Justin as we were. I'm even afraid to see him alone. I keep having these conversations with him in my head. Like he'll ask me if I regret what we had together? And I'll say I do regret it. Look what it led to. It's like wishing I'd never been born. It's like . . ."

I went on for a while more before I realized that David was asleep. I found a pad of paper on Amy's bed and I wrote notes to myself. I wanted the name of the umbrella boy with the nice smile. It began with a B. I needed an engagement ring. Amy had to get that picture—the one of us around the barbecue—developed. I wished we'd taken pictures of the table and the presents. But I did have the cake receipt somewhere at home. And the big main house . . . had the police been in it?

I was still scribbling when the others came up. We whispered so as not to wake David, but it would have taken a brass band to do that.

"Poor David," Caro said. "Vinnie looks worse, though."

"Amy, what was in that newspaper? The page you stuck in your pocket?"

Amy said it wasn't that important. Some reporter had tried to find Simon Cassidy, the ferryman, and couldn't. His son was running the ferry, and the son said his father was due for a vacation and he'd gone fishing and he had no intention of telling where.

"I guess I thought how it goes to show," Amy said. "I guess I kind of liked seeing what the Lamberts can do with people. Because I can't get my mind off Curtis Jeffers. That's the guy I bought the pot from."

"Poor Amy. Oh, the boy with the nice smile? Brian."

"I'm obsessing too," I said. "About the big house. The bed in Justin's room. The bed."

It was like the problem of Curtis Jeffers. You couldn't solve it without shining a bright light on it. I did remember making the bed with Justin's help but being distracted by something when we did it. I wasn't sure about the pillows.

"Give up," Bitsie said. "If we get tripped up by anything, it will be some dumb detail we never even worried about. So why worry? It's always about the wrong thing."

Talking and undressing, we forgot David was there. When he came to, Bitsie threw her naked self under her blanket.

"How long did I sleep?"

"About half an hour. David, you've lost five pounds at least. Aren't you eating?"

"I have this burning knot right here. I'll be all right. I got some Tums from the housekeeper."

"Vinnie's falling off his feet. He's getting tighter, not looser, and things are going all right, aren't they? So why is he so irritable?"

Caro did well, keeping her voice light. David stretched and yawned and grimaced. "He's been calling the state capitol. Getting the picture. You know Vinnie and his contacts, they hear everything. Sure, he's upset. They're flinging so much dirt some of it is bound to stick. Dirt. He's thinking of his wife, hearing it."

"Dirt. We went there to screw, is that it?"

You could always count on Bitsie to reach the bottom line first. David bit his lip.

"Well, one thing they're saying is that Justin isn't Old Henry's son for nothing."

"Don't give us the details," I said dully. "I guess we'd have to expect it. Be prepared."

Caro slipped into the bathroom. David said he was going back to Justin, and breakfast was eight sharp, and he'd knock to see that we didn't oversleep. He left, and we let Caro stay in the bathroom, crying, until we told her that was enough, it had nothing to do with her, come out this minute.

Finally we slept. I thought I heard Tandy's voice, but I was only dreaming. Her plane had been delayed. She arrived the next morning, while we were having breakfast. I heard her come in. I heard her say, "Where is he?" and her heels, clattering on the floor, then running upstairs to her husband.

We talked about it later because we couldn't talk about it then: how people brace themselves for a bad experience by imagining the worst of it ahead of time. We couldn't talk to one another in the enormous limousine they provided for us; it held eight people, and one of them was Dr. Mellors. We had two hours of travel, mixing a painful silence with vapid conversation. There was plenty of time for imagining.

The mob of reporters and photographers in front of the funeral chapel, cawing like crows. "Over here! Look up, that's a girl!" The sight of her coffin. Meeting her brother and his wife, such a small family, made even smaller. Seeing Justin. Standing in the rain in the cemetery. Oh, and the coffin, always that. We hoped it would be closed. We were too afraid to ask.

But Wednesday would play itself out, with this new understanding: none of it was as hard to bear as that silent ride to Fort Leeds and the imagining.

It all went so smoothly. Minions of the Lambert family had spent three days making sure of that. They'd chosen a small funeral chapel instead of a church, which was public. It held only fifty people, and none of them could be there out of cold curiosity or sensation hunger. Most of the mourners were Lucia's age, class-mates from Kilmer High. They had passes with their names on them. They were admitted last. When we arrived, Justin and Tandy were already seated in the front row, their navy-blue shoulders touching. We sat two rows back. I couldn't see his face and I didn't want to. I wanted to keep seeing Lucia, little flashes of her, winking off the fresh bright faces of her old friends.

The coffin was closed, and a mound of pink carnations lay over it. The minister stood in front of it, black-robed, pink-winged. All rise. We read together. Psalm Twenty-three, the Lord's Prayer, "Rock of Ages."

He didn't know her. He spoke of anybody's brief and blame-less life, and memory, and keeping faith. It fit. He didn't have to know her. The carnations were palest pink, like a blanket for a newborn baby girl.

Justin sang the last hymn. I could hear his voice.

Half a dozen state troopers were at the cemetery gates, to see that only our cars entered. It happened naturally: Justin and Tandy on one side of the grave, us on the other. We didn't look across; we didn't not look across. When they lowered the coffin, we stepped forward, with our bag of petals, and her brother took some, and her sister-in-law too. They showered down, softer than the rain, and they stuck like snowflakes to the green strip of turf that hid the wood of the coffin. We bowed our heads while the minister prayed. There was a blank five seconds while we stood there, looking down. Then there were hands at our elbows, arms at our arms, guiding us away, making us match quick steps to the waiting cars.

They do that. You have to leave right away. I think they bring the coffin up again, to remove the quiet machine that lets it lower so gently, smooth as silk.

We wanted to see her brother. We'd only had a handshake

at the door to the chapel and saying our names, very low. We hardly knew what he looked like. But the first car to leave the cemetery was his, and Delano, the lawyer, and two other young men were in it as well.

Smooth as silk, that mesh of spun power, but strong as steel. "In seclusion," Vinnie said sternly, when we asked him if we could stop for a minute at her brother's apartment. Then he pulled out a piece of newsprint from one of his sagging pockets. He read, " 'The family of Lucia Bennett requests a private period of mourning. No visitors, please. Gifts of food and flowers will be appreciated at Fort Leeds Pediatric Hospital, Pavilion for Asthma and Lung Disorders.' "

"Very appropriate," said Dr. Mellors. "I suppose you can write, though."

"I'm going to call," Amy said grimly. "No one can stop me."

"Talk to Delano," Vinnie said. "You'll have to. They have a new number. Unlisted."

He closed his eyes and said he was going to sleep. David said the same and put his head on my shoulder. The inside of the limousine was gloomy because of the tinted windows and the rain, and we all found ourselves nodding. It was a reprieve of some kind. Besides, anything was better than trading insipid comments with Dr. Mellors.

It was over. It was two o'clock, and we would be back on the estate by four. All that was left was seeing Justin.

We were back in the room, changing out of our city clothes and shoes. We had fresh cotton skirts or clean white pants to wear, thanks to Mrs. Shearing. The funeral had washed us out, and we sat quietly on our beds or on the little chairs, reading the papers. We didn't talk. We just spoke occasionally.

"The scuba guy gave another interview. Bragging. Jerk."

"It didn't even rain here. The sun's coming out."

"Rachel? How you holding?"

I was holding without effort. I was waiting for what I knew would be the last of it. It helps to know that, and my heart didn't skip a beat when David came in. He had changed too. Over the white Lacoste shirt his narrow, clever face looked exotic. He wasn't a handsome man, but he was good-looking. People always said we looked well together. They said that about Justin and Tandy, too.

"Everybody ready? The pool; Justin chose it. It has chairs, and there's no way anyone can get close enough to hear us. And he said he wanted to be outside. In the air."

I stood up. I said, "Is he there now?"

"Waiting with Vinnie."

We went down the back stairs and across the lawn. A cool breeze stirred our skirts, our hair. We were girls still, and it was summer still, and the breeze was riffling the surface of the dark green pool.

He stood up when he saw us approaching. The pool was invisible from the house, and one by one we went to him and kissed him. I went last. My kiss was no different from the others. He looked all right to me, but only at first. Then I saw the pupils of his eyes were just tiny dots, and he seemed to be seeing around me and beyond.

"I've got a few tranquilizers in me still," he said. "Just what's left from this morning. Rachel? Sit by me."

It was easier that way. We didn't have to read each other's faces. We sat in a circle of chairs around a table with a glass top. Our feet kept touching, under it.

And then we were all solemn and silent. We had to be; it was just four nights—four nights!—since we'd sat around another table, planning the accident.

Caro seemed the bravest of us all, then. She said later that it was just her sense of sin. It didn't come from the cover-up and the lies thereafter; I guess you'd have to be Catholic to understand that. It came because she had let herself fall in love with Vinnie, a married man, and because she had been a willing helper to my love affair with Justin, who was another.

"Justin," Caro said, "you're saving us all. Sacrificing yourself. I can't bear it. I was just as much at fault as you were."

"Don't, Caro," Vinnie said.

"We don't have much time," she said. "I must say it."

"I know you mean it, too," Justin said, and his voice was calm and measured. "I can't change that for any one of you. But this is the way it's going to be. That's past changing."

"We know," I said. "We all know."

I didn't turn to him; I spoke to everyone, and the air, and the sky. The sky was a deep, ruthless blue, the color of sublime indifference. I said that I was grateful to him too, but that after this I couldn't see him anymore.

"David told me that, last night, while we were waiting for Tandy. I won't try to hold you. I would if I thought I deserved you. I don't."

"It's for your sake. Think how you'll be watched."

"Mine *and* yours. You're young. You can have a beautiful life."

That was all we said, about us. Bitsie's eyes were swimming.

"What can we do. Ever enough for you."

"That's easy. Keep together. Keep the secret. Let the Judge tell you how to handle things in public. He knows what will play and what won't, and you can trust him."

"The drugs," Amy said. "Listen, I'm not trying to make myself important. Only seeing my car on the tube. Knowing it was me bought the pot. *I'm* the most frightened. I know it! Curtis Jeffers, that's his name."

"A loose end, right," Justin said. "The three of us have gone over it. The Judge is out of this one. But we have a plan and we'll act on it and that's all I'm going to tell you, Amy. It'll be all right."

"Okay. That's some relief. Okay. Just so I know. You're going to do something."

"Then there's the big house," I said. "Where we were. I've been worrying about that. If anyone goes around. Snooping. Looking."

"Oh, Rachel," Vinnie said, "you should have mentioned it. It's okay. I went there Sunday morning. Upstairs. Shipshape. No problem."

I sighed; I couldn't get out more than that. Stupid, how that rumpled bed had obsessed me. I saw it again for a moment. I had to choke down a surge of fear and disbelief. I wanted to pound the table with my fist like a bratty Lambert and terrorize them all and curse and shout! I couldn't stand knowing that that was to be our last time, our last, last time.

I took Justin's hand.

193

"Can you tell us?" I managed to say. "What it was like after we left you to go back to the motel? You were all alone. We should never have left you all alone."

David and Vinnie looked at each other. Justin said, "That's just what those two keep saying. Believe me, it wouldn't have made any difference. I could feel it coming, even when we were at the bridge. It felt like I was watching a movie. I was doing things and seeing myself at the same time."

The pressure on my hand came from his hand. The warm fingers over mine were his.

"I noticed my eyes when I shaved this morning. My first shave in three days. I know my eyes look strange. Out of focus. But I see perfectly well. Only *that* night was different. I wasn't seeing normally. Close things looked far away. People looked like dolls. It was the first sign, and I should have told somebody."

"You must have been frightened. Feeling like that."

"Not at all. It seemed . . . interesting."

He never lost that controlled, measured way of speaking. I guessed it was the tranquilizers. He groped for a word now and then. Otherwise, he seemed like the old Justin, and the hand in mine was dry and strong.

Justin said that Mellors called it a "fugue state." Something like shell shock, but different. You can do rational things in that state, but it's as if you've become another personality. And when that state lifts, you can't remember what you did in it.

Justin said that's what we would hear at the inquest. It was the clinical entity that would explain what happened after the accident and why he didn't wake up Vinnie and David, right away, to tell them. The best part of such an explanation was that Mellors really believed in his own diagnosis. "Classic," he called it, and whatever didn't fit he just attributed to the "mild concussion." Of course there had been no such concussion. The lump on his head came from banging into a wall, when he was wrestling with Vinnie and David.

"What's the name for what really happened to me?" Justin asked us. He didn't know, he said. He might never know, and that was our mutual fix, wasn't it? Don't know, can't ask. But he could tell us what it felt like. It felt like a whirlwind. It sucked him up, higher and higher, and he felt . . . like God. A god. Superior to everyone and everything. The only honest man in the world. The only one who knew what really happened. And he had to tell. He had to lecture Vinnie and David, because they were stupid and cowardly, and they were trying to stop him. He *thought* he was lecturing. He was only raving and ranting, trying to convince them that he'd been driving.

He had to convince them. He had to invent the details, like how he'd kept diving for her and nearly drowned himself. And yet at the same time he *knew* he was lying! A part of him knew. The rest of him was in the whirlwind, insisting they hear, insisting they do what he wanted.

But there was another element. He felt they were weak and he was strong. He had to protect them. It was imperative, protecting David and Vinnie. When they pleaded and argued and tried to remind him of what really happened—the bridge, the broom, the car turning over—he didn't think he had to listen. It was that superior feeling. He had contempt for them. He kept telling himself, Poor guys, they're saying these dumb things, and I have to help them; *they're in real trouble and I'm not*.

He never thought of us. He didn't think we were ever at the cottage. Even Lucia wasn't real to him. She was just someone in the car, someone he'd tried to save after driving off the bridge.

Not a fugue state, Justin said. Not amnesia. Just going crazy, somehow. Just being in a place where nothing matters but the sound of your own voice. Weird. Your own world. And all of it staying with you, when you wake up, remembering everything. Remembering to be careful. Remembering to pretend to Mellors that you couldn't talk yet.

I'm not writing down everything he said, but I don't think I've left out what matters. Some other things mattered more. There was the way he kept looking around the table, sweeping his head slowly, from one end of the arc to the other. There was the way his hand didn't move in mine, not a quiver, never tightening, never relaxing. There was the way he seemed to be talking about someone else, and above all there was what he didn't say.

195

He never once said he was sorry. And when he finished, I knew it wasn't the cold wind that made the hair on the nape of my neck stir and stand on end.

This wasn't Justin. Every word out of his mouth was rational and to the point, but it was all flat and unemotional. It was a recitation. It was a drugged recitation from a person who was still in shock, and the enormity of what he'd done, and what it would mean to him, still hadn't registered. He wasn't connecting it yet, not to the gun and the girl in the past, not to the suffering he would endure in the future. That calm was not his own; it only encased him, like a sheath of sculpted marble.

"You'll be all right," he said. "All of you. The inquest will be a challenge, but it will go well, I'm sure of it."

"I'm sure too!" I cried. "We're not worried. We're all . . . a team. Like you and Vinnie and David. And we'll be loyal to one another, all of us, forever and ever."

"That's good to hear," he said. "Well. Getting late. I'd like to spend more time, but they've got me scheduled like the Eastern Shuttle."

It was one of his campaign breakaway lines; it came out in the old way. But for an endless moment we all felt stricken dumb, all caught in the same awareness of a fair, large, heavy-limbed statue that spoke and moved its blue glass eyes.

He had let go of my hand. David came around to pull out his chair and Vinnie helped him to his feet. He loomed. He swayed.

"All that time in bed," he said. "Still a little shaky. You all go ahead. I want a word with Rachel."

Slowly, stiffly, as if unwilling to surpass him, the others moved to the far side of the pool and became a frieze of figures against the sky. The pool was black in the fading light. His hair was honey.

"Rachel? Whatever I can do for you. Anything. Just ask. The others too. Now or later. Jobs, if you need them. Money. For anything: emergency? travel? You might want to get away for a while. No problem, ever. What I have is yours, as long as I live."

"I know," I said. "We know we can depend on you. We always have. I wish I had something to give you in return."

"You just keep well," he said. "I'll need to hear that."

196

"I intend to," I said. "That's a promise."

We were close enough to touch each other, but we didn't. For a minute we just stood side by side, looking at the dark water in the pool. It was magnetizing. Even in broad daylight you couldn't see the bottom or guess how deep it was. And then his words fell like petals on my cheek, because his voice went low and dreamy and I looked up at him because I thought he was going to kiss me. But he didn't.

He said, "Don't worry, Rachel. I'll never take that way out. I'll go on. I'll serve my time."

We walked toward the others. Those were his last words to me. I never saw him alone again.

The six of us got drunk that night. Someone in power, the Judge, or Old Henry, had decided it would do Justin good to get out of the house for dinner, and all the Lamberts and their circle went to the Judge's place in one of the funeral limousines. Its tinted windows ran them safely past the few bored reporters still hanging around outside the gates.

John asked David if we wanted wine with dinner. Yes, we do, David said, but there was only one bottle, and after dinner, with the doors closed, we went on drinking brandy from the decanters on the sideboard. We swaggered over it, like kids with the grown-ups gone. I didn't like it—it burned—but it was available without asking John.

We were talking about the schedule. We were all to leave in the family's cars for home at eleven in the morning. Justin was going back to Seaview and the arraignment, and then he'd go back to the city too.

"We've got a press conference for him at six. He'll read something bland about his 'ordeal.' Four minutes, and six more for Q and A."

We all groaned.

"It won't be a free-for-all. They'll give him a break. No TV, but we'll have our own crew taping. If it comes out okay we'll offer it to the locals for the ten o'clock news. Maybe the big networks will want it too."

"You did all that from here?"

"Not such a ball-buster. I called two guys back from vacation."

"Oh, but how will he do, look, sound?"

"You saw him. What do you think?"

We agreed that he'd be all right for a short talk and some cream-puff questions. But up ahead—

"He'll do what he has to do," Vinnie said gruffly. "He'll keep the flag up. It's decided that the Senate primary is a lost cause, what with all the rumors, the innuendos. But there's the party to consider."

"We don't want to lose control," David said. "He's the head of the party in this state, and the inside opposition has to know he's *not* giving that up. They have to hear it, loud and clear."

I didn't think the brandy was having much effect on me yet. It tasted so lousy I was just sipping. But all at once it was flowing like hot syrup in my blood.

"I want you to shut up, both of you," I said. "The king is dead, long live the king, right? I have to sit here and listen to it! All you care about is propping him up and shoving him out front so he can make it easy for the next guy."

"That's not fair, Rachel," Vinnie muttered. "The next guy could be him, and it's *his* future in politics we're about."

"We're telling it like it is," David said. "You want us to treat you like you can't hear it? Come on, you want that?"

"I don't like your tone of voice."

"I don't like yours."

"You won't like this either. You wanted to know my opinion

199

of him, remember? *My* opinion. He's shattered. He's just stuck together with tranquilizers. It's clear to me that he never got over shooting that girl, and if he didn't break down for one thing, he'd break down later for something else. And unless he gets some *real* help he's got no more future in politics than . . . than the butler."

"You're no psychiatrist."

"I'm not a family fink like Mellors, either! He's a *nothing*, David, you said so yourself. He'll tell them what they want to hear. He won't help Justin deep down, where he needs it."

I poured myself some more brandy. I didn't look to Caro or Amy or Bitsie for backup; I didn't care that David and Vinnie must think I was drunk. I knew I was right, and anyway I trusted them, come whatever.

"Pressure," I said. "Stress. It was going to happen. And I was part of it. No one can tell me different."

"You're saying he's weak," Vinnie said. "That's what it comes down to. Weak."

David poured himself another drink. It was easy to see he wanted to get off the subject; it was easy to see that he and Vinnie had talked it to death.

"She doesn't mean that," David mumbled. "She's talking about his mind."

"His soul," Caro said gently. "Souls aren't weak or strong. Only saved. Or not saved."

"This is worse than the funeral," Bitsie said. "Let's get off it. I don't know what went on in Justin's head, then or now, and I don't give a damn. But I do know the Lamberts always made things easy for him, and so did everyone at this table, and so when things get tough and he falls apart we're all to blame, and if that's no excuse for a drink I don't know what is."

Next to Lucia, Bitsie was our best party girl. We drank, started talking again about the primary, got to arguing. We killed the decanter and then poured half of another into it, for looks. Then we saw one another, each cross-eyed and groggy, and we were afraid the family would come back and find us like that, so we went to our rooms.

"Last time," Bitsie said, falling on her bed. "Last night in kiddie prison."

Amy got the hiccups. Caro monopolized the bathroom sink for washing Vinnie's white sweater. It was filthy, but mostly nylon, so it would dry by morning. Caro was borrowing it because it had gotten chilly and her blouses were all sleeveless tank tops.

I fell asleep without remembering why Caro had no sweater of her own to wear. The brandy had stuffed my head with cotton, and the cotton smothered every unpleasant thought. I suppose, for those hours, I was living in the world Justin now lived in, a padded world where there were no sharp corners, no hard edges, no grim connections. Drunk as I was, I pitied him. The next day he would stand before a sympathetic judge and take his sympathetic sentence and go home, read a speech, have dinner, sleep. He'd go on like that for a while; Tandy and the Lamberts would see to it. The motions would be painless. Work, go home, eat, sleep. He'd have days like that. Then little by little they'd take him off whatever it was that soothed and buffered and walled him in.

And then he would know. And wake up in hell.

We had our city clothes on for that last interview with the Judge. There was a real fire in the marble fireplace, burning low against the cold snap and taking the chill out of the quilted leather sofa. No matter how vividly I remember other details of the Lambert estate—the manicured woodland, the uniformed servants, the antique silver that Old Henry collected and that was used even at breakfast—nothing resonates quite like the memory of a morning fire in a marble fireplace in the middle of August.

But the house seemed smaller. Justin had left for Seaview with Tandy, David, Vinnie, and Delano, and all the stretch and tension had gone with them. Outside the library window the sky was rinsed pale blue and everything looked clear to us, including the Judge. We weren't afraid of him anymore. If his manner had all the old silkiness, it was starched silk now, crisp and matter-of-fact. Point one: he was our lawyer. Point two: he was and he wasn't.

"Your legal fees will be paid by the Lamberts, but not to my firm. Delano and Delano will represent the Governor. To avoid the appearance of a conflict of interest, we'll meet in the offices of Shaw, Ross. Officially, they'll represent you. Unofficially, I'll be in charge.

"I'll give you two numbers to call in any contingency: one to my home, one to a private line in Delano's office. Don't use the office switchboard, ever. Don't use the switchboards in your own offices, either. I suggest you get in the habit of phoning one another at your homes only. I suggest, most strongly, that you not be seen together in public, all four of you, ever. That's important. Not even three of you. Twos. No more than that.

"I will only call you at your home numbers. On Monday, I'll call to set up hours for the next seven Saturdays. The inquest is set: October eleventh. Seven sessions on Saturday mornings, in the offices of Shaw, Ross, Tenth and Broad. Please keep those Saturdays free. Only Delano and I will be present, and together we'll walk you through every step of the inquest. You'll be bored, I assure you, after the first few times. You'll think I'm a prosy old fool, nattering away at the same points. I'm used to it. Careful people are often boring.

"Remember that an inquest is not an adversary proceeding. It's entirely the DA's show, and it's the judge on the bench, not your own lawyer, who can interrupt, ask questions, bring up his own objections. A good judge can keep the DA from running off at the mouth or grandstanding for the record. As yet, we don't know who the judge will be. We can only hope we get a fair one.

"Well. I suppose you're dreading the real world—not that this isn't real!—I mean your own worlds, and people, and questions. Perhaps I can be of some help there. Perhaps I can give you an inkling of what you'll have to put up with and how you can deal with it. May I try?"

He was a courtier himself, the Judge, skilled in a thousand shades of deference, even the minimum due to us. But perhaps it wasn't a minimum? We *were* important. I remembered Vinnie, glaring at us on the beach that day, expecting someone to get hysterical, cry, blow it.

Girls.

"Please give us your suggestions," I said. "We *are* worried. About what to say."

He took each possibility in turn: the press, the office, party people, friends, family members—all of them, down to the last anonymous phone-caller or piece of nasty mail. He was sorry how soon we'd find it out: there were people out there with nothing better to do but make their drab lives more exciting by trying to make contact with people like us.

"The Governor's statement is all we know about the accident."

"It's a tragedy. She was a wonderful person."

"This is harassment. If you call me again, I will have the call traced by the police."

"With the inquest coming up, I've been warned not to discuss even small details. That's the law, even if I don't understand it."

We were totally absorbed, listening, memorizing. The pat phrases would be our talismans, and we knew that the more we said them, the easier it would get.

"I suppose," the Judge said, "that someday you'll want to do something in your friend's memory. I did that myself once, for a friend who died in the war, World War Two. With a couple of other men, I set up a little fund in his name at his college. Not a lot of money. It just threw off a few hundred a year, for a prize. Philosophy. A philosophy prize. He was a philosopher."

A kind of happiness filled us. We had never thought of that. It would be something to do.

"That's a great idea," I said. "We could do it in her high school. A fund? That sounds like a lot of money."

"Well, it doesn't have to be," said the Judge. "It could be a onetime thing. You ask people to subscribe. Dedicate it."

I heard Amy whisper, "Asthma."

"Let's give something to a hospital for asthmatics," I said. "Hospitals put up plaques, I've seen them."

"Yes indeed," said the Judge. "That might be better. Poor child. I suppose you could say it was asthma, really, that caused her death."

"You could," I said.

There was a silence that cracked and snapped like the logs burning in the fireplace, and then there was the Judge, not sitting on the desk anymore but pacing in front of us, lean as a whippet, and pointing to us, pointing with his long thin forefinger.

"You won't make it, you know," he said quietly. "I don't

203

mean the inquest. I mean after. You're so damnably young, and you think this is the hardest life gets. Believe me, it gets harder. A conspiracy is only as strong as its weakest link. One day one of you will find life too hard. And break."

It was like a wave of ice-cold water, swift, stunning. We were thinking of what we'd do for Lucia's memory and we weren't ready and he knew it, slick whippet, spinning, pointing, making us cower.

And his voice, always clear, soft or loud, high or low, every syllable piercing.

"Think of the danger you're in! Imagine one of you coming forward, for God knows what reason! The heart has reasons. Guilt. Fear. Madness! A mind turned against itself like a weapon of vengeance. Blind to consequence! Deaf to family, friendship, self-interest. You know what happened to Justin. Can you sit there and truly believe it could never happen to *you*?

"I can protect you against that possibility. I know the safeguards a secret needs. There are ways. Instruments. Legal instruments that will bind you more surely, more tightly, than mere promises. Tell me what really happened at Lighthouse Point. I will not betray you. And you will be really safe, safe now and safe in the future from the one who may bring you all to ruin."

I thought, for many years, that it must have cost him a lot to say those things. I thought of him as overmastered, for once, by his curiosity and his thwarted will, and I saw his baffled brilliance come to this: he was begging to hear the truth, not for our sake but his own.

But I'm older now. Getting older means you learn the price, and I see now that his plea, with its flimsy promise of protection, cost him nothing. He just knew it was time to turn over the dice, so he took a final throw, hoping for a lucky seven.

Back then it made me feel sorry for him. I even believed he wouldn't betray us. And I said, "I'm not speaking for anyone but myself now. I think you're wonderful. I think you're the best friend Justin could have, and the best friend we could have in this. I'd like to kiss you."

That's when Bitsie leaped up, crying, "Blondes first!" We all kissed him; for a moment we clustered around him and saw his assurance turn into reddened confusion. Then I took one arm and Bitsie took the other and we went into lunch.

I don't think Amy was right, saying that the Judge just ate veal and looked sad and sat there, planning the phone taps. I think he really was sad. I think he thought up the phone taps later.

23

It would always be a matter of pride to us how little those phone taps mattered. Before a week passed—a week of being back in the city—we had decided never to discuss anything about Lighthouse Point on *any* phone, including our own. The Judge himself had started it, with his warning about switchboards, and with Bitsie and me living together, and Amy and Caro the same, it seemed like a good idea to go whole hog.

We set up a schedule: Tuesday and Thursday nights at our place, for dinner together. That, plus the Saturday hours in the Judge's office, would give us all the time we needed to talk about it.

We told David and Vinnie, Don't call. Just come, if you want, Tuesdays and Thursdays. They came often; they needed it as much as we did.

Vinnie found the tap in our house. We were all sitting

around waiting for the spaghetti water to boil, and David was telling us how well Justin was doing. Vinnie said he had to call Brenda.

"Holy shit," we heard him mutter at the desk. He'd recognized the click. We thought he'd gone bananas, shaking the phone and yelling for a screwdriver. He pried the thing out of the receiver.

Not a word, we said proudly, not a word; we made a rule.

It had to be the Judge, we decided, and Old Henry had to know too. Why leave a stone unturned when you have the means to overturn mountains? Lambertland, Bitsie reminded us, and from then on that's what we all called it, and we laughed and we marveled at their nerve, their quickness. Anger and outrage would have been beside the point, and what does that show about us, except how far we'd slipped into their circle? We knew by now that they didn't pull strings; they pulled ropes, hawsers, cables made of steel and gold, and the Judge had a smile on his face and a spring in his step when he told us the name of the magistrate who would most probably be assigned to the inquest.

"A very fair fellow." The Judge beamed. "It's just on the grapevine, but let's hope it turns out to be fact. We'll consider ourselves lucky."

Some grapevine. Some lucky. But the Judge was smiling, and we did too.

That Tuesday sent Vinnie and David running to Caro and Amy's place to check their phone. It probably wasn't tapped; with six girls sharing it, it must have looked like a loser, and unnecessary too. The phone in the row house would do for all four of *us*. But how about Vinnie's and David's?

Vinnie was shrugging into his raincoat; he said there was no way they'd try it on him or David.

"Oh, really," I said sarcastically. "You're so damn sure. Just us, right? It wouldn't be honorable, on you and David."

"Something like that," he said, and he was serious too.

It was a grave, shaken Murph Steuben who greeted me when I came in to work that first Friday morning. I had thought, naïvely, that the five or six days that had elapsed since the accident would

207

be in our favor; people would have had all that time to talk the subject into the ground. But a big scandal doesn't work that way. The first spate of sensational news is like a bomb, exploding; it pulls the public into ground zero; the blare is too deafening for speculation. The real talk comes later. My indolent, amiable old pol of a boss was now in the thick of it, and when he saw me his eyes filled with tears. He led me into his office and shut the door.

"It's awful, Rachel. What they're saying about him. To me, and I was at his christening!"

"Vinnie told us. Well, not all. Just a few things, and they were bad enough."

Murph told me some more. It helped, hearing them from someone so faithful to Justin who also respected me. I sat in front of Murph's battered old desk feeling more at home than I had the night before, in my own house. I worked here. I had an identity of my own. I was a team player, good with people, fair with num- bers . . . a responsible, ambitious, twenty-six-year-old person, not a girl.

"They're talking booze, they're talking blondes, they're even saying that maybe he could have saved her if he'd kept his head and gone for help."

"Sure," I said bitterly. "On what's practically a desert island. When it would have taken him God knows how long, maybe fifteen minutes, to get back to the house."

"The bridge isn't near the house?"

"Nowhere near. Not a phone, not any other house. It's all wild. Even the lighthouse isn't working. I can't believe people are talking about calling the Coast Guard! Don't they know the Coast Guard turned the lighthouse over to Parks and Recreation a million years ago?"

"They'll get to know it," Murph said grimly. "I've got five people to call and tell, and they'll tell twenty-five others."

"Do what you can. Oh, Murph. It looks bad, it *is* bad, and there's no way to stop people from thinking it was even worse. It's the end of him, isn't it?"

"In this state? It doesn't have to be. He's a Lambert. If it wasn't so close to the Senate primary—"

"He'll finish the term. God knows what he'll do after that. The next governor—"

"Could be Matty Ferguson," Murph said. "Oh, yeah. Matty. I wonder how many jobs a sixty-year-old golfer can get. I'm going to be out on my ass."

"Me too, then. So we've got a year or two. Murph? I'm going to work. We're going to sell Toyota on the Glens Cove location. Watch."

"Work, darling. It's the best thing of all. I'm kind of sorry I missed learning how."

There wasn't much of summer left. The linen suits and blouses went to the back of the closet, and before Labor Day came the big wrap-up stories in *Time* and *Newsweek*. Our pictures came out sharp and clear on those shiny pages, and under my constant anxiety about Justin a new worry stirred: would someone see my face as Robin White's? And would that someone want to let the world know?

But the letter with the Dover postmark was only from Sonya Warshowsky, my old guidance counselor, and it said she was thinking of me, and if I needed help she was still at the same address. I got notes from old friends in New York, and these notes were kind too; I answered them the day they arrived. All of us learned the same lesson: the people who care about you wish you well, and the rest don't matter anyway.

I had to be seen a lot with David. We went out to dinner in popular places, and the fake ruby on my third finger left hand would shine in the candlelight like a drop of port wine. David would tell me about Justin. He was working well this week, much better than last. He was talkative yesterday, kind of subdued today. He'd asked about me or he hadn't; he was shrugging off the rumors or depressed by them. Sometimes I would press the real diamond ring hidden by my silk shirt, so hard it would bite into my skin. Sometimes David would see my expression and murmur, "Easy, Rachel. Calm down." He thought it was worry. It was grief, a grief that would well up inside me like nausea, so that I'd grimace and twist my mouth. Bitsie asked me, nicely, to stifle the tic, so I learned to clench my teeth until the feeling went away.

Reporters pestered us; photographers hung outside our offices at quitting time, taking pictures that seldom ran. There were stares and whispers, but the inquest up ahead was a focus for us, a promise. Over, we kept telling one another, it's almost over. And our sessions with the Judge worked to make us lose that sense of awful expectation—would anything new come up?—that kept us, awake and asleep, off balance.

There was only what we learned about Lucia. That was bad.

At our first meeting with the Judge in the Shaw, Ross office, the Judge told us that Lucia's room would be sealed tight in a matter of days. The district attorney's office had made some procedural errors in filing for the inquest, or else the room would have been sealed long before.

"There's no key," Caro said. "Besides, the door to that room barely shuts, much less locks."

"You live in the same house, I take it," the Judge said. He consulted some notes. "And Amy too. Well, the procedure doesn't depend on keys. Keys can be duplicated. The deputy comes with tape and wax and state seals and closes the door, the windows. If the inquest ever leads the court to think there's significant evidence in that room, there won't be any chance of its being tampered with."

"It's a tiny room," Amy said. "And a huge mess, anyway. She never threw anything out. She had Christmas cards from the year she moved in."

"My God," Bitsie said. "I wrote her two letters from Puerto Rico, and do I want *them* back. They're from the time I went there with you-know-who."

Bitsie made some circular motions with her index finger, all around her head. I suppose the Judge thought she was referring to some deranged companion, but we knew she meant Ravi, her old boyfriend, who was sane but wore turbans.

"As your counsel," the Judge said, "I must warn you not to enter Lucia's room now. There are two other young women living in the house? Best to avoid even the appearance of an impropriety."

Bitsie set her jaw. The minute we were out on the steamy sidewalk in front of the Shaw, Ross office she said she was going straight to Lucia's room and grab those letters.

"No, you're not," Caro said. "You heard what the Judge said."

210

"You bet I heard," Bitsie said. "He said I had like two days to get my letters out. That's what he *really* was telling us. About anything in that room that could be used against her or us or the Lamberts. Call a cab, Caro, I'll treat."

The four of us argued for a while and finally agreed: the next day was Sunday, perfect timing, when Amy and Caro's two other roommates in the house would be gone and we certainly wouldn't have to worry about anyone coming around on official business. We'd all meet in Lucia's room and if Caro disapproved so much—Bitsie said—she could stay downstairs and pretend she didn't know what we were doing.

That was all Caro needed. When Bitsie and I got to the house, we found her in Lucia's room, sitting on the bed, crying.

"It's only that I've been dreading this for days," she said. "It's like she'll walk in, any minute."

"And trip over something and fall on her kiester," I said. Lucia's little room had to be seen to be believed. It always looked like it had been burgled by poltergeists. Shoes booby-trapped the rug; every drawer was open; the closet would rain lethal boxes, ski poles, and tennis balls on anyone dumb enough to open it, looking for clothes. Her clothes were on the bed, the chair, and the floor.

The letters were under the bed, in a cookie tin. Bitsie found her own scrawls from Puerto Rico and breathed a great sigh and then said, "Look here. I didn't know she kept a diary."

The cookie tin also held a little book with a tooled-leather cover and a broken lock.

"Just like her." Amy sighed. "I'll bet she lost the key the first day. Put it back, Bitsie. Or maybe throw it away. I keep a diary myself. I couldn't bear to let anyone else read it."

"There might be nice things in it. She used to write poetry. Things her brother would like to read someday."

"If she had a sister, yes. Not a brother. I vote we deep-six it. That's what I'd want done with mine."

"A brother could treasure something loving. We should leave it for him."

"A diary. There could be things about us too. Oh, hell, put it away for now."

211

"We don't have time. We have to decide. People from the DA's office could come tomorrow to seal this room up."

It was raining. The ceiling fixture and the rickety bridge lamp didn't add much to the gray light coming through the window. The general mess looked simply defeating, and none of us wanted to stay in it anymore or sort it through. But there was the diary.

"Her last thoughts could be in there. I want to read them. Maybe it's wrong, but I do."

"She might have had a premonition? I believe in that."

"What matters is her privacy, damn it! Screw premonitions; if she had any, they didn't do her any good."

I don't remember, now, who was on what side of which issue. We went back and forth, as we always did, arguing, changing sides, more or less backing into the kind of consensus that never quite gets spelled out, but that everybody goes along with. I remember that Caro had hold of the book and she was riffling through it with one finger.

"August eleventh. The last entry. The day before we left. I feel like I'm doing something wrong."

"Oh, read it, Caro. It drives me nuts when you get so scrupulous! *That* day only. Just that."

I felt the narrow, untidy room enclosing me like a crypt. We were all on edge, oppressed by the disorder and the stale-smelling dust that we'd stirred up by poking around under the bed. Her room was dead too. Caro started reading.

" 'I stick to my vow. I must never write his name. But I'll see him Saturday and I'll want him to notice me, touch me, hug me. And he'll never guess what I feel! I feel sixteen. I feel like last Christmas. I know I don't have a chance even though I know he thinks I'm pretty. He always says that to me. Pretty doesn't matter. He has beauty, and he hardly knows I'm alive. That doesn't matter either because I love him enough for two. His mouth on mine. I can still feel it after all these months. He tasted me. Sucked on me. He crushed me in his arms. I could feel my legs coming apart. No one ever made me feel that way before. I love him!!! Now & forever. Till tomorrow, my sacred, secret love.' "

212

When Caro finished reading, we just stood there, gaping at one another. And then we had to ask.

"Vinnie?"

"David?"

"Justin?"

My mouth was so dry I couldn't speak. I knew it was Justin. I remembered Lucia watching us, behind her magazine, that Saturday afternoon out on the lawn with the big house behind it. This time I saw passion in her smile. And if Justin and I never . . . if she went on loving him . . .

"Of course it was Justin," Bitsie was saying impatiently. "Vinnie wasn't her type, married or not. David was available."

"She meant Rachel," Amy said. "She meant that Rachel was the beauty and she was just pretty."

"Give me that," Bitsie said, but she didn't wait for Caro to give it to her. She reached and grabbed. "Kiss. Christmas. Shit, it starts with New Year's."

"Sure," Amy said. "The Christmas statehouse party. That five-to-seven; we all dropped in. It was still going at nine. Everybody whooping it up and drunk as skunks when Justin arrived. He kissed all of us."

I tried to laugh. "Even me."

"That had to be it. She says it. 'Even after all these months.' "

"We'll see about that," Bitsie said grimly. She handed me the book. "This is for Rachel. She should read it. We'll go downstairs."

I sat down on the bed. I had put my hand out. It was automatic; I was dazed. If Bitsie had told me to fling the diary through the window I would have done that too. I riffled through the pages. More than half were blank and most had only a few lines on them. Lucia hadn't liked writing any more than she liked reading.

"This won't take long," I said, and they left.

I stayed in Lucia's room for just fifteen minutes, and even so I read everything twice. There was poetry about love and vows and walking alone in the rain. There were entries that said only two words: SAW HIM. There was a two-page description of a tour she'd given some senior citizens, and how HE had passed by in

213

the rotunda and joined the tour and taken everyone back to his office. There were many entries about what she was wearing on pages marked with a big asterisk and exclamation points and the phrase MORE COMPS! Compliments.

One page had an imaginary letter to him. The inspiration was Barry Manilow. *My darling*, it started. *You will never receive this. As seagulls fly to the sun and never reach it, so do I . . . .*

That's all there was. The vow never to write his name was pathetic: anyone old enough to read would have known it was the Governor. But in the rest of it—in every babyish capital and dopey verse—there was the shock of recognition. This was how I had felt about him when I came down from New York. This was the hapless infatuation I had once carried around in secret, like an invisible, intoxicating bouquet.

I went downstairs and threw the book on the kitchen table. The three of them were sitting around it as if they were waiting for a séance to start. It was nearly noon, early for a wine bottle on the table and four glasses. Bitsie pushed one at me.

"Take a drink. What's in it?"

"Nothing you'd call another fact. See for yourself. She wrote down every time he talked to her. A lot of poetry. But anyone would know it was Justin. She even described his looks. She pasted in his horoscope on his birthday! We have to get rid of it. Burn it or something."

"You can't burn leather," Amy said. "Listen, I read this somewhere. You put it in water till the ink runs. Then it's safe for the garbage."

Caro got a dishpan full of hot water and put the book in. For a minute we all looked at the water starting to swirl thin lines of dye. I realized that I was covered with cold sweat and that Caro was so pale her freckles looked like dabs of milk chocolate. Dear God, what a thing for the DA to get his hands on! Dear, merciful God, to let us find danger and let us dissolve it. I think even Amy thought that. Then we sat there for a while, saying what had to be said.

Forget love, we said. Forget crushes and feeling sixteen. All that was bullshit and more bullshit because love was nothing compared to bad luck and dumb pride, and any truth about that fatal

214

Saturday had to include the fact that Lucia couldn't bear looking less than perfect in Justin's eyes. She couldn't deal with having him know that she was sick and getting sicker. So was it on his account that she'd overdone the steroids to hide the wheezing? Was it for him she'd stayed at Lighthouse Point, waiting for the next pill to kick in?

Did she die for someone who hardly knew she was alive?

These things weren't hard to say. But there was a dull weight on my chest where other things lay unspoken. And it hurt when Caro tried to lift it.

"He didn't encourage her," Caro said. "We'd have known. Amy and I, we lived with her; we'd have known."

"One wet kiss," Amy said. "He was half crocked, like the rest of us. Big deal."

"I wouldn't be so sure," Bitsie said.

"But this is terrible," I heard myself say, feeling drunk already on one glass of wine. "I don't even feel sorry for her. And I know I should."

"You should stop feeling sorry for everybody," Bitsie said. "I don't mean just for Lucia. Justin too. What a pair, him and her. What a pair of fuck-ups."

"That's harsh, Bitsie. Why do you make yourself sound like such a bitch?"

"I am a bitch," Bitsie said. "It's what they teach you in boarding school. And you're through with him, Rachel, you promised, so why shouldn't I say what's true? Justin Lambert wants everyone to love him, and I mean he turns on the charm for every stray dog and parking attendant. He teases and flirts with the goddam world, so why not her too?"

"That's just politics. Stroking for votes."

"It's his life. Charming people. Saying what they want to hear. He's been a star for so long, he's all Hollywood."

"Oh, shit," Amy said. "Dry up, Bitsie. Every time he sees me he says I ought to get contacts and show off my beautiful eyes. Do I make a thing out of it?"

"If you wanted him you would; that's my point."

"Listen, the diary explains one thing, anyway. Why did she stay on and on in that lousy job? She got to see him, that's why."

215

"Rachel's read it all. It wasn't that much."

"She was so gone on him it was enough. Better than nothing."

"I'm like stunned. I can't believe Caro and I didn't guess she was so nuts about him."

"I didn't think she had it in her. To be so secretive."

"It was fantasy, that's why. Like a crush on a movie star. She was probably a little ashamed of it. And then there was Rachel—"

They were all talking at once, but suddenly they stopped, stricken, because I was there, not talking, only looking at the pan full of inky water.

"Oh, Rachel," Caro said. "Please. Don't look like that. A crush. A dumb crush."

To say what was on my mind had not yet become a habit. I'd had too many years of hiding things. To be open and honest with people I liked was a luxury I was just learning to afford. I said, "But it's something to think about, right? And my opinion isn't worth any more than one of yours. I don't think he came on to her. But believe it or not, all it does is remind me—"

There was the sound of shoes on the wooden porch. Men's shoes. No one was expected, so Bitsie leapt to her feet and shoved the dishpan in the oven and Amy went to open the door.

"I have a court order, miss," we heard a man say. "Sorry to bother you on Sunday. Our section's working overtime."

"Well, hand it here and you just stand there while I read what it says," we heard Amy say loudly. Caro and I had time to clear away the wine and glasses, and then we all came out on the porch while he explained what he had to do with the tape. Then Caro and Amy took him upstairs and Bitsie took the pan out of the oven and wrapped up the diary in aluminum foil and put it in the garbage pail. Then she had to stand at the sink for a while to scrub the dye off her hands.

"That's that," she said. "So come on. You were saying, before the interruption, it reminded you . . . ?"

"Give me a break, Bitsie. This is no fun."

"Reminded you of what?"

"Of what Justin told me. After the first time. The first time I slept with him. The first time he told me he loved me."

"When was that? Where? I've forgotten."

"Three years ago next week. In that upstate hotel. It was morning. Still dark. He was tiptoeing around my room, getting dressed, and I was in bed watching him."

"What did he say?"

"He said he would never have had the nerve to tell me he loved me if he hadn't guessed how I felt about him. You and I were already roommates and you didn't guess, did you?"

"No. I didn't have a clue back then."

"I could hide it from you. Not from him. I can't help being reminded."

"So be reminded. Sure he knew. About *you*. About *her*. About everyone he hooks. So think of her swooning every time he was in sight. And him getting off on it. Telling her how cute she is, how pretty, what a heartbreaker. Encouraging her . . . he wouldn't think twice about it! He can't help being what he is."

"Shut up, Bitsie. I don't need this."

"You need to stop idolizing him. He cheated on his wife, didn't he? He could cheat on you."

"Never. Even if he did, I'd still love him."

"Stop that too. Please, Rachel. Use this! Get mad. Get a little goddam angry."

I got up to make coffee. I knew there was no point in trying to argue with Bitsie. She was in one of her kick-the-cat moods, lashing out at everybody. She was trashing Justin, and she was an inch away from trashing Lucia as a tricky little bitch. Hot pants. Hanging around the statehouse with mouth wide open, always bouncing, hair, tits, a born tease, and him teasing back; the mutual massaging, yes, he liked it, it was his nature. . . .

Maybe those were Bitsie's thoughts. But they were in my head and I knew I owned them. I just didn't know what to do with them then, except bury them six feet under with everything else that was dead, ruined, over.

"Drink some coffee," I said. "You're getting sloshed. You

217

think if you dump on him you'll help me somehow. I'm sorry, but it's not working."

"You're sorry for living," she muttered, but she shut up.

The days before the inquest went by slowly, slowly, and still the ominous question mark named Curtis Jeffers had no answer. Amy had to see him too; at least once a day Curtis would stroll through her newsroom collecting copy or distributing mail. She'd catch him staring at her or winking, or at least she thought he did; just catching the smart slap of his Bally mocs coming down the aisle could give her the shakes. She ate badly; she needed pills to sleep.

One of the editors on the paper, half drunk and only half joking, promised Amy that if she told him the whole story, he'd split the Pulitzer Prize with her. Amy had just walked away without answering; she didn't even feel insulted; all she could think of— she told us later—was what *Curtis* could tell a reporter, and for much less money.

"Justin promised," she'd moan. "He said they had a plan for making sure of Curtis. Why haven't they done anything?"

"Maybe it's too early," we'd answer. "Vinnie said you shouldn't worry, just last week. David says it'll be all right."

"I have this pain," Amy said. "Like someone's been stapling my stomach."

Her face had gotten so thin the horn-rims hid half of it. We were all worried about her. I told her I was seeing David for dinner, and now that it was nearly a month since the accident I was going to demand either some action or some explanation. Or was a month's silence on the young man's part proof positive that we didn't have to worry? For sleepless, shaking Amy, it wasn't any proof at all. It was as if she had delegated herself to do all the worrying for the four of us.

I attacked David the minute we sat down in the restaurant. What were they waiting for? Or were they just conning Amy, trying to calm her down because there was no plan and no way in the world of approaching Curtis without harming ourselves?

"It's all done already." David sighed. "Two weeks ago Friday. No, Thursday. I'm pretty sure we're home free."

"Two weeks ago!" I cried. "And you didn't tell us? How did you do it? What was the plan?"

David picked up my hand and examined it as if it were something weird that the waiter had brought with the hors d'oeuvres. He said morosely, "The plan had two parts. This is part two. It's where you ask about part one, and I say forget it, it's over, the details aren't important, and I hear they do Veal Oscar nicely here."

"You have surely suffered some massive blow to your common sense. The details *are* important. To Amy, particularly. Have you seen her lately? She weighs ninety pounds."

"I've reassured her and so has Vinnie, and it's her problem, not trusting us. Yours too, lady. It's all to your benefit, not knowing too much. So back off. Try feeling grateful. Try saying thank you."

"For being treated like an idiot? All right, you did something not quite kosher, right? Money? To him? God, David, I'd expect this goofball paternalism from Vinnie and Justin. Not from you."

We argued all through dinner. But I could sense, behind his stubbornness, a barely suppressed excitement and a real hint of swagger. Oh, they'd done something neat. And he wanted to tell me as much as I wanted to know, and so together we wore away at his resolve until just a face-saving minimum was left.

"Remember," David said finally, "how we used to do it? Suppose this. Suppose that. Just spitballing, throwing ideas at the wall, starting every sentence, with 'I know this sounds stupid, but here goes anyway.'"

"I understand," I said. "A scenario. A sketch. One out of hundreds of brainstorms. Okay. So suppose. . . ."

Suppose, David said, they waited to make their move until Curtis went on the late shift, leaving the newspaper office at two in the morning. Suppose two men, white men, were waiting on the sidewalk for him. They always go in twos; that's on every cop show. Suppose they were real cops, or ex-cops, or even good actors; it didn't matter. If you have money and power and a long list of people who owe you a favor, you can find what you need.

"Mr. Jeffers? Police. Like to talk to you."

Or Special Narcotics. Or T-men, or FBI. Whatever went best with a badge flashed for a second in dim streetlight at a frightened boy.

They'd ask him to talk in their car. A friendly chat, a note-

219

book to consult. We know you're dealing, they might say. We have a list of your customers right here. You go to school at State. Your scholarship's worth so much. And mother's maiden name and brothers' ages and all kinds of stuff they could get from Personnel with the right phone call.

They'd scare him to death, wouldn't they? Then they'd ask him to make a deal, even scarier. Inform. Name his contacts, maybe set up a meet. They'd tell him to think it over, and we'll be in touch.

Only the kid would never see them again. And he'd thank God for it. If he'd ever had any idea of coming forward with Amy's name, or using it to extort money from her, he'd drop it flat. He'd think the law already knew all about Amy, one of the customers on the "list." He'd keep quiet. He'd even quit pushing, maybe. Hadn't Amy once said—and didn't it seem like a hundred years ago?—that her dealer had enough cashmere sweaters to last him a lifetime?

Amy went mildly manic when I gave her the news. Between guilt and fear, she'd spent a month conjuring up the image of a certified pusher who would rise at the inquest to point her out. Even so, she didn't start to sleep normally until the Judge got the final list of witnesses.

But we all had our private haunts and goblin nightmares of the inquest courtroom. Caro dreamed of her blue sweater waving wet arms around Lucia's head and Bitsie was nagged by a three-dollar cake pan she'd left in the cottage, for a maid to notice, maybe, and suspect. And I, of course, had Justin, who would have to testify, and who could be kept—no matter by how friendly a magistrate—in the witness seat for hours or even days. He could break out of that marble sheath. He could break down in front of everyone. And the very thought of any further humiliation for him made me want to weep.

"Remember what I said about an inquest," the Judge told us. "I'll have no standing in the courtroom, even though I'll have a seat up front. Justin will give his testimony first, and the DA may take a few hours, or even days, on it. The presiding judge can ask questions too. But you won't see Justin or hear him. You won't be in the courtroom with him. In fact, the four of you won't be seen together in Seaview till the last possible moment. I don't want to set you up for the press."

As the eldest of Lucia's housemates, Caro was to testify first, right after Justin. The Judge would send a car to the city for her, when Justin began testifying. She'd be at the shore and on hand, no matter how short Justin's time was. The rest of us would drive down in two cars as soon as Caro was called to the stand.

"David and Vinnie?"

"Afterward. It's not manners. In this state the degree of relationship to the victim determines the precedence."

He added, rather wryly, "Being with the victim at the time of death is a prime relationship."

The victim. Months later, when the inquest transcript was released, I saw how often that word was used. Or "the deceased." Or "the passenger," "your patient," "your friend," "former resident"—it was as if they'd lost her name. It reduced her, but it helped us. We all felt the same in that courtroom. It was surgery, and the cold legalisms were anesthetic.

The ocean winds, still full of sun and salt, blew our skirts around as we each went in and out of the courthouse, and the reporters would wave and whistle. They were bored; the press had no entry to the proceedings inside. "Good luck, gorgeous!" they would call; it sounded friendly but the Judge had warned us.

"You can cry," he'd told us. "You can cry, faint, insult the bailiff's mother if you want to. But for God's sake, don't let them catch you smiling."

And still it wasn't over. The presiding judge wrote a two-page opinion, finding no malice or negligence or reason to question death by drowning. But he didn't release it for two weeks, and we were dizzy with suspense, no matter how often we were told it had gone just fine. Then David called me with the news.

The first thing I said was, "How did Justin take it?"

"Stoic. Not up, not down. He put up a good front for Tandy and the kids. Very hearty. But I could tell."

"It's not over for him. God knows when it will be."

"Same deal for all of us. We just have to move off it."

"I'm going to try. David? How is he?"

"Like I said. Stoic. He's working hard, though. He's keeping the party in line."

"That's good. Tell him I'm doing fine."

"I will. You are. Oh, I forgot. When he heard? Tandy was right there so he couldn't say much. He just said, 'Thank you, David. Thank the girls, too.'"

"Thank the girls," I repeated. And when I hung up I had to keep saying to myself that Tandy had been right there, and the children too, and how could I expect some special message, meant just for me? It was stupid to have hoped for that. Stupid. Nuts. Unrealistic.

But it broke my heart anyway. I suppose one occasion is as good as another, for that.

That was a hard year. We tried to take up our ordinary lives again, but we floundered and gasped, like divers pulled too suddenly to the surface. Pressure can break you; pressure can hold you together. Once the inquest was over, and we said our good-byes to the Judge, we had our license for impulse, our fools' freedom.

One day Amy announced she was moving back to Chicago. The job wasn't better—it turned out to be much worse—but at least it was elsewhere. One night Caro said she was thinking of signing up for another hitch in the Peace Corps, and she left, going back to Brazil and the first glimmerings of her real vocation. One morning Bitsie sat in front of me eating corn flakes, laughing and crying between mouthfuls and sometimes covering her ears to keep from hearing me.

"I don't want your advice, I know what I'm doing," she said, and later that week she eloped with a man she'd only known for six weeks. The marriage didn't last six months.

I saw them go, one by one, and in spite of the loss I didn't blame them. I wished I could do something too. For all my brave talk about work, I hadn't realized what I'd feel like without Justin. Everything dimmed. Nothing looked worth fighting for. When we lost out on the Japanese contract, I knew a kind of defeat that frightened me. I couldn't make myself care.

Yet I went on clinging like a barnacle to the shell of my house and following Justin's fortunes through the press, and David, and Murph. It was a secondhand existence; my dull, sad letters to Caro and Amy and my calls to Bitsie brought back worried responses. Sell the house, they said. Get out. Go somewhere, it's a big country; New York, you have friends there.

I couldn't, yet. The Christmas holidays came and went, and I had the experience of spending Christmas day at Vinnie's, a cozy family dinner, with David at my side and Brenda, Vinnie's wife, trying to be amiable. She was a nice quiet woman without a dissembling bone in her body, and I could see she'd invited me for Vinnie's sake, over her suspicions, her doubts, and her anger. That night, after he took me home, I asked David how much my house was worth.

"Prices are going through the roof here," David said. "You've got the corner, with garage. I'll bet you can get two hundred thousand."

"Wow. I never asked Justin. What did he pay?"

"Less than a hundred."

"If I sell, I'll give him back the difference."

"If you try that, I'll have you certified. What's the matter with you, Rachel? He doesn't need it. He'll sign it over to one of Tandy's Junior League charities. You're just depressed. You should see a shrink."

"No shrinks. None of us can afford to take that kind of chance. All right. Two hundred thousand. What's the tax on that? Must be a lot."

"Not so bad if you reinvest in another place to live."

"I'll think about it," I said. "I might buy something in New York. I'm thinking about that too."

"I'll miss you. But it's not a bad idea."

224

"I'll miss you too. Clean sweep. I don't know what else to do. It's awful here."

"Oh, Rachel. I know you're miserable. And yet we've been so lucky!"

"I keep reminding myself. It's no help, is it?"

"Not really. I'll find you an agent. It was nice at Vinnie's, wasn't it?"

"Not really. Brenda hates me. I represent it to her."

"I'll find you an agent. Call you tomorrow on it."

"Thanks. I have to get started. I can't live the rest of my life at a funeral."

I remember the bitter cold that night, sitting next to David in his car, in front of my dark, empty house. It was all right when I was inside it; just the going in was bad.

"I'm going to get a dog," I said suddenly, "and get rid of that goddam cat. She's too self-sufficient."

David laughed. "Look who's talking."

"I can take care of myself. That's not the same thing. How about you? What will you do when his term is up?"

"I'm going back to school. Get an MBA. At least I'm considering it. Justin says there's a dozen spots in the family empire that could use me. Not politics. I've lost my taste for it. Banking, maybe."

"I don't see you as a banker. Listen, David. Using the Lamberts . . . doesn't it bother you? The idea of it."

"I've thought about it. I'm not sure. In one way, yes. In another . . . I've been talking to Vinnie. He's been into his lawbooks."

"What for?"

"He's a little obsessed. Not what you'd expect, from Vinnie. He digs and digs on his own, because who's he going to ask for help?"

"I'm not following. Help on what?"

"On just how guilty the six of us are. And what we're really guilty *of*. Like we were ordinary people? Okay. We tampered with a dead body. We didn't report a death. We faked a car accident and collected the insurance. Well, Amy collected, but we colluded. Are you counting? And the pot and the hash, more than two ounces, easy."

225

"My God," I whispered. "I never thought about it."

"Good for you. I have. Vinnie has. It could come out to a couple of years, but with a good defense—and a confession—we'd probably all get off with fines and suspended sentences. Plus paying back the car insurance."

"Maybe not. Maybe we'd really go to jail."

"It's moot. It's not an issue, unless you're into Vinnie's head. *He's* been weighing it up."

"Weighing. Against what?"

"Against what else we've done. Perjury under oath. Entering into a conspiracy to obstruct justice. That's what we did, *in court*. They don't let you off with a fine for that. The sentences would really be stiff. Don't you see, the first way makes us just frightened jerks trying to protect Justin and then confessing when we're caught. But the Judge's way? Cold-blooded liars conspiring to obstruct justice."

"It wasn't the Judge's way! It was ours. Justin didn't leave us any way out, taking the blame."

"That's the truth. But it's no excuse. Justin didn't use force. Nobody held a gun to our heads in the courtroom."

The car was so cold. The house key in my hand was a thin piece of ice. David and I had had lunch or dinner, alone, maybe ten times since the inquest, but we'd never talked like this. I think it was being in the dark. I think it was because we weren't acting for anyone.

"My head is spinning. But I see what you're driving at. It's the Lamberts, isn't it?"

"You bet. They've got us, don't they? The minute we lied under oath, we did something much worse than pushing a car off a bridge."

"And they know we lied. So even if they don't know *what* we lied about, they've got us. We can never come forward without taking the consequences."

"Amen. So you see what I meant when I said that about keeping the profit on your house. Or why I might take a very good position in some bank or insurance company they just happen to control. They used us. They used us good."

This time I was the one who started laughing. I felt braced and refreshed, wide awake in the dark. It really was funny. All that time, worrying about the Lamberts "throwing us away" to save Justin!

They hadn't had to do that.

We did it to ourselves.

David must have thought I'd lost it, the way I was laughing.

"Oh, dear," I said. "Just think about it. You and Vinnie had us saying it, over and over, and it was really the truth. We really should have had our own lawyers."

So that was the last surprise, and I took it in, and wrote about it to Amy and Caro and Bitsie with a strange, cold kind of exaltation. I felt as if I'd reached, finally, the bottom line and the hardest understanding. It sustained me through selling the house, moving to New York, meeting Sidney Miller, and feeling alive again. He wanted to marry me; he was attractive and interesting; being wanted, for a while, was enough. I was grateful to Sidney but I couldn't let myself cheat him forever. He deserved better. I didn't love him.

The best part of those years in New York was knowing— only gradually, and with a kind of incredulity—that I was rich enough not to work. I'd taken most of the money from the sale of my house and put it into a co-op apartment on Manhattan's Upper West Side, and by the time I sold it—I'd moved in with Sidney— another remarkable rise in values had overtaken me. I put the money into bonds; the income was enough to pay half Sidney's rent and all my expenses for graduate school. I was sick of politics and PR, and if I could never again feel mirror-new, I could at least elect a different career. I'd always wanted to teach. When I got the appointment at Columbus College, I was halfway through my doctorate, and all through with Sid Miller, a man whose bitterness, I knew, wouldn't last.

Mine didn't either. There'd just be the pangs of disappointment, when I met with David.

How's Justin? That's good. Give him my best.

There'd be the dreams from which I'd wake nearly happy, for being reminded of happiness.

There'd be my friends, twining their lives with mine so that they seemed to be all the family I'd ever need.

A peaceful life. The sleepy hollow of my college town enclosed me. I was useful, safe, free to travel every summer and love lightly and go out on Sundays looking for the perfect farmhouse to buy and restore and live in, alone.

Alone. It didn't frighten me. I was used to it by now. When I thought of love—and I did, sometimes—it was like looking at a travel agent's brochure, of a place so costly and difficult to get to that for all those wonders, all those fascinating monuments and heart-stopping vistas, it was too far away; it couldn't be worth it.

Look what it led to.

PART
THREE

25

I had always been able to push my way through a crowd of darkened memories to the safe and spacious present. But after that long lunch with David at Windows on the World I found it hard to calm down. I had to write the letter I'd promised to Bitsie and Caro and Amy, telling them everything David had said about the Lamberts and their new hopes for Justin. After that came a nervous flurry of follow-up phone calls and then I started reading four papers a day and leaving the TV news on even when I took my bath. I couldn't hear the phone ring without a jolt of apprehension. All in all, it was not too different from the way I'd felt and acted ten years before, waiting for the inquest to begin.

But the days went by without any mention of Justin Lambert and the presidential primary and I gradually relaxed. True to his word, David called with brief no-news-is-good-news reassurances and after two major hailstorms, which flattened every tulip on campus, the weather brightened and softened and my spirits lifted on its gusty winds. I felt reprieved, and reckless with it and when I called David in late May he caught the change.

"You sound cheerful," he said. "What's up?"

"I'm going to meet my editor in New York again," I said. "And collect my advance; I told them not to mail it to me. I want to cash that wimpy check at Bergdorf's, that's what I want to do, and then buy you a fancy feed. Name the place, you've got it."

"When?"

"Next week. Thursday."

"Oh, hell." David groaned. "I'm going to London next week for a meeting. Change the date."

"I can't do that. The editor told me *he's* going to London for a long vacation."

"I'm out of luck then. Incidentally, I spoke to Vinnie yesterday. Not a peep out of the Lamberts. All quiet on the western front."

"Just what I wanted to hear. Is it gorgeous there? It's gorgeous here."

"It's raining," David said. "Listen, don't buy that editor lunch. I get a rain check."

"Sure you do," I said happily. "But I just realized. The editor? He's going to London and his name is David too. Isn't that a really weird coincidence?"

"No," said David. "Your publisher has a branch in London, and David is the commonest name on the East Coast."

Because he was speaking from the office, I didn't take his time to argue the point. I did, I knew, have the habit of looking for meaning in the most trivial kinds of coincidence. David thought it was softheaded of me; he said people who did that were just trying to make their lives look interesting. And he didn't change his mind either, not even after I went to New York that next week and walked up to Bergdorf's and got off the elevator, by accident, on the wrong floor. I certainly did not want to be on International Couture, where my publisher's check wouldn't buy the buttons on a Chanel suit. I amused myself anyway for a few minutes by counting zeros on the price tags. The tags were hard to read in all that down-lighted dimness. Then I came around a low Lucite wall with a bunch of calla lilies on it and walked right into Tandy Lambert.

I was wearing sensible shopping flats and she had to bend down to kiss my cheek. She was beaming; she shone at me, with her wide, white smile and bright gold hair like a smooth helmet with every strand in place. She had never been slim, and now she was truly matronly. Yet nothing about her had coarsened; it was as if her classic good looks had just expanded with time.

"Rachel! What a surprise! How have you been?"

"Just fine," I said. "Imagine, what a coincidence, I got off at the wrong floor, I was going to Shoes—"

"Shoes is where I'm going now; come on, let's go together. I've got to match this miserable scrap of lace; it's all they'd give me off my new dress."

We stepped into the elevator together, getting pushed to different corners in the crowd. I had all the time I needed to work off the diamond ring and put it in the zippered pocket on the outside of my purse. There was a young man waiting in front of the elevator.

"Here you are, Mrs. Lambert. They told me you were coming right up."

"Rachel, this is Mr. Tyler. He always helps me and my big feet. He'll help us both."

We sat down and began trying on shoes, and in two minutes we were both talking at once and jumbling up shoes and people and laughing.

"Tell me about Bitsie. We got the marriage announcement; is he nice?"

"Very nice. Let me try triple A, bone if you don't have patent. I read that Marion graduated with highest honors; you must have been proud."

"Oh, points are back, I hate points. She's thinking of graduate school: economics. Is Caro still teaching?"

"She's running the place too. Are these as bad as I think they are?"

"Awful, orthopedic, take them off. So Amy—"

I bought two pairs of shoes. Tandy bought strappy satin

233

evening sandals in gold, black, and dyed-to-match. I was usually so hard to fit that the two pairs were a triumph, and with this, and Tandy's easy, assured presence, I felt my tension wash away. A kind of hopeful excitement took hold of me. I was living for the pleasant present moment and Justin didn't figure in it except for this: maybe Tandy could tell me something about his plans.

So I nodded eagerly when she said, "Four o'clock, and I'm famished. Could you have tea, Rachel? We'll just pop upstairs; they have this new place."

We took another elevator. I'll mention seeing him on TV, I thought; that's the way to bring it up.

The new place was just a few tables near the hairdresser's, with mammoth vases of flowers and waiters out of *Chariots of Fire*. Tandy ordered tea and tea sandwiches and I did the same. Small wafers containing watercress and smoked salmon, four each, arrived immediately. If you bit one in half, you'd nick a finger.

I told her about my work and the new textbook that had brought me to Manhattan. She brought me up to date on her children and the United Fund. She was heading two related committees and it was getting impossible to recruit younger volunteers, what with all the bright young women who had real careers. Like you and your friends, she said. You're practically the next generation, she said; *we* give time, *you* give taxes.

Then she said the new dress she'd just had fitted was for a big party, her party, for her fiftieth birthday, and when I told her how little she'd changed, she patted a hip and said if bigger was better she shouldn't complain. And their thirtieth anniversary was coming up soon!

Time, we said, how it's speeding up, the milestones, one after the other. She looked at me a little shyly over her teacup.

"You haven't married, Rachel? Or did I miss it? I know there's only so much you can put on a Christmas card."

"I'd have found room for that." I laughed. "No, no marriage. I'm still looking."

"It didn't work out with David. That must have been sad. Of course he hardly talked about it when you broke up. But whenever we see him, he always mentions you."

"I should hope so," I said. "We're still the best of friends.

234

But the engagement . . . that got lost, back there. I don't know how else to describe it. We lost it."

"Back there," she repeated, and the echoed words seemed to hang in the air between us, like a bit of salt spray or a patch of fog that only we could taste or see.

"You and David did seem so right for each other. Even your looks. And the exact same interests. It was a disappointment to all of us. I hope you don't mind my saying it."

"Of course I don't mind. And yes, in some ways we were just right. I guess there weren't enough of them. We drifted. All that pressure did some damage. That was a hard time."

"Lighthouse Point. It was hardest on Justin, though. He'd go over it and over it. What he could have done. What he didn't do."

"I can imagine. But we all went that route. Trying to rewrite history? You too, I guess."

I said that in sympathy, but it must have come out wrong. At least I thought so for a split second because she made such a dry little grimace of distaste.

"Me? Oh, no. Maybe I did sometimes wish I hadn't gone to Europe that summer. Or come back earlier. But I'd stopped trying to rewrite Justin's history for years and years before Lighthouse Point. I just gave it up. Gradually. Like smoking."

I must have looked as puzzled as I felt. I must have slopped some tea on my skirt because I saw the stain, later.

"Well," I said, awkwardly, and while I groped for a neutral phrase she went on.

"It was Bitsie, wasn't it? He was looking her over at the country club pool when she was just sixteen. I knew when she grew up and went to work for him that he'd get something going."

My jaw dropped. She didn't even change her tone of voice. But it knocked the very breath out of me and I found myself squeaking.

"Who? What? Did you say Bitsie? But that's crazy, Bitsie and I lived together! Whatever gave you such an idea?"

"I just told you. He'd had his eye on her. My sister-in-law, Edith, didn't think so though. She thought it was Lucia, like everyone else."

"Oh, I know what Edith thought. She was just as wrong as

you are. There wasn't anybody, there was nobody. My God, Bitsie, of all people!"

I was sputtering. Tandy bit her lip.

"I've upset you. Edith said you slapped her face when she accused Lucia. When she told me, I actually giggled. Couldn't help it! I'd always wanted to hit her, myself. Don't leave, Rachel. I believe you, about Bitsie. Just an old stupid suspicion. But meeting you here . . . I couldn't resist asking."

I suddenly realized that I was halfway out of my little gilded chair, and I must have been for quite a while. My legs ached. I sat down. She sighed.

"Can you catch our waiter's eye? He thinks he's royalty or something. We need hotter tea. And more sandwiches. And you have to say you accept my apology. Please say you do. I don't know what got into me. Oh, I *am* sorry."

Her face had gone all blotched with color. She put her hand to her mouth as if to stop herself from saying anything else. She looked about to cry, and I saw that she was no less upset than I was and no stronger, either.

"Oh, please," I said. "You don't have to apologize to me. Blurting things, that happens; I do it all the time. Anyway, maybe it was for the best. Yes, look, it *was* for the best. At least I could tell you the truth."

For a minute we sat in silence, recovering.

"The truth," Tandy said. "Yes, I do know it. I've just always thought it was so ironic, there being *no* girlfriend of his at Lighthouse Point. Because he was heading for it. He'd had so many close calls before. You *must* have heard, Rachel! One of his early flings even tried to blackmail him. He was in Congress and it was common gossip in Washington, and it reached my parents. Daddy was furious. Daddy wanted me to leave him, then and there."

I wanted to wet my dry mouth with some tea but I was afraid to handle a cup. I was trembling.

"I didn't know. Blackmailed him? Why didn't you leave?"

"I had a second baby on the way. I loved him and I didn't want to leave, not for that one or for all the others, after."

All the others. And the daughter who had graduated from college five years ago wasn't even born yet. I shook my head in disbelief. It was pretending; I couldn't doubt her. But a sharp sliver of envy had got stuck in my chest; I hadn't felt *that* for years; it was for the way she had said "Daddy." Her father, hurting for her.

"I never heard any of this about him," I said quickly. "None of us did. The five of us—Tandy, you remember how tight we were! If one of us had heard, we'd all have known about it."

"Well, he'd gotten more discreet; he was in his forties by then. And you girls were so much younger. Into hero worship and that kind of thing. But I think people get to hear the things they want to hear. Or that they're ready to understand."

"That's true," I said slowly. "The hero worship. We would have discounted stuff like that. Put it down to jealousy or dirty politics or something. Unless it came from Vinnie and David, and they—oh, never, they were absolutely loyal to him."

"You probably think I'm being disloyal. Perhaps I am. I just think I owe you the background, after what I said about Bitsie."

"She's still my dearest friend. I won't tell her."

"I would appreciate that. Not that I care if she knows what a fool I can be. But it's nasty, to be suspected. And I'd like it if you wouldn't pass on what I said about Justin's affairs, either. I know what people say. But what *I* say—"

"Please don't worry. You have my word."

"Thank you," she said softly. "You're awfully nice, Rachel."

I knew then that she didn't believe in my previous ignorance. She thought I'd just been sparing her feelings by pretending not to know what her marriage was like. She was composed again, with calm hands and fair cheeks, and I suppose she thought she was safe in the company of someone as kind as she was.

"I'm happy you're out of politics," she said, "I never had the taste for it. Or if I did, it soured pretty fast. The worst of it was when he was in Congress. What a place! They all sniff around the pretty staffers and they all cover up for one another. They call it 'keeping it in the family,' you see. Like a club, with everybody safe inside the Rayburn Building. And the press plays along because they're in the club too. Justin was sleeping with Louise Soames, the columnist, on and off, for ages, and not even a rumor got into print."

I knew Louise Soames. She'd come by several times during

the campaign; she was what men like to call a "terrific broad." She'd sit around the office, waiting to interview him, and we all liked her, for her stories, her foul, funny mouth, her wild, graying Afro. We thought she was great. We also thought she was old.

I would no more have believed that Justin ever slept with her than that he'd ever slept with Margaret Mead.

"They're tougher now, the journalists," I managed to say, and I mentioned a couple of recent scandals in Washington. But Tandy just shrugged; maybe the press was more outspoken, she said, but only when some affair got so blatant they couldn't keep the lid on. If we had more time, she said, she could tell me a few current stories that would curl my hair. I said it was too curly already, and we laughed and she looked at her watch and said she had to get back to the fitting room and have more seams let out.

I said yes, I had to think of my train too. But neither of us moved to go.

"I think I've shocked you," Tandy said. "Not the facts, but *me*, going on like this. It seems all right, though, doesn't it? I hardly ever see anyone from those days, except David. The public days, I mean. And we always thought you were special. Justin told me once that you hadn't had an easy childhood. Downright difficult, in fact. And here you are, a writer, a full professor. You made good use of hardship."

She wasn't trying to flatter me. It was part of her kindness, to bring out something like that.

"I wasn't special," I mumbled. I wanted, suddenly, to get away from her and not hear any more, and I looked wildly around the enclosure exactly like the poor trapped creature I felt I was.

"Oh, your train," Tandy said. "This is my treat, Rachel. Oh, dear, where is that awful waiter?"

He gestured that he'd be right over and went on talking to the cashier.

"It must be turning fifty," Tandy went on. "You get some perspective. Men, marriage. I made plenty of mistakes. I made it easy for him, the lying, the broken promises. I was too passive, too much the martyr, always doing what I was told to do. I see that now. But I did shock you, didn't I?"

I had to answer her. I had to meet all this honesty with my

238

Judas face and practiced deceit and a diamond ring hidden in five seconds with a thief's cunning. I felt soiled in my skin and I knew it was pathetic, the way I tried to make myself cleaner.

"I just feel more . . . sad. How we all mess up in one way or another. Because a long time ago I had an affair myself with a married man. It ended badly. It *should* have ended badly. And the older I get, the more ashamed of it I am."

"Oh, my dear."

"Yes. It was the worst time of my life. It *froze* me, somehow, and maybe it's why I haven't married. Don't tell anyone, please. I do care what people think. I shouldn't have brought it up."

"Of course I won't. Is it over and done with?"

"Absolutely. Years and years ago. But shock . . . yes, you're right. I always thought you were so reserved."

"I usually am reserved. I suspect I often seem kind of *blank* on account of it. But it did help hide my unhappiness, all those bad years. Some men seem to reach the dangerous age pretty early, don't you think? Maybe, for me, it was better sooner than later. The children. I know it must sound old-fashioned, but I thought a breakup would hurt them terribly. I was probably kidding myself. But it gave me the strength to stick it out. And now we're really living a good life together, a private life mainly, Justin and I."

She drew those last syllables out a little, as if she savored even the sound of them.

"That's wonderful," I said, and I meant it.

But I knew I only meant it for her.

She put her gold MasterCard on the little tray with the check. I reached into the sleeves of my jacket. I'd drunk what seemed like a gallon of tea and I asked the waiter for the ladies' room.

"I must dash," she said as she signed the check. "They're probably fuming down there, waiting for me to bring them the shoes. To get the hem right, such a fuss over nothing. Thank God the store's open late tonight. I'm glad I didn't miss seeing you, Rachel."

"I'm glad too," I said. "Please give my best to Justin."

With the table between us we shook hands and nodded, smiling, as if some valuable contract had been happily settled. She

239

went in one direction, and I went in another, through the hair-dresser's to the bathroom. It was just for their customers; I could lock the door. I sat down, closed my eyes, and pounded my knees with my fists. Then I cried and then I walked out to the reception desk with my smeared makeup and pink rabbit eyes for everyone to see. I didn't care. I asked the receptionist if the salon was open late, like the rest of the store, and could someone do my hair? She gave me a hasty, worried glance and said she'd get Mr. Michel to take one more client.

Mr. Michel gave me a warm wet cloth to put over my eyes during the wash. Ah, madame, he said, there was so much air pollution in New York nowadays that many ladies suffered with their eyes. I must keep them closed against the blow-dry, too, and he would not make the conversation.

"We have tea," the girl who washed my hair said. "Let me bring you a cup. They make it with real leaves outside, and it's delicious."

"I know," I said wanly, but I took the cup when she brought it. Everyone was being so nice to me; for the sake of these solicitous strangers I got hold of myself and kept hold until I got back to Columbus College. I was locking the car door when I realized what I'd done. I'd gone and missed a precious opportunity. I hadn't remembered to ask Tandy about Justin's plans.

It was all the excuse I needed to give way to another fit of weeping. But there is only so much of that you can do, and when it was over, I sat down in the kitchen and tried to take stock. It was impossible to think straight; to help myself I went into the living room and opened my typewriter. There would have to be a letter, and it would have to be a long one.

"Dear Ones," I typed, "I met Tandy Lambert by some miserable fluke in Bergdorf Goodman's. We had tea and talked for nearly an hour."

No secrets, we'd promised. What one hears we all hear, we always said. If it even touches on Lighthouse Point, spit it out and let us decide if it's important.

Of course there'd been less and less about Lighthouse Point to share as the years went by. Our closeness held, without it. The sharing just meant the most to me, who had the most to hide.

I ripped the paper in half and shut the typewriter. I'd use

the phone. I'd tell David too, the next time he called. How about this for coincidence! Tandy! And trying on shoes, and having a nice chatty cup of tea, oh, just catching up, this and that, old times, and I was all set to sneak in a leading remark about Justin's future when she upped and ran back to her fitting.

I couldn't sell her out.

It wasn't even a hard call. I knew that the fancy rationalizations would come to me later, and that they wouldn't much matter next to the need I had to keep my word to Tandy Lambert. I was still raw with surprise and pain and bewilderment, but I knew I was more than ever in her debt. I didn't, now, have to wait till I turned fifty to use my perspective on the past. I sighed, a great shuddering sigh with a wail in it. I could feel myself giving up the ghost. Oh, Justin.

Staffers, journalists, even a blackmailer . . . no wonder he'd never expressed the slightest guilt about Tandy to me. I had thought that was on my behalf: he didn't want to make *me* feel any guiltier. But the cheating was really an old, established institution; it was part of his being; he'd probably have *told* me about the others if I'd asked! It hadn't occurred to me. How could it? I was twenty-three, twenty-four, -five, -six. The world I'd built for us was a first world; everything in it had to seem fine and new; I thought he was *born* for me the day we met, and in that ignorant delusion I saw the heart of youth. It isn't only that you don't have the right answers. You don't even want to ask the right questions.

But I was different from those others, wasn't I? He loved me. He'd wanted to marry me. I could close my eyes and hear his whispered supplications. *You're what I need. I love you. You are my love, my dear, my little rock, I'll get a divorce, say it, tell me, get a divorce. . . .*

He might have meant those words when he said them. Only I'd never put him to the test. And he must have said the same things to at least some of the women before me. So I wasn't unique; I hadn't been that important; and all my crying hadn't come from a grown woman for a toppled idol or a lost love. I had bawled like a child with the sting of whipped pride, a stupid, stubborn pride that even ten years of his silence hadn't taken to the defeat it deserved.

Bitsie had had his number all along.

It's his life, charming people. Encouraging them. He just tells them what they want to hear.

I suddenly had the dead-cold certainty that he would run for President. That prize, that platform: hadn't he always managed to overcome his reluctance for prizes and platforms a tenth as small, a hundredth as flattering? Three terms in Congress, two as governor—yes, he always said yes, and he was going to say it again, even if he denied it a hundred times beforehand. And soon there would be more floaters arranged, more visibility achieved with the African appointment, more planted speculations in the press. The lack of news from the Lambert interests didn't mean a thing. They'd make their move when they were good and ready.

I remembered Tandy saying, with such quiet confidence, that she and Justin were really living a good life, a private life at last. The memory made me feel absurdly relieved. I wasn't a *total* idiot; I hadn't blown any precious opportunity to ask her about Justin's future plans.

Unless she was the best actress in New York, she knew less than I did. He must be lying to her, as usual, for his own convenience, to avoid the tears and protestations until the last possible minute. It was cruel and selfish. She'd be so unprepared. The announcement, when it came, would break over her like a curling wave of ice water, and she could sink, swim, or freeze in it, those were her choices; she knew her history and I was sorry for her, but not a hell of a lot sorry. She'd stuck to him? She was stuck with him, too. I wasn't and I could take credit for it, because no matter how often or how much I'd wanted a word or a gesture from him that would show he still remembered me, I hadn't lifted a finger in ten years to get one lying word or one cheap gesture. I'd let him alone and I'd kept his secret and my distance, and by God I could keep my pride too.

Some of it, anyway. Enough so that I knew I was finished crying.

26

"I can't discuss it now," David hissed into the phone, for the third time. "Let me call you back."

I knew he had people in his office with him, but I didn't care. I spoke so loudly they could probably hear me.

"Dammit, you said you'd call me back yesterday. And I hung by my phone all night."

"I've lost contact, as I've said, many times," David answered. I could tell he was gritting his teeth. "I'm doing my best to restore it. Thank you very much for your concern, and I'll get back to you as soon as possible."

He hung up on me. I knew I deserved it, but I stomped away from the pay phone in the corridor like the Bride of Frankenstein, wild of hair and eye, and when I came into my classroom my students quailed in their seats, expecting overdue vengeance in the shape of a pop quiz. I did wish I had a quiz ready. My lecture notes were already mashed like Kleenex in my right hand. I went ahead anyway. School was almost out; the kids were always half deaf in this season of savage flowering, birdsong, white clouds flying outside the prison windows.

The paragraph in the *Times* the day before said that Justin Lambert was unavailable for comment, but "sources close to him" were predicting his interest in starting up a campaign for the presidential primary. It wasn't on the front page, but it was part of a page-one story, and the strongest emotion I felt was the grim satisfaction of having expected it.

I had a date for the evening, but I broke it. I had a letter, too, from Jean-Claude at Stanford, full of cute misspellings and demands that I write more often and give him some definite date for the visit I promised him this summer. I stuck the letter in a drawer with the other one I hadn't answered. I was back in my house by five o'clock, trying to figure out David's schedule. I wanted his phone to be ringing when he walked in.

He called at nine.

"I sent Fiona to the movies," he said wearily. "Jesus, Rachel, what's gotten into you? Don't you understand English? I was as thrown as you were by the story. They cut me out of the loop, damn them. Vinnie too, and he's down there, on the spot. They're not talking to us."

"I wasn't thrown. So what are we going to do?"

"Do? What is this, *Star Trek*? We can't *do* anything."

"He hasn't got a chance. And we have to put up with their lunacy anyway? Have the press after us again. Have the whole mess dug up and plastered all over. For nothing! Or is it that they're thinking of putting him in position for something else? Like Vice-President?"

"I thought of that. But it's completely the wrong track. His state is safe. Nothing to gain there. And if the winner wanted him, which is doubtful, he'd do better making it a surprise choice. Like a vote of confidence. It's a stupid long shot, even in that scenario."

"David? Where are you? Do you still feel the same?"

"Double it. I'm pissed. Justin hasn't returned any of my calls.

He's ducking me, and he's been back from Africa for ten days. How do you think that makes me feel?"

"Mad. Hurt. Pissed is the word."

"So give me a break. Stop acting like it's all my fault. We're helpless. We'll just have to sit tight and watch them crash."

"We could do something."

"What?"

"Threaten them. Tell them we'll talk."

"Is this you, Rachel? What the hell do you mean? Talk? We can't talk. You know why."

"It's ten years. Maybe we can. Maybe there's a statute of limitations on perjury. On obstructing justice."

David snorted. "So maybe it's too late to prosecute us. It's not to late to ruin us! I can't believe I'm hearing you right. Weren't you just saying you didn't want the press after you again? Being plastered in the papers? What do you think you'd get if you went public now? You want a spot on Donahue? You want to sell your story to the movies? You want Tandy to know about you and Justin? Rachel? Are you there? Say you're kidding."

"I'm not kidding," I said. "About threatening them, that is. Of course I don't want to go public. I'd sooner die. I mean that. But it might work on the Lamberts. Just the threat of it."

The silence between us stretched and swelled, like a full sail. Suppose this. Suppose that. But there was no fear in it this time. We weren't afraid that Justin would run. Dismayed and disgusted, outraged and unhappy . . . but not afraid. We weren't so young now.

"I have to think, Rachel," David said. "Whatever comes up, let's make it clear. We act, all of us together, or we don't act at all. Right?"

"Right. You or Vinnie could go to Old Henry. Tell him the six of us think Justin shouldn't run. Tell him—"

"I'm thinking. Maybe you ought to see Justin yourself. Tell him yourself. Weigh in. It just might tip him."

"I could talk to him," I said. "Yes. It might do some good. I should have thought of that. Not you."

"Old habits."

"Useless old habits. I'm not what I was, ten years ago."

245

David laughed. "I never noticed. But thanks for letting me know."

We said good-bye and let's-sleep-on-it. I paced around the living room for a few minutes and then I called him back.

"Sorry," I said. "But just as long as Fiona's at the movies . . . I thought of something. Something I want your opinion on. You know, I always thought Justin was a politician. I mean a real one. With savvy. Smarts. So how come he can be so *wrong*, so *dense*, about his chances in a thing like this?"

"That's easy. And it's not just my opinion either. Ask anyone. Justin was never what you and I would call a politician. He was in politics, that's all. Like the crown prince, no sweat, no hustle. He's got charm and stature and he gets out the vote. He likes leading, too. But he's not a player. He could never get worked up about the strategy, the party, the inside dealing. He left those decisions to other people, and you don't catch a real politician doing that."

"Other people. Like you and Vinnie."

"Thanks for the compliment. But no. Maybe ten, twenty percent. The rest was from the family and their advisers. His father. Who used to be good at it too."

"But not anymore? Why?"

"Feeling his age, I guess. Getting reckless. Listen, Rachel, I'm glad you called back, I forgot to tell you the most important thing. I've done some checking. The Lambert people haven't taken any polls. Not one. They haven't gotten a single reading on how people feel about Lighthouse Point. And him, in it. Care-a-lot, care-some, don't-care-at-all."

"They don't want to know."

"They don't want to know."

I sighed. "Well, you answered my question. Keep in touch. I won't hound you at the office anymore, promise."

"Good. And speaking of questions . . . you answered one of mine."

"Which one?"

"I didn't ask it out loud. But I was wondering if you're really objective enough to handle seeing him again."

"Him who?"

246

"I hate wise guys. Good night."

"Oh, don't hang up. Justin. Seeing him again. Of course, I can handle it, David. My God, it's been ten years. Do you expect me to fall flat on my face? Kiss his Harvard ring?"

"No, but I have a long memory. If I ever saw a woman in love, it was you with him. Dum-dum, gaga. You were walking into walls."

I laughed, rather loudly. "You're remembering a girl, not a woman. I was a kid. At least I was a kid up until Lighthouse Point. That was instant middle age, in my opinion."

"Okay, but you know what I mean. I just want you to be prepared. It could be . . . traumatic."

"Traumatic. Oh, boy. *That* is slightly offensive. You'd think I've been living in a convent since then. May I remind you—"

"Don't give me the body count," David said. He sighed. "I think of it, sometimes. How much Justin wanted to marry you. He'd talk about it to Vinnie and me, did I ever tell you? About how you weren't anything like the others."

"The others," I said carefully. "Yes. I know all about them, no thanks to you."

"It wasn't my place, back then, to bring that stuff up. I guess the stories had to get to you, though. After all, he'd been stepping out on Tandy long before my time, even. I just wonder, occasionally, where we'd all be if you'd married him."

"God knows. What I know is that I don't regret it, and that's the truth."

David said he felt the same and in spades. There was a sudden series of loud noises in the background.

"That's Fiona, banging on the door. She can't work a double lock."

"I'm sure it doesn't show, on camera. Is it ever late! Good night."

"Good night."

A good night is what it wasn't. I went to bed, prepared for what the French call a *nuit blanche*, a white night, where you never quite sleep and never quite wake, and slow trains of thought are interspersed with brief and timid dreams. I've learned to rest through such nights, quietly, without tossing or checking the clock.

247

My eyes stay mostly closed, and behind them I can see things.

I saw myself facing Justin again quite calmly, because he was no longer the person I once loved. Perhaps that man had never existed except in my imagination; perhaps that illusion still deserved some loyalty. Well, I could give the past its due. I couldn't, any longer, keep warm in its flame.

I saw David's eyes widen as I told him the truth about meeting Tandy. Too bad that would never happen; I would never tell. But dear David . . . I didn't like holding out on him. It was good to know he was always in my corner and on my side. Only I'd paid a price for that, hadn't I? Having David in my life had kept Justin alive in me too. He was Justin's friend, a Lambert insider, and he'd fueled that low, guttering flame with news and reminiscences and his tactful courier's niceties. I might have been better off without those.

"You're looking great, Rachel. I'll tell Justin."

What had David said about the others? That I was different, that he'd actually talked about marrying me. Well, so what. But good, too. Pride is always hungry, it wants to eat: realities, supposings. . . .

What if Lighthouse Point had never happened? How much longer could we have gone on, Justin and I, just as we were? I might have gotten tired of that secret, closed-off life. Left him. Found someone else. Sick, finally, of crumbs off the table, stolen hours, never enough sky.

If I had married him . . . what was the phrase David had used? Oh, yes, "stepping out." Funny phrase, from David. Real Nashville. If I had married Justin Lambert, would he have stepped out on me?

The ifs and the mights. It wasn't my game, usually. It showed how much I'd changed. The past had been some kind of shrine for me; I was new at the business of turning it into a playground, a puzzle, a game. Fun, almost. You can treat the past like Lego. Same shapes, different objects. You can make a house, a car, a chair. . . .

Toward morning, I saw Lucia.

For a minute I was so happy! I thought she hadn't died.

She was in bed. Her blond hair was fanned out like a great

gold tassel on the white pillow. Her eyes were open. I saw their blueness looking at me over the arched brown back of a heavy man. I couldn't see his face but I knew he had blue eyes too. I knew it was Justin. He covered her. She had fallen to him like a ripe fruit, full of hope and yearning; he had only to put out his hand to have her in it. Easy. No guilt, no effort. It was his nature, the lazy greed, the careless taking.

Yet she would whisper in her bliss, Poor Rachel.

I wasn't dreaming. It was a vision, cast from my soul like a colored slide on the screen behind my eyelids. There are things in our pasts—smothered suspicions, ugly fears—that keep a desperate energy. They live like plants on the ocean floor, in a darkness rich with intuition. They want to come true. They want you to think they happened.

I was breathing as if I'd been running hard. When I was really awake, I got up and made my breakfast in the greenish light of dawn, too early for the cheerful voices of Jane and Bryant. But the quiet felt right. I wasn't tired or worried. All the same, I had the notion that some intangible things I'd counted on were now gone forever and that I had to feel their leaving. I couldn't name them; I didn't even try. I was absorbed in a profound solitude that I didn't want to escape from or rise above or talk myself out of. I just wanted to get used to it. I just knew I felt lonely, lonely to the bone, the way I'd felt that year Mama sickened and died after only a few short weeks, going, going, gone, so quick, just like that, and then you have to say a real good-bye.

Amy's clipping arrived that morning. It was from the *Clarion-Dispatch*, our old home-state paper. It contained a disclaimer from Justin Lambert himself, dismissing the "rumors" and the "speculation" about the primary. He had no intention of seeking any office at all. He was encouraged about the latest news of the President's health.

That was one paragraph. The next ten consisted of statements from various party officials and other citizens, upstate and downstate, all claiming an interest in having their ex-Governor "test the waters" and "keep his options open."

Of course there was no mention of Lighthouse Point. Of course the Lamberts controlled the paper.

I called Amy the next day. Express mail had delivered my letter to her.

"I wasn't as concerned as you were," she said. "Now I am. For my own reasons. My children. They're five and seven. And you know how damned precocious they are. It's them I worry about. Reading about it. Hearing things. The teasing."

"You have my letter. What did you think? About threatening the Lamberts. About me talking to Justin."

"Go for it. What have we got to lose? They can't hurt us. Anyway, they can't hurt me."

"If we do do something, do you want to be in on it? The four of us. The old way. So nobody's left out."

Amy snorted. "Oh, Rachel," she said. "It's been ten years! Grow up."

In their own words, Bitsie and Caro said the same things. Bitsie was more concerned about her new husband than her son, and Caro didn't want any publicity for her order. But if worst came to worst, they'd ride it out. And in the past few weeks they'd done a little informal polling of their own, and they couldn't find a human being who thought Justin Lambert was what the country needed. Some even said, Justin Lambert? Which Lambert is that?

It was, in a way, amusing to me. I had to understand that I was the only one of us who still cared if Justin made a fool of himself. The others didn't give a damn.

"Frankly," said Bitsie, "that's the bright spot, if he runs. Think of all those arrogant Lambert bastards, getting the horselaugh."

"I'm starting to wonder now myself. Bitsie, am I being a fool too? Overreacting?"

"No," she said sternly. "I think stopping him is great, worth a try. Now don't get mad, Rachel, but there's something else. It's good for you. It's about time you saw him. It's enough, already."

"I'm not looking forward to it."

Bitsie sounded eight years old, giggling. "You must have heard my mother. She was at a club party last week, and Justin and Tandy were there. Mother says he's gotten fat."

"Never. Not fat. Heavy, maybe. Besides, I saw him on TV, back in April."

"So did I, and all you really got was head and shoulders.

Anyway, you know how he eats when he's nervous. I'll bet he's plenty nervous nowadays."

"He's got plenty of company in Pennsylvania. Listen, did your mother actually say *fat?*"

Two days later, David called.

"Don't poor-mouth me," he said. "I know you're loaded. And we've got Vinnie's schedule to consider, and being careful, the three of us, being seen together. So use that private air service in Harrisburg and zip up to LaGuardia Wednesday noon, the seventeenth. Vinnie will do the same from the capital. We'll all have a terrible lunch in the airport restaurant and talk it out."

"I hate little planes."

"So drive, take the train to New York, take a cab back to LaGuardia. Lose the day, get tired. You don't hate little planes. You're cheap."

"I don't make a hundred thousand a year like some people I know. Oh, all right. Which restaurant?"

"Upstairs, in the main terminal. You haven't seen Vinnie in how long?"

"Five years. He didn't make Bitsie's wedding."

"I haven't seen him for four months. But we're on the phone a lot. Funny, how cheerful I feel. Even after I finally cornered Justin. Or at least he called me back."

"What did he say?"

"He said he was dead set against it. He said it was all coming from Smith and Trager and Old Henry, and he was letting them make noise because it wouldn't come to anything anyway."

"But—"

"But nothing. I didn't believe him. He was just saying what I wanted to hear. And it got to me. All these years . . . I really think I deserve better. I've always been honest with him."

"I guess I'll have to tell you what Amy said to me. On a related matter."

"What?"

"Grow up."

I was ashen when that little plane touched down, through a patchy fog and fine drizzle and crosswinds that sent it lurching ten feet sideways on the runway. David and Vinnie thought I looked hilariously white and grim, and after one martini I found I could join in the joke. Barely.

"I'm never going back," I said. "Not that way. Vinnie, it's wonderful to see you. Show me pictures of the kids."

We ordered our lunches and I caught Vinnie up on Amy's business, Bitsie's marriage. I said I'd seen Caro just a few weeks ago, looking smart.

Vinnie was puzzled. Smart?

"It's a strict order with these funny flukes in it. They dress like everyone else. Pants. Sweaters. Long hair, but it has to be put back."

I twisted my own mane into a severe knot to show him how it looked. Vinnie nodded. It was ten years since he'd laid eyes on her.

"She's happy?"

"Very. She says so. People come from all over to see those kindergartens she runs."

"I'm doing fine too," Vinnie said, but in such a quaint, formal way that I knew I was to tell Caro. "I've hired five new people. We're consulting on the Bay cleanup and the new monorail."

"You never miss politics?"

"Fat chance. I'm up to my neck in them. How do you think you get consulting contracts?"

"Dumb question. Shows you how far I'm out of it."

David opened the topic. "Vinnie thinks the two of us should talk to Justin. Not you alone. But he can't be in on it. He's a hostage. He still lives there."

"That makes sense," I said. "But you're a hostage too, David. You work for them."

"So they'll fire me. You know I've never felt good in that job. I was going to quit anyway."

"How can we arrange it? It can't be a surprise."

"Wish it could be. We might get no for an answer."

Vinnie cleared his throat. He said, "I think I can do it. No phones. Me, on the spot. I'll make an appointment to see him on this monorail thing, at his office. He has an office in the family bank. Then I'll tell him the real reason for the visit. You."

There was a sudden open pit yawning in my stomach.

"Well, me. But David too, if that's best."

"I won't tell him David's coming. He'll probably guess what you want to say to him, but he won't be sure. He might think you're in trouble, money or something. If he knows David's on tap, he'll get too suspicious and hide."

"What's the office setup?" David asked. "It must be new; he was working out of his house last time I was down."

"It's new. The space opened up last year. A big office, with a private entrance off Fifth Street. It doesn't even look like it's part of the bank. Ground floor. He's got a secretary, but she's just a kid; she won't recognize Rachel."

"Why did I ask you to help me see him?"

"You were afraid of using the phone or a letter. Like in the old days."

"All right, but what will he do when he sees me walk in with David?"

David grinned. "He'll plotz," he said. "But too late. We'll have him, alone. He'll see you have backup. He'll know he can't put it on your just being vindictive or whatever. It's us. We mean it. We'll do what we can to keep him in retirement."

It certainly was a terrible lunch. We kept asking for more rolls and butter. I was hungry, but I didn't care. I was keyed up and listless, by turns; I kept looking out the huge glass windows of the restaurant that showed nothing but grayness, fog and rain, and a few runway lights winking softly. There were phantoms out there. They wanted to get in, the shy ghosts of girls and young men, one dead, the others merely superseded, lost, alike in this: they weren't real. David had gray hair. Vinnie's olive skin had grooves in it. My hand on the table showed raised blue veins like little ropes. And none of us needed Justin anymore.

"What are we doing this for?" I asked suddenly. "We ought to make it clear. I'm starting to feel funny. Not sure. Motives matter, don't they? What's it for? Or who?"

"Justin," said Vinnie and David together. They didn't laugh.

"Me," I said. "Not just Justin. I get sick thinking of the publicity. I'm starting to write the articles in my sleep. LIGHTHOUSE POINT: WAS JUSTICE SERVED?"

"Brenda," Vinnie said. "And the kids, they're teenagers. I

don't count. I live there, I work there, and believe it or not, some of the rumors help. People think I'm some kind of goddam saint, sticking by Justin. Keeping my mouth shut. So for me it's my wife. She had to put up with a lot, and for years, too. If he had a real shot at the Presidency—Jesus, I hate to think. But he doesn't. So I don't have any mixed feelings. Not one."

"David?"

"Rachel," David said. "I'm glad she's taking a stand. It's about time. And me. I've been wanting to get out from under the Lamberts for maybe five years. I keep seeing my tombstone with four words on it: HE WORKED FOR THEM. So maybe my motives aren't the purest, but so what? I haven't had the guts to quit, but at least now I've found a good cause for getting fired."

Suddenly Vinnie said, "You know, we're talking blackmail. The Lamberts won't take it lying down. They'll try to get back at us. I've been up nights trying to figure out how."

"Me too," David said. "But unless I'm missing some marbles, I can't see how they get to us without damaging themselves. So they kick my ass out of the foundation and screw up my references. So they tell Vinnie he's in for a lot of grief, going for consulting work in their territory. Vinnie's free to play dumb and give them a lot of crapola about how hard he tried to stop us. As for Rachel and the other girls . . . hell, what can the Lamberts do to them? The girls are way out of their orbit. Anyway, we're six people, right? Are they going to invite us all out on the family yacht and push us overboard?"

Vinnie nodded. "That was always the safety," he said. "The number of us. But don't think it hasn't occurred to me, since we started this business. Threatening *them*! Suppose we were only one person? Or two, at most, who knew what really happened that night? I ask you."

"Brazil," David answered thoughtfully. "Yes, if I were the only one, it would be Brazil. And a new name and a big mustache."

"That's ridiculous," I said.

"It is," Vinnie said. "Because Brazil isn't far enough. I'd go to Russia. And ask the KGB for protection."

They both started laughing. They picked up the scenario and started running with it and I just sat there, thinking how stupid

255

they sounded, grown men, and even how stupid they looked, grinning like idiots at their own grasp of bad melodrama. "A Knock at the Door!" "Stalked and Hunted!" "Two Guys Who Knew Too Much!"

When I told them, finally, to knock it off, Vinnie said quietly, "Oh, Rachel. You still trust them, don't you? You think people like that are so rich they don't ever have to be bad. You're wrong. David and I know. The Lamberts are different. They're so rich they never learned to be good."

David shifted uneasily. "Let's change the subject," he said. "Let's work out the dialogue. Point by point."

We had to let Justin know we were serious. We had to be sure he knew that we understood his ambivalence, his genuine diffidence about running, even if the other people around him didn't. Hadn't he told David over and over that he didn't want to try for the nomination? We respected this. And we were sure he'd respect our position, in turn. We didn't think he had a chance. We didn't want Lighthouse Point raked up again. But if worst came to worst and the press came after us, we'd fight fire with fire. We'd talk. We wouldn't tell the whole story, but we'd put out so many dire hints, so many intimations of sadder-but-wiser reflection, that Lighthouse Point would look like a brand-new and nasty issue.

"Tactful," David kept saying. "It has to be done with tact. Affection."

"Hearts and flowers," I kept saying. "Not like we're trying to push him around. He gets enough of that from the family."

While Vinnie demanded, "Who's kidding who here? You think you're going to a tea party? Make the pitch and clear out fast."

But there was one point we didn't discuss. I guess, after Lighthouse Point and ten years, we just took it for granted. It was something we all knew for a plain fact, and we didn't want to spell it out. For what? If we didn't like talking about it among ourselves, how could David and I ever summon up the brutal intention of saying it to Justin?

President. It was the biggest job in the whole world. The other men were right for it.

He wasn't.

The college year always drew to its close in the same way. There would be great chords of organ music sounding at odd hours as the organist practiced her Handel; a last editorial in the college paper knocking—in advance—the commencement speaker; the sudden appearance of innumerable cars and vans parked all over the green lawns of the campus quadrangle. The seniors were leaving. They were taking everything they hadn't sold at the Swap Shop with them: mattresses and mongrels, bikes and chairs, cartons of books they couldn't part with and would never read again. Then the hour would arrive when the boys—men, now—would stand around in awkward quiet, just close enough for a final handshake or back thump. The girls—women—would hang in for a while too, but clumped close together, in noisy groups. It always fascinated me to see the students like this, coalescing by sex, regressing back to junior high. Most of them knew this was the end of their schooling. No more homework, no more books. . . . But this time it would be forever, and so they puttered and lingered until sadness made them irritable.

"Come on, this is stupid, let's go, we're history."

Commencement made me sad too. But at this time of year I was usually busy with packing to travel: Russia, Spain, Greece. I took tours or hitched up with colleagues or went alone; I'd take my sweet time, traveling; I'd come back feeling refreshed and different and poor again. I always spent too much, buying things. The first thing I'd do when I got to the college was get over to the bank, and check my balance, and open my safety-deposit box to count my bonds. I'd sit for a while in the little cubbyhole they give you, counting. I'd know I was all right. I'd take the diamond ring out of the metal box; I always kept it there when I traveled out of the country. I'd breathe on it, polish it, slip it on my finger. There. I was home.

But I had no plans to travel this year unless I counted the promise I had made to Jean-Claude before he went off to Stanford. I had said I'd meet him in California in August. I could certainly remember saying it; the trouble was I couldn't remember why. Had I liked him that much? And if I had, how come I hadn't answered his last letter? As a matter of fact, I had opened it with all the enthusiasm I usually give to my bill from VISA.

Well, I thought righteously, I had the book contract, and a reckless first-draft commitment and a carrel in the library with my name neatly lettered on the slot, and reference books and note cards, all lined up. The easy part was over. I had to work. If I worked I could safely make good on that promise. So I went to work, but even Jean-Claude's last phone call hadn't made me set a date to meet him. All it did was make me whine about how busy I was and how lucky some people were to have nothing to do but plan vacations.

I also had to stay put, to hear from Vinnie. After a week, I still hadn't heard. David said it was because Justin had gone back to Canada; after that, it was Vinnie who was out of town; any day now, David said, and you think you're the only one with an itchy foot? *I* have vacation time coming, a lot of it, and I'd like to use some before the Lamberts drop an anvil on me.

"But the thing is, I'm losing my nerve," I said. "Well, not nerve exactly. Impetus. The drive."

"You'll get it back," David said. "When we have a date. And Vinnie said he'd call you first. Any day now, I'm positive."

Vinnie called the next day. I was in the kitchen, cooking my dinner.

"It's all set," he said happily. "Sorry it took so long. Did David tell you why?"

"Yes," I said. I was poking at some vegetables in the pan. "He told me. So when?"

"June thirtieth, at three o'clock in Justin's office. He kept asking *why* and I kept saying you hadn't given me any details and I didn't think it was my place to ask for any. Just that you wanted to see him strictly in private. And with school out, you could make it anytime it suited him."

I went on stirring the eggplant pieces so vigorously several fell on my foot.

"How did he act?" I asked. "Did he mention the primary?"

"He didn't mention it. He acted normal. So I stuck to my agenda. Asking his advice about the city council and the monorail problems."

"Advice. I guess he still knows the score, around the city."

"Enough to make it a legitimate topic. But he wasn't really interested in my worries. People think we're still tight, but he does the bare minimum to help me. Always has, since Lighthouse Point. You know what I really think? I just make him uncomfortable. I think he wishes I'd moved away, like the rest of you guys."

"But he said he'd see me."

"He didn't hesitate. '*Sure*,' he said, '*any time you say*.' "

So it was set. I had four days. I went on making dinner, thinking how different that conversation would have been if it were a woman calling me. A woman would have told me how Justin looked. What kind of expression he'd had, hearing I wanted to see him. How many times he'd asked "What for?" We would have talked an hour about it. As it was, Vinnie's call lasted just three minutes, time enough for me to burn everything in the pan.

I hadn't been back to that city for nine years. When Bitsie still lived there she'd always preferred to come up to New York to get together. She knew all my sofa beds, in all my apartments, including the one I shared with Sidney Miller. Then she moved away too. When I thought of the place at all, it was always in connection with Justin, and better not thought of. Only sometimes I'd put myself to sleep going into its houses. I'd walk up the steep brick stoop of my row house, or into the apartment I'd shared that first year with Bitsie, or onto the shabby porch of the wooden bungalow where Caro and Amy and Lucia had lived. It was always an ankle trap of fallen bicycles and paint cans. The houses were real to me, even the governor's mansion. I could still remember the smell of floor wax in the big ballroom. But only the houses held. The place itself, the living city, had become blurred to a strangely accurate congruence with reality: I'd never gotten to know much about it. I'd lived in my work, in my friends, in my tranced interior world where the only light came from Justin. And if I'd stayed there, I would have stayed the same, because nothing can grow in such a world, not even love.

I thought of that as the days ticked away to the thirtieth of June. I thought how I was a different woman from the one who used to live there and how I had nothing to fear from facing Justin. He was as far away from me, almost, as Tin Town. I had dealt with that, hadn't I? I could deal with him.

So I heartened myself with pep talks and keeping-a-good-self-image, and then it was the morning of June thirtieth and I woke up in a sweaty panic and reached for the phone.

"David? Did I wake you? I—um, feel lousy."

"Don't tell me. You're sick. You can't go."

"I'm not sick. I just—um, feel lousy."

"You said that."

"It's *six*-thirty? Oh, I thought the clock said eight-thirty. Fiona must think I'm some kind of nut."

"She might. But she went back to Toronto to visit her mum. I'm not at all unhappy about sleeping alone. I *told* you."

"I forgot."

"Get up and get dressed, Rachel. Take a walk or work on your book. You'll meet me at the airport at one. Everything is going to go all right, and please do not try this number again. I consider this an obscene phone call."

I managed to laugh. "Last one you get from me. See you at one."

I lay back in bed. Six-thirty. I'd only had five hours' sleep. And I was not only a nut, I was going blind. I could have sworn the clock said eight-thirty. But at least I didn't wake Fiona, who slept in—when she wasn't being photographed—until the soaps started. Fiona wasn't there. That was a break. Maybe she wouldn't come back, if David didn't ask her to. He probably wouldn't. He'd told me once—rather morosely—that the only thing they had in common was that they both thought her left side was better for close-ups.

David wasn't very good at sleeping alone—or living alone, for that matter. He ought to learn, I thought smugly. He ought to stop inviting every gorgeous moron he meets to move in. *I've* managed to live alone all these years, why can't he?

I lay in bed, yawning and lining out some improving advice to give David. I got indignant, in advance, thinking that he'd tell me to mind my own business. So maybe I wouldn't say anything? I suddenly felt that the stupidest thing I could do on this ominous day would be to annoy David. David was precious. It wasn't just that he'd be with me for the confrontation. He was precious in himself.

For some reason this train of thought embarrassed me. I got quickly out of bed, and the morning went by with only one unpleasant incident. Jean-Claude called. He thought he might go to Paris in August, if I continued to be so evasive about giving him a definite date for my visit. For a few minutes we exchanged threats and whines, and when I said I was in a terrible rush he answered me in French and hung up. My French is not good, but I guessed some of the words would not be in my dictionary.

I drove to Philadelphia and met David's plane. It was hot and muggy and I'd dressed for comfort as well as the occasion. I thought I looked all right, but I felt a pang when David said, "What is this, a Mafia funeral? What's the get-up?"

We were walking to my car. I said, "This is a sinfully expensive silk dress. It's cool and comfortable. It happens to be black. What's the problem?"

261

"You never wear black. You always wear colors."

"I do not. I have a lot of black. I have a black coat. I have a black velvet dress, four black sweaters, a black jacket—"

"Spare me. I've never seen you in any of them."

"How often do you see me? A few times a year? What's wrong with the way I look?"

"I'm sorry I mentioned it. No, let me drive. It's not the black, anyway. You're white as a sheet."

I pulled down the sun visor and checked. He was right.

"I'm nervous," I said. "I'll put on some blusher when we get there. No, I'll do it now. Don't start, I'll make a mess."

I brushed some color on my cheeks and renewed my lipstick. We got on the turnpike and started south.

"Did you have lunch?" I said. "I couldn't."

"I had a heaping bowlful of Maalox, thank you."

"We're a pair," I said. "Well, I'm not even worried. The worst that can happen is that he'll agree with everything we say and then do what he wants to do anyway. We won't even get a chance to pitch a few threats. That'll be the worst."

"Seeing him again? How about that?"

"No problem. Definitely. I'll have to control my face, though. If it's true what Bitsie's mother told her. Did I mention it? She saw him at the club. She says he's fat."

"That's since March then. Late March. Well, it could happen. So if you're not nervous about seeing him, what are you nervous about?"

"I'm nervous about you constantly telling me I'm nervous. Let's not talk. Tapes or radio?"

We played tapes all the way south. It was two o'clock when I saw the city. You make a wide U off the turnpike and come over a ridge, and you see it beyond the river.

"My God," I said. "Look at all those buildings. Skyscrapers. I can't believe it. Nine years."

"That's the Lambert insurance company. The big one with the bronze pediment. Oh, it's changed. A monorail! I thought Vinnie was kidding."

"We're so early. Nearly an hour. Let's drive around."

We made the circuit around the outer belt. We saw the

new shopping malls, the widened ramps, the places they used to call North Fields and South Fields on the traffic reports. They really were fields then. There were houses all over them now. Going into the downtown area we ticked off the missing landmarks: the Orpheum theater, Blaner's Department Store, Bowl-o-Rama (razed for a hotel), an office building, another statehouse annex. Curtain walls of glass and aluminum shimmered in the heat, looming like cliffs over the capitol. Its famous gilded dome and elegant spire seemed shrunk to the size of an olive with a pin on it.

"Pardon me for sounding old," David said. "But I think it's awful. They've mugged the statehouse."

"It does look puny," I said. "Go past my old house. We still have time."

The garage was gone. It had been turned it into a rec room, with sliding doors. The blinds were up and I could see pine paneling and a couch piled with newspapers and cushions. And where once our row of houses had lorded it over the opposite side of the street, it now looked humbled in the face of a new row, higher, bigger, with three full stories each, pillars and porticoes, shutters and windowboxes, gleaming brass rails outlining fieldstone steps. I was stunned. My two-hundred-thousand-dollar house had become a poor relation.

"Williamsburgh Mews," David said. "I heard about it. It's the best address in town. The mayor bought in."

"Wait until I tell the guys," I said. "I wish I'd brought a camera. Amy will not believe it."

"That's it," David said, swinging the car around. "Ten of three. And we have to park."

"I'm glad we did this," I said. "I'm ready. For whatever else has changed too."

There was still a parking lot in back of the Lambert bank. There was a small brass plate on the door on Fifth Street. It said J. LAMBERT. It was so new it was hard to read. I let David walk in first, to a large anteroom, done up in that ubiquitous cream-and-hunter-green. There were some mahogany chairs, a small desk, a pretty young girl, everything fresh as paint.

"Miss Warshowsky? Mr. Lambert will be with you in a minute."

David and I took seats. The young girl turned to her word processor and began tapping the keys. If she wasn't expecting David, she didn't show it. I inspected the inside of my purse. David tied and retied his shoes. After several years, we looked at our watches simultaneously. Three-fifteen.

Justin almost never kept people waiting. David asked the girl if Mr. Lambert knew we were there.

"I buzzed him," she said. "He might be waiting for this."

She picked up a few papers and walked through a door. Then she came back and said, "Please go right in."

I thought it was funny: she came out with the papers still in her hand. I tried to concentrate on that because I suddenly felt my heart tugging on whatever keeps it in place. It was beating in my throat. We walked in, and the door shut behind us.

The inner office was a large room, bare of clutter, a war room before the war started. David's eyes, my eyes, swept it from corner to corner: the conference table, the TV sets, the computer consoles, the precinct maps on the wall. We must have looked ridiculous, standing there, looking for Justin. Justin wasn't in the room. There was only his desk and his father, seated behind it. For however long I live, I will always be grateful to David for speaking first.

"This is a surprise, sir," he said. "We expected to see Justin."

"You won't," said Old Henry. "Rachel, how are you? Pull up a couple of chairs. A surprise? I'm sure it is. But I'm not surprised to see you, David."

"I decided to come along at the last minute."

"Oh, really? You bought your plane ticket to Philadelphia last week."

I sank heavily into the chair David pulled over for me. I had one clear thought, Gloves off. Old Henry was angry, and neither the new silvery whiteness of his brows, the sunken cheeks, nor the slackness at his throat could make him seem less formidable.

"I don't appreciate being spied on," David said. "And we could dispute what I meant by 'last minute.' But I won't waste your time. Is there any reason we can't see Justin?"

"He was called to Washington," Old Henry said. He lit a

cigar, not looking at the match, only staring at David from beneath those whitened brows. "At the last minute, in your use of the phrase. You can say what you have to say to me."

I found my voice, somewhere in the vicinity of my appendix scar.

"This visit was on my account," I said. "I haven't anything particular to say to anyone but Justin. If he's not available, we'll leave. And make another appointment."

"You can take it from me that he wants *me* to hear what you have to say. I don't have it in writing. But you have my word for it."

David was leaning back in his chair, his legs stretched out, his arms behind his head. It was a pose; it was provocative; it was not the way people sat in front of Henry Lambert.

"Who told you about the ticket?"

"Your secretary. I had someone ask her if you were planning to travel in the near future. You see, Justin told me he was expecting a visit from Rachel. *I* suspected she wouldn't be alone. If I didn't know before what this is all about, I knew then. You're still leaning on him, David? And you're using Rachel to help you?"

"We're not alone. We represent the others. The six of us. We are all dead set against his running."

"He knows that. I know that. You've made yourself clear before. You're here for something else. And let me tell you that I don't admire the way you've used this young lady as a decoy. Justin was genuinely worried. He thought she might be in some kind of trouble. You're not, are you? You look very well. Prettier than ever."

He blew smoke at the ceiling; he looked at me with a kind of benevolent sternness. Of course women let themselves be used. That was their nature, and they were more to be pitied than censured. He smiled at me most kindly.

"I am well," I said. "And believe me, this visit was my idea. Mine. I wanted to tell Justin myself how much we're all dreading what can happen. Having Lighthouse Point brought up again. Not just for own sakes. His."

"That's very unselfish of you," Old Henry said. "But Justin isn't dreading it. He knows he's surmounted it. He can go on surmounting it, even though it certainly will get brought up, as you say. It won't harm him. Not now."

"Everyone I know thinks it will," I said. "Everyone I know thinks it will stop him cold."

"We must know different people," Old Henry said. "I promise you, the smartest heads in the party think otherwise."

He spoke the way you speak to a child who's worried it will rain for tomorrow's picnic. I was dismissed. He turned to David.

"So what's new, David? Or did you really come all this way to repeat yourself?"

He looked at his watch and didn't hide the fact that he'd looked. He had the gift of time, too, to bestow or withhold, and I knew he'd kept us waiting on purpose.

"I'll let Rachel tell you," David said. "She wasn't kidding. This was her idea."

I took a deep, noisy breath. There was no point pretending not to be nervous.

"I'm sorry Justin's not here to get our message himself," I said. "Will you give it to him? Please."

"Of course, my dear."

"Tell him that if he persists in this stupid, useless, selfish idiocy, the four of us—Amy and Bitsie and Caro and I—will tell every reporter who calls that the truth about Lighthouse Point never came out. And that if we had to do it over again, we'd add a few details that might interest Lucia's brother."

It wasn't spontaneous; I'd had many days and nights to think of what I'd say and how I'd say it. I only thought that it would all go in gradual, measured steps. I hadn't intended to be so blunt. I hadn't intended to watch an old man grow pale and hear an old voice reduced to a cricket's chirp.

"You'd do that? David? You'd do that?"

"Probably not, sir," David said. "Most probably I'd just stand by and let the girls do it."

"This is ridiculous. This is bluffing. You'd suffer the consequences. You were under oath."

"As the Judge kept reminding us," I said. "Of course, we didn't understand. Now we do. So we wouldn't say anything that

266

would put our testimony in doubt. Not what we swore to. More like what we left out? Because nobody asked? Something like that. We'd say just enough to give it some spin. Energy. Get people thinking about *Justin's* story."

"Party people, especially," David said. "They have heads, as you said. They can use them, to spot a loser."

The silence stretched. Would I have felt as mean and hollow if it had been Justin in front of me? Old Henry was seventy-nine. The great dome of his head was shaking, slowly, slowly, from side to side, a bell of doleful ivory.

"I don't believe this. I don't believe it."

But we knew he did. And we could feel his longing, then and there, for a tall, thin figure, a bony, pointing hand, a low, precise, musical voice with a purr in the middle, a whip at the edge. He wanted the Judge, Leland Hofstedter, dead for five years but still Henry Lambert's private lighthouse, the one who gave the proper warnings or changed the courses or kept them steady. Without the Judge, Old Henry knew what he wanted but not how to get it. Not this time.

But he did what he could. He said he needed a drink and would we join him? The bar was behind that shuttered door. David could do the honors.

I asked for a vodka and tonic. I closed my eyes, waiting for the drink and waiting for the childish lump in my throat to go away. That was the only other door in the room, and somewhere, in the back of my mind, I'd been hoping that Justin was behind it, in another room. He'd come out, any minute! He'd come out and stand next to us, facing the desk, on our side.

It wasn't going to happen. He'd taken his father's advice and the easy way out and made himself scarce. And I knew he didn't want to see me and he never had, not ever in all these years. I was like Vinnie to him, just another person who could make him uncomfortable. And if there was space in his selfishness for the feeling of gratitude, it was probably for the last favor I had done for him: I had left town.

We all had a glass in our hands. We drank in silence like wine tasters, seriously. A little warmth crept through me. I looked at David.

"We're sorry about this, sir," David said. "And I know what I owe the family personally. My job. But I'm leaving it. Very soon. I have a few projects to clean up."

Old Henry's glass was empty and there was some color back in his face. He knew what to do on many things, still.

"The only thing you've got to clean up is your desk in New York. Do it and go. Your disloyalty is beyond me."

"I'm being loyal to Justin. I always have been. *We* have been. We saved him once, didn't we? You'll never know exactly how, but we did it. We're doing it again."

The old man's eyes blazed with anger.

"Saved him? Goddam your arrogance. If it weren't for *you* there'd have been no party. No accident. No need for whatever it was you all cooked up so that *my son* blamed himself for everything! And yet I never, until this minute, accused you. Well, I do now. This isn't the first time you've betrayed him."

I heard David's helpless sigh. He had turned bright red, as if he'd been slapped on both cheeks. I cried, "It wasn't like that!" and now Justin's father looked at me and me only.

"Rachel. Let me appeal to you. Hasn't there been enough payment from our family? Did it ever occur to you that my wife died brokenhearted not a year after Lighthouse Point? That accident shortened her life. Her nerves. And her heart. It was all too much."

"I thought that," I said. "It was the first thing I thought of when I heard about it."

"Casualty after casualty," Old Henry said softly. "Rachel, you can put a stop to this. Don't let David do your thinking for you. I know Justin's chances aren't all that high. But he'd make a great President! It's wrong to let the past dictate every letter of a man's life. We can all do better than we've done. People live and learn and make up for what they've lost. I've lived a long time, and I've never met a person who wasn't worth a second chance."

There was dignity in his pleading, and sincerity in every syllable. He believed what he was saying. But all I could feel was a queer, choked bitterness that scalded my throat and kept me dumb while he went on talking. It was his voice. He could sound exactly like Justin when he chose to, the warmth and resonance of the family voice only a little muffled, as if spoken through gauze. But hearing it underlined the plain and painful truth I had never grasped before this minute: Justin was not and never would be the man his father was. Justin didn't have the guts to face me. And even if he had, he could never, not in a hundred years, summon up the integrity of passionate ambition of this old man. He wouldn't even have had the words in which to frame it.

He'd always had speech writers—for the passion as well as for the words.

His father was something else. Old Henry had gotten ambushed, all alone; he'd seen us shoot down his fondest dream in twenty seconds. But he could keep his head, plead his cause, and even touch my heart, and if any Lambert was the real thing, he was it. The real thing was what a President had to be.

"I'm sorry, sir," David said. His voice was sad and firm. "I have the utmost respect for you, but I believe it's best for everyone—and I include Justin—if Jemsen or Dempsey gets the nomination."

For a minute we all kept silent. There was just the sizzle and flare of a lighter and the leathery scent of a fresh cigar. We'll be here for hours, I thought. He won't give up; he'll try again.

Surely it's by the strength of their bequests that the dead remain immortal? Leland Hofstedster had left the Lamberts a legacy of sound counsel, and even without him Old Henry could recognize the limits of power and the outlines of a bad case. We *were* dangerous. It would take some fancy footwork and some hard thinking to come up with any further strategy against us—if, indeed, any strategy deserved a try. And because the Judge had touched our lives too, we knew this as well as Justin's father did.

He blew a plume of blue smoke so forcefully that David and I both coughed. He stood up and we did too, and I felt myself grow light, light as air, because at long last he was standing, coming around the desk, taking my arm. He motioned to David to precede him to the door. David opened it, and it was then I felt how strong the old man's hand was, how it clasped my bare flesh like a sensual bracelet of bone and sinew.

He was holding me.

"You won't refuse me a minute alone with Rachel, will you,

David? Or five, at most. I have something to say to her that I think she'd prefer, herself, to hear in private."

"We don't have any secrets, sir," David said. "Rachel will—"

"That's her business," Old Henry said, but David may not have heard it, because the door closed on him quickly and the hand on my arm slid smoothly to my own hand and led me to a chair.

"Sit down, Robin," he said. "I'll sit next to you. I hate getting behind these goddam clean desks."

Robin!

He handed me the glass I'd been drinking from—it was still half full—and then he went to the bar to make his own. I could hear him, behind me, the ice cubes tinkling, the hiss of the soda siphon, but he didn't come around to sit down. He spoke from behind my back, and I understood it for what it was: a sporting gesture, a chance for naked shock to cover itself.

"We were more worried about a trial after the inquest than we ever let on," he said. "We didn't want to make you girls any more nervous than you were. But we were damn worried, let me tell you, and we did the routine thing. Be prepared, as the Judge always said. We got background checks on all of you. Yours was the most thorough. Had to be, right?"

"No," I managed to say. "I don't understand. Why me?"

"The Jewish thing, the New York thing. We were just being realistic. Radical politics? Communist relatives? People who don't like people like me and my family, wouldn't that be a possibility? So we traced your mother through your next-of-kin note in the Barnard files: Angela White. The name switch didn't register any-thing; we just thought she'd remarried. Sent a man down to Dover to finish the check and he got the story. How poor you were. The old couple you worked for. And about your father, too, dying in prison. That must have been awfully hard on a little girl. But it didn't stop you, did it, Rachel? I admire you."

He came around and sat down then, and I had a face ready for him, with the blood back in it, and another question on my lips, the one I knew he'd expect.

"Who else knows all this?"

270

"The Judge, who's gone. The investigator, who's still alive, still working for me. A quiet man . . . that's why he's still working. And me. I never told anyone else."

"If this is some kind of offer, I'm not taking it. You can tell the whole world about me. I'll still keep my stand on Justin's running."

"It's not an offer. Give me some credit, my dear. If I made you an offer—a deal—it would be a lot better than just these scraps of ancient history."

"Then why are you telling me what you know?"

"So that *you* know I understand you. Respect you. Why, Rachel, there isn't a rich man in the world who doesn't think he's somehow gypped his children by making life too easy for them. There's a kind of stuff—grit—that rich kids hardly ever have."

It sounded like sentimental generalizing, but it wasn't; he was talking about himself and his son. There was no point in not agreeing with him. I nodded. His smile was wry and resigned. He sighed.

"Edith's not bright. I think she drinks to feel smarter. But my own father had a saying: Even a stopped clock is right, twice a day. Edie knew there was a special girl at Lighthouse Point. She thought it was Lucia, like the rest of them. But *I* thought it was you."

"It wasn't any of us," I said, but he just shook his head and looked at me across the space dividing our two chairs as if he were seeing me for the first time, as if I were a woman who had just happened to sit next to him, on a train, in a theater, across a mahogany table laid with heavy silver.

What luck, his eyes said. You being you, and me being here.

It was practiced, perfectly clear and perfectly inoffensive, and for a few seconds I could forget who he was and how old he was too.

"Me and the Judge," he said. "We made the same guess. We always did have the same taste in women. Spirit. Independence. And once he said to me, 'Hank, she might have made a difference.'"

Was he guessing, bluffing, trying to get me off balance again, as he'd done by calling me Robin, just once? I think he was bluffing. But I'll never be sure.

271

"You're flattering me, Mr. Lambert," I said. "But if I heard you right, there was a lot of *difference* to make up. We agree on that at least. The way I see it, no woman could have really helped Justin. There was too much to change, wasn't there?"

I couldn't say more than that. If I'd brought up the accident with the gun I would have betrayed an intimacy with Justin's life that would only have strengthened his case. I wasn't softening; I knew this man was ruthless and would use the slightest edge against me. But I had that home-free feeling back; I knew I could end the conversation and walk out when I wanted to. Yet a part of me also wanted, then and there, to stay with him longer. To talk and talk. To tell him everything, and hear everything from him, and blame, and kiss, and forgive and forget.

Fathers? Justin was twenty years older than I was. You look backward, and then you see.

I wanted to give Old Henry something.

"Justin's still a young man, politically," I said. "If you set your sights lower? You could depend on us."

"Thank you, Rachel," he said. "I doubt anything like that will come to pass. I'm tired. Bone tired. But that's a really decent last word."

He got up and held the door for me and closed it before David leaped to his feet. The secretary's desk was empty. "Some five minutes," David said. "What the hell was that all about?"

"He guessed about me and Justin. Nothing but guesswork. No facts, no threats. He just wanted to see me react and maybe admit it. I hope I didn't disappoint him too badly."

"My money's on you," David said. "Let's go."

"I'm hungry," David said, when we were out on the street. "It's four o'clock, where do we go?"

We walked up Main. We didn't recognize the name of a single restaurant we used to go to, although some of the buildings themselves were still standing. At Main and Ninth we stopped and stared. Where Chatterton's had been there was an excavation the size of a Superdome.

"Guess everyone found another place," David said thoughtfully. "Watch, whatever one we pick will turn out to be the new Chatterton's."

"At least your mother moved to Florida," I said. "We can't run into her. Oh, hell, we'll do Chinese. That has to be safe."

We found a Ming Palace left over from the old days. It had become a treasure trove of campy blue mirror and vinyl, and it was very dark. We slipped into a booth and ordered soup immediately.

"I was afraid I'd faint, back there," I said. I felt lightheaded with hunger, and the drink. "I guess you don't know that about me. I faint."

"That's interesting," David said. "I didn't think women fainted anymore. I thought it was all on account of corsets."

"Low blood pressure," I said. "I have that. David? I was disappointed. Shocked, too. That he'd do that to us."

David knew I meant Justin. "I never thought of it. Shows you. Well, he'll get the message. We got it through. I was disappointed too."

"It's so . . . cowardly. He couldn't rally himself. Just ducked. I'm not even angry. It's kind of sad, that's all."

"I feel the same. It would have been easier, telling him. Old Henry, now. I felt bad. He was always decent to me."

"Is it possible Justin *won't* know? That Old Henry won't tell him? He could sit on it. Pretend it didn't happen."

"No. He's not that kind of man. He's tough. Maybe he'll test it on a few of his honchos before he tells Justin. They'll smell the coffee. He did already. I could tell he knew we were serious. Or at least the bluff was too dangerous to call."

The place was shabby and comforting, dark, quiet. It would probably be torn down soon. It would be change, if not progress. I felt the slow drag of melancholy. Another finality. We're history here. With an effort, I asked David what he would do. He'd been fired. Would he get severance?

"I don't have a contract," he said. "I think no. And I don't have a lot in the bank, either. I think you should pay for this dinner."

"I was going to offer," I said frostily. "With or without the hard-luck story. I owe you a lot. I could have been alone in there. I could have blown it."

"No, you wouldn't have. But I'm glad I was there. It would have been better, though, if Justin were. So I could see you with him again."

273

"What's that supposed to mean?"

"I'd know if you were still involved with him."

"That's ridiculous. I already told you. I'm not. I haven't been for . . . oh, quite a while. I don't say it didn't take time. And some reality. These last two months? I think I got to know him better than I ever did when we were together! He's weak and selfish. A taker. The family uses him, and he uses the rest of the world. Maybe I can explain him, but I can't excuse him, not anymore. And having him outright avoid me? The last straw, and I didn't even need one."

I was warming my fingers on the teacup. The restaurant was still nearly empty, and the air-conditioning was ferocious.

David reached over and took the little cup.

"Hold my hands, Rachel. I'm nervous as hell."

"Why? It's over. We did fine."

"I don't want anything to be over. I want to go on sitting here, with you."

I took his hands. They were thin, fine; they always looked tanned, somehow. An immense shyness possessed me; I could feel my face growing red; at the same time I knew the satisfaction I sometimes felt when I put in the last letter on the Sunday cross-word puzzle.

Oh, I thought. This is why I didn't want to go to California.

"It's nice, yes," I said. "I feel exactly the same."

We sat there until we both felt awkward. We didn't know what to say after that. I paid the check. We drifted out to the street. The office buildings were letting out; the streets were crowded now with people going home. We walked slower than they did, as if we were tourists with all the time in the world. We sat in one of the new pocket parks and watched the people. At first he kept his arm across the top of the bench, not quite around my shoulder but touching me. Then it fell around me and I could rest my head against it.

"We'd better go," David said. "I think I remember some kind of sign in that parking lot."

We'd walked a mile away from it, and my feet were hurting when we got there. The sign was conspicuous next to the thick iron chain that stretched across the entrance.

274

Bank Customers Only—Towing After 6 PM.

The lot was empty. They'd towed it.

"Son of a bitch," David said. "I'll bet that old bastard gave them specific orders."

I was holding my shoes. It was still hot and muggy. David said we could call Vinnie and take a cab out to his house. They'd find room for us. Anyway, Vinnie was waiting to hear.

It was a sensible plan; I said no to it. I wanted my car *now*. We'd waste a whole day, tomorrow, getting it out of the pound. Waste, waste, David said, you'd think you were losing a day's pay. You're on vacation; I'm out of work; we have all the time in the world. Anyway, he said, it's too late, they'll make us wait until morning anyway.

"I don't want to go to Vinnie's," I said. I felt ugly, tired, and dumb. "I don't know what I want, but it's not a whole evening making conversation with Vinnie's family. I just want to be alone."

"Thanks a lot."

"I meant alone with you."

"Say that again. Slowly."

"I want to be alone with you."

"Come on, then. I'll spring for one toothbrush."

"Toothpaste too."

"They give you. Little packages. Shampoo."

So we spent the night in the city. It was lovely. I was astonished at how lovely it was. I took off the diamond ring and put it in my wallet; I told David I was going to sell it; no, I said I was going to send it back to Justin. What did he think I should do?

"Don't rush me," David said, "I'm thinking," and when I stopped laughing I told him my real name and why I changed it.

One lovely thing after the other. Toward midnight, we stood together for a long while at the window of the hotel room, looking out at the city, all the newness, and the dome and spire of the statehouse fitted out with floodlights so that—small as they were— they glistened like real gold.

He ordered breakfast in the room the next morning, and I hid in the bathroom when I heard the knock on the door. I wanted a quick shower anyway, and when I came out I saw a table all set with white linen and a few roses in a glass vase. David was talking to someone on the phone. I asked if that was Vinnie. He shook his head and put his hand over the receiver.

"My mother, in Miami," he said. "Get over here and say hello. I've just told her the news. She's crying with happiness. She always thought I'd marry a model from God knows what background."

I thought it was a dirty trick then and I still do. But I took the phone. If there was any way out, I didn't look for it. I said, "Mrs. Freed? This is Rachel Warshowsky. . . . Oh, yes, it's certainly been a long time. . . . Thank you. Thank you very much. I'm happy too. You won't believe this, but it was very sudden."